Moonlight on Nightingale Way

An *On Dublin Street* novel

SAMANTHA YOUNG

piatkus

PIATKUS

First published in the US in 2015 by New American Library,
a division of Penguin Group (USA) LLC
First published in Great Britain in 2015 by Piatkus

1 3 5 7 9 10 8 6 4 2

Copyright © Samantha Young, 2015

The moral right of the author has been asserted.

A CIP catalogue record for this book
is available from the British Library.

ISBN 978-0-349-40880-4

Printed and bound by CPI (Group) UK Ltd, Croydon CR0 4YY

Papers used by Piatkus are from well-managed forests
and other responsible sources.

MIX
Paper from
responsible sources
FSC
www.fsc.org   FSC® C104740

Piatkus
An imprint of
Little, Brown Book Group
Carmelite House
50 Victoria Embankment
London EC4Y 0DZ

An Hachette UK Company
www.hachette.co.uk

www.piatkus.co.uk

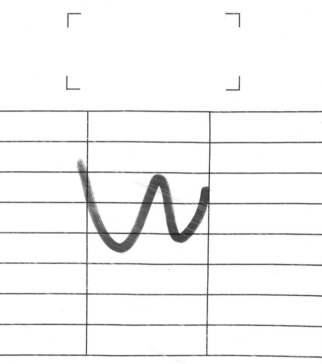

Samantha Young is a *New York Times, USA Today* and *Wall Street Journal* bestselling author from Stirlingshire, Scotland. She's been nominated for the Goodreads Choice Award for Best Author and Best Romance for her international bestselling novel *On Dublin Street*.

Visit Samantha Young online:

www.authorsamanthayoung.com
www.twitter.com/SYoungSFAuthor

On Dublin Street Series
On Dublin Street
Down London Road
Before Jamaica Lane
Fall from India Place
Echoes of Scotland Street
Moonlight on Nightingale Way

Hero

Castle Hill (ebook novella)

Moonlight on
Nightingale Way

CHAPTER 1

I stared at the bright pink thong draped across the hand railing on the landing I shared with the new neighbor I had yet to meet. My first semi-introduction to him was last night when my work was ground to a halt by the high-pitched squealing coming from next door.

My neighbor's girlfriend was loud during sex.

Very, *very* loud.

Although frustrating, there was nothing I could do but wait for it to end. It took so long (I had to give them points for stamina), it was time for me to go to sleep and I'd gotten hardly any editing done.

Now the squealer's thong was drip-drying on my handrail.

Aghast at the thought of my clean and well-maintained stairwell suddenly turning into the set for *Shameless*, I could do nothing but stare at the offending item in horror.

The sound of my neighbor's door opening jerked my attention from the thong to his door.

Stepping out of the doorway, phone to his ear, was an exceptionally tall man. My eyes roamed over the broad shoulders and muscular biceps and stopped on the black tattoo that took up a good part of his right forearm. It looked Celtic in design and appeared to be a sword with a semicircle arching over it and connecting on either side of the hilt.

"Talk to Dad," the man murmured, drawing my gaze from his tattoo to his face. "Whatever you decide, I'm on board."

His dark hair was close-shaven, and he was sporting heavy scruff that only made his rugged features that much more so. His large build and the scruff were too much in my opinion. I preferred my men leaner, clean-cut, and far less intimidating.

Suddenly I found myself trapped in his gaze as he looked up and spotted me.

I froze, flustered by the heat that suffused my cheeks under his perusal. He had the most extraordinary eyes I'd ever seen. They were clear and light. Beautiful, unusual violet eyes rimmed with black lashes. Those eyes softened his looks somewhat.

I found myself released from his gaze as he dragged it down my body and back up again. From there I received a polite nod that made me bristle. Perhaps my reaction had something to do with how dismissive he was. Altogether irritated and not at all good at handling it, I glanced back at the thong and bit my lip. I couldn't have underwear drying on my landing.

I just couldn't.

I looked back at him as he continued his conversation. "Excuse me," I said quietly, annoyed, wanting to interrupt but still somehow too well mannered to do it forcefully.

Still, my quiet words brought his gaze back to me, and he frowned. "Shannon, I'll call you back . . . Aye . . . 'Bye, sweetheart." He lowered his phone from his ear and slipped it into his pocket. "Can I help you?"

I stuck out my hand and formally introduced myself. "I'm Miss Grace Farquhar." I pointed to my door with my other hand. "Your neighbor."

Lips pressed together in a hard line, he slipped his large hand into mine and engulfed it. A shiver rippled across my shoulders, and I immediately regretted offering my hand to him. "Nice to meet you, *Miss Grace Farquhar.*"

"Hmm, quite," I murmured, tugging my hand back and trying not to appear as flustered as I felt. "And you are?"

"Mr. Logan James MacLeod."

He was making fun of me. I ignored it. "Well, Mr. MacLeod." I tried for a pleasant tone, but I could feel the thong glaring at me from the hand railing and fueling my annoyance. "I would greatly appreciate it if your girlfriend would desist from air-drying her unmentionables in the public stairwell." I pointed a finger at the thong, not attempting to hide my distaste.

Logan stared at the thong. "Shit," he murmured.

"Logan!" a female voice shouted from inside his flat. "Do you fancy going out for breakfast?" The voice was suddenly accompanied by a body.

A young woman stepped out onto the landing wearing nothing but a man's shirt. It was buttoned just below the ribbon on her bra, revealing a rather impressive cleavage. Everything about the woman was curvy and feminine, and her short but trim legs were tan, her long hair was dyed a shiny platinum blond, and she had what appeared to be mile-long fake eyelashes expertly affixed to her eyes.

She was my opposite in every possible way, and I suddenly realized why Logan MacLeod had dismissed me upon sight.

"What's going on?" She blinked her wide baby-blue eyes up at Logan.

Logan sighed. "Did you put your thong out here to dry?"

She nodded. "The air's drier out here than in the bathroom. I thought it would dry quicker."

I watched the two of them, fascinated by my neighbor's growing annoyance and his girlfriend's obliviousness in the face of it.

"Are you nuts?"

She wrinkled her nose. "No. What's wrong with *you*?"

"We just met last night, and you're air-drying your knickers on my landing."

"And?"

Logan looked at me as if asking for help. I could only stare at him in bemusement. He turned back to what I now gathered was a persistent one-night stand. "It's rude and it pissed off my neighbor." He jerked a thumb over his shoulder toward me. "Not to mention it's a little too soon for doing your laundry here. As is breakfast. Now, if you don't mind, I've got stuff to do."

Affronted by his less-than-diplomatic brush-off, his one-night stand grabbed her thong and dashed back into the flat, yelling out a stream of expletives. By the time she'd changed into a formfitting pink dress and high heels and was tottering angrily out of his flat on unstable feet, Logan was visibly angry.

He looked almost menacing.

I shivered at the air of danger around him.

"Fuck you, you bastard!" She stomped down the stairs and then threw another look over her shoulder, this time at me. "And you, you snobby cow!"

My lips parted in shock as she stumbled out of sight. "Well, wasn't she delightful," I said, stunned.

"*She* was a Class-A cling-on."

"Perhaps you should be more selective when choosing a sexual partner for the evening," I suggested helpfully.

Apparently it wasn't helpful. Logan MacLeod turned his intimidating glare on me. "Are you judging me, plum?"

Cheeks blazing, I whispered, "Plum?"

"Plummy." He raked his eyes over me, and his lips twisted into a grimace before he explained. "Posh."

"I'm not posh." I stopped myself from stamping my foot in indignation that he would even mention it. I was raised in Kensington in London, and it was true I was very well-spoken, but that had nothing to do with the fact that for whatever reason, he was being very antagonistic.

"You're the poshest person I've ever met, plum."

"I am not."

"I think I'd know," he said.

"Do you have a distaste for the English, Mr. MacLeod?"

He narrowed his eyes. "I don't have a distaste for anybody because I don't judge people." There he went again insinuating I judged people. We'd only just met!

"Neither do I."

"Oh? So you weren't judging me based on the knickers drip-drying on the banister, then? Or that those knickers belonged to a one-night stand of mine? Are you judging me for having casual sex, Miss Farquhar? Or merely on my choice of casual-sex partner?" He took in my blouse with the floppy bow tied at the neck and my high-waist, wide-leg trousers. "Was she not classy enough for your liking?"

"I'm com-completely confused," I stuttered. And mortified! I hated confrontation.

"Let me make it clearer. A friendly neighbor would have introduced herself when I moved in. A friendly neighbor would have welcomed me to the building before rattling on about a pair of knickers. So what is it? Are you not friendly, or did you hear something about me that got your own judgy little knickers in a twist?"

"I have no idea what you're talking about." I shook my head. "I just didn't want a thong on my landing." Feeling my blood heat, my cheeks blooming ever brighter, I had no recourse but to turn around and shove my key in my door to get away from the brewing argument. I had no idea why he was so defensive or why he irritated me to melodramatic levels, but he did, and I didn't know how to deal with it.

" 'Bye . . . *Miss Grace Farquhar.*"

I slammed the door shut. Leaning against it, I discovered I felt out of breath, like I'd just run all the way up the stairs. I huffed at the ludicrous pounding of my heart.

My stairwell was no longer a safe place.

. . .

I was exhausted.

It was sheer fortuitousness, then, that when I lifted my foot to step out of my door, I was actually aware enough of my surroundings to spot the pile of vomit on my doorstep.

I jerked my foot back and wrinkled my nose in disgust.

My gaze shot across the hall to Logan's door.

That bloody swine.

Not only was he the reason I was exhausted, but he was now the reason I had to step over bodily waste to get out of my flat.

Last night I'd heard the ruffian outside on the landing, trying to shut up his cackling female companion. It had been two weeks since our encounter, and in that time I'd spotted him with three different women. Player. Absolute Player with a capital *P*.

After hearing him shush his lady friend, I'd waited for the inevitable noisy bedroom gymnastics to begin. To my delight there was silence, and I managed to work through three chapters of the romance novel I was editing.

I thought all was well and fell into bed around three thirty, setting my alarm for eleven thirty. I was shamefully awoken at six o' clock in the morning to 'OH GOD, OH GOD, LOGAN, OH GOD.' Like the man needed to be compared to God. His ego was already biblical.

Logan MacLeod was an arrogant pain in my arse.

Two rounds of OH GOD later, I was wide-awake and could not get back to sleep.

Now I was a walking zombie, and I'd almost zombie walked my way into the vomit he or his companion had deposited on my doorstep.

All morning I'd argued with the arse in my head about him keeping me awake with his sexual antics, but like always, I'd eventually calmed down. I hated disagreements with people. The therapist I'd seen in my early twenties had told me my aversion to confrontation was born from the fact that I was constantly seeking the approval of others. For years I'd sought to win both of my parents over with little success, and that need for them to like me filtered into my relationships with everyone. I hated to be hated and so I avoided making people unhappy in any way.

I'd worked hard to overcome it because it could be damaging, and my job as a freelance book editor certainly helped, because as a good editor I had to be absolutely honest in my constructive criticism. I'd grown a thicker skin when dealing with my clients, but I still had a hard time pissing anyone off in my personal life.

And I really didn't want the hassle of dealing with a pissed-off neighbor.

But now I was pissed off.

Well and truly.

Imagine vomiting on my doorstep and not bloody well cleaning it up! I glared at Logan's door.

It wasn't as though I actually wanted anything to do with the man. Airing my complaints to him wasn't going to have an adverse effect on our relationship because we didn't have a relationship and we never would.

Logan MacLeod was going to clean up the mess he made, and I could give a damn if he thought me the most irritating woman in the world.

Anger simmering in my blood, I hopped over the vomit, locked up, and marched to his door. I pounded on it.

Nothing.

I pounded harder before I could regret my decision to confront him.

Two seconds later I heard movement inside, followed by a muffled curse. The door suddenly swung open, and there he stood in all his glory. I blinked, fighting the heat that bloomed on my cheeks, but failed. Logan MacLeod had opened the door in nothing but boxer briefs, and I had never seen a man like him in real life. There was not an inch of fat on him. Just pure, hard muscle.

Cut. My friend Chloe would say he was cut.

Logan rubbed a hand over his short hair, drawing my attention from his six-pack to his sleep-roughened face. "It's Sunday fucking morning," he said, squinting at me. "If you're going to speak, speak."

The heat in my cheeks flared hotter. Despite my blushing, I mustered on. "I am well aware it is Sunday morning," I said in my quiet voice, wishing for once that I'd inherited my mother's authoritative one. "After working into the wee hours, I was rudely awoken at dawn by your inconsiderately loud antics. I then stepped out of my door and missed the pile of vomit on it by inches. I can only assume it was deposited there by either yourself or the cackling female you brought home last night." I was shaking badly, and I didn't know if it was from anxiety or anger.

No one had upset me like this in a very long time.

"Fuck." He dragged his hand down his face and then peered past me. "It was . . ." He frowned. "My friend."

I rolled my eyes, realizing he couldn't remember his one-night stand's name.

"I meant to come out and clean it up first thing. Sorry. I'll do it now."

His apology deflated me somewhat. I stared dumbly at him.

He blinked sleepily, looking much too attractive for someone who was just awake. "Is there anything else?"

"No. I appreciate you cleaning it." I turned away and had put only one foot on the stairs when he stopped me.

"You don't have to be so antagonistic, you know. You should consider removing that stick from your tiny arse."

And just like that I was enraged all over again. I stopped and looked at him over my shoulder. "Excuse me?" I wasn't quite sure I'd even heard right.

"You talk down to me. And there's that pinchy-mouthed look you give me instead of a smile every time you pass me in the hall."

Pinchy-mouthed? I sniffed at the insult and turned to leave again, not deigning to give him a response.

"And that," he called out to me as I descended the stairs. "That haughty little sniff is extremely fucking annoying."

I halted, shocked.

Because it suddenly occurred to me that I wasn't my usual pile of anxiety over the fact that this person found me wanting. No. Instead triumph coursed through me that he was just as aggravated by me as I was by him.

I looked up to find him standing out on the landing scowling down at me.

Despite my red cheeks, I managed an irritatingly *haughty* swish of my hair over my shoulder and snapped out, "Good."

CHAPTER 2

There was no possible way I could manage to hide my distaste and I didn't even want to. This was in response to Chloe's, "He sounds hot."

She was referring to Logan MacLeod. I'd just spent the last ten minutes complaining about his antics and what he'd said to me that morning to my friends Chloe, Aidan, and Aidan's fiancée, Juno. How Chloe managed to pick "hot" out of all I'd just said, I had no clue.

"Oh, please." Chloe huffed at my expression. "You secretly think he's hot."

"I think he's appalling," I said, *appalled*.

"Well, I'm proud of you for sticking up for yourself," Aidan said, and Juno curled deeper into his side on their sofa.

I'd met Aidan eleven years ago, during our first semester at the University of Edinburgh. He, more than anyone, knew what a big deal it was for me to speak up for myself, and he knew exactly why. Chloe was my roommate in first year, and the three of us had grown close during our four years at Edinburgh. A bit of a chatterbox, flirtatious, and energetic, Chloe was our opposite, but together we worked. In fact, if it hadn't been for Chloe, Aidan would never have met Juno.

Juno was a postgrad student from Canada. She was here working on some engineering . . . thing . . . that I still didn't understand and had met

Chloe on a night out. During one of her moments of utter perceptiveness, Chloe recognized something in Juno that she thought would appeal to Aidan. She introduced the fresh-faced, shy, exceptionally intelligent Canadian to Aidan, and it was pretty much love at first sight. They'd been together for five years and were planning to marry when Juno finished her postgrad. For now they were settled happily into the somewhat swanky Stockbridge flat, courtesy of Aidan's income as a professional rugby player.

I was the single one among us, as Chloe was also engaged. Her fiancé, Ed, worked in energy efficiency. He'd spent the last six months in Sweden working on developing some brilliant new technology that would help reduce energy costs in everyday housing.

Chloe was lonely without Ed. And when Chloe was lonely she liked to play matchmaker. For me. Not that it was such a hardship to put up with her matchmaking. I was single and "looking."

Plus . . . it was Chloe. I'd do anything for Chloe, Aidan, and Juno. As they sat around me in Aidan and Juno's lovely flat, I looked at them and I saw my family. They knew me better than the one I'd severed all communication with seven years ago.

"Thanks," I said to Aidan. "It actually felt good to stand my ground."

"If he gives you any more problems, you just tell Aidan," Juno said, offering his services up. "He'll deal with it."

Aidan didn't protest, because the truth was, he would deal with it. Despite his reserve, he took shit from no man, and he didn't allow any of us to either. Plus, he was huge, even bigger than Logan. No one—unless an idiot—would try to mess with him. Excluding one extremely drunken night at uni, I mostly thought of him as an overprotective big brother. He was more family to me than my own brother, Sebastian, who was never protective. In fact, he was the opposite.

I threw thoughts of Sebastian aside and gave my friends a reassuring smile. "It will be fine. I'm just tired and cranky. I have that date tomorrow night, and I really hope I manage to get some sleep so I don't end up looking like the walking dead."

"Date?" Aidan said.

"The guy from my gym."

Chloe snorted. "I still can't believe you made a date with a guy who pervs on women in a yoga class."

"He wasn't perving. He was thinking about joining the class."

Aidan grinned. "Right."

I glowered at them. "You all think the worst of everyone."

"And for someone who was raised by Dracula and one of his brides, you see the best, even when it's not there," Chloe said.

"Not always," I grumbled, thinking about my neighbor.

"So where is the yoga perv taking you?" Juno said.

I ignored her teasing. "His name is Bryan and he's taking me to dinner."

Chloe grunted. "You don't sound that excited about it."

"Of course I'm looking forward to it. Bryan seems very nice." And he did. He was also quite good-looking.

"Nice?" Juno gave me a confused smile. "Sweetie, nice? No. Your first thought about this guy should be 'wow.'" She shrugged. "When I met Aidan, it was very much a 'wow' for me."

Aidan smiled down at her. "Back at you, darlin'."

"Ugh. Stop." Chloe waved her hands at them. "No cutesy, lovey-dovey crap right now. I haven't had sex in five weeks, and Miss Farquhar here hasn't been laid in three months."

I colored. "Thank you for sharing that."

"Just because you haven't gotten laid in a while doesn't mean you should settle for this guy," Juno opined.

"Who says I'm settling?" I threw my hands up in disbelief. "None of you have met him."

"We don't need to," Aidan said. "Your last five dates have all borne a scarily similar resemblance and the personality of a wet blanket. You keep selling yourself short, Grace. Can you blame us for being skeptical about *this* guy?"

"And when Aidan says 'scarily similar resemblance,' he means guys who are punching way above their weight dating you," Chloe added.

"No, they weren't. That's such a shallow thing to say. It's not all about looks, you know. I'm not exactly Angelina Jolie myself."

Aidan made an irritated noise and reached for his mug of coffee. He took a drink rather than saying something that might upset me. Chloe, however, cursed and snapped, "I could kill your bloody mother."

"Yes, well, get in line," I muttered, taking a sip of my own coffee and avoiding eye contact with her. I did not want to have that particular conversation.

"My brother's friend Joe saw your photo on my Facebook page. He said he thinks you're beautiful." Juno grinned at me.

I blushed and squirmed uncomfortably. "He did not."

She laughed. "He did so. I asked Ally to bring him to Scotland next time he visits me."

"Don't be silly." I huffed at the thought.

"Is this Joe hot?" Chloe asked.

"Oh yeah."

"As much as I appreciate the compliment, I think I'll still go on my date with Bryan, if that's okay. I can compromise on a lot of things, but having an ocean between me and my boyfriend isn't one of them."

"How about a landing?" Chloe teased.

I wrinkled my nose at her wayward thoughts. "Logan MacLeod is the least likely candidate for boyfriendhood of any man in the entire world."

She raised an eyebrow at me, and I flushed again when I realized I'd practically shouted it. "Famous last words."

"No, not famous last words," I insisted, feeling that immediate aggravation ignite in my very blood at the thought of my neighbor. "Logan MacLeod is uncouth, probably riddled with sexual diseases, and he's not at all to my taste. And I am definitely not to his taste. You should see the women he sleeps with. They're all sexy, tan, blond hair and big boobs. He thinks I have a stick up my arse because the hem of my skirt sits below my crotch and I do up the buttons over my cleavage."

Chloe's eyes were round as I ranted on. She turned to Aidan and Juno in seeming wonder. "I have to meet this man."

"Why?" I snapped.

"Because he's clearly got something intriguing about him if he can do this to you." She gestured to me in a vague way.

"Do what?"

"This," she insisted, repeating the vague gesturing.

I clenched my teeth together. "What is *this*?"

"I don't know what it is. I just know it's *something*."

It had been suggested in the past by people who didn't really know me at all well that as an editor who spent her days editing romantic fiction, I might have unrealistic expectations of men. Anyone who knew me— *really* knew me—knew that wasn't true. Although I was actively looking for the man I wanted to spend my life with, I wasn't looking for a fantasy man. I *was* looking for someone understanding, protective, and funny. I didn't expect perfection. I just wanted to *like* the person I was dating, and I wanted him to be *kind*.

Bryan was neither funny nor kind.

"So the bitch took the fish, even though she never bought the fish," Bryan finished, his nostrils flaring.

I blinked, wondering how my mentioning that my hake had been delicious had somehow gotten us onto the topic of his ex-girlfriend. Again. So far Bryan had turned all of our conversations on this abysmal date back to his last two ex-girlfriends.

He seemed to be a very angry little man.

Bored, I somehow found myself kicking the hornet's nest. "But didn't you say you won it at a fun fair for her?"

He scowled. "That's not the point."

"Surely a gift once given cannot be taken back?"

"Ugh, that's such a fucking female thing to say."

I stuck my hand up at the passing waiter. "Check, please."

Exhausted from the terrible date, all I wanted was to get home and snuggle up to watch the latest episode of my favorite reality singing contest, which I'd recorded from the weekend.

I was hurrying up my stairwell when, to my horror, *his* door opened.

Logan stepped out, surprising me with his attire. He wore a beautiful black suit and a black shirt. The top button was open on the shirt and he wore no tie, but still he was very smart—it was the most civilized I'd ever seen him. I had to wonder if he worked at night, and if so, what exactly it was that he did.

I drew to a stop at the top of the stairs, and Logan jolted when he saw me, his gaze raking over me, his lips parting slightly as though he were in shock. Like him, I was wearing black. A black Alexander McQueen dress with a pleated knee-length skirt and a V-neck that showed off a modest amount of cleavage. The dress was a remnant from my previous life, and it was pure class. I loved it. I'd loved it for almost ten years. For once my honey brown hair hung loose over my shoulders, and my makeup was soft in dusky pink shades, which suited my light complexion.

I flushed when those extraordinary eyes of his connected with mine.

"Back from a date?" he said, sounding surprised by this.

"Yes," I answered out of politeness.

"I take it the date didn't go well?"

"Why would you think that?"

"Because you're home alone."

Feeling my cheeks redden, as they had a tendency to do around him, I slipped past him, rummaging through my clutch for my keys. "It may come as a shock to you, Mr. MacLeod, but not all of us sleep with someone on the first date."

"How boring."

I jerked around at his teasing tone and found his eyes glittering at me. "It's called respecting a woman."

"It is called not living life to the fullest." He started to descend the stairs. "Maybe if you got yourself laid, you'd relax a wee bit."

I sniffed, denying even to myself that his perception of me stung. "I am perfectly relaxed."

"Oh, you sound it," he called up, his infuriating chuckle trailing up to me as his head disappeared from sight.

"Argggh." I smacked my clutch against my door before throwing it open and slamming it shut behind me. The clutch went sailing down the hall of my flat in my anger. "Damn the man!"

Next time I was bloody well going to get in the last word.

CHAPTER 3

"Bugger, bugger, bugger," I muttered as I attempted to retrieve my keys from my purse while trying to juggle three shopping bags filled with food.

A large hand suddenly tugged on the handles of one of the bags and I jerked my head up in fright. My gaze clashed with Logan MacLeod's. "Wha—"

The bag was in his hand and the second and third followed quickly into his other.

I stared up at his serious expression, bemused. "I didn't even hear you come up behind me." He certainly moved quietly for a big man.

Instead of speaking, he gestured to the front door of our building.

Flustered, my hands shook a little as I tugged my keys out and selected the right one. I let us inside. "I can carry them now. Thank you."

His blank face and refusal to give me back the shopping bags forced me to keep walking. I stopped at flat one on the ground floor and knocked. Logan halted in confusion. Before I could explain, the door to the flat opened and I was faced with my favorite neighbor, Mr. Jenner, and his cheery disposition.

"Ah, Gracie, there you are." He grinned at me, his smile faltering a little when he glanced beyond me. "Oh, you have company?"

"Mr. Jenner, this is Mr. MacLeod. He just moved into the building. He very kindly offered to carry your shopping."

I heard Logan's grunt behind me and didn't know whether it pertained to my diplomatic retelling of the situation or the fact that the shopping bags weren't for me.

"Oh, how kind." Mr. Jenner smiled at Logan. "Come in. Come in."

I looked at Logan and he stared at me, his eyebrow raised in question.

"I do Mr. Jenner's shopping for him every week. I can carry them inside if you like." I held out my hand for the bags.

"I've got them." He brushed past me, and I followed him into Mr. Jenner's flat.

The elderly gentleman lost his wife a few years ago, only a few short months after I moved into the building. His son had arranged for a cleaner to visit once a week, but she wanted more money to do the shopping, so I had offered to do it for free because the Jenners were kind and welcoming to me from the moment I moved in.

I watched Logan as he glanced around the small, well-kept flat, wondering if he was really listening to Mr. Jenner's chitchat as he followed our neighbor into his kitchen.

I realized I had been so busy watching Logan *I* hadn't heard Mr. Jenner's chitchat and was thus confused when Logan offered, "I'll take a look at it."

"Look at what?" I said, immediately diving into the bags Logan had placed on the counter. I started putting the perishables away in the refrigerator.

"Mr. Jenner's washing machine is playing up. I'll have a look at it."

"Are you qualified to do that?" I said, still curious about exactly what it was he did for a living.

"Yes. I have a Ph.D. in washing-machine technology."

I rolled my eyes at his sarcasm.

"That's very kind," Mr. Jenner said, clearly oblivious to the undercurrents of tension between me and Logan.

"I'll do it now, if that's okay?" Logan shrugged out of his jacket at Jenner's grateful nod.

I didn't particularly want to stick around to see Logan do a good deed. It might put a dent in my annoyance, and I wanted nothing to penetrate my dislike for my new neighbor. One good deed did not outweigh the growing tally of complaints I had against him. "Well, I'm off, then."

Mr. Jenner smiled. "Thanks again, Gracie. You're an angel."

I returned his smile but found mine wobbling a little under Logan's fierce regard. Ignoring his quizzical, burning stare, I waved good-bye without looking at either of them and dashed from the flat.

All those moments would be lost in time . . . like tears in rain.

I stared at the sentence for the fifteenth time, trying to think what it was that niggled at me about it, why it was so familiar, but I couldn't concentrate.

I couldn't concentrate because U2 had been screaming at me from next door for the last two hours. Every time one of their songs faded into the next, the lull was filled in by the sounds of laughter.

Logan was having a party.

"All those moments would be lost in time like tears in rain," I muttered, tapping my finger against my computer mouse. "All those moments. All those moments . . . All those . . . Arrggggh!" I pushed back from the computer and glowered at the wall connecting my flat to *his*.

It occurred to me that earlier I'd let myself soften a little toward him when he'd casually offered to help Mr. Jenner.

Well, never again.

He was an inconsiderate oaf.

Last night I'd started thinking that it would take visiting a therapist again to deal with my gradually mounting resentment against my new neighbor. But I made the decision in the morning that it would be much cheaper for me to change my work schedule than to visit a therapist. I'd have to work in the afternoon from now on, and that was that.

Okay, so I wasn't really as blasé about having to rearrange my schedule as I was trying to convince myself I was. I knew it would take me days, if not weeks, to come around to a new work and sleeping pattern, but I could see no other choice since a hell-raiser had moved in next door.

Upon that decision, I was up in the morning to run my errands so I could get back in the early afternoon to finish a manuscript that was due back to one of my authors that evening. It was a Saturday, and I'd much rather spend my Saturday with Juno and Chloe, who were buggering off to St. Andrews for the day, but I had work to do.

I was tired, I was disagreeable, and I wasn't in the mood to face any annoying neighbors. So of course I was delighted when my neighbor Janice appeared on the stairs just as I was locking my door.

Janice climbed up the stairs to my landing and stopped at the sight of me. "Did you hear?" she snapped without preamble.

I pulled on my patience like a winter cloak against her icy chill.

Janice lived on the floor above me with her long-term boyfriend, Lukash. I rarely saw Lukash, and thankfully, I didn't have that many run-ins with Janice. She was a defense lawyer for the Scottish courts, she was humorless, and she was . . . Well, there was no other word for it. She was a bit of a bitch really.

"Hear about what?"

"Your next-door neighbor." She gestured to Logan's door, eyes blazing with fury.

So he'd pissed someone else off. I wasn't surprised.

"The ex-con," she spat.

Now I *was* surprised. "Excuse me?"

Janice stepped toward me. I immediately wanted to back away from her. "Mr. Jenner told me that Logan MacLeod mentioned to him that he'd done time. Apparently, the idiot assumed we all knew of his prison time.

That bloody old goat downstairs doesn't even seem to think it's a problem. He just went on and on about that thug fixing his washing machine."

I curled my hands into fists. "Mr. Jenner is not an old goat."

"That's not the point." Janice waved my defense off. "Aren't you terrified you're living next door to a convicted criminal? I went straight onto the phone to Mr. Carmichael, but he insists that thug is a friend of his and that we're actually safer with him as a neighbor. Can you believe it?"

Mr. Carmichael was our landlord. Although I'd never met him personally, he was a very good landlord. If anything went wrong in the building or our apartments, it was fixed immediately. "Perhaps he's a good judge of character. And maybe we *are* safer with Mr. MacLeod here." I couldn't explain why I found myself defending Logan. He was certainly a very inconsiderate neighbor, and I was intimidated by him on occasion. But truly frightened?

No. Never.

Janice grunted. "Oh, you're all idiots. You forget I defend people like that man. I know exactly what kind of person he is. *I'll* be looking for a new place to rent."

Oh, finally some good news.

I just managed to stifle my smile. "Okay. Have a good day, then." I skirted around her and hurried down the stairs before she subjected me to any more of her judgmental bile.

I had just entered the supermarket when Aidan called and asked me if I fancied grabbing a quick coffee. I knew saying yes was deliberate procrastination, but I talked myself around to it because coffee might wake me up a bit and thus give me more energy for my work later.

The low spring sun cast the outside of the coffee shop in a beautiful soft light. I shaded my eyes against it and saw Aidan sitting at one of the little metal tables. He'd already ordered me a coffee.

I smiled gratefully as I slipped into the seat across from him. "You are a rock star." I immediately wrapped a chilled hand around the hot cup and sipped at the smooth drink.

Aidan squinted at me against the light of the sun. "You look knackered."

I grunted. "Thank you."

"Is it that neighbor of yours?"

I thought on the news Janice had imparted this morning and decided not to mention it to Aidan. It would concern him. He would jump to conclusions.

Perhaps . . . well, perhaps I should be jumping to conclusions, too, about the fact that my neighbor was a convicted criminal, but I didn't know what he'd been convicted of, I didn't know why Mr. Carmichael seemed so sure of the man's character, and I'd always found it best to reserve judgment until I had all the facts. For instance, I did know Logan MacLeod was arrogant, annoying, and loud. I could judge him all I wanted about that. "He seems intent on living life to the fullest."

"Meaning?"

"He's very loud."

Aidan shrugged. "Well, perhaps he doesn't know how loud he's being. Just say something."

"If I do, he'll just assume I'm being difficult."

"You?" Aidan said. "Difficult? You wouldn't know how to be difficult."

"I don't want to talk about Logan. Why are you lot so interested in my bloody neighbor?"

He grinned. "Because of your reaction to him."

"Oh, not this again. Ever since Chloe introduced you to Juno, you've come to think of her as the queen of perception. I'll have you know she gets lots of things wrong. All the time." I sipped at my coffee and then deliberately changed the subject. "How's Callum?"

Callum was Aidan's teammate. I'd dated him a few years ago for a couple of months, until we both realized we didn't have a lot in common and were actually very boring as a couple. We were definitely better off as friends. A few months after we broke up, Callum started dating Annie, a very outgoing, outdoorsy sports journalist. They'd been together ever since and were planning their wedding.

Aidan's face fell. "Callum and Annie broke up."

"Oh no!" I said, aghast. "Why?"

"Believe it or not, you and she share a very similar family situation, except she still talks to hers. Her parents are dominating and negative, and they've completely tried to take over the wedding. They also started putting pressure on them about grandkids, and not like other parents' kind of pressure. It turns out they own Annie's house. Callum didn't know that. Her mum and dad have threatened to force them out if Annie isn't pregnant within their first year of marriage. Apparently, they believe that having children will prove that Callum is serious about Annie. Unlike marriage."

"Oh my gosh," I murmured, feeling a deep empathy. Other people might think it ridiculous that any parent would act like that—perhaps even disbelieve that such parents existed—but I knew from personal experience that they did.

"Callum kept waiting for Annie to stand up to them. They had already discussed that they were going to have at least a year to themselves as a married couple before they'd try for kids. He could give a shit about the house. He's ready to walk away from it all. But Annie . . . she won't, and she keeps getting pissed at him when he asks her to stand up to her family. Finally Callum got sick of the arguments. He felt trapped by her parents, and he can just see that that's what he's in for, for the rest of his life, if he marries Annie."

"That's awful," I whispered, my chest aching for Callum. "Bloody families."

"They're not all bad."

"No," I agreed. "Especially if you self-build them."

Aidan chuckled. "I have heard that self-building is the smart thing to do."

"As long as you choose good-quality materials, you can't go wrong."

"Am I the good-quality material in this analogy?"

I just grinned, because he knew he was.

I thought on Annie and wished I could go to her and tell her how much better her life would be if she took a chance on Callum and made *him* her family instead.

There would be relief.

Nothing but sweet relief.

It was around two in the afternoon before I eventually climbed the stairs to my flat, carrying my small bag of shopping. I was already editing in my head and was thus jerked out of my own little world at the sound of laughter as Logan's door opened.

I paused in surprise at the sight of the tiny, gorgeous redhead stepping out of his door in front of him. She was not at all his type. She was wearing too many clothes, for a start.

The laughing redhead stopped at the sight of me. She smiled. "Hello."

I was too polite not to return her smile. "Hello." I moved toward my door, but she stopped me again.

"I'm Shannon. Logan's little sister." Her violet eyes gleamed at me in friendly amusement. She stuck out her hand to me.

I shook it. "Grace. It's nice to meet you."

"You're Logan's next-door neighbor, right?"

"Aye," Logan grunted beside her.

I glanced up at his suddenly surly expression and felt a frisson of satisfaction. It was wonderful I annoyed him as much as he irritated me. It really was the only thing that made his inconsiderate noise levels bearable.

"You're not at all how he described you." Shannon grinned up at her brother before turning back to me.

I inwardly questioned the mischief in her stunning eyes and wondered what exactly Logan *had* said about me. "Probably not," I concurred.

"So what do you do, Grace? Logan's the manager at Fire, the nightclub on Victoria Street."

I knew where Fire was. I'd been dragged there to dance several times by Chloe. Why on earth did Shannon feel the need to tell me what Logan's occupation was? The job made sense, considering the late hours he kept. "I'm a freelance book editor." I looked up into Logan's eyes and added pointedly, "I work from home."

"Oh, that's great," Shannon said enthusiastically.

Why, oh why, hadn't this friendly sweetheart moved in next door instead of her grumpy older brother?

"It can be." I took a deep breath, suddenly finding courage in Shannon's presence—or her possible role as buffer. "I work late hours. I couldn't last night, however." I tried not to falter under Logan's imperious expression. "Your party was very loud. I'm not a fan of U2 at three in the morning, I'm afraid."

Shannon pinched her lips together and looked up at her brother. He stared back down at her, not saying a word in response to my "accusation." Shannon shook her head in admonishment. "Try to be a bit more considerate, eh?"

He crossed his arms over his chest. "Take it with a pinch of salt, Shannon. Miss Farquhar here is a professional complainer."

"Logan!" Shannon looked affronted.

I took even more courage from her reaction. "I complained about your one-night stand's thong drying on my landing and about your other one-night stand getting sick on my doorstep. I *haven't* complained about the numerous nights I couldn't work because of the very loud sex coming from your flat."

His sister stared up at him with round eyes filled with horror. "Logan?"

He glowered down at her but remained quiet. He didn't need to speak. The words "I answer to no one" were written all over his face.

The sound of footsteps interrupted the tense moment, and we all turned as Janice walked down the stairs onto our landing. I braced myself.

The attractive brunette nodded at me. "Grace." She then turned her chin up in such a haughty manner it was almost comical. She sailed past Logan and Shannon without acknowledging them.

As the sounds of her heels faded upon her descent, Shannon whispered, "What was that?"

I shifted uncomfortably, hating to be the bearer of bad news. Even if it was to Logan. "I'm afraid Mr. Jenner made the mistake of mentioning Logan's time in prison to Janice. Mr. Jenner is so nice, you see. He doesn't realize that people like Janice . . . well . . . *aren't.*"

The news caused Logan's whole body to tense. Even his facial features tightened.

Shannon paled. "We thought everyone knew already. Are you saying *now* they know?"

For some reason I could not fathom, I felt an unpleasant sensation in my stomach and suddenly realized I felt bad for Logan.

Who would have thought?

"It makes no difference," I hurried to assure them both. "Janice . . . well, we all know how unfriendly she can be. I wouldn't worry. Everyone else will be fine." I shrugged, not knowing what else to say. "It was lovely to meet you, Shannon." I turned toward my door and then stopped. I glanced over my shoulder at Logan, who was staring at me in a way that made my breath catch.

He looked . . . disarmed.

I shook off my reaction to his reaction and said in what I hoped was a diplomatic tone, "If you could try to be a little more quiet, I'd appreciate it."

Logan gave me a sharp nod. "Party noise I can lower. However, how loud women are in my bed is out of my control."

"Oh, Logan." Shannon made a comically disgusted face at his arrogance, and her brother broke out into a massive grin.

Once more I felt breathless at the sight of him smiling widely down at his sister. It was the first time I'd ever seen Logan MacLeod smile in a way that was pure and real and not tainted by mockery.

What a sight it was to behold.

Suddenly he looked at me, and our gazes locked.

Frantically I searched for a way to release myself.

Breathe, Grace. Breathe!

I blew out air between my lips and forced myself to lower my gaze. I opened my door and stepped inside. "As always, I'm charmed, Mr. MacLeod," I said, wishing I'd injected more sarcasm into it.

I closed my door before he could say or do anything to throw me off-balance again.

CHAPTER 4

Just as I expected, Logan's past became a nonissue once Janice moved out of our building. It seemed everyone, like me, was reassured by Mr. Carmichael that we were in no danger with Logan in the building. Despite my aggravation with my neighbor, I couldn't help but wonder what it must be like for him in everyday society as an ex-convict. It would seem he'd fallen on his feet regarding a job—Mr. Carmichael owned Fire and had obviously offered Logan a position there. But surely that was about knowing the right person. Not everyone was a Mr. Carmichael. Janice was a great example. So whenever Logan had to fill out a form or explain absences for whenever it was he did his time, he had to face judgment.

In a way he was still doing his time.

I knew how deep the cut was when people refused to see beyond their own perceptions and judgments of you.

Despite myself, I think I really did feel bad for him. However, and I would never admit it out loud, I was incredibly curious to know what it was he'd been sentenced for. Clearly, it was a misdemeanor in conviction terms, right? Or Mr. Carmichael wouldn't be so assured of his stability. Maybe that was naive of me, but I was blissfully ignorant in my naïveté and quite happy to be.

It helped that, as promised, Logan attempted to be more considerate with his noise levels. There was one instance over the next few weeks of loud sex, but there was no music or partying. When we passed each other in the stairwell, we offered a polite nod of acknowledgment, mostly because ignoring each other would be bad manners.

Life was returning to a sense of normality and I was even working at night again.

What I wasn't doing was getting out much.

After the disastrous date with Bryan, which was really the fifth in a long line of disastrous dates, I felt more than a little gun-shy, but I was also bored. Chloe's fiancé was home for a bit and Aidan was in focused "training mode."

So when Chloe called me up at the beginning of the week to ask me if I fancied getting fixed up with a colleague of hers, I reluctantly said yes.

To my pleasant surprise, John was handsome in an old-fashioned kind of way and nervous upon meeting me in a way that was endearing. Half an hour into our dinner date, however, I was growing concerned by the quick rate at which he was consuming wine. It seemed he needed the alcohol as fortification to converse with me, and it also seemed he just didn't know when to stop.

And John and alcohol apparently weren't a good mix.

His dark eyes had been friendly and kind when he approached me in the restaurant. They were warm, even if his gaze did dart around the room anxiously as we chitchatted while deciding what to eat.

By his third glass of vino, however, a mocking light entered the backs of his eyes.

"I've seen pictures of you, you know," he said.

I looked up from my pasta, wondering what on earth he meant. "Excuse me?"

He grinned, the smile off-kilter, lazy with wine. "On Facebook. Chloe shows me her pictures on Facebook. I've always thought you were very pretty."

I blushed at the compliment. "Thank you."

John suddenly ogled my chest, and I tensed. "You could dress a bit sexier though—don't you think? You've got a cracking figure, but we can't really see it."

Hiding my flinch at the far-too-close-to-the-bone comment, I looked at his almost-empty wineglass and wished I had it in me to say something, but I didn't want to cause a scene in the restaurant. I met his glazed stare with one of quiet reproach. "I like my style just fine."

He held up his hands defensively. "Oh, I didn't mean to be insulting. I was just suggesting that you might not be single if you dressed a bit better."

I almost choked on my food.

"And you might look better with your hair down. You look a bit uptight with it up like that."

I squeezed my eyes closed, trying to block him out, because unfortunately, his criticisms were a trigger . . .

The butterflies swarming in my stomach threatened to upend all the nothing in it. I'd never felt so nervous. I hadn't been able to eat all day.

My first school dance.

I stared into the mirror, fidgeting with my hair and my dress and wondering if I should have worn my hair up and if I should have worn the black dress instead of the purple one.

"Why is there a boy at the door?"

I whirled around, my pulse instantly racing at the sight of my mother leaning against my doorframe. She was frowning at me as she swirled a glass of red wine in her hand.

"I thought you were having dinner with Mrs. Ferguson this evening."

Mother scowled at me. "Clearly I'm not. What are you hiding? Why are you dressed in that hideous monstrosity?"

"I got asked to go the school dance."

She snorted. "By the short boy at my door? He has acne." She wrinkled her nose in disgust.

I flushed and looked away. "His name is Michael and I like him."

"Does he come from a good family?"

"Why?" I looked up, scared because Michael's dad was a dentist and his mother was an actress on a soap opera. It was hard to know if that made them a "good" family or not.

"Because," she sighed impatiently, "I need to know if, despite the acne, this boy is worth my advising you out of a dress that makes you look like you have four thighs instead of two." She stared at me suspiciously. "Have you been sticking to that diet I told you to start?"

I trembled. "The nurse at school said it's not meant for a fourteen-year-old."

"Why the bloody hell does the nurse at school know anything about your eating habits?"

"I—I fainted at school."

Mother rolled her eyes. "Dear God, how maudlin."

My finger curled into the fabric of my dress, crushing it. I was slender, and still it didn't seem to be skinny enough for my model-thin mother.

"Well?" she snapped. "Who is this boy?"

"His mother is Andrea Leeds."

"The actress?" Mother tilted her head in thought. "I suppose it could be worse. Well, you can't wear that." She put her glass down on my desk and sauntered over to my wardrobe. "Let's see if we can't find you something that gives the illusion of a figure. Boys want girls who look like girls, you know, Gracelyn. You won't ever be sexy, but we can but try to make you feminine." She stared doubtfully at my wardrobe selection. "We'll also need to do something with your hair. You look like a bloody waif. You're getting it cut next week."

I touched a strand of my long hair. "I don't want to cut it."

Her head jerked around, her dark eyes flashing angrily. "As long as you're under my roof, taking my money and representing my name, you will do as I say. Understood?"

"Yes, Mother."

"Bloody children," she muttered, turning back to the clothes. "I'd never have had any if it weren't for your goddamn father and his need for heirs to his bloody *empire. But does he give a shit that it's me who's left to deal with your stupidity? No, he does not . . ." She trailed off, lost in thought.*

Tears burned in my eyes, but like always, I fought against them and the painful lump in my throat . . .

"Oh fuck," John groaned, running his hand through his hair in distress. "I'm just saying all the wrong things. I say these things, and in my head they sound helpful, but they come out all wrong." He leaned across the table, and his elbow hit the bottom of his dessert spoon. It pinged up off the table. He didn't even notice. "I think you're gorgeous, Grace. I really do."

I smiled weakly at my drunken date. "It's all right. Let's just finish dinner."

Thankfully, John prattled on through dinner without critiquing me again, although he also never asked me anything about myself. He talked a lot about his job and his parents and his love of rugby. In fact, the only time he asked me a question was when he gushed, "What it's like to be friends with Aidan Ramage?"

"Friendly?" I offered, not knowing how to answer the question when his tone bordered on sycophantic.

His "admiration" for Aidan didn't salvage the date. I understood how hard it could be to meet new people and how nerves could make the nicest person act like an idiot. But dating a lush was just not for me. Especially not one who reminded me of my mother.

"Let me walk you home." John swayed a little as we stood outside the restaurant. It had been a late dinner, so now the sky was dark and the moon was out. The restaurant was in Old Town and only a few streets away from my flat, and the area was still buzzing with people. I didn't mind walking home alone despite the drizzle in the night air. In fact, I would have preferred it.

"I'll be fine."

"No, I insist. You're by the university, right?" He turned and began walking.

I sighed and hurried after him. "You really don't have to walk me home."

"It would be ungentlemanly of me not to see you home. There are creeps out here, you know." He threw me another lazy, drunk grin.

I just stopped myself from rolling my eyes.

"So." John stuck his hands in his pockets and looked at me. "Do you like your job?"

I was surprised by the sudden interest in my life. "Um . . . yes. I love keeping my own hours and . . . well, I get to read and shape books for a living."

He wrinkled his nose like a little boy. "Books. Yak. Aren't you bored all the time?"

"No." I huffed in annoyance.

"What about your parents? They still in England?"

"Yes."

"What do they do for a living?"

"My father works in the media, and my mother is a housewife."

"A housewife, eh? Your dad must make a bob or two."

Or a billion. "Hmm."

"Got any brothers or sisters?"

I stared up at his profile, annoyed that he'd decided to get nosy. "A brother. You?"

"No, thank God. What does your brother do?"

"He works for my father."

"What's his name, then?"

"Oh, look!" I said a little too brightly. "We're almost at mine." I stopped. "Well, good night, then."

"Oh no." He shook his head and shot me a grin that caused an unpleasant shiver to ripple over me. "Let me walk you to the door."

Knowing exactly what he was expecting when we got to the door, I shook my head. "I think we should just say good night."

Instead of agreeing, he turned swiftly on his heel and started down Nightingale Way. The street was quite dark, shaded by all the buildings and interspersed sparsely with street lighting. Much of the light cast over the wet cobbles was offered by the ever-helpful moon. Feeling uneasy, I followed John.

"What number are you?" he called back to me.

"I'm right here." I slowed to a stop in front of the blue door to my building. "Thank you for dinner."

John did a little skip back to me. "I could come up for coffee." He grinned down at me hopefully.

I gave him an apologetic smile. "I've got work to do."

"Oh, come on." He edged closer to me, and I stumbled back against the wall. "Ask me up, Grace. You know you want to." He fingered the collar of my light coat, and I instinctively slapped his hand away.

"I'm going inside. You should leave."

He held his hands up in a surrender gesture but took another step toward me.

My stomach flipped, and I glanced right and then left. The dark street was empty. "Really, John. I'd just like to go inside. Good night."

"You're nervous," he said softly. "I get it. I had to have a few glasses of wine to loosen up tonight, I was so nervous about meeting you, but we don't have to be nervous, Grace." He brushed his fingers across my cheek, and I flinched away. "We're two adults just looking for company."

"No. You're drunk, and I want you to leave. Now, please step back."

The door to the building opened before John could react. A large figure stepped outside, and when he shut the door behind him and turned his face, the moonlight revealed Logan. He stopped a moment at the sight of me and gave me a nod before turning his back. He was dressed for work. And he was leaving.

Fear forced my mouth open, and I was just about to call out Logan's name when he halted and turned around. He looked at me, expressionless, and then he looked at John. Despite the blank look on his face, I knew right away he'd deduced the situation when, without a word, Logan pulled his keys out and opened the door. He pushed the door open and stepped toward me. "Grace," he said.

Relief flooded me, and I knew I couldn't hide it just as I hadn't been able to keep the panic from my face when I thought he was leaving. I darted past him and inside, glancing over my shoulder to see John take a step toward the door. Logan blocked the doorway, and I watched, fascinated, as he intimidated John into retreating without saying one bloody word.

John ran a shaky hand through his hair, suddenly looking anywhere but at Logan, and then he spun on his heel and started striding a little unsteadily down our street.

Logan entered the building and closed the door. We just stared at each other for a second before he gestured for me to move.

I started down the hall, hearing him fall into step behind me. He followed me all the way up the stairs until we reached my flat, and he watched as I fumbled for my keys in my purse. When I managed to get ahold of them, they rattled in my trembling hands.

Logan's warm hand curled around mine, and he gently eased the keys from my grip. He opened my door for me. "You all right?"

"Yes, thanks." I gave him a small, grateful smile. "I just feel like I've been stuck in episodes of *Sex and the City* on my last few dates. There are some bizarre men out there." He didn't reply, and I shifted uncomfortably. "Well, thanks again." I moved to go inside, and he said my name. "Yes?"

Logan was no longer expressionless. There was a tautness to his features and a shadow of dark purple in his eyes. I recognized that look. He was angry. "Never let a drunk man walk you home again."

Flummoxed that his anger seemed to be born from concern, I could only nod, tongue-tied.

He stared at me pointedly, and I stared dumbly back at him.

Logan sighed impatiently. "Close your door, Grace. I'm not leaving for work until I hear the sound of your lock turning."

"Oh." I flushed at my silliness and eased the door shut. I turned my lock and put the chain in place. "Good night!" I called through the door.

"Good night, Miss Farquhar," he returned, and I heard the rumble of dry amusement in his voice before the sounds of his footsteps faded into the distance.

The sun felt wonderful on my skin. The waves were crashing to shore. I had no worries, no responsibilities, just never-ending time and white sands.

Life was perfectly, gloriously cliché in its utter heavenliness.

"Grace."

I squeezed my eyes tighter shut against the sound of the masculine voice in my ear.

"Grace." The voice became more insistent. "Grace, wake up."

Suddenly my sun lounger was flipped on its side, and I awoke with a jolt. Breathing hard, I blinked against the darkness of my bedroom, and as my eyes adjusted to the light, my heart started to hammer harder against my chest. Logan was sitting on my bed.

"What?" I whispered in fright, leaning over to switch my bedside light on. I wasn't imagining it. Logan MacLeod was sitting on my bed, wearing nothing but a pair of faded old jeans. I forced my gaze to his face. "What are you doing here?"

His violet eyes were hot on me, his silent presence potent.

My breath caught.

My lower stomach clenched against the burst of tingles between my legs.

"Logan?"

He placed a hand slowly on either side of my hips and leaned forward until his face was so close to mine our lips were almost touching. A fierce hunger flashed across his face, and I gasped, feeling arousal shoot through my body.

He wanted me.

Suddenly he grasped me by the nape of the neck and hauled me against him.

His mouth captured mine. I instantly melted into him and wrapped my arms around him, my fingers pressing into the muscle beneath his hot skin.

His kiss was hard, demanding, almost punishing, and I reveled in it. Logan groaned, the reverberations causing my nipples to tighten in reaction, and I shuddered. My reaction ignited something inside of him, and he shoved me roughly onto my back before hauling the covers off me. I stared up at him in aroused astonishment as he tugged on my pajama shorts. He slid them deftly down my legs, along with my underwear, and then he was braced over me, nudging my thighs apart as he stared down into my eyes. Logan's hands encircled my wrists, and he pinned my arms above my head as he pressed his jeans-covered erection between my legs.

"Grace," he whispered hoarsely, the word filled with need.

"Logan," I pleaded.

His right hand left my wrist to draw down his zipper. He shoved his jeans low enough to release his erection and then returned his hand to my wrist to pin me to the bed.

Logan slammed inside me before I could draw another breath. I cried out at the pleasure-pain that surged through me.

My legs parted, urging him to go deeper. He did. He pulled back out only to thrust in even harder. His rhythm was fast. It was rough. It was molten.

It was unlike any sex I'd ever had before.

I gasped for more as Logan pounded into me, his features fierce and taut with lust.

The headboard rattled against the wall as Logan fucked me toward climax. As the orgasm tore through me, I cried out his name so loudly, I was sure the whole building heard me.

Lost in some lust-fogged hyperspace, I distantly felt Logan still. And then he shuddered on a throaty groan that made my inner muscles clench around him. He threw his head back as he came, and I watched him in awe. Finally, he finished and his head lowered.

Violet eyes pierced right through me, and he gave me this mocking, calculated smile. "I told you all you needed was to get laid."

My eyes flew open, and I couldn't see anything or hear anything but the rushing waves of blood in my ears.

I launched myself across my bed and fumbled for the light switch on my bedside lamp. Soft light flooded the room, and I gazed around.

I was alone.

I was also covered in sweat.

My body was lit with arousal.

I flopped back against my pillow, my cheeks inflamed and the erotic dream burned into my brain.

I'd had a sex dream about Logan MacLeod.

With a moan of absolute mortification, I covered my eyes with my arm as if somehow I could block out the memory of the dream.

But I couldn't.

I'd had a sex dream about that grumpy, irritating, arrogant, inconsiderate ruffian of a man! How was it possible? He wasn't even my type! No.

No.

NO!

"Oh God," I groaned as I thought of something even worse.

How on earth was I ever going to face him again?

CHAPTER 5

_____

H is considerate streak was over.

I glowered at my reflection in the gilded silver mirror in my bedroom.

The person looking back at me was unrecognizable.

I looked like hell.

Because of him.

Only hours after I was jolted awake by the dream I needed to stop
acknowledging ever happened, I was awoken by the noise coming from
Logan's bedroom. Loud—extremely loud—sex.

"THAT'S RIGHT. RIGHT THERE. OH BOY. RIGHT THERE.
OH, LOGAN. OH, LOGAN. OH, LOGAN . . . AHHHHHHH!"

And she was American. He was obviously branching out.

Not that I cared. Nope.

I was, however, surprised and outraged when the next night I got
even less sleep because the American was back, and she and Logan went
three rounds of "RIGHT THERE."

And she returned last night for more rounds of it.

Seventy-two hours of no sleep.

It did not look good on me.

If he bloody well returned with the American again, I was going to . . . "What, Grace?" I curled my lip at my exhausted reflection. "Shout at him? Let him have it? Scold him? Because you've done so well at it in the past."

What if the American did make a fourth appearance? I lowered my gaze, unable to look at myself anymore as I stood there with my messy hair, wearing sweatpants and a long-sleeved shirt because I was too tired to iron something decent.

Was Logan MacLeod finally settling in to become a one-woman man?

I turned around and strode out of my bedroom, my mood darkening to the black-hole level. Marching through my flat, I snatched up my purse. I needed chocolate and coffee. There was no way I was getting through the day without either one of those.

Locking the door behind me, my shoulders instantly hunched up around my ears at the familiar sound of Logan's door opening.

Oh God, was life really this unfair?

Feeling my cheeks bloom with heat at the thought of Logan seeing me so disheveled, I turned slowly around.

He was staring over at me as he locked up. "Grace."

"Mr. MacLeod." I glanced away, willing the memory of that bloody dream away.

"You all right? You look like shit."

And that was it.

The straw that broke the back of that damn camel everyone was always piling straw on top of! Looking at him, seeing him standing there, well rested despite his sexual gymnastics at the crack of bloody dawn, I saw red.

"I look like shit?" I took a bristling step toward him.

Logan raised an eyebrow at my tone.

"Do you know *why* I look like shit?"

"No, but I suddenly have a feeling I'm to blame." He crossed his arms over his chest, clearly not amused.

"Yes." I nodded frantically, the lack of sleep making me frenzied in my anger. "You are to blame!" My voice echoed off the concrete walls of our stairwell, but I was past caring. "Seventy-two hours. Seventy-bleeding-two hours I have been awake."

"That's not my problem, and frankly, I'm not in the mood to deal with this . . . hysteria." He walked toward the stairs, dismissing me.

"Don't you walk away from me."

He stopped. Turned. He raised an eyebrow. "Am I supposed to be frightened? Christ, Grace, it's like getting bitten by a butterfly."

I huffed, furious that he was making fun of me when my standing up to him was a momentous accomplishment. "How dare you! For the last three nights I've had to put up with the constant loud sex from you and your bloody American. I just want peace and quiet! I want some bloody goddamn fucking sleep!"

My words seemed to soak into the coldness of the stairwell, ringing against the walls, stunning Logan.

After a moment's silence, during which I at once berated myself for losing my ladylike cool and mentally shook my hand for taking a stance, Logan cleared his throat.

"Have you got a glass up against the wall?"

"Excuse me?" I shook my head, confused.

"How did you know I've been fucking an American?"

My mouth dropped open at his obtuseness. "Because. I. Can. Hear. Every. Word. She. Says."

"Och, no. You must be straining to listen."

My anger reignited. "Are you mad? Why on earth would I be straining to listen?"

He shrugged. "I don't know. You tell me."

"Are you always this deliberately irritating?" I huffed, mirroring his stance by crossing my arms over my chest.

To my surprise, this caused Logan's lips to twitch, and his eyes started dancing with humor. "I only seem to irritate you." He cocked his head to the side. "I wonder why that is."

"Because," I whined, my head lolling with exasperation and tiredness, "I'm sleep deprived, and it's all your fault, you bloody wretched man-whore."

"Well, this is a whole other side to you. It's quite unpleasant. I may have to speak to the landlord about it. I can't take this kind of abuse."

My head jerked upright and I glowered at him. "I swear if you don't start taking this seriously I will push you down those stairs."

"Now you're threatening my life." He *tsk*ed. "That won't do at all."

"Now!" I yelled. "Now you decide you have a sense of humor?"

"Uh, excuse me." A soft, young voice interrupted our argument.

Standing a few steps down from our landing was a girl. A very pretty girl with dark hair and olive skin. She was dressed in a school uniform, and she looked a little pale—when she swallowed hard, I realized she was nervous.

I glanced at my watch. The girl should be in school. Concerned, I took a step toward her, but she was staring up at Logan in scared awe. "Can we help?"

Instead of answering me, she took a shaky step up toward us and light flooded over her face. I drew in a gasp. Behind her glasses, she had the most beautiful eyes. *Violet* eyes surrounded by thick black lashes.

My gaze jerked to Logan, who was staring at the girl in stupefied confusion.

"My name is . . ." She gulped, her chest rising and falling in shallow, fast movements. "I—I'm Maia." Maia licked her lips and clutched tighter to the strap of her shoulder bag. "You're Logan MacLeod, right?"

He nodded dumbly.

"Well, I think . . . I think I—I'm your kid. I'm your daughter."

I sucked in a gasp, never taking my eyes off Logan. His expression shuttered.

"I don't have a kid." But he sounded uncertain.

Agog that in seconds my argument with him had turned into a life-altering revelation for him, I took a moment to shake off my curious stupor. I was intruding on an incredibly private situation and I needed to leave. "I should leave you to talk."

Logan's hand wrapped around my upper arm, drawing me to an abrupt halt. "Grace. Stay."

Since there was really nothing else I could do, considering he was holding me physically hostage, I nodded and tried to relax so he'd let me go. He didn't.

Maia appeared near tears, but I watched her throw her shoulders back despite her fear. Her voice trembled. "Maybe we should go inside to talk."

I didn't even know the girl, but for some reason I felt a surge of pride toward her for her bravery. A sense of kinship, actually. "I think that's a good idea." I pressed against Logan until he looked down at me. "Let's take this inside. Or do you want every one of your neighbors to know your business?"

As he continued to just stare at me, I knew he was in shock.

"Come on, Logan," I joked, trying to draw him out of it. "If we stay out here, I'll start to feel less special about being the only neighbor to be a part of this."

He blinked out of his daze and nodded. He pulled me with him to the door as he opened his flat and nudged me inside first, releasing my arm only once I was in.

I glanced over my shoulder to see him gesture to Maia. The girl strode inside still wearing bravado as a mask. Not a very good mask, but I admired her all the same for trying. I gave her a reassuring smile. "Would you like a cup of tea?" I offered, not even sure if Logan had tea.

"Um . . ." She licked her lips nervously. "Water, please."

"I'll get it," Logan said immediately. "Grace?"

"Oh, I'll have a coffee if you've got it. Milk, one sugar."

He nodded and waved a hand at us. "Living room is straight ahead."

Turned out Logan's flat was a mirror image of mine, which would explain why his bedroom wall abutted mine. There were still boxes lying unpacked. There was nothing on the walls, and the only major piece of furniture in the sitting room was a massive L-shaped black sofa.

"It'll be okay," I said to Maia as she stared around the room, looking terrified. "We'll get this all sorted."

"Um . . . who are you?"

I sat on the sofa and waited for her to join me. She did so slowly, staring at me with those wide, beautiful eyes of hers. Her glasses were a little too big for her delicate features. I swore I could see Logan's sister Shannon in her face though. "I'm Logan's next-door neighbor. Grace."

She frowned. "I thought you were his girlfriend."

I raised an eyebrow. "Why would you think that?"

She shrugged. "You seem close."

Now it was my turn to frown.

"Here we go," Logan said as he came into the room carrying two mugs and a glass of water. He handed the water to Maia, giving her a kind smile.

It occurred to me what a sweet thing that was. This girl had just arrived on his doorstep, announced herself as his daughter; he was in shock, probably petrified, and yet still he was trying to reassure the girl.

Inwardly I grumbled as I took the coffee from him. He was such a complicated bugger. "Thank you," I muttered.

Logan sat down on a large box across from us and sipped at his coffee. An awkward silence fell between us.

"Maia," I said, "who is your mother?"

Logan tensed at the question as Maia turned to him to answer. "Maryanne Lewis."

The way he jerked back at the news suggested he knew exactly who Maryanne Lewis was. "No," he muttered, seeming to shake his head in disbelief. "Maryanne . . . Yeah, she got pregnant, but she told me she didn't want to keep it, that I had no choice. She was getting an abortion. She disappeared. I never saw her again!"

Maia's mouth trembled, and I instinctively reached for her hand. "How old are you, Maia?"

"Fifteen."

"Logan?"

He nodded at me slowly, his eyes bleak. "It was almost sixteen years ago. We were only seventeen." He stood up suddenly. "Fuck. Fuck, fuck, fuck!"

Maia leaned in to me, looking frightened, and I put an arm around her. "It's okay. It's just a shock for him."

Logan glowered at the wall, and I watched him take slow, even breaths as he tried to calm himself. "How could she do that to me? How could anyone do that?"

"She told me she lied to you." Maia pulled gently away from me, and Logan looked at her sharply. "We've been living in Glasgow all this time, but I can't stay with her anymore." Desperation suddenly bled into her words. "I can't! She saw you in the paper, and that's when she told me who you were. They said you were put in prison for attacking your sister's boyfriend because he beat her up and tried to rape her."

I sucked in a huge breath, and Logan's eyes flew to me. We stared at each other as I processed this. Someone tried to rape Shannon? Attacked her? I was horrified.

"You were a hero. Protecting her like that. And you got punished for it. My mum puts me in harm's way all the time, and no one gives a damn. You could look after me better than her."

Logan's attention was forced from me at this unwelcome information. He stared hard at Maia. "What do you mean 'harm's way'?"

Maia ducked her head, threading her fingers together anxiously. "Mum's a junkie."

I closed my eyes. This was getting more melodramatic by the second.

"What do you mean 'a junkie'?" Logan asked quietly, danger in his words.

"Heroin."

"Oh God." I felt sick.

"I can't live with it anymore." Tears started to fall down her pretty cheeks, and I felt a coldness creep into my bones at the expression in her eyes. Such despair for such a young girl.

"Logan," I whispered, looking up at him, pleading, though I didn't know why.

He looked trapped. Terrified. I could tell he wanted to escape.

It was frightening to see. He was usually so together, so in control.

"What can I do?" he snapped at us. "I admit the eyes . . . You look like . . ."

"Shannon," I offered helpfully. He glared at me. Clearly it was not helpful.

"Your sister?" Maia said, her eyes brightening with curiosity.

Logan groaned and rubbed his hand over his short hair. "I don't know for certain if you're my kid."

I just managed to contain my snort, but he shot me a dirty look anyway, as if he knew exactly what I was thinking.

"How did this happen? Two minutes ago I was just . . . You can't stay here, Maia. I have to take you back to your mum, and then I'll have to talk to her about all of this."

Maia stood up. "Please. I don't want to go back. That's why I'm here. You don't know what it's like there."

Faced with her fear, Logan could only stare at her helplessly.

When the silence stretched between them, turning physically painful to be around, I stood up. "Maia, you can't stay here with Logan. It isn't right. He could get in trouble. He'll have to take you home until this can all be sorted out."

She bowed her head, her dark hair falling like a curtain and hiding her face. But we both heard her quiet sniffles.

Logan gave me a look as if to say, *What the hell else can I do?*

I gave him a bolstering smile.

And for my troubles . . . "You're coming with us," Logan said to me.

Oh no. "To Glasgow?" I squeaked. No. Absolutely not. I was exhausted. I did not need to witness an emotional roller coaster on top of my exhaustion.

"Yes."

"No. I . . ." My refusal trailed off when Maia abruptly looked up at me, her watery eyes begging me.

They both needed a buffer.

Great.

"Okay." I reached for her hand and gave it a squeeze. "I'm coming with you."

You know in those old Western movies when they shot scenes of bales of hay blowing down empty main streets of small towns? The wind would whistle in exaggeration, the only sound to break through the silence . . .

Let's just say it came to mind as Logan drove us to Glasgow. I didn't even know he had a car. I didn't know enough about cars to know exactly what it was. I just knew it was some kind of Volkswagen and it was at least five years old. It was dusty from disuse.

We were twenty minutes into the journey and Logan had informed me it would take about an hour and twenty minutes to get to Maia's council estate. Someone had to talk. The silence was becoming unbearable.

"You know, I've only ever been to Glasgow city center. For shopping. At Christmas. Oh, and I've been to the theater and out for drinks. There's so much going on in the city center, you just forget how big the rest of the city is."

I got nothing.

"Did you know it used to be the fourth-largest city in Europe?" I rambled on. "That was quite a feat, considering how tiny we are as an island. I think it was the largest after London, Paris, and Berlin, and it was also called the 'Second City in the British Empire' in the Victorian era, and of course it's Scotland's largest city and the third largest in Britain, so it's really no wonder I haven't seen much of it, I suppose, although I lived in London and managed to see quite a bit of that growing up. I could ha—"

"Grace," Logan interrupted. His eyes were still focused on the road in front of him, but I could see he was struggling not to smile. "We've got it. Glasgow's big."

I heard a small giggle from the backseat, and instead of feeling embarrassed by my nervous ramblings, I smiled. I'd gotten a giggle out of Maia. Or Logan had. Or *we* had. It didn't matter who or what; it just mattered that on an exceptionally trying day, the shy little lost girl in the backseat had laughed.

I turned a little in my seat to look behind me. Maia's sad eyes stared into mine. "Do you do well in school, Maia?"

She nodded cautiously.

I had a feeling she did. I gave her a smile of encouragement. "What subjects do you enjoy?"

"I like maths and physics. Mum doesn't get it. She liked art at school."

"I liked maths and physics," Logan said quietly. "I was good at maths and physics."

Maia stared at the back of his head and offered shyly, "I get A's."

I watched his face soften. "Good," he murmured.

That awkward silence began to fall again.

"Well, I'm rubbish at maths and physics," I said. "I had a tutor." I made a face. "He was this horrible pretentious boy in the year above me." I'd hated him. Lawrence Trevelyn. Sebastian had dared Lawrence to put his hand up my skirt and cop a feel during a lesson. I'd felt violated and frightened by the whole thing, and it had taken me a good while to let a boy get near me again.

I shuddered.

"You all right, Grace?" Logan suddenly asked.

I caught him glance at me quickly, his brows puckered. Surprised by his perceptiveness I couldn't say anything for a moment.

"Grace?"

"I'm fine." I turned to Maia and smiled again, brushing the memories off. "Do you like English?"

She shrugged. "It's okay. I'm not as good at it. I only get B's."

"Well, I've got a degree in it if you ever need help. I'm a freelance book editor." I said it without thinking, and I sensed Logan tense beside me.

Maia, however, looked hopeful. "Really? That's cool. And you'd help me, really?"

Oh bugger. I'd gone and put my foot in it now. Logan had only just met the girl. He had no idea what was going on, what the future held, and here was his silly neighbor attaching herself to his . . . possible child. Feeling guilty, I had no recourse, however, but to say, "Of course. I'll give you my number so you can give me a ring if you ever have a question."

Some of the light dimmed in Maia's eyes. "Right," she muttered, and looked away.

I turned back around and caught Logan's annoyed look. I flushed and glanced away.

Perhaps silence was best after all.

I don't know what I'd been expecting. Rumors of the dangers of Glasgow were just that. It was like any big city. It had its crime, its good areas, and its not-so-good areas. It was often exaggerated. I was reassured about the exaggeration as we drove through the well-kept council estates of areas that had been depicted in the media as "rough."

Even when we drew up to the high-rise flats Maia had directed Logan to, I was filled with optimism. Part of me wanted to put Maia in the "overly dramatic teenage girl" file. Was her mum really a junkie, or was she just making stuff up because she'd had an argument with her mum and was upset about finding out who her dad was at such a fragile age?

I ignored my gut, which told me Maia wasn't that kind of teenager.

I didn't want anything she had said to be true.

For her.

And for Logan.

There was graffiti on the walls of the high-rises, but you got graffiti in lots of places these days. That didn't mean anything.

When we entered one of the high-rises, the smells of garbage and urine hit my nostrils and my stomach began to sink. When we reached the first floor, I came to a complete standstill at the grim sight of the heavy-duty iron gate that had been attached over the front door of a flat.

What kind of place was this that you needed that kind of security?

Logan nudged me. "Come on."

"Why?" I pointed at the gate before hurrying to catch up with them.

The muscle in his jaw clenched. "Either the flat of a well-known criminal, or because of their close proximity to the ground floor, they've suffered numerous break-ins."

"This isn't a nice place, is it?"

"No, it's fucking not." Logan's gaze followed Maia as she led us up to the next floor, and I could see his concern mounting.

Maia stopped halfway down the long corridor of the third floor and drew in a shaky breath. "This is it."

Although it had no metal grill over the front of it, the door had been kicked in at one point. Not only were there rubber marks from the soles of shoes, but the wood had buckled and cracked near the bottom of the door. The words "hingoot," "junkie hoor," and "brass monkey slut," among others, were graffitied on the door. I didn't understand what anything but "junkie" and "slut" meant, but I could tell by the darkening of Logan's expression that the other stuff wasn't good.

Reluctantly, Maia took out her keys and let us into the flat.

As soon as we walked in, I was hit by the smell.

"Holy fuck," Logan muttered, and we shared a horrified look.

It smelled of stale sweat, cigarettes, piss, and vomit.

"I try to clean." Maia's complexion had paled, and there were tears of shame in her eyes. "I do. Honest."

Tears pricked my own eyes, a lump of sympathy and anger burning in my throat. I squeezed her arm, but I had to look away from her so I could control my emotions.

"My, is that you!" a voice screeched from the back of the flat.

At that Logan stepped forward and put his hand on Maia's shoulder. He looked like a giant next to the slender teen. I wasn't exactly tall at five six, and she was even shorter. She was only about five three. He led her forward gently, and I followed, taking everything in.

The faded, stained carpets were so threadbare at the edges they were pulling away from the baseboard. We passed a tiny kitchen that looked like it hadn't been modernized since the late eighties. There were stains all over the counters and even the walls, but the surfaces were wiped clean and there were no dirty dishes in the kitchen. There was evidence that Maia was trying her best here.

There were two doors on the other side of the narrow corridor, separated by yellow-stained walls. One door opened to a small, sparse but tidy and clean single room with posters of bands on the wall. Maia's room? The other door caused Logan's brow to furrow deeply as he passed it. Curious, I took a look inside and just managed to squelch a yelp of surprise.

There was a skinny naked man sprawled on his front across a rumpled bed. Around the bed the carpet had been swallowed up by beer cans, cigarette trays, clothes, and rubbish. There was a dresser at the bottom of the bed that had seen better days, and the bedside table closest to me was missing a drawer. It was also covered in gashes and score marks.

I felt ill at the sight of the needles scattered across the top of it.

Unfortunately, we were only greeted by worse when we walked into the small sitting room. Sprawled across what actually looked like a fairly new leather sofa was a skinny mess. The dark-haired woman was dressed in a dirty, oversized white T-shirt and skinny jeans. Her thin hair was pulled back in a disheveled ponytail. She wore no makeup, and when she opened her mouth I could see her teeth were yellow and decaying.

"My God." Logan closed his eyes against the image of her.

Maryanne Lewis clearly no longer resembled herself. Although I had no clue what she'd looked like back when she was with Logan, I could see from her delicate features that she'd once been pretty. But now she looked ten to fifteen years older than Logan, and her sharp cheekbones stretched out her papery skin so she looked gaunt, ill. The color of her complexion was gray. Just . . . wrong.

There were a couple of open bottles of vodka in the room, empty beer cans, dirty ashtrays, unwrapped food, dirty plates, and more needles.

This was bad.

Very bad.

If anything, Maia had *played down* her home situation.

Maryanne narrowed her eyes. "Who the fuck are you?" She stumbled up onto her feet in jerky, frenetic movements. "My, who the fuck is this?"

To my surprise, Maia stepped in to my side, almost but not quite burrowing there. Despite my discomfort and apprehension in her mother's presence, I put my arm around Maia, offering her support.

"Maryanne, this is my dad."

I had to give Logan his due. He didn't flinch at the word. "Maryanne." He stepped toward her, and she jerked back, her eyes wide and glazed. She was agitated. Her skin looked clammy, and she was scratching at her arm constantly.

I didn't know much about drugs, but I had a suspicion she was in withdrawal.

"Fucking bastard," she snapped, stumbling away from him. "Logan. Logan. Oh my God, what did you bring him here for?" She glowered at Maia and then moved toward her.

As I shoved Maia behind me, Logan stepped in front of us. "Maryanne . . . when was your last hit?"

"Too fucking long. Too fucking long. I told that wee bitch to go and get Kells for Dom and me. Where's my fucking money? Eh? Where is it, you wee cunt?"

"Watch it," Logan warned, his tone dangerous, and Maia cowered against my shoulder.

"Who is Kells?" I asked Maia softly.

"Her dealer," she whispered, and there was a rustling before I felt her press something into my hand.

I looked down at a wad of cash. "Logan," I muttered. The idea of a mother sending her fifteen-year-old daughter to a drug dealer settled like oil in my stomach.

Logan glanced over his shoulder, and I held the money out to him. He took it, understanding what it was without my having to tell him. When he turned back to Maryanne, he said, "Is she mine? Did you lie to me?"

"I want my money!" Maryanne screeched.

"Is she mine?"

"Money!"

Logan threw it at her feet and grunted in disgust as she scrambled to pick it up.

"Give me your phone," she begged as she stood up. "Mine needs to be charged and I can't find my charger. Give me your phone."

"So you can call your dealer? No way. Now, answer me." He took a menacing step toward her, and she blinked up at him blankly. "Is Maia mine?"

"Give me your phone." She pleaded again, scratching at her head. "Please. I'm fucked." She stumbled over the coffee table, reaching for a bottle of vodka. "Kells said he would be here yesterday, but he never fucking came. He never fucking came."

Logan turned to us, drawing my distraught gaze to his haggard face. "We'll never get a straight answer out of her when she's like this." He looked over my shoulder to Maia. "I don't know what to do. I can't leave you here, but I can't let you stay with me until we work out this paternity stuff. The only option is Social Services."

"No." Maia pushed away from me, backing up from us. "I've heard stories about it. Worse than this. Please. At least I know what to expect here."

"Maia, it's not all bad in foster care. It would just be temporary," Logan tried to rationalize with her.

"No!" She covered her face, her shoulders shaking as she started to sob.

I don't know what possessed me to speak up. Perhaps it was seeing Maia's mother treat her as badly as my mother had treated me, but in a much worse environment. Or perhaps it was the carefully controlled mask Logan was wearing that slipped every now and then to show his fear. Or maybe it was just I was a decent person who couldn't bear the thought of leaving a child to this. Or maybe I hadn't slept in seventy-two hours and wasn't thinking straight.

Maybe it was all of the above.

"I have a suggestion. Why—"

"My, where's your phone?" Maryanne suddenly stumbled into the middle of us, reaching for Maia. She tugged at Maia's wrists and then slapped her head before Logan could pull her off. He shoved her none-too-gently onto the sofa.

"And stay down," he warned.

"Where's your phone?" Maryanne screeched.

Maia wiped at her tearstained face. "I told you," she whispered. "You smashed it a few weeks ago."

It was time to move this along. "As I was saying, Maia, although it would seem Logan is your dad, we're not one hundred percent sure about that. Surely you can see how inappropriate it would be for a grown man to live with a fifteen-year-old girl who isn't family? However, I'd be happy to let you stay in my guest room until Logan can confirm the paternity." I was shaking badly as I looked up at Logan, not sure I even really comprehended how much responsibility I was offering to take on here. "That way she's close by but not living with you until you have the paternity results."

He nodded slowly. "Aye, that might be . . . But what about school?"

"You'll have to get Maryanne's permission to enroll her at school in Edinburgh until you have legal claim."

"She won't even know I'm gone," Maia murmured.

We heard a groan from the nearby bedroom, and at the widening of Maia's eyes, I said, "Look, let's iron this all out in the car. We should get out of here."

Seeing sense in that, a subdued Logan led us out of the flat, and we all did our best to ignore the sound of retching coming from the sitting room as we left.

CHAPTER 6

If the silence had been awkward in the car, it was painful as we stood outside on our landing with Maia. Both she and Logan had been pensive the entire drive, internalizing whatever was going on in their heads. Me? I was trying not to have a panic attack.

"Maia, why don't you go on inside." I handed her my key. "Logan and I are just going to have a quick word, and then we'll be right in."

She glanced at Logan and then back to me, clearly worried.

"Go on. It'll be fine," I reassured her.

Nodding reluctantly, she turned and put the key in my door.

I looked at Logan, who was staring at me like I was a car coming toward him at a hundred miles per hour with my full-beam headlights on. I gestured to his door. "Let's go in."

Without a word he did as I asked, and I followed his heavy footsteps into his sitting room. He turned and faced me, hands on his narrow hips. "What the fuck am I going to do?"

"Logan—"

"I can't take care of a teenager."

"Logan—"

"No, Grace, you don't understand." He swallowed hard, and I found myself struck dumb by the fear in him. All this time I thought Logan

MacLeod feared nothing, was intimidated by no one, was somehow untouchable. It was unnerving to see him vulnerable. I didn't like it. For some absurd reason, it made me want to fix his situation. Which was probably why I was in this position. He glanced away, running a hand over his short hair. "A few years ago, aye, maybe I could have done this. But I'm not that man anymore."

That's when I think I understood.

Logan MacLeod had been in prison. So who was he before that? And how much had it really changed him?

"It must have been difficult," I said. "Being punished, treated like a criminal for merely protecting your family."

His eyes hardened. "Don't. Don't you do that. Don't you do what she's doing." He pointed to the wall that adjoined my flat. "Don't glorify the situation."

He wanted my bad opinion? Well, that didn't make sense. I remembered how he jumped down my throat when we first met, and I knew now that he thought I was aware of his time in prison. Back then he misunderstood and he was pissed off at me for judging him and thinking badly of him. Now he *wanted* me to think badly of him?

Confused, I shrugged. "I guess I really don't know what the situation was. But I do know what Maia's situation is, and I'm fairly certain she's your daughter, Logan. She deserves better than what she's got. Right now better is you."

He squeezed his eyes closed and kind of collapsed on his armchair. After taking a minute, he looked up at me. "I could call my parents and ask them to take her in."

"No, you bloody will not!"

I jumped, startled as Shannon stormed into the sitting room, her eyes sparking with anger. My eyes rounded slightly at the sight of the man following her into the room. I almost blushed, he was that good-looking. No one should be that good-looking. Although much like Logan in the scruffy, tattooed department, his masculine beauty was bordering on perfection. He was the kind of man I usually got tongue-tied around. He gave me a nod of acknowledgment before settling behind a very unamused Shannon. He put his hands on her shoulders and squeezed lightly, silently offering her support.

"Shannon, what the hell?" Logan said.

"If you didn't want me here, you shouldn't have called me to tell me about your long-lost daughter."

I shot Logan a questioning look.

He sighed. "When I stopped for petrol, I phoned her."

Shannon's eyes softened when our gazes met. "Hi, Grace. Thanks for being here. This"—she patted the arm of the supermodel behind her—"is my fiancé, Cole."

"Nice to meet you." He held out his hand and I noted the leather bracelets and aviator watch he was wearing, along with the chunky silver ring on his middle finger. He was *that* guy. Cool, tattooed, can-pull-off-man-jewelry guy. I tried not to blush and failed as I shook his hand.

"Nice to meet you too." I smiled shyly and turned quickly back to Logan.

His eyes were narrowed on me.

"Back to what you just said," Shannon snapped, dragging her brother's intimidating gaze off me to her. "Like hell are you sending your own kid to our parents. You'd do a much better job yourself and you know it."

Logan got to his feet. "Since when are you anti-parents again? First you ask me to walk you down the aisle; now you think I'm better parenting material than them? I thought we were over this."

"Over this?" Shannon whispered, and something in her voice, in her eyes, made me tense. Cole heard it too and pulled her back against him protectively. "They abandoned me when I needed them the most. They blamed me for what happened. I may play nice to keep this family together, but I will never forget what they did. And neither should you. Is that really what you want for your own daughter, Logan?"

Suddenly I found myself finding kinship with another MacLeod girl in less than twenty-four hours. I didn't know the details, but I was smart. I could put it together. It sounded like their parents blamed her for her own assault, for whatever asinine reason. But I'd been there. I got it.

I wanted to reach out a hand and tell her so.

Luckily for Shannon, she had the gorgeous Cole at her back, and the fierceness in his eyes as he held her told me he would take down anyone who tried to hurt her. I felt an ache in my chest and realized sadly that it was envy. I slapped my conscience for the unjust feeling. If anyone deserved happiness with a good man, it was someone who had gone through what she had.

"I'm not saying they're perfect," Logan said, appeasement in his tone. "But they did raise us. I'm not ready for this, sweetheart. I'm just trying to get my life back together. I'm not set up to be a dad to a teenage girl."

"Then you need to get ready," Shannon advised, her chin jutting out stubbornly.

Logan scowled. "That's easy for you to fucking say."

"Hey." Cole's voice held warning, as did his eyes.

Logan wasn't fazed. "Don't 'hey' me. You both waltz in here and it's obvious you've got grand plans for me as a dad, but I'm trying to tell you I can't do it."

"Who are you?" Shannon jerked away from Cole to get in her brother's face. "Because I don't recognize this guy."

"Don't come into my house and start," Logan warned softly. "You've known about this five seconds and you've clearly not given it proper thought."

Shannon didn't even flinch as her brother towered over her, all bristling and angry. I was so impressed by her. "I know what you told me on the phone. I know that there's a ninety nine-point-nine-percent chance that this girl is yours, that she looks like me, that she's my niece, and that we've missed out on being there for her for fifteen years. I know she's been stuck living with a junkie of a mother, and I know there's a possibility that she's been through hell." She touched his arm, pleading. "She deserves a chance. You both do. And we deserve a chance to have a say in where she stays. She's my family too."

Logan jerked away. "You're not even listening to me."

"Logan—"

Before I could stop myself, I stepped in, cutting her off. "There's a greater issue here."

All three of them stared at me as if I had all the answers. I tried not to turn red with embarrassment under such expectation. "The greater issue for Maia is being with her father." I locked eyes with a resistant Logan. "Maia chose you, Logan. If you abandon her when she needs you . . . Believe me"—I blinked back tears, remembering my own abandonment—"she'll never get over the rejection."

The room was still as my words sank in, and while I was unsure of Shannon's and Cole's thoughts, I felt like I knew where Logan's had gone. The questions in his eyes.

He was wondering if I'd been abandoned.

And it was almost like he cared.

I was confused by the overwhelming sense of connection that passed between us. For a moment it was like we were the only two people in the room.

Shannon cleared her throat, and I shrugged off Logan's intense scrutiny as he turned to his sister. She nodded at him. Logan glanced over at Cole. He nodded too. "You know she's right."

Logan took a deep breath. "Right. Well, looks like a lifestyle change is in order." He looked around his sitting room. "I'll need to do something with this place, turn the second room into an actual bedroom. And fuck . . . I'll need to talk to Braden. I can't work those hours anymore."

"You know he'll do anything he can to help you out," Cole assured him.

"I know." Logan looked at me. "I also know you offered to let Maia stay with you until I have the paternity and the legal stuff sorted out, but you don't have to do that. I get that we were all caught up in the moment, but it's too much to ask."

"She could stay with us," Shannon piped up, looking excited by the prospect. Cole nodded his agreement, a small, tender smile curling the corner of his mouth.

It occurred to me then that they were giving me an out. What did I know about looking after a teenage girl, anyway? And one who was connected to Logan MacLeod? Did I really want to get any more involved with my neighbor?

No. I did not.

I stared at the wall, thinking of the girl on the other side of it.

"I really don't mind." The words just poured out of me before I could stop them. "It means Maia is right next door to you, so you can see her anytime you want while you get it worked out. And I think . . ." I offered him a confused shrug. "I don't know. It sounds presumptuous, but . . ," I trailed off, not knowing how to explain what I was feeling.

Logan did. "Maia's attached herself to Grace." His gaze was soft on me, and I found myself flushing. He'd never looked at me like that before. "She's comfortable with her. I think she feels safe with her."

Although Shannon looked disappointed, she smiled through it. "Then Maia should stay with Grace for now. I'd still like to meet her though."

"Maybe tomorrow, sweetheart. Let's give her some time to adjust." Logan reached for his sister and pulled her in for a hug. "Thanks for being here."

Shannon hugged him back. "*That* . . . Knowing that's the right thing for Maia right now . . . *That's* how I know you can do this. You have been there for me more than Dad ever was, Logan. You can do this. It's who you are."

His arms tightened around her and I felt tears prick my eyes. I brushed them away quickly, but Cole caught me. He grinned cheekily at me.

"What?" I huffed, drawing Logan's gaze as I wiped at the tears. "I'm really bloody tired, okay? It makes me emotional."

They all grinned at me now, and I rolled my eyes, turning away from them. I looked at them again only to say good-bye as they were leaving. Cole was almost out the door and Shannon had just passed me when she abruptly turned around and came at me.

I tensed, relaxing only when she put her arms around me.

"Thank you."

I hugged her back. "You're very welcome."

She pulled away and smiled. Hope glimmered in her beautiful eyes. "This is exactly where he was meant to be," she whispered, and walked away before I could ask her to explain.

The door shut behind her and Cole.

"What did she say?" Logan said.

I shook my head. "Just thank you."

He didn't look convinced, but he dropped it. "What now?"

"Come over." I gestured to the door. "I'll make you and Maia dinner."

He did that staring-at-me-intently thing again. "Why are you doing this? Is it for Maia, or for me?"

Blame it on my exhaustion or temporary insanity, but I found myself confessing a little of my story to him. "Because to a certain extent I've been where Maia is. I know what she's going through. There was no parental figure there for me, *trying*. You're going to try, and I admire that. I'd like to help you both, I guess."

Logan was quiet so long I was starting to feel stupid for revealing that about myself.

"We better go next doo—"

"You're a good woman, Grace Farquhar," Logan interrupted solemnly. "I won't forget this."

Not sure how to respond to his words or the way they pressed down on my chest in painful pleasure, I smirked. "Um . . . you might not think that once you taste my cooking."

. . .

Maia was standing in my sitting room before the bookshelves that lined the full length of one wall.

She was so still and tense that Logan and I could tell something wasn't quite right even with her back to us.

"Maia, are you okay?" Logan said gruffly.

"Maia?"

She looked over her shoulder at us, tears in her eyes. "You have so many books."

Confused, I nodded. "I do like to read."

"But it's like a library. You own all these books."

"Yes, I do."

"And you have really nice furniture." She gestured to the room.

I looked around at my place, drinking it in as if from her perspective. I took pride in my home, not just because it was who I was, but because I worked from home and so I liked to be surrounded by nice things. My style was shabby chic. Everything was pretty but comfortable. Lots of cushions and throws and books and artwork.

"It does look like a fucking magazine spread," Logan muttered, staring around at everything.

"I'll take that as a compliment," I said dryly.

"And it's clean," Maia added. Fresh tears pooled in her eyes. "This is how other people live. With books and nice things and clean. Why didn't she give me that?" she begged. "I loved her. She should have loved me and given me that." Her tears broke free, but before I got to her Logan did. He was across the room and pulling her into his arms in under a few seconds.

He let her cry it all out as I stood there crying for her too.

But I was also hopeful for her, because only ten minutes ago Logan MacLeod had been a scared-shitless ex-con, and now he was stepping up for Maia, comforting her without even having to be asked.

There was a possibility Logan was a natural at this stuff. His sister certainly seemed to think so.

For Maia's sake, I hoped so.

"Is this all right?" I said, pulling back the duvet on my guest room bed.

Maia was looking a little shell-shocked again. "It's really nice."

The guest room was decked out with a mahogany sleigh bed and matching furniture. The walls were a soft lilac, and the accent colors for the furnishings were black and silver. I loved my guest room and was more than thankful I had it set up and ready to go.

Dinner had been awkward. I had had no grand expectations of anything else. It was going to take time for Maia and Logan to get used to each other. Logan asked questions about school and her hobbies. She muttered more stuff about maths and physics and something about a choir, but it was like pulling teeth to get information from her. I think it had all just hit her.

Plus, she and Logan were both exhausted, and Logan had to leave early to get ready for work. It was only eight o' clock, but Maia's lids were drooping, so I'd insisted she get ready for bed.

We had a lot to do the next day and we all needed rest.

She dumped her book bag on the floor as I handed her a pair of clean pajamas.

"You can borrow those for now. Tomorrow we'll need to do some shopping. We'll just get you a few things until . . ." I trailed off, not knowing how to complete that sentence without sounding insensitive.

"Until Logan gets the paternity results back," Maia finished for me. "It's okay. I'm not stupid. I know it would be insane of either of you to spend too much money on me for it to come back that I'm not his kid."

"I think we both know that with those eyes of yours and that face that is scarily similar to his sister's, the chances are you're Logan's. But that doesn't mean this will all work out legally. We're being cautious because you might not get to stay with him, and I just want you to be prepared for that."

Her lower lip trembled, but she nodded and slumped down on the bed. "Why are you helping, Grace? I mean, you and Logan aren't together, and from the questions he was asking you at dinner, it doesn't even seem like you know each other that well."

I sighed and sat down next to her. "Honestly?"

"The answer to that is always yes."

I smiled at her response. "Okay. Noted. The truth is, Logan moved in here only a few months ago, and we've been at loggerheads for most of it. But I don't think he's a bad guy. In fact, I'm fairly certain that he's one of the good ones." I thought of all his women. *Well, for the most part.* "But mostly I'm doing this for you."

"Why? You don't even know me."

"Because I've been where you are—looking for family because the one I was born with let me down in a way you can't forgive."

She stared up at me with those wise violet eyes. "They hurt you too."

I nodded. "I made a new family here with my friends. I just want the same for you."

Silence enveloped us, but this time it was the sweet kind, made even more so when Maia reached across the bedspread and slipped her hand into mine.

———————

CHAPTER 7

"I don't really need this." Maia stared at me with those big woeful eyes of hers as she stood in a changing room.

"It's cute." I gestured to the dress she'd tried on. It looked particularly cute with her grungy biker boots. "We should get it." I patted my purse and reminded her, "Logan's credit card."

She looked down at the ground. "I just don't want him to be mad at me for spending too much money."

I'd been having so much fun with Maia that morning, making her breakfast, taking her shopping, that I'd temporarily forgotten how scary and confusing this must all be for her. Just because she initiated the whole thing didn't mean she wasn't terrified it could all blow up in her face. "Logan won't be mad. We've barely bought anything. He knows you need at least a week's wardrobe. That's what we're doing."

The nod she gave me was reluctant, but we ended up buying the dress along with a pair of jeans and a few shirts. She changed out of her uniform and into a set of her new clothes. Afterward I led Maia away from Princes Street and up onto the path that ran along the outskirts of Calton Hill, where we would have privacy.

I had woken up that morning to the sound of my kettle boiling at five a.m. Maia was in my kitchen, making herself a cup of tea, moving from one foot to the other with nervous energy. Her eyes were bloodshot, and that, along with how early it was, told me the girl had gotten hardly any sleep. I thought the best thing to do was get her out of the flat. Logan had given me his credit card before he left the previous night for work, and I'd thought Maia would be like most teenage girls, and that shopping would take her mind off things.

It had not.

She had so many thoughts right now I could practically hear the buzz of them over the sound of the busy city-center traffic below us.

"You can talk to me," I announced. "If you want to talk to me about anything that happened at home. I understand if you're not ready yet for that. I just want you to know that I'm here."

She stared out over the city, and for a moment I thought she might not answer. Finally she spoke. "Maybe you could just tell me more about you?"

It occurred to me then that for all Maia knew, I was a crazy person she was entrusting with her well-being. I didn't think she believed that, but I could understand her hesitation. She had been desperate to get away from the situation with her mother, and that meant taking a big risk, such as living with me. "Sure. That's only fair. What would you like to know?"

Finally she looked at me. "You're an editor? For, like, a publisher?"

"No. I'm a freelance editor. I mostly do editing for self-published fiction writers, but I also copyedit academic papers."

"And you make a lot of money? You have nice things."

I grinned at the nosy question. "I make just enough. Most of that nice stuff I found while bargain hunting, and a few pieces are from a previous life."

She frowned. "What does that mean?"

Although this was a topic I usually shied away from, I knew to earn Maia's trust I was going to have to show her I trusted her in return. "My parents have a lot of money."

I watched as she processed this. "But you don't talk to them anymore," she deduced.

"No, I don't."

"Can I ask why?"

"You *may*," I corrected her with a reassuring smile.

She blushed a little and looked away. "*May* I ask why?"

"Well, it's not something I like talking about, but . . . my parents are not very nice people."

"When did you stop talking to them?"

I searched her face, wondering why she wanted to know so much. "About seven years ago. I went to university here at Edinburgh, and when I graduated I returned to London. I tried to be a part of the family, but it . . . Let's just say I was better off back in Edinburgh, where I felt more at home with the friends I'd made here. I stayed in a flat with a number of them for a while, and then they all started pairing off and getting engaged. By then I'd built up a clientele and was making good money editing, and so I found my little flat on Nightingale Way."

Maia came to an abrupt stop, and I halted too, looking back at her quizzically. "So you did it," she said softly. There was something in her tone. Something akin to awe. "You made a life for yourself outside of your family. You really did it."

I understood now. "Yes. I really did." *And you will too.*

Her eyes grew big, luminous, and there was something hesitant in them. "Can . . . *May* I ask what your family did that was so awful?"

I looked out over the city I loved and sighed. "Some other time perhaps."

When Maia didn't reply, I glanced sharply back at her, afraid I'd hurt her feelings. Instead her sad smile was one that offered understanding.

"That was quick." Logan was stooped over, his elbows leaning on the railing of our landing as he watched us climb the stairs. I looked up at him, and my smile faltered when I took in his appearance. He looked as exhausted as Maia.

"Turns out Maia is not much of a shopper." I threw her a teasing smile as we stepped onto the landing to join Logan. I held up the bags in my hand. "I had to force-feed her."

He straightened up, eyeing the bags and then Maia. "Did you get everything you needed?"

She nodded shyly.

We *had* gotten her everything she needed. Clothes, underwear, shoes, and toiletries.

Logan reached for the bags Maia was carrying. "Let me help you with those."

I smiled at the way she watched his every movement with big round eyes, completely fascinated by him, before I let us into my flat. They followed me inside to the guest room, and I dumped the bags on Maia's bed. Logan followed suit, and he took in the room. "This is nice. Do you like it, Maia?"

"It's really nice," she agreed quietly.

"Oh, here." I dug in my purse for his credit card and handed it to him. Our eyes met, and he gave me this little smirk. I laughed. "Don't worry. We were kind."

His smirk turned into a tired smile, and I ignored the little pang of feeling it produced in my chest. "I'm sure you were. Have you guys had lunch? I thought I could take you out."

"We haven't. But you know . . . I've got some work to do. Why don't you take Maia?"

We locked gazes again, and that little pang I felt quadrupled at the gleam of gratitude in his eyes. "That sounds great. What do you think, Maia?"

She nodded, and I could see her trying to mentally bat away her nerves like she had done in our landing yesterday when she'd confronted Logan. *My gosh, was that only yesterday?*

"What do you fancy?" Logan said as he guided her out of the room.

"Um . . . a cheeseburger?"

"Oh, my kind of food, girl. I know where we can get a good burger."

"Have fun!" I called after them.

Maia gave me a wave at the door, and Logan lifted his chin toward me in what I assumed was a macho good-bye. When the door closed behind them, I bit my lip.

What the hell was I doing?

"What the hell are you doing?" Aidan yelled.

I winced and pulled my phone away from my ear.

"Grace? Grace!"

"I'm here," I snapped. "Stop yelling before you blow out my eardrum."

"I was shouting at my teammate, who is acting like a complete arse," he said. "Sorry. I'm in the locker room. Anyway, I probably should be yelling at you. Would you like to explain to me what on earth made you think it was a good idea to take in a strange homeless girl who may or may not be your annoying next-door neighbor's long-lost daughter?"

I'd decided it was best to call Aidan and let him in on my current situation, because he'd be pissed off at me if he found out about it much later. However, I was now rethinking that decision.

"Well, when you say it like that, it sounds nuts."

"Because it is nuts."

"Look, they needed my help."

Aidan grunted at that. "I'm coming over to meet them."

I frowned at the thought. "I don't think that's a good idea. Maia is overwhelmed as it is."

"I'm sorry this girl is going through all this and I think it's amazing that you want to look out for her, but I'm looking out for you. I'll be over at yours in a bit to meet them. No arguments."

I smiled because it wasn't so bad having someone care about me. "Fine. But I'm not feeding you."

He was quiet a moment. "But I'll be hungry."

I snorted, knowing he was pouting like a little boy on the other end of the line. "Fine. I'll feed you."

"Do you have feelings for this guy? Is that what this is?"

I froze at Aidan's question, hot oven tray held aloft in midair. "What?"

"Um . . . Why don't you put the sausage rolls down before you answer that?"

True to his word, Aidan had come over after his training, and I'd decided to heat up some snacks like sausage rolls and little mini samosas for our lunch while Logan was out with Maia.

I had not expected to be hit with a question I really didn't know how to answer.

Putting the hot tray down, I tugged off my oven gloves and turned my back to put them away so I didn't have to look Aidan in the eye. "It's not like that. Impossible though it may seem, I think Logan and I might be friends."

"Just friends?"

I laughed, but even to my ears it sounded hollow. "Of course." I turned around to look at my friend. "Aidan, I'm not his type at all."

"That's not what I asked." He leaned across my kitchen counter. "I don't want you to get hurt."

"Oh, I won't." I waved off his concerns. "Logan is not my type either." I adamantly ignored memories of the dream I'd had about him, or the fact that every time he shot me that crooked smile I felt a flare of pleasure-pain in my chest. I didn't know what it meant, but I knew I was damn well going to ignore it. "I'm just helping out a neighbor. And mostly I'm helping out Maia. I think you'll understand once you meet her."

I began to plate up our food, and Aidan was quiet until I sat down beside him. "What do you mean?"

I cocked my head to the side in thought. "She reminds me of me."

My friend smiled. "Then I'm sure she's worth all the effort you're putting in."

I returned his smile with a grateful one of my own and then caught him up with the situation to date.

It wasn't much later that we heard my front door open, and my ears pricked up at the sound of Maia's giggle. Relief whooshed through me. I had to admit I'd been anxious for her, and for Logan, wondering if they could get over their awkwardness around each other long enough to enjoy lunch together. From the sounds of that giggle, things might have gone all right for them.

"I'll ask Grace," I heard Logan say. "She'll back me up."

I smiled at Aidan's raised eyebrows and called out, "Back you up about what?"

"About music from—" Logan suddenly cut off his reply as he and Maia entered the kitchen. His eyes narrowed on Aidan. When I looked at Maia, her expression was almost an exact mirror image of her father's.

I swallowed my laughter. "This is my friend Aidan Ramage."

"The rugby player." Logan's voice seemed to rumble with suspicion.

"Rugby player?" Maia said softly.

"Aidan plays for Scotland," I explained to her. "He's one of those friends I was telling you about. We've been friends since first year at university."

Aidan was standing now, towering over me, eyeing Logan and his daughter.

"Aidan, this is Logan MacLeod and Maia."

"MacLeod," Logan added. "Maia told me her surname is MacLeod."

"But that . . ." I frowned. "Does that mean you're on the birth certificate?"

"I'll find out tomorrow. I'm heading to the register office on Princes Street."

"Nice to meet you both," Aidan broke in. "I understand it's an interesting situation here."

Logan drew his eyes over him, carefully, deliberately, and really quite intimidatingly. "It's a private family matter."

Aidan shrugged at the warning, not at all intimidated, but also not offended. "Grace is involved, and Grace is *my* family," he said pointedly.

I knew Logan understood, but he didn't seem any happier about it. Maia was worrying her lower lip with her teeth, gazing up at Aidan as if he were about to take everything away. One of the reasons I loved Aidan was because he was a pretty perceptive guy. He smiled disarmingly at Maia, and she blushed to her roots. "I just wanted to check in and make sure Grace was okay." His gaze drifted back to Logan.

Logan's shoulders seemed to relax somewhat. "I understand. I meant no offense."

Aidan grinned good-naturedly. "I wasn't offended."

"Did you guys have a nice lunch?" I said, deliberately changing the subject before I was stifled by the testosterone in the air. "Did you get your cheeseburger?"

Maia nodded. "And then we went to the National Museum on Chambers Street because I've never been before."

I raised an eyebrow at Logan. "Good food and a trip to the museum. Who are you trying to impress?"

His lip quirked up at the left corner at my teasing. "Maybe I like culture and was just trying to impart some."

"Yes, you're full of surprises," I said sardonically.

"You have no idea." He flashed me a full-on wicked smile that hit me straight in the gut and I blinked, stupefied for a moment. "Maia, why don't we head next door and let Grace visit with her friend."

"Guys, please stay," Aidan encouraged. "I'll be leaving soon anyway."

Maia was the first one to make a move toward the counter. I noted her eye the mini savory snacks we hadn't gotten around to eating. "Help yourself, sweetheart."

"Don't mind if we do." Logan brushed past me and began searching cupboards for plates. He pulled out a couple and pushed one toward Maia. They both began loading snacks onto them.

I chuckled. "Was that cheeseburger not very filling?"

Logan threw me a look out of the corner of his eyes that simply said, "I'm a man."

Maia giggled and bit into a sausage roll. I caught her eye and she shrugged. "I'm just really hungry."

"That's because you're my—" Logan cut off abruptly, suddenly looking very uncomfortable.

We were silent, all knowing he was about to say "daughter."

"Hey, stop hogging the food," Aidan said loudly, breaking the awkward silence. "I've just come from training, you know. I'm starving."

Logan jumped on Aidan's offer of a save and started asking questions about rugby. Aidan even managed to get Maia asking him questions.

When Aidan was leaving a little while later, I threw my arms around him and hugged him tight. He'd reminded me today why I adored him. "I love you to bits." I squeezed him.

"Love you, too, Grace," he said gruffly, squeezing me back. Reluctantly, I let him go, and he slipped quietly out of the flat.

"He an ex?"

I spun around, startled by Logan's appearance in the hallway.

I shook my head, because technically he wasn't really. One time didn't count. "No. Aidan's like family. And he's engaged to a woman he's madly in love with."

Logan processed this and then shrugged. "Nice guy. Glad to know there's someone looking out for you."

"Thank you," I said, surprised by his comment.

He cleared his throat. "Aye, anyway . . . I wanted your opinion on something."

"Shoot?"

"Shannon wants to meet Maia tonight, but I'm not sure it's a good idea yet."

I loved that he was so concerned for her feelings. I walked toward him and patted his arm reassuringly. "Trust your instincts, Logan."

"I'm thinking we should wait until the paternity results come in."

"I would agree."

He nodded. "I'll call her." I walked away, but he said my name, stopping me in my tracks. I glanced over my shoulder in question. "Thanks for everything."

Once more the gratitude in his eyes affected me. In fact, I was hit with a wave of attraction so big I could only mumble "you're welcome" before I had to walk away from him. I closed my eyes and prayed to God Aidan's concerns were unfounded.

This thing with Logan and Maia . . . *Would* I end up getting hurt? What on earth had I let myself in for?

CHAPTER 8

Logan stood on my doorstep the next morning holding a padded envelope. His features were tight with anxiety. "The paternity kit arrived."

I stepped aside to let him past. "It will all be okay," I promised.

He didn't respond. He was too focused on getting to Maia. I followed him into the kitchen, where we both stopped at the sight of Maia sitting in her new pajamas, scooping up spoonfuls of cereal with one hand while she held a book from my collection with the other. Her nose was practically pressed to the pages.

I'd discovered that Maia was like me in more ways than one. If I got engrossed in a book, the world around me ceased to exist. This morning, as Maia wandered into the kitchen with a young-adult novel in her hand, she'd barely grunted a "good morning" to me while I poured her a bowl of cereal and a glass of fresh orange juice.

"Maia," Logan said. When Maia didn't respond, he looked at me, his eyebrows raised.

"She's reading," I said, as if that explained everything. Logan stared blankly at me. I sighed and wandered over to Maia and gently plucked the book out of her hand.

She gazed up at me in confusion.

"Logan's here," I said.

"Oh." She whipped around on the stool and smiled at him. "Mornin'."

Logan gave her a bemused smile in return. "Good book, is it?"

"Hmm?" She frowned before understanding cleared her expression. "Oh, yeah. I borrowed it from Grace. It's cool."

"Well, I'm sorry to disturb your reading, sweetheart." Logan slid onto the stool next to her, and I set about making him a coffee to help bolster him through this huge moment. "But the paternity kit arrived. I need you to take a swab of the inside of your cheek so I can send it off for the test."

Maia's spoon fell into her bowl with a clatter. "Okay. So . . . how long will it take? You know, for the results?"

"I'll send it off today. The company I'm using has a forty-eight-hour turnaround, so we'll know really soon."

I watched her closely as I slid Logan his coffee. She had paled considerably.

"Maia, it's going to be okay," I said.

She looked up at me with tears in her eyes. "I should probably brush my teeth first." She took the plastic packet Logan was holding out to her with the swab inside it. As soon as she disappeared out of the room, Logan took a deep gulp of coffee.

"Thanks," he murmured, setting the mug down. "This is . . ." He glanced back at the door. "She looked terrified. She was practically crying. I . . . What's going on? I thought she wanted this."

"Exactly." I slid onto the stool Maia had just vacated. "Logan, she's not scared that you're her dad. She's scared you're not."

He thought about this, and slowly the muscles in his clenched jaw relaxed.

"What about you?" I said. "How are you feeling?"

"Whatever happens happens." He shrugged.

"Logan," I warned. "Macho bullshit does not fly in this flat."

He raised an eyebrow at me. "Macho bullshit?"

"Yes, macho bullshit. I can smell it a mile away."

He looked into his mug of coffee like it had all the answers. "There have been a lot of ups and downs for me these last few years. I've learned to deal with those. I can learn to deal with this. It's a lifestyle change." He shot me a wry look. "I had to break things off with the American."

Ignoring the weird sense of satisfaction I felt at his announcement, I tried to be nonchalant. "Why?"

"It wasn't serious between us, and right now it's a distraction. I have to focus on Maia." The violet in his eyes darkened. "C'mon, Grace. We both know this paternity test is going to tell us this kid is mine. My life as it was is over. I make this commitment to that wee girl in there, then I better mean business. What kind of arsehole would subject their kid to the fucking carousel of women I've had in and out of my life these past few months?"

I didn't know what to say to make him feel better, because the truth was that life as he knew it *was* over. I got up to refill his coffee, and as I passed him, I squeezed his shoulder. "You're one of the good ones, Logan MacLeod."

All those moments would be lost in time . . . like tears in rain.

That sentence was still bugging me. I chewed my lip, wondering what the hell my fascination was with the damn sentence. While Maia seemed perfectly content to curl up in my guest room reading her book for the day, I was able to get on with my work. This manuscript was due back to the author in a few days, and I was going over all the bits I'd highlighted to return to before sending the edits back to her.

The sound of my front door slamming shut jerked me out of the manuscript.

"It's just me!" Logan called from the front of the flat.

"Back here!"

My eyes darted around my bedroom. Thankfully, I didn't have any embarrassing pieces of underwear on show. Which was good, because Logan sauntered right in and came to stand behind me with his hands on the back of my computer chair.

"How did it go?" I said, craning my neck to look up at him.

He was too busy frowning at my computer screen to answer me. "'All those moments would be lost in time . . . like tears in rain.' Why do you have that highlighted?"

I shut my laptop. "I have it highlighted because something about it bugs me."

"Did you Google it?"

"No." I frowned. "Why?"

"Because it's a quote from *Blade Runner.*"

Recognition jolted through me. "Oh my God, it bloody well is." I stared up at him, annoyed. "Ugh. The last thing I need to deal with right now is an author trying to plagiarize cult classic films." He smirked and then stepped back, taking a seat on the end of my bed. I pushed away thoughts of my author and what I was going to do to deal with it—after all, it could be accidental. Hopefully. "Logan, what happened at New Register House?"

He heaved a sigh and reached into his jacket. He pulled out a piece of paper and handed it to me. It was a copy of Maia's birth certificate. I scanned it. "Logan. This . . . You *are* named as the father here." I looked up at him, thrilled for him. "You realize this means you have legal rights now—don't you?"

"It does?"

We turned to find Maia leaning in my doorway unsurely.

Logan nodded at her. "It does."

"That's good, right?"

"It's good, sweetheart." He shot a look at me, and I had a feeling he'd come in here to talk it out with me, to vent perhaps, but he definitely was not going to do that with Maia here. From what I'd already witnessed of his thoughtfulness around her, he wouldn't want her to think he was troubled. He clapped his hands on his knees and stood up. "Why don't you and I go out for a bit before my shift tonight? Catch a movie or something? We can let Grace get on with her work."

Maia's eyes lit up. "Yeah, okay. That sounds good." She gave me a little wave and hurried off to get her shoes and jacket.

I looked over at Logan, who hovered in my doorway, gazing back at me. "This will all be okay."

His mouth turned down at the corners before he said, "If you say it enough times maybe you'll make it true."

I managed to get only a couple of hours of work in and did not get much done in that time. I kept forcing myself to focus on the work, but Logan's face flashed across my eyes more times than I could count. He was swimming against a stormy tide, and all I wanted to do was reach out and help him to shore. But my reassurances didn't seem to be helping. They just felt empty.

I was jolted from my musings and my work by my phone ringing. It was Chloe. Calling to berate me.

Aidan had told her everything.

"Are you nuts?"

Yesterday I would have said no. Today . . . "I might be."

Chloe *tutt*ed on the other end of the line. "I *knew* you had feelings for this guy."

I went straight into denial mode. "Feelings. *Pfft.* I barely know him. I'm doing this for Maia."

"Who you also barely know. I need to meet this Maia."

"No," I snapped, my mother bear instincts kicking in. I attempted to reel in those instincts, softening my voice when I continued. "You *want* to meet, Maia. There's a difference. I can't let you meet her right now, Chloe. Not just yet. That kid is going through a complete life change. I don't want to overwhelm her any more than she already is, especially not with my overly suspicious but well-meaning family members."

"Precisely," Chloe said. "I *am* your family. It is my duty to make sure you're not being taken for a ride."

"Yes, Aidan said the same thing."

"Speaking of . . . *he* got to meet Maia."

"We were practically ambushed. Plus, no offense, sweetie, but Aidan is much more diplomatic than you."

She sniffed haughtily. "I'll try not to let that hurt my feelings."

"Chloe." I fought to find the words to explain. "You have this big personality, and Maia . . . well . . . doesn't. And she's scared and—"

"I get it," she interrupted with an exaggerated sigh. "But if you get hurt in this, I'm cracking some heads."

I chuckled. "I will warn all involved parties."

"You think I'm joking, but I'm not, Grace. You, more than anyone I know, deserve kindness and respect. If I get even a whiff of 'user' off these people, I'm stepping in."

"Do you think I'd help them if they were those kind of people?"

"I guess not, but—"

"Chloe." I stopped her from arguing further. "I love you."

She sighed again. "Love you, too. Call me when it's safe for me to intrude."

I laughed, feeling more grateful for her than ever. "I will do that."

We hung up and I stared at my phone, wishing I could find a better way to reassure my friends that I was okay and that I wasn't making a mistake helping Maia and Logan out.

"Your friends are worried."

I jumped, startled. I whirled around and found Maia standing in my bedroom doorway, wearing her jacket and shoes. She'd obviously returned from the movies with Logan. There was no sound of him, so I assumed he was in his flat, getting ready for work.

"Maia." I held a hand to my chest, willing my heart rate to slow. "Sweetie, it's rude to eavesdrop."

She threw her shoulders back defiantly. "I heard my name." And just as quickly as she displayed it, that defiance wilted right out of her. "Your friends don't want me here, do they?"

This was a girl who'd felt wanted by no one for so long. This was not a small issue to her. I gestured to my chair, and she slowly made her way to it. Once she was sitting down, I sat across from her on the end of my bed.

Maia stared up at me with those sad violet eyes of hers, and I wanted nothing more than to take away all the shadows from them. "My friends are just looking out for me, just like I'm trying to look out for you. They'll understand why I'm doing all this as soon as they get to know you."

She frowned. "But you don't really know me."

"True." I grinned at her bluntness. "But sometimes we meet people and we just click with them. There's a connection and you can't explain it. It's just there."

"And we've clicked?" Maia said, eyes now lightening a little with obvious hope.

I felt this painful little ache in my chest for her. "Yes, we have." Something unsettling occurred to me. "Haven't you clicked with a friend—*friends*—before? You haven't spoken about anyone you might be leaving behind."

Maia suddenly looked very weary. "Friends want to know everything about you, and I couldn't tell them about Maryanne or bring them back to the flat to hang out. It was just easier to be a loner than to deal with the questions. It did me no good trying to hide it, though, because kids from the area know about Maryanne and they told everyone. There are very few people who want to hang out with the daughter of a junkie."

The depth of Maia's loneliness hit me.

It choked me.

It made me want to shake some bloody sense into her wretched mother.

More than anything, however, I was in awe of Maia. She'd had no support, no encouragement, from anyone, as far as I could tell, and yet somehow she had dug deep and found the courage to come here and confront Logan. She was only fifteen and she'd taken the reins of her destiny in hand. I didn't have that courage at her age.

I felt tears prick my eyes, proud of her in a way I couldn't explain. "You are a remarkable and very special person, Maia MacLeod. Do not let anyone tell you different. And whatever happens next, never ever be ashamed to let anyone know you. You are worth knowing."

Maia gazed at me, eyes round with surprise. And just like that she burst into tears.

I got up and pulled her out of the chair, and I held her tight as she sobbed against me. It took everything within me not to cry along with her.

That's when I realized that this kid had gotten deep under my skin in a very short time. My life had changed too. Because I knew that no matter what happened with Logan, I wouldn't let my connection with Maia break. If she needed family, I wanted to be that for her, just like Chloe and Aidan had stepped up to be mine.

CHAPTER 9

"Maia, I'm your dad." Logan stood in my sitting room, holding up a single piece of paper, staring down at Maia with a careful expression as he imparted his life-altering news.

It was the morning after Maia had cried in my arms, and I'd just made her a cup of tea after our breakfast together. Logan had let himself into my flat and without further ado announced the results of the paternity test.

Maia's cup trembled in her hand, and I reached over to gently take it away from her. "What does this mean now?" she said. The color had risen in her cheeks, her whole face bright with expectation.

Logan didn't keep her waiting. "It means that between this and the birth certificate, I have legal rights as your father. I'm going to enforce those rights. I'm going to your mum's today to tell her you're moving in with me. If she wants to discuss it, we will. If she wants to fight it, she can, but she will have a fight on her hands."

"Really?" Maia whispered, almost as if she didn't quite believe it.

"Maia, she kept you from me for fifteen years." His eyes were hard with determination. "And as far as I can see, she's not done right by you. It's my turn to look after you. I can't promise you I'll be very good at it, but I can promise I'll try my very best to make the next fifteen, thirty, fifty years better than the last fifteen."

As I tried to blink back my tears at his speech, Maia launched herself out of her chair and straight at Logan. He stood stunned for a moment as she wrapped her arms around his waist and burrowed her face against his chest. Seconds later he slid his arms around her and held her tight.

I had to look away so I wouldn't turn into a blubbering mess.

"Grace."

I glanced up at them again to find Maia had stepped away from her dad, looking almost embarrassed by her outburst of affection. Logan noticed and put his arm around her shoulders and drew her in to his side. She smiled shyly up at him, but he'd turned to me so he didn't notice the adoration he was receiving. "Are you okay to let Maia stay with you while I turn the second room into Maia's room?"

"Of course," I answered easily.

"Okay." He blew out air between his lips and looked down at Maia. "I'll need the details of your last school, sweetheart, so I can arrange a transfer to a school here."

She nodded eagerly.

"You'll need more clothes. If Grace can't take you, I'll get Shannon to. She's dying to meet you." He reached out with his other hand and stroked her cheek with his thumb. There was this dazed, tender light in his eyes, and I think it was just finally hitting him that Maia was his. She was his daughter. His voice was gruff with emotion when he spoke again. "I'd better go see your mum."

"I'll come with you," I blurted out. I didn't want him to go back out there alone. I didn't want him to have to face it on his own after everything he'd already gone through.

"What about Maia?"

"I'm fifteen," she piped up. "I can look after myself for a few hours. Believe me."

Logan frowned. "How would you feel about spending a few hours with Shannon?"

I wasn't sure that was a good idea, considering Maia had never met her aunt. However, she spoke up before I could say anything. "Okay. I want to meet her." I scrutinized her to make sure she was telling the truth, and as far as I could see, she was. In fact, she was positively giddy. Jittery. Like a kid on Christmas morning.

I guess, in a way, this was a bit like that for her. Instead of presents, she was getting a family.

"Here? Or at Shannon and Cole's?" Logan said.

"Um . . ." She bit her lip. "Here, please."

Excited she might have been, but she was also still nervous. Logan seemed to understand she'd be more comfortable meeting his sister somewhere that felt familiar and safe to her. "Okay. Let me give her a call."

He did it right away, and we heard him telling her it was to be just her. In other words, Cole wasn't invited this time. She must have agreed, because he got off the phone and nodded at Maia. "She doesn't have a class today, so she'll be right over."

Not too long later my doorbell rang and Logan disappeared to let Shannon in. He led her into the sitting room, her violet eyes shining, her cheeks flushed, and her bright red hair falling around her shoulders in a mass of gorgeous waves and ringlets. She scanned the room, and as soon as she spotted Maia, she strode over to her.

Without a word, Shannon tugged Maia into her arms and held on tight. I looked at Logan to see how he was reacting to the heartwarming scene. Just like this morning, his expression was carefully blank.

I was starting to worry about that.

Shannon eventually let go of Maia long enough to step back and then cup her face between her hands. Maia looked at Shannon as if she were some beautiful, magical fairy. Shannon was looking at Maia in much the same way. "Just look at you. You're so grown-up and so beautiful. Isn't she beautiful?" Shannon grinned at us.

I nodded, and Logan murmured, "Yeah. She looks just like you, Shannon."

Maia's eyes grew round at the compliment.

"Except for the hair." He smirked.

They both giggled, the sound exactly the same, and I burst out laughing at their twin expressions of amazement and excitement. I had a feeling they were going to be fine, and I started to relax about leaving Maia alone with Shannon.

"Well, you two better hit the road." Logan's sister gestured toward the door.

Logan nodded and walked over to give both Shannon and Maia a kiss on the cheek. I followed suit, squeezing Maia's hand and giving Shannon a grateful smile before hurrying after Logan as he started his determined journey back to Glasgow.

Like the last time I was in Logan's car with him, there was total silence. Unlike last time, however, I wanted to give him the quiet. He needed it to process everything that had happened. So I gave him quiet. And he took it. For the entire ninety minutes.

When we eventually pulled up to the familiar block of flats, Logan parked and switched the car off. He looked at me.

I gave him a small, wobbly smile. "Are you ready?"

"I want her to fight me."

He didn't have to clarify his statement. I knew exactly what he meant, because I wanted Maryanne to fight him too. For Maia's sake. It wasn't about him not wanting to take care of Maia. No matter what happened, he was going to do that. But we both wanted Maryanne to give some indication that Maia meant something to her. My mother had never fought for me. It was a special kind of agony knowing your own mother didn't love you. It was always with me. A ghost haunting me, a demon taunting, "If your mother can't love you, who can?"

I fought that demon, or whatever you wanted to call it, every day. Most days I won. Still . . . I didn't want Maia to have that fight.

Logan gave me a militant nod. "Let's do this."

By the time we reached the door, I had butterflies in my stomach and not the good kind. It didn't help that Logan banged on the door like he meant business. I stared up at his stern expression and reminded myself that I didn't actually know him that well, and I had no idea what his reaction to this situation was going to be without Maia around as a buffer.

Oh shit.

I guess that made me the buffer this time.

Not even a few seconds passed before the lock turned and the door swung inward to reveal a tall, skinny fellow, wearing nothing but a pair of ratty gray jogging bottoms.

His thinning dark hair was unwashed, his face unshaved, and there was a strong odor of stale sweat reeking from him.

"Aye?" he grunted, scratching his bare belly. Not that he had much of one.

"Is Maryanne home?" Logan said, politely enough.

The skinny man's answer was to leave the door open, turn around, and walk away.

Logan took that to mean we could enter, and I followed him inside the flat. I was instantly hit with that stench we'd smelled last time we were there. I instinctively huddled closer to Logan as we walked down the narrow hall and into the living room. The skinny man flopped down on an armchair across from us. Maryanne was lying on the couch watching television.

She looked up, her expression giving nothing away.

"Remember us?" Logan scowled at her.

Her eyes narrowed. "What the fuck do you want now?"

I eyed her carefully. She seemed less jittery than last time. I didn't know enough about substance abuse to understand what that meant. Was she high? Was she not high? Who knew?

Logan forged ahead. "I got a paternity test. Maia is mine."

"Good detective work." She snorted, and the skinny man laughed.

Logan ignored them both. "I also got a copy of her birth certificate. You named me as the father on it. You gave her my name."

"So?"

"I have legal rights, Maryanne. I'm enforcing them. Maia is living with me from now on. Permanently. Do you have anything to say about that?"

Maryanne just stared at him.

Skinny Man frowned at her. "You gonnae take that?"

"What's it to you?" Logan said, his tone quietly menacing.

I shifted a little closer to him, sensing the fight in him.

"Nothing." Skinny Man shrugged and then grinned idiotically. "Wee My was nice to look it, that's aw."

Logan lunged, but I was faster. I put myself in front of him, my hands pressed to his chest. "Don't."

He grabbed my wrists, glowering over at Skinny Man. "If you fucking touched her, I'll kill you."

"Naw, man." Skinny Man got up out of his chair, backing off. "Mare, tell him I didnae touch her."

Maryanne grunted. "What would he want a wee bairn for when he's got me?"

Logan was still tense.

I pressed harder against him, forcing him to look at me. Our eyes locked, and I felt all his pain and frustration and impotence over Maia's history wash over me. I curled my fingers into his shirt and leaned closer. "They're not worth it," I whispered. "Let's just go."

He blinked at my words, and I felt him relax, his hands uncurling around my wrists. He looked over at Maryanne. "Does this mean you're not fighting this?"

"Does it look like it?" She gestured around the room. "What the hell can I do for that wee lassie, eh? She's better off with you. Why do you think I told her about you? She doesnae need me."

I shook my head. "You have no idea how wrong you are."

"Get oot ma house, fancy pants."

Logan tensed again. "This is it, Maryanne. If you ever coming looking for Maia, you'll have to go through me first."

Her answer was to turn up the volume on the television.

Logan could only stare at her in disgust.

I dropped my hands from his chest in order to take his hand in mine, and I led him out of the flat.

And I didn't let go until we got to the car.

There was more tense silence between us as Logan drove back toward Edinburgh. We were perhaps twenty minutes in the car, however, when he suddenly pulled off the motorway and into a service station car park.

He turned off the engine and just sat there.

I waited, giving him time.

And then, "Who does that?" He slammed his hand on the steering wheel, his chest moving up and down rapidly as he took haggard, quick breaths.

I'd seen him tense, concerned, anxious.

But not like this.

I didn't know if it was purely about Maryanne, but I suspected it was everything. It was a buildup of everything from the moment he'd opened that paternity letter. Maybe even from the moment Maia had turned up on our landing.

"Logan." I touched his arm, forcing him to look at me. "Anything you do is going to be better than what Maryanne has done for Maia."

His eyes blazed. "I could have done this no problem a few years ago, but I'm not that guy anymore. The laid-back guy who could take on anything."

"You keep saying that. Was prison really that bad?"

He clenched his jaw and looked out of the windshield.

"Logan?" I pressed.

"It . . . I had to become a different man in order to get through it."

"How?"

He sighed heavily. "I don't want to talk about it. It's done."

"It's not done," I disagreed, hearing the irritation in my voice and not caring. "You have a teenage girl waiting for you at home now. A week ago, okay, fine, I would have dropped it, let you keep whatever shit that's stirring inside of you to yourself, but it's not just about you anymore."

Logan turned his head and glowered at me. I tensed, waiting. And to my surprise he began to talk. His voice was gruff, low, however, like the words were dragged from deep down in his belly. "I'm not a criminal, Grace."

There was a pain in those words he couldn't hide, and I felt the burn of tears in my eyes in response to it. "I know that, Logan."

"No, you don't." He shook his head and looked away from me. "I wasn't that kid. I wasn't that teenager, and I certainly wasn't that man, and I didn't surround myself with men like that either. The men inside . . . So many of them aren't even men. They're just scum who think because they like violence and like playing with knives and drugs that it makes them men. I was breathing in scum for two fucking years, listening to them and the vile, ignorant things they talked about. Things they planned to do when they got out, the men they planned to fuck up, the women they planned to hurt. And I listened to them plan to hurt one another. Because it's war." He turned to stare at me now, his nostrils flared with anger, with the memories. "It's a war in there. And if you don't want to get fucked-up, you have to make them fear you."

I shivered at the look in his eyes. "What does that mean?"

"It means I had to find a balance. I wanted out early for good behavior, but I also had to make sure no one messed with me. I spent every day in the gym bulking up and allied myself with certain men."

"What kind of men?" I was almost afraid to ask.

"The kind of men who are real hardened criminals. The kind of men who have done very bad things, Grace. One of my closest friends in there—and we still talk to this day—was in for manslaughter. It was his third conviction since he was fourteen. That's the kind of men I let into my life. What kind of man does that make me?"

I ached all over for him. "The kind of man who did what he had to do to survive."

"You say that, but you don't know what I was party to in there."

"And I don't need to." I shook my head. "Not unless you really want to tell me. Because otherwise I don't care. I don't need to know. It doesn't change who I think you are." I rested my hand on his leg. "Logan, it was two years of your life. Two terrible years, I know. But in the grand scheme of things, two years should not define who you are."

His fingers tightened around the steering wheel. "You're forgetting the reason I was in prison."

Sensing I hadn't quite won this round with him, I said, "Then tell me about it."

"I was at work," he said immediately. "I used to be head mechanic in a garage. Shannon came in . . . stumbled in." When he gazed at me this time, he looked truly haunted. "Fuck, Grace, you should have seen her." He shuddered and looked down. "Her top was ripped, her jeans undone, her face . . . Fuck, her face. Bloody, swollen. And her arm was hanging funny. Dislocated." He wrenched his eyes from the floor to my face. "I grabbed her, shouted at someone to call for an ambulance, and as we waited, she told me her boyfriend had done it. I can't explain it. I've never felt rage like it. She's Shannon." He seemed to plead with me. "She's my wee sister. She's the kindest person I've ever met until you. She means the world to me. I wanted to kill him. He tried to rape her. He beat the shit out of her. And later I found out it wasn't the first time he'd hit her. The thought of her fighting him off, trying to get to me so I could protect her . . . the thought that I wasn't there . . ." He trailed off, his emotions getting the better of him, and I waited as he attempted to get a handle on them.

"I had only one thought," he whispered. "To find him and give him back as good as he gave." He cleared his throat, his face turning hard. "They call it bloodlust. Maybe it was, because once I got ahold of him, I couldn't stop. A colleague, a friend of mine, he followed me. Dragged me off." Logan glared at me now. "I put Shannon's boyfriend in a coma. What kind of man does that make me, Grace? Fit to be a father?"

I had a feeling he wanted me to be outraged. Disgusted. Take Maia away. Seeing him so raw, so exposed, and so ashamed of himself was too much. I didn't want him to feel that way about himself. And so I sought to help in any way I could.

A story I had told no one, not even Aidan, came to mind, and I found myself telling it to Logan. "When I was fifteen I woke up one evening and there was a boy in bed with me. He had his hands on me, touching me. I fought him off, hearing laughter around me, and when I managed to get away from the boy, to get out of the bed, I discovered my brother, Sebastian, and a few of his drunken friends in my room. He'd brought them into my room to deliberately do that to me. My parents weren't home." I looked at my lap, trying to hold back the tears. I hadn't realized how painful it would be to say the words out loud. "I ran out of the room and locked myself in my bathroom, and I could hear them laughing the whole time. The one who had touched me, I knew him. He was my brother's best friend. He stood outside the bathroom and taunted me until my brother got bored and pulled him away. I was terrified." I forced myself to look at Logan, and he was staring at me, incredulous, outraged. "Sebastian did things like that all the time. He thought it was a game. We're both lucky he didn't get me raped." I stared solemnly into Logan's eyes, hoping the point I was trying to make would have an impact. "Life is shades of gray, Logan. I don't know if what you did was wrong. The law says it is, but I just think you were acting on an instinct that most people have. If I could choose between how Sebastian acted or how you acted, I'd choose your actions. That's all *I* know."

"Jesus, fuck, Grace," he said hoarsely.

"I know good and bad, Logan, trust me. And deep down you do too. And you know you're a good man. You know it. And I'm not going to tell you any different." I brushed impatiently at a tear. "We both know Maia deserves you. You deserve her."

My heart leapt into my throat as I was abruptly pulled across the passenger seat and into Logan's arms. He wrapped his hand around my nape and pressed my head into the crook of his neck, while his other arm fastened tight around my back. I had no choice but to slide my arms around him and hold on.

I let his solid, secure warmth rush over me.

I breathed him in.

And I wished that this moment didn't feel as perfect as it did.

CHAPTER 10

As I stepped out of my flat I realized I was relaxed for the first time in what felt like forever. I was going to meet up with Aidan, Juno, and Chloe for a coffee before starting my work for the day.

Maia was at school.

Her first day of school.

Thankfully, her time off school ran at the same time as Edinburgh's Easter break, so it didn't even really feel like she'd missed out on much. She was starting a new school in the last term of the year, which was a little awkward, but there was nothing that could be done about that.

Logan hadn't wasted any time in arranging Maia's new life here with him. He got her transferred to Muirhead High School, which was a twenty-minute walk through the Meadows and into Viewforth. Logan had dropped her off this morning, but she had been quite insistent that she walk home alone and that she would walk to school by herself every morning thereafter. Her father was not happy about this. I think he kept forgetting she was fifteen years old and used to taking care of herself. I'd tried to tell him that, but he'd just grunted at me and led Maia down the stairs and out of the building.

Although he and I had spent quite some time together these last few days with Maia, the closeness we'd experienced in his car seemed like a distant memory. I got the feeling Logan was uncomfortable with what we had shared with each other. Perhaps he felt strange about letting me see him so vulnerable, or perhaps it was because I'd let him see me so vulnerable. I could go over and over it in my head, and I could let myself get embarrassed for giving him a piece of myself I hadn't given to anyone, but I wasn't going to let myself go through that. If Logan wanted to be macho and weird about the whole thing, then I'd let him. I wasn't going to drive myself crazy overthinking it.

The truth was Maia was a big distraction from the "car moment." Her moods were all over the place. She'd go from being excited, happy, and filled with anticipation, to worried, anxious, and locking herself in her room to cry. I guessed it was partly caused by the fact that she was a teenager, a girl (and on her period), but I knew it was also hugely to do with the fact that her mother had given her away without a fight. She confided in me a little of what life was like with Maryanne. Maia had practically raised herself, from taking herself to the opticians when she realized her eyesight was worsening, to stealing money out of her mother's purse to pay for school clothes, shoes, and food. The new transition was forcing her to deal with her memories, and thus her emotions were heightened.

Maia's moods were infectious, and so I was absolutely exhausted.

As much as I enjoyed being a part of this new chapter in Maia's life and getting to know her, I was looking forward to the normality of having a cup of coffee with friends and then catching up on my work. In fact, I was more than a little behind.

I was in the middle of locking my door when I heard Logan's door open behind me. He stood in his doorway wearing a black T-shirt with the logo from the nightclub he worked at etched across his chest. His dark blue jeans were worn and hung on his hips in a rather attractive way. I'd never really thought much about men in jeans, but in that moment I realized that certain men just sold them to you. Logan definitely sold those jeans.

He had a bit of a short beard going on again, and I found I liked it. A lot. Despite the tiredness behind his eyes, he really was bloody gorgeous.

When had he become my type?

I looked down, dropping my keys in my bag, avoiding his gaze so he couldn't see what I was thinking. "Hi."

"You going out?"

I glanced up at him because he sounded agitated. "Are you okay?"

"Maia's bed was delivered an hour ago."

"That's good." I felt a little pang in my chest at the realization Maia would be moving out soon.

"I . . . um . . ." He rubbed a hand over his hair. "I want her room to be, you know . . . I need paint. Things . . . stuff . . . that girls like."

He looked so adorably lost and confounded I couldn't help but laugh a little. "Are you asking for my help?"

"I can ask Shannon if you're busy, but I just thought . . . you know Maia a little better."

Maia had spent more time with Shannon, and the two of them got on very well together. Over the weekend Logan had taken Maia to meet Shannon's fiancé, Cole, and some of his family. She'd been flushed with excitement when Logan dropped her off at my flat afterward, and she filled my ears with descriptions of Cole's gorgeous sister, Jo, and her husband, Cam, and their little girl, Belle. From what I could tell of Maia's accounts, they'd all been extremely welcoming to her. I was thrilled for her. She'd never experienced anything like Logan's friends and family.

However, despite getting to know them all and loving it, Maia still clung to me. She wanted me to be included in everything and was disappointed when I insisted she go with just Logan to meet his friends and family. I tried my best to give them father-daughter time, and I knew Logan appreciated it. But the truth was, Maia was living with me, and so far I'd spent a great deal of time with her and I was the one she chose to show her vulnerable side to. It was my shoulder she chose to cry on when everything became too overwhelming.

So yes, I probably did know her better than anyone.

"She likes green. She's not too girlie. She's quite mature in her tastes actually. Stylish." I sighed inwardly, knowing I was an idiot. *I'm doing this for Maia, not Logan!* "I'll have a look at the bed and make a quick call while you get your shoes on."

He raised an eyebrow. "You're sure?"

"Yes, I'm sure." I shooed him inside and followed him in, pulling my phone out of my bag.

I called Chloe. She was not happy. Her screeching melted away for a second, and suddenly I heard Aidan say, "Do what you have to do, Grace. We'll catch up with you later."

I smiled at his understanding. "Thanks. I'll talk to you soon."

By the time I got off the phone, I was standing in Logan's spare room. It was the same size as my guest room, and it was now dwarfed by the beautiful white Shaker-style bed frame and mattress that sat in the middle of the room.

"What do you think?"

I glanced over my shoulder and found him leaning in the doorway. "I think it's lovely. I hope you have dust sheets to cover it so you don't get paint on it."

"We'll add those to the shopping list."

"I think this is going to be a very large shopping list," I said wryly, following him out of the flat.

We'd just hit the ground floor when Mr. Jenner's door suddenly opened and he leaned outside. "I thought I heard your voice, Grace." He smiled. "Logan."

"Mr. Jenner," we said in unison.

"I heard we have a new addition to the building."

"My daughter," Logan said.

I smiled up at him.

"What?" He frowned.

"Nothing." I looked over at Mr. Jenner, still smiling. Already it seemed to be getting easier and easier for Logan to use the word "daughter."

"Oh, very good," Mr. Jenner said, grinning at Logan. "Nice to have family around. Speaking of my lack thereof . . ." He threw me an apologetic smile. "I couldn't ask you for a favor, Grace, could I? I've run out of a few things."

I held out my hand. "Of course. You know it's no problem. Do you have your list?"

He had it in his hand. I tried not to laugh as he passed it to me.

"We'll probably be a few hours. Is that all right?"

"Oh, of course. That's no problem. You're an angel."

I smiled at him, Logan said good-bye, and we heard Mr. Jenner's door close behind us just as we stepped out of the building.

"Do you ever say no to anyone?" Logan said.

It was my turn to raise an eyebrow at him. "And where would you be if I did?"

He blinked at my response and then threw his head back in a bark of laughter.

I couldn't help grinning. And I did so, ignoring the swell of attraction I felt toward him.

The man could probably heal the world with that laugh of his.

We stared down into the boot of Logan's car. It was packed with stuff, as was the backseat. It wasn't just stuff for Grace's room, either, but bits and pieces I'd picked out for the rest of his flat to give it some warmth. Right now it looked half-empty and unlived in. Logan needed to turn the place into a home.

"Do you think we got enough?" he said dryly.

I smirked. "I hope so, or you can say good-bye to your savings."

"On that note." He shut the boot and gestured to the computer store. "Does Maia need a laptop? For her school stuff? I mean, she needs a phone, but does she *need* a laptop?"

"Well, Logan, no one *needs* a laptop," I said. "The question is can you afford a laptop?"

He frowned at my nosy question.

"You asked," I huffed. "I'm just saying . . . Her birthday is in a few months. If you want to make up for unintentionally missing the last fifteen, a laptop would be a lovely way to do that. But not every birthday should be of laptop magnitude," I hurried to add.

Logan looked undecided.

"Maia's just happy to have you right now. She doesn't need a laptop."

He slanted me a look out of the corner of his eye. "Okay."

"Okay?"

"Yeah." He nodded and then spun around to look across at the other side of the giant retail park. "Fancy having some lunch before we hit the supermarket for Mr. Jenner?"

I should probably have been getting back. I had work to do. "Sounds good."

We started walking toward the Tex-Mex restaurant.

"So about a phone for Maia . . . Do I just buy one? Or should I let her pick it?"

I grinned. He was trying very hard not to sound anxious, but I could hear it anyway. "Do what you think is best."

He made this little growling noise that a few weeks ago would have intimidated me. Now it just made me grin harder. "I can feel you laughing at me."

"Moi." I stared up at him round-eyed and innocent. "I wouldn't dream of it."

"Aye, right." He held open the door to the restaurant, staring me down the whole time.

I pretended to be cowed.

After we ordered, the waitress moved away and Logan and I were left just staring across the booth at each other.

He looked very serious all of a sudden.

"What?" I said warily.

"You haven't mentioned your family at all, with the exception of that fucker who doesn't even count as a brother."

Uncomfortable under his sudden intense scrutiny, I shrugged. "My friends—Aidan, Chloe, and Juno—are my family."

"What about your blood? Your parents?"

"I don't speak to them."

He cocked his head in curiosity. "Why?"

Why did he suddenly want to know about me? I'd gotten the impression that he was avoiding any really personal discussions between us when he threw up a wall after our outpouring and hug in his car the other day. "Why do you want to know?"

Logan shrugged and took a sip of water. When he placed the glass back on the table, he said, "You're my friend."

That surprised me. "Yeah?"

He gave me a lazy grin, and something rippled low in my belly in response to it. "Yes."

Shoving away that ludicrous reaction to him, I gave a huff of laughter. "Who would have thought?"

"Certainly not me. I was pretty sure you were a shrew."

I narrowed my eyes. "You were no picnic either, Logan MacLeod."

He grinned again, and it occurred to me I'd seen him smile more in the last few days than I had the entire time I'd known him. "I've missed that," he said.

"What?"

"You saying my full name in exasperation."

I giggled. "I don't think you'll have time to miss it. I'm pretty sure you'll be hearing it again soon."

"Stop changing the subject."

"I didn't!"

"Someone did."

"It wasn't me."

He gave me a low-lidded no-nonsense look. "Why don't you talk to your family?"

Trying for nonchalant when I felt anything but, I rolled my eyes. "My mother is cold and my father is distant. I didn't like life in London with them, so I left them behind for a real family here in Edinburgh. End of story. Okay?"

He was quiet a moment. I didn't know if he was processing that information or gearing up for more questions . . . and then he surprised me again. "Thank you, Grace."

"For what?"

It was his turn to give a huff of incredulous laughter. "For everything."

Just like that I found myself locked in his gaze. The air around us seemed to thicken until I was feeling a little breathless. My skin was flushed and I felt a shiver skate down my neck, following a tingling path around my back to my breasts.

Logan's eyes darkened with heat.

"Unfortunately"—our waitress appeared at our booth, and I practically jumped out of my skin—"we don't have any more of the . . ."

I wasn't listening to whatever she was saying to Logan. I was too busy wondering what the hell had just happened.

The waitress broke the moment between Logan and me, and right away he jumped into asking me about my work, and if I'd spoken to the author who had tried to plagiarize *Blade Runner*. From there we chatted and joked about our work, about Maia, and avoided anything too personal.

After our supermarket run, we dropped by Mr. Jenner's to give him his shopping and then Logan disappeared into his flat to start work on decorating Maia's room, and I darted into my flat to start my own work.

I think I reread the same chapter ten times.

Before I knew it, Maia was home from school.

I immediately called Logan over.

"What?" Maia stared at us as all three of us stood in the living room. She'd come in, dropped her book bag in the living room, sauntered into the kitchen, and then reappeared in the sitting room with a glass of orange juice in her hand. She looked very smart in her uniform — a black blazer with the Muirhead badge on the left chest pocket, a black shirt, a green and black striped tie, black skinny trousers, and black boots.

"Well?" Logan said, sounding impatient. "How was it?"

She shrugged. "It was fine."

I rolled my eyes. "You've got to give us more than that. How were classes? How were the teachers? Your peers?"

"I'm taking mostly the same classes I was taking back in Glasgow, except for media, which they let me take here. The teachers were teachers, and everyone was fine. I think I made a friend. What's for dinner?"

I narrowed my eyes at how blasé Maia was being. I knew for a fact after our conversation about her friendless history that making a friend was a big deal. Why wasn't she acting like it was?

"That all sounds great." Logan looked at me, pleased, and I didn't want to burst his bubble by suggesting there was something fishy going on, so I grinned back.

"Great." Maia shrugged again. "What's for dinner?"

"My shift change to days starts tomorrow, so I'm not working tonight. I was thinking—but only if you're up for it—in honor of your first day at school, you might want to eat out? Shannon and Cole invited us out to a restaurant with them and Cam and Jo. What do you think?"

Her eyes lit up, and I saw that sparkle I'd been hoping to see when she was talking about school. "Okay. Sure. Grace, you're coming, right?"

I almost blushed, wondering if Logan was groaning inside at the thought. I was sure he'd seen enough of me for one day. "Oh no. You go and have dinner with your family."

"I want you to come," she insisted with this mulish expression on her face. That was new.

"Maia," I began, "I'm s—"

"You should come," Logan interrupted me. "You should be there to celebrate with us."

"Yay!" Maia clapped happily, and Logan's whole face brightened at the sight of her excitement. "We'll get ready."

He chuckled. "Okay, then. I'll be back at six o clock to pick you up."

As soon as the door closed behind him, I turned to Maia. "One, you can't keep inviting me along to things with your father. Two, what really happened at school today?"

"Oh my God, it was amazing!" She rushed toward me, her whole face glowing. "These two girls started talking to me right away in my first class. They're so nice and we're, like, into the same music and have the same taste in films and actors and everything. They don't like all that stupid boy-band stuff, you know? They like real music. They've even been to live gigs. They're so cool!"

I was relieved that she'd met people she clicked with, but I was still confused as to why she hadn't shared this with Logan. "Why on earth didn't you say so when Logan was here?"

Her smile died a little. "I don't want him to think I'm a silly wee girl who gets excited over stupid stuff like this. I don't want him to be bored with me."

"Maia." I shook my head in wonder at how muddled her mind was right now. "Logan wants to hear this stuff. He wants to know how happy you are. He doesn't think it's stupid girlie stuff. You don't have to pretend to be someone you're not because you think it will impress your father. He's proud of you, especially when you're being yourself."

She chewed her lower lip with her teeth for a bit and then cocked her head to the side and said, "Yeah?"

"Yes. Now, you must promise to tell him all about . . ."

"Leigh and Layla," she supplied.

"Leigh and Layla." I grinned. "Well, those names will be easy to re-member."

. . .

Maia had been right about Cole's older sister, Jo. She was one of the most beautiful women I'd met in real life, and I'd lived in London and met lots of gorgeous women. From what I could tell, her beauty ran deep. As soon as she saw Maia again, she drew her in for a hug and started asking her about school immediately, seeming genuinely interested in anything she had to say.

I was introduced to her husband, Cam, first. While Shannon and Cole were a few years younger than me, Cam was apparently nearly forty. The guy did not look it at all. Unlike Cole, who roughed up his classically handsome looks with scruff and tattoos, Cam was truly rugged. His tattoos and scruff just made him more so.

"I've heard a lot about you from Shannon and Cole," Cam said, shaking my hand. "You take being a good neighbor to the next level."

"You would know all about that," Jo teased him as she pressed into his side. She smiled at me, and for a moment I was a little dazzled by her. "I'm Jo, Cole's sister."

I shook her hand as I looked up at her. She was tall and even taller in her four-inch heels. "It's really nice to meet you both."

I didn't know what else to say. I felt a little intimidated by the gorgeous couple.

Luckily, Cole saved me by coming over to shake my hand. "Nice to see you again, Grace."

I blushed.

He turned to Maia, who was at my side. "Maia." He winked at her. She blushed.

Logan groaned and glowered at his sister. "We need to get you a new fiancé."

Shannon grinned, looking more than a tad smug. "He can't help that he's gorgeous."

I think Maia and I blushed even harder.

"Oh God. Don't be filling his head with that nonsense." Cam gave Cole a teasing shove toward the table. "It's big enough."

"I'll have you know I have just the right amount of ego," Cole shot back before pulling out Shannon's chair for her. I noted Cam did the same for Jo and Logan did the same for Maia.

It was such a gentlemanly thing to do. And here I thought chivalry was dead.

Before I could pull out my own chair, Logan slid around Maia's and did it for me. I smiled at his kindness and settled in across from Jo.

"Where's Belle?" Maia said immediately, looking disappointed.

I had to rack my brain, but I was sure Belle was Jo and Cam's daughter.

"Oh, our friends Hannah and Marco are babysitting Belle. They have two boys and a daughter, Sophia, who is close to Belle's age. They're like cousins. They're really close," Jo explained.

"Hannah is Cole's best friend," Logan added for Maia's benefit. "She's a high school English teacher."

Maia's eyes widened. "At my school?"

Logan shook his head. "She doesn't work there."

"Thank God," Maia murmured, and then blushed when everyone laughed. "Sorry. I just really don't want to know one of my teachers outside of school."

"Hannah can always help you though," Cole said. "She's happy to tutor after school."

"Thanks, but Grace helps me with my English homework." Maia grinned up at me, and now I had everyone's attention.

"Oh? What do you do, Grace?" Cam said.

"I'm a freelance book editor. Mostly self-published fiction but some academic papers as well."

"Really?" Jo leaned forward, looking extremely interested. "Our friend is a writer, and she's thinking about self-publishing this series her publisher doesn't want. She's been looking for an editor."

Yay for me! Dinner had suddenly turned into a potential client. "Oh, well, I'll give you my number to give to her, and my Web site. What's her name?"

"Jocelyn. She writes under 'J. B. Carmichael.'"

My jaw dropped.

Jo snorted.

Her snort was quickly followed by muffled laughter around the table. Clearly my face was a picture.

Considering J. B. Carmichael was a number-one *Sunday Times* bestseller, however, I think I was entitled to my surprise.

"You're friends with J. B. Carmichael?" I said.

"This feels like déjà vu." Cole grinned cheekily at Shannon, and she threw her napkin at him for some bizarre reason.

Jo ignored them. "Yes." She smiled. "Can I still give her your number?"

"Wait." I glanced down the table at Logan. "Is J. B. Carmichael our landlord, Braden—your boss's—wife?"

"Yeah."

"And you just didn't think it was important to mention that his wife was a bestselling author?"

Logan's eyes glimmered with amusement. "Not really."

"Have you not seen her flat?" Maia jumped in for me. "It's, like, overflowing with books. Including J. B. Carmichael's books. You could have told her."

Cole found this even more hilarious.

"Can we maybe stop calling her 'J. B. Carmichael'?" Cam asked the whole table. "It's weird."

"Agreed." Jo nodded and turned back to me. "Can I give Joss your number?"

Joss, I mouthed. "Joss." I managed to utter the word. "Yes. Yes, you can definitely do that."

Holy crap. There was a possibility J. B. Carmichael could be my client. That would look amazing on my Web site!

"We've lost her," Logan said.

I rolled my eyes at him. "You have not. I'm here." I grinned huge. "I'm just happier than I was ten minutes ago."

He burst out laughing but was stopped from responding by the pretty waitress hovering over him. She grinned down at him, cocking her hip toward him. Logan's own grin deepened.

I felt an unpleasant sensation in my stomach.

"Can I get you guys drinks?" the waitress asked the table while looking into Logan's eyes. She was just his type. Petite, blond, with exaggerated curves.

"Water for the table," Logan said.

"Anything else?"

"Guys?" he asked us without taking his eyes off her.

I wanted to punch him.

Hard.

"I like your tattoo," the waitress said. "Does it mean something?"

"It definitely means something." He grinned suggestively at her.

Shannon shot him an annoyed look before turning to us. "A bottle of wine?"

We nodded.

"Red?" Jo asked.

We all nodded again.

"A bottle of the house red," Logan said. "Maia." He finally wrenched his eyes away from the waitress to look at Maia. He frowned when he found her glaring daggers at him. "What do you want to drink, sweetheart?"

Instead of answering, she buried her nose in her menu.

He looked at me for answers and I glanced down at Maia, unable to look him in the eye. I had no right to feel jealous or hurt by his flirting with another woman. Maia . . . she had a right to be confused by how it made her feel. I imagined right now she wanted Logan all to herself. "Diet Coke, sweetheart?" I asked her softly.

She nodded.

"Diet Coke," I said, snapping open my own menu.

I heard him mutter the drink to the waitress, and as soon as she left, I felt his burning stare. I ignored it and looked up at Jo and Cam. "So Logan didn't tell me what you two do for a living."

"I work with my uncle Mick. I'm a painter and decorator," Jo said.

This surprised me, but I tried to hide it. I imagine looking the way she looked, she was used to people making all sorts of snap judgments about her. "That must be fun working with family."

She nodded. "It can be, yeah." She nudged Cam with her shoulder. "Cam's a graphic designer."

"Oh? Do you work for yourself or . . . ?"

"Both. I work for a marketing company full-time, but I also codesign with multimedia artists."

I knew Cole was famous in the tattoo industry because he was the top artist at INKarnate, a tattoo studio in Edinburgh of national acclaim. I wondered if he was inspired by Cam and asked. From there the two of them kept me entertained, with Jo and Shannon interjecting every now and then, but I was very aware of a silently pissed-off Maia at my side and her confused father on her other side.

I was also aware it was time I started taking back my own life, because there was no *if* anymore regarding whether I was going to end up getting hurt. Only *when*.

CHAPTER 11

"Why are you looking at me like that?" Maia said, throwing Logan and me a wary smile.

She'd come home from school to find us standing in my sitting room, waiting for her. It was a week since I'd gone shopping with Logan, and it was his day off again. We'd spent it putting the finishing touches on Maia's room.

Logan's face was perfectly blank.

I refrained from grimacing at him and smiled brightly at his daughter instead. "Logan has a surprise for you."

I wouldn't hold his sudden lack of enthusiasm against him, because I knew underneath that stoic reserve, he was a pile of nerves. He wanted Maia's room to be perfect for her.

Maia's eyebrows rose at the announcement. "Okay."

"This way," Logan piped up, marching toward her. He put his hands on her shoulders, gently turned her around, and put his hands over her eyes. He started guiding her out of my flat. She giggled, and I saw his shoulders relax a little.

I hurried past them to get my door and laughed at them as Logan attempted to guide her out. She tripped on the doorjamb, and Logan's arms went around her to stop her from falling. She craned her neck to look back up at him, laughing, and he grinned down at her.

"Maybe I'll just cover your eyes once we're in our flat."

She didn't miss the emphasis he put on the word "our," and she turned back to me with bright eyes.

"Come on, then." I hurried ahead and opened Logan's door.

Once we were all inside, Logan insisted on covering her eyes again, and it took them twice as long to get through the flat to Maia's room. He guided her in and said, "I hope you like it, sweetheart," and then removed his hands from her eyes.

Maia blinked a number of times, her eyes growing rounder and rounder as she gazed at her new bedroom.

Logan had painted the whole room a soft, soothing green. The white Shaker bed was centered to the room, and we'd found matching bedside cabinets, bureau, and wardrobe. In the corner of the room was a small, extremely cute green velvet reading chair I'd fallen in love with and promised Logan Maia would love too. I'd dressed her bed in a white cotton duvet set that was trimmed in forest green and champagne. Draped across the bottom of the bed was a forest green velvet throw, and I'd arranged five scatter cushions in all shapes and sizes, in greens and champagne, on top of her pillows.

Pretty gold lamps with silk champagne shades set off her bedside cabinets, and I'd bought her some perfume and makeup and arranged it on her bureau. In her many conversations about Leigh and Layla, I'd discovered who her favorite bands were. We'd found posters for a few of them, framed them, and put them on the walls. Above her bed was a piece of canvas abstract art that was painted in the colors we'd decorated her room in.

We waited with bated breath for her reaction.

The wonder on her face suddenly dissolved into tears.

Logan shot me a panicked look.

I smiled at him in reassurance and before I could say anything Maia slowly walked over to him, her mouth trembling, her chest heaving as she tried to control the tears, and she threw her arms around him. Right then she seemed so much a little girl, and tears pricked my eyes.

Logan relaxed into the hug, holding her securely in his strong arms. He kissed the top of her head and said softly, "I take it that means you like it?"

She nodded against his chest. "I love it. It's beautiful." Her mumbled praise rose up to reach our ears. There were a few more sniffles and choked emotions before she pulled away from her dad and swiped at her cheeks. "Thank you."

My heart squeezed in my chest when I realized Logan's eyes were bright with emotion. He cupped her face and whispered, "Welcome home, sweetheart."

I couldn't stop the tears and, frankly, I wasn't ashamed of them. I was so moved to be a part of this moment.

Maia smiled shakily at me. "I better go pack."

"Yeah."

She rushed toward me and hugged me tight before hurrying out of the flat.

And just like that I found myself wrapped in Logan's arms. I made a startled noise before relaxing into him. Sliding my own arms around him, I tried not to think about how warm and strong he felt against me, the muscles in his back hard beneath my fingertips. He smelled bloody wonderful too.

Damn it.

The hug didn't last nearly long enough. He pulled back but not to step away. Instead he cupped my face in his hands like he had done Maia, and his thumbs swiped at the tear tracks on my cheeks. I felt a little lost looking up into his beautiful eyes. "There's no way for me to thank you properly," he said, his voice gruff.

"You don't have to thank me," I whispered, struggling to find the strength to speak up over the reaction my body was having to his nearness.

I was tingling.

All over.

In places Logan really shouldn't be making me tingle.

Those tingles turned to full-on shivers as he lowered his hands, his thumbs whispering a trail down my neck and along my collarbone. He let go, only to settle his hands on my waist.

My lips parted in surprise, drawing his gaze.

I couldn't breathe.

A vibrating noise shattered the intensity of the moment, and I frowned in confusion.

Logan stepped back, no longer meeting my eyes. "My phone," he muttered, digging into his jeans pocket for it.

More than a little discombobulated by what had or had not just happened, I started backing out of the room. "I'll just, uh . . . go see how Maia is getting on."

Shaking my head, I hurried out of the flat.

What the hell had that been?

He wasn't all flirty, so it couldn't have been sexual. In fact, I knew for certain it wasn't sexual, because he wasn't attracted to me. I shook my head again and charged into my flat, suddenly annoyed.

I wish the man wouldn't be so bloody affectionate with me!

That was it. I'd been right a week ago at the restaurant when he'd flirted with the waitress. Sure, as soon as Maia went into a huff with him over it, he stopped it, but it still reminded me of a very important fact.

I was not Logan MacLeod's type. I never would be.

And, frankly, in any other dimension he wouldn't be my type. I'd been thrown at him in circumstances beyond my control.

Well, no more!

I needed to create distance from him without creating distance with Maia. I could do it.

I *had* to do it.

Shoving the moment out of my head, I moved into the doorway of my guest room to see Maia packing her clothes into the suitcase I'd left out for her. "Nearly ready?"

She looked up and gave me a tremulous smile.

"Sweetie, are you all right?"

She shrugged, and then she was crying again. "I'm going to miss you."

I walked into the room and drew her into my arms. "I am not going anywhere. I will be right next door, and you can come see me anytime you want."

I let her cry for a little while longer, and finally she pulled away to start packing again. "I'm a wee bit nervous," she admitted.

"That's perfectly natural. But you and Logan are going to have an amazing time making up for lost years." I gave her a teasing smile. "Still, try to take it easy on him."

Maia giggled and nodded. She gave me one last hug, and I walked her to the door. Logan was waiting in his doorway, and he came over to take the suitcase from her.

It was only a few steps, but it felt like miles as I watched him lead her across the landing. She gave me a watery smile and disappeared.

Logan nodded at me, and I gave him a little wave before shutting my door.

Sliding down the door, I landed with a little bump on my bottom as I stared despondently down my hall.

My despondency did not last. I didn't have time for it because any concerns I had about not seeing Maia (and yes, maybe Logan too) were put to rest when it became perfectly apparent than neither she nor her father had any intention of forgetting about me.

Two weeks later I was standing in my kitchen. The first week in May had passed us by, and I found myself doing something familiar.

Eating dinner with Maia and Logan.

Somehow we'd fallen into this pattern together. After school Maia usually spent time at either Leigh's or Layla's house for an hour before coming home to me. She'd do her homework and I would help if I could, while I got dinner started in time for Logan to finish work. If I was too busy with my own work to cook, I ordered takeout for us all.

"Layla said what?" I shook my head, thinking I'd heard wrong.

"Layla said that she thinks our history teacher, Mr. Tatum, is having an affair with the music teacher, Mrs. Rogers."

I shared a worried look with Logan.

We were sitting around my kitchen counter eating Chinese takeout. "And did Layla witness something that made her think this?"

"Yup. She said Mrs. Rogers fiddles with her wedding ring every time she's talking to Mr. Tatum."

"How bored must this girl be to notice that shit?" Logan looked as flummoxed as me.

"I think the more important point here is that Layla should not be spreading rumors based on a woman fiddling with her wedding ring."

Maia shrugged. "I didn't say it."

"Well, maybe you should get Layla to stop saying it."

Maia bugged out her eyes at me. "It's Layla. Only the British Army and a Challenger 2 tank could get her to stop talking."

Logan choked on the bite of food he had just taken.

I took a sip of water to hide my smile. When I felt composed, I faced her again. "Maia, spreading rumors is wrong."

"I know. I won't do it," she promised.

"Pass the prawn crackers." Logan gestured to me, and I slid them over the counter to him. "I found out who was stealing at work," he said as he piled rice and chicken onto a cracker.

"Oh?" Money had been going missing from the bar take on and off for the last week or so. It was driving Logan crazy, and I knew it was partly to do with his inner sense of responsibility and the fact that he had a criminal record and money was missing from his place of employment. Braden had gone out on a limb for him by giving him the managerial position at Fire, and I knew Logan didn't want to let him down.

"One of the nightclub promoters started . . ." He stopped and shot a look at Maia. He did this a lot when he was about to say something before remembering his fifteen-year-old daughter was in the room. "Started a relationship with one of my bartenders. She found out somehow that I have a past record and thought it would be easy enough to steal the cash and that I would naturally be blamed for it."

I felt my blood heat with fury and noticed Maia's cheeks turn red with her own. "How did you find out it was her?"

"Luckily, the bartender she was slee—in a relationship with noticed a change in her funding situation. He got suspicious and caught her last night when he was shutting down the bar. She thought his back was turned."

"Bitch," Maia snapped, furious.

Logan just nodded in agreement.

I rolled my eyes. "Maia, don't use that word." I looked at Logan. "But she's right. Did you get the police involved?"

Logan shook his head. "You know Braden. I think he was worried it would stir trouble for me, so he told her that she could pay him back or he could go the police. She's paying him back."

Maia huffed, pushing her food around her plate. "People suck."

"Only sometimes," he told her. "They make mistakes. Everyone does."

Sensing she was going into broody teenager mode over the unfairness dealt toward her dad, I decided to change the subject. "Speaking of mistakes, I made one today."

"Yeah?" She looked up from her plate.

"Hmm. I listened to that bloody awful band you like so much."

"Uh!" She made a noise of outrage. "Which one?"

"The Charmed Umbrellas . . . Potatoes . . . Walking stick." I shrugged, teasing her.

"The Charitable Rifle," she huffed. "They are not bloody awful."

I looked at Logan. "How do they get away with a name like that? It doesn't even make sense."

He shrugged, his lips twitching.

"Jeez, Grace, you're showing your age." Maia was giving me what I referred to as her "hell no" look.

I gave her my own "hell no" look back. "You did just not say that. I will have you know that twenty-eight is not that old."

"It's *thirteen* years older than me." She grinned cheekily.

"Now you're just being mean."

Logan lost his battle and grinned at his food.

Before Maia could respond, the doorbell rang, interrupting us. I frowned. "I wonder who that is."

Who that was, was a tall, leggy, curvy blonde. She was wearing skinny jeans, stilettos, and a tight-fitting sweater with a deep V-neck that showed a very good cleavage. She wore no jacket and didn't need one, considering we were having quite a warm May. Her wide blue eyes grew round at the sight of me. "Uh . . ." Her brows drew together in confusion. "I'm looking for Logan."

She was American.

My stomach plummeted.

Was she *the* American?

"Come in," I found myself uttering out of ingrained politeness. I stepped aside, letting her into my flat, and her strong perfume wafted over me.

Her stilettos clacked against my wooden floors as I led her into the kitchen. She stopped in the doorway, and Logan's lips parted in surprise.

She gave him an intimate, cheeky smile. "Some old guy downstairs said you might be here." Her smile dropped as she took in Maia, her expression turning confused when she looked at me.

He dropped his fork on his plate and slid off his stool. "What helpful neighbors we have."

An awkward silence fell.

"Uh . . . Sharon, this is my daughter, Maia, and my friend Grace. Guys, Sharon." He walked over to her and leaned in to her to ask quietly, "What are you doing here?"

"Well"—she put her hand into her large handbag and pulled out a device—"you left your iPad at my place this afternoon, and I thought you might need it."

"Fuck. I was looking all over the office for that. Thanks." He took it from her.

I felt sick.

All this time, he'd been seeing the American after he said he wasn't.

I felt . . . betrayed.

I knew that wasn't fair to Logan because that wasn't what we had, but still . . . I guess you can't help how you feel.

"Dad, who is this?" Maia demanded snottily. It also happened to be the first time she'd called Logan "Dad."

He stared back at her a little dazed. "Uh . . . a friend, Maia."

"Well, we're having dinner. She's interrupting."

"Maia." His voice lowered with warning. "Don't be rude."

"I'm not the one being rude," she muttered, and turned around on her stool, pushing her food around her plate with her fork.

She was glaring at that plate with a fierceness that concerned me. Logan was really going to have to be careful when it came to introducing women into her life.

"Sharon—"

"I better go," she said, throwing me an apologetic smile. "I'm sorry to interrupt." She leaned in to kiss his cheek. "It was nice seeing you again."

Logan walked her out, and I felt my frustration mount every time one of her heels clacked against my floorboards.

When Logan returned, Maia looked up at me. "Can I be excused?"

I stared over her shoulder at Logan, and he nodded wearily.

"Sure." I smiled patiently at her and took her plate away.

Without another word, Maia got up and left the flat to go next door.

Logan rubbed the back of his neck, uncomfortable. "That wasn't supposed to happen."

Feeling dread at the fact that I was the one he wanted to talk to about this, I turned my back on him and began emptying mine and Maia's food into the bin. "If you have a woman, I think it best you ease her into your life with Maia. For future reference."

"But I don't . . . Sharon . . . I haven't . . . Look, Sharon and I haven't been together. I did break it off with her. Today was a slip."

I didn't say anything.

"I'm saying I spent two years in prison, and when I got out, I may have been trying to make up for the fact that I hadn't had sex in two years. When you get used to it regular . . . She called me, and I went to her place on my lunch break and—"

"I don't need to know the details." I shot him a look over my shoulder, trying to hide my fury. "We're friends, but we're not that close."

"I'm just saying it happened. It's not serious, and it won't happen again."

I started loading the plates into the dishwasher now. "Does *she* know that?"

"She's here on a six-month visa. We both knew it was temporary. Would you turn around? I hate talking to your back."

I braced myself and spun around, leaning against the counter for support. "Unless she's dreaming of the rough-around-the-edges Scotsman popping the question."

Logan stared at me like I was nuts.

I gave a huff of unamused laughter. "What? You don't think women think like that? Many women have romantic fantasies and notions, and as much as we understand the reality of a situation, there's always these little things called imagination and hope, and they make us think crazy things such as wanting a manwhore nightclub manager to marry us and give us a permanent visa."

Logan processed this. "No?"

"Yes."

"Okay, well, it's definitely finished, then."

"The horror. However will you find your next booty call?"

Logan burst into laughter and got up off the stool. Still laughing, he took his empty plate and put it in the dishwasher. When he stood up, we were way too close for my liking. He grinned. "Thanks for dinner."

I watched him walk away, thinking perhaps I hated him a little, and I hated myself for hating him when it wasn't his fault I had feelings for him.

"Oh and, Grace." He glanced over his shoulder. "Don't ever say 'booty call' again."

CHAPTER 12

"Do I know you?" Chloe dragged her gaze down the length of me and back up again with exaggerated attitude.

"Don't." I sighed and slipped onto the stool next to her at the bar. After Logan had left, I'd called Chloe to arrange an emergency night out. I needed a drink and I needed my friend. I did not, however, need her to be snarky. "I know I've been preoccupied lately and I'm sorry, but . . ." I trailed off. The truth was, I really hadn't been the greatest friend. "Actually, I'm just sorry."

Chloe made a face. "You got yourself a life, Grace. There's nothing to be sorry for. I was just teasing."

The bartender interrupted. "What can I get you?"

I slumped, leaning my elbow on the bar and my chin in the palm of my hand. "Talisker and ginger ale, please."

Chloe sucked in her breath beside me. "You're on the whisky? Okay, whose head do I need to be cracking?"

"Mine." I groaned and squeezed my eyes closed. "Shit, Chloe. I'm letting myself fall for Logan MacLeod and I need you to help me stop."

"I knew it!"

My eyes popped open to glare at her. "No gloating."

She hid her smile behind her glass and took a sip of the fruity-looking cocktail she was drinking.

"Stop smiling."

She huffed. "Right, you grumpy cow. Tell me why I'm stopping you from falling for Mr. MacLeod. I saw a picture of him on Facebook. Can I just say . . . *wow.*"

My brows puckered. "Facebook?" How on earth did she find him on Facebook? Logan had a Facebook account? That didn't sound right.

"I friended Maia after we talked on the phone the other day and—"

"You talked to Maia?"

"Yes. When I called you, she picked up. We had a wee chat. She's a cutie."

Trust Chloe to make friends with Maia after one conversation. "So you added her to your Facebook? You do know you're thirteen years older than her?"

Chloe made a face. "I didn't friend her to friend her. I friended her for the purpose of snooping, and it paid off."

"Ed really needs to get a job closer to home," I murmured.

She ignored my dig. "Maia posted a selfie of her and Logan."

I perked up. The thought of Logan posing for a selfie with his daughter made me feel all warm inside. "Let me see."

Grinning, Chloe reached into her clutch and pulled out her phone. She played around with it for a few seconds and then passed it to me. She had brought up Maia's profile on Facebook, and sure enough, her profile pic was a selfie of her and Logan.

It was adorable.

Maia was grinning widely into the camera, her cheek pressed to Logan's as he gave that little smirk of his that was sexy even when he didn't mean it to be. I scrolled through the comments and started to frown. "Look what these children are saying about Logan."

"They're fifteen and he's hot."

"It's Maia's father, not . . ." My mouth hung open. I pushed the phone in Chloe's face, pointing to a comment. "Where did she learn about that? That is inappropriate. That . . . Bloody hell, that's Layla." I was aghast. "Okay, I think I need to curb how much time Maia is spending with that little dirty-mouthed . . . *girl*."

"Ooh nice, Grace. You really got vicious there."

"I'm not going to be vicious about a fifteen-year-old, even if she is cruder than porn."

"Is it possible to be cruder than porn?"

"Depends on the porn," the bartender said with a cheeky smile as he put my whisky in front of me. "Tab?"

I thought about Logan and Sharon. "Yes, please."

"Back to the subject at hand," Chloe said. "I don't want to stop you from falling for this guy. Personally, I think he's good for you."

"How can you possibly think that? You haven't even met him."

"I know that you have this fire about you that I've never seen before. You have these new people in your life. You have Maia, whom you clearly adore."

I decided it was time to tell her about Sharon the American.

"Och, that's nothing." Chloe dismissed it with a wave of her hand as soon as I was finished telling her about the events of the evening.

I was affronted by the dismissal. "You're clearly not listening. I am not Logan's type. At all. And he's not even my type. I don't know how this happened. But I do know that he's never going to see me as anything but a friend, and I'm going to end up getting my heart broken if I don't do something quickly."

Chloe raised an eyebrow. "Did you hear what you just said? He's not your type. And yet here we are discussing how you have feelings for him. Who is to say that he hasn't developed feelings for you?"

I shook my head, frustrated by her attempts at encouragement rather than discouragement. "He flirts with women he finds attractive. I've witnessed it. He has never flirted with me. Ever. Chloe, all of his women look the same. And they don't look like me. If he's not looking to get serious with his type, he is definitely not looking to get serious with me. He's just going to have shady hookups on the side with women he doesn't want to bring home to his daughter. I'm not going to be a shady hookup, and I wouldn't want to be."

Chloe scowled. "What the hell is it you want me to say?"

"I want you to help me get over him. Before all of this I'd been on one bad date after another. A few of those you sent me out on. I'm asking you to dig deep and search hard and find me the best bloody date you've ever found anyone. It's time to remake the magic of Aidan and Juno."

My friend did not look happy. "But—"

"But nothing. Logan is a dead end. Find me a through road!"

Her eyes widened with amusement. "Fine. I'll find you the most perfect date ever."

"That's what I'm talking about." I clinked my glass against hers, feeling better already.

As Maia helped me load the dishwasher a few days later, she turned to Logan, who was sipping a beer at my counter. We'd just finished dinner together. Again. "Since it's Friday, can we watch a movie tonight?"

"Have you done all your homework?"

"Most of it. I thought I'd finish the rest on Sunday. There's not much to do. Ask Grace."

I glanced over my shoulder to find him looking at me questioningly. "She speaks the truth."

His lips curled up at the corners and his eyes slid to his daughter. "Then we can watch a movie."

"You too, Grace. Dad bought a new armchair and it's awesome, but I'll let you have it."

I chuckled at her generosity.

"No chick flicks, please," Logan added. "Don't need the two of you ganging up on me."

"We'll vote," Maia said. "And I promise not to vote for a chick flick. They're crap anyway. It's always about two idiots who apparently don't understand the art of communication."

"There is nothing wrong with a good chick flick," I argued, but I did it laughing at her assessment of the chick flick. "But unfortunately, I can't vote because I can't come over tonight."

"Why?" Maia looked disappointed.

"I have plans."

"Oh. Well, change them."

I laughed, but Logan said her name with warning and shook his head at her. "Perhaps Grace is spending time with her other friends, Maia. Remember she has those."

Maia snorted. "Oh yeah. I forgot she had a life before we took it over."

The two of them smiled mischievously at each other.

"You two are so funny," I said dryly. "And wrong."

"About?"

"My plans. I'm not seeing my friends." I felt a fluttering in my belly and I knew it was part nerves for the date tonight and part excitement that tonight might mean the end of my infatuation with Logan. "I have a date."

My announcement was met with utter silence.

Maia was looking at me horrified, and Logan's face had gone blank.

"A date?" Maia spat out as if it were a dirty word.

I gave a huff of laughter. "Yes, a date. I do go on those sometimes. I have to hide my horns and cloven feet to do it, but somehow I manage."

"With who?" Logan practically barked from across the counter, his expression no longer blank. He was glowering. Hard.

I blinked rapidly in surprise at the bark. What was this? Was Logan daring to play protective big brother?

Oh God, could my life get any more pathetic? I'd been relegated to "familial" in his book.

"A colleague of Chloe. She set us up. She said he's wonderful."

Apparently, he was a divorced father of two, and he was looking for something serious again after a year in the dating pool. As soon as Chloe heard that she said she knew she had to set us up. She said he was just what I needed.

I felt another burst of butterflies at the thought of meeting him.

"A blind date?" Logan was still scowling.

"Yes."

"Because you've had such great luck with those in the past."

I made a face at his reminder that he'd saved me from the last one. "Witness one bad one and you think you know everything."

Maia suddenly marched across the room toward the door. "I'm going to pick a film," she threw over her shoulder before disappearing.

"Maia?" I called out, concerned by her reaction. In response I heard nothing but the slamming of my front door. I shot a confused look at Logan.

He shrugged. "Don't ask me. I'm still trying to figure out half of her moods."

I chewed on my lip and slid onto a stool. "Maybe she feels like I'm abandoning her by not staying to watch the movie with you."

"Maybe."

"I hate disappointing her, but she has to appreciate that I have friendships outside of you two and that when I see other people it doesn't mean I'm abandoning her."

Logan nodded. "I'll talk to her about it."

"Thank you."

He sighed and got up off his stool. "It's like another language and there's no one to teach it to me."

"Teenage girl?" I smiled sympathetically.

"No. Women in general."

"Well, that's because we're far more intelligent than men. It's hard for you simple creatures to keep up." I smiled beatifically.

He narrowed his eyes on me. "Very droll, Grace." He turned to go and then seemed to think better of it. "So who is this guy you're seeing tonight?"

"His name is Colin. He works at the estate agency with Chloe."

"He sounds like a dick."

I snorted. "How did you get that from those two pieces of information?"

"The only Colins I've ever met have turned out to be dicks, and estate agents are no better than smarmy salesmen."

"He has a good job, he's divorced, and he has children. He's not a dick."

"That makes him sound like even more of a dick." Logan turned fully around now to argue.

"He sounds like he's responsible and willing to commit!" I felt my temper genuinely start to rise at his overprotectiveness.

"Really? Responsible? So who is looking after his bloody children while he's out on a date with you?"

"I imagine his ex-wife is. He divorced her, Logan. He didn't kill her."

"No, of course not. Why kill her when he can keep her around as a glorified nanny while he fucks beautiful, impressionable women." He gestured to me in irritation.

I was stunned silent for a moment.

There was an undercurrent of true anger under his ridiculousness, and I felt stifled by the way he saw me. I might as well have been Shannon for the proprietary way he was treating me and talking down to me.

"I am not impressionable!" I snapped, and hurried from the room. "You can see yourself out! I have a *date* to get ready for."

If in the back of my mind I thought it strange that Colin had asked me out for drinks rather than dinner, I was determined to shove it aside and think he was just trying to make the whole first date thing more relaxing.

I should have listened to the back of my mind.

When I first saw him I thought him handsome, with his tall, dark, clean-cut good looks. Charming as well, as he stood up from the bar to shake my hand and press a kiss to my cheek. He smelled good too. He also couldn't tear his eyes away from my cleavage.

And he did not look old enough to be a divorced father of two.

As I settled into a booth across from him with my glass of wine, I immediately said, "So Chloe tells me you have two children."

He practically choked on a sip of his pint. "Excuse me?" He coughed into his hand, eyes bright with mirth.

Chloe was going to die as soon as I got my hands on her.

I gave Colin a strained smile. "Not divorced either, then?"

He shook his head, grinning. "What the hell kind of nonsense did Chloe tell you?"

"Please tell me your name is Colin."

"My name *is* Colin and I work with Chloe, but I've never been married and I don't have kids."

What kind of game was my friend playing here?

"Your name is Grace, right?" he teased.

I stared into his warm brown eyes and found myself nodding. I didn't know what Chloe was up to, but Colin seemed congenial enough. "I don't know why she said those things."

"Chloe has a weird sense of humor. She does tell me I'm the second work colleague of hers you've been on a date with though."

I thought I detected something suggestive in his eyes and tone, but I shrugged it off, deciding I was paranoid. "It's a large estate agency," I joked.

He chuckled and nodded before leaning across the table. "This place is a bit pretentious. Why don't we just cut to the chase and go back to my flat?"

I blinked at the suggestion. There was no denying the heat in his eyes. Apparently I wasn't paranoid. "Pardon?"

"I mean I can buy you another drink if you want, but I just thought why waste some of the night, right?"

A few months ago I probably would have quelled my inner outrage, stuttered and blushed and somehow got myself out of the situation, apologizing like it was all my fault. Anything to avoid confronting the truth of it.

Therefore I could only blame Logan's influence for forging past my fear of confrontation and asking straight out, "Are you telling me you're only here on this date to get laid?"

Colin shrugged and nodded, like it was obvious. "Chloe knows I just like fun. Nothing serious. I'm sure she told you that . . . no?"

I grimaced. Yes, I was definitely going to kill her. "No. She did not."

"So . . . this isn't a hookup? You don't want to go back to my place, then?"

Somehow I managed to refrain from throwing my drink in his face. He hadn't even given me five minutes of conversation before deciding he wanted nothing more from me than a quick bang in the sack. As far as I was concerned, his way of doing things was just a glorified form of masturbation.

I gathered my purse and jacket and gave him a tight smile. "No. I'm afraid it would only be a disappointing experience for the two of us." I stood up and stared down at him with a gleam in my eye. "I only enjoy the really dirty stuff, and I have to be able to know and trust a man before I'll let him do absolutely *anything* he wants to me in bed."

I sashayed out of the bar, leaving him staring after me with his mouth hanging open, and I laughed as I stepped out into the night air. I glanced back over my shoulder at the bar and shook my head, still grinning. I didn't know what came over me in there, but I liked it.

Not enough to stop me from killing Chloe, however.

That momentary triumph of making Colin feel like he'd just missed out on something exciting dissipated as I walked home.

I was back at square one.

Chloe, in her infinite wisdom (not!) had put me there. Thinking about it, I realized exactly what she was up to. She had made it perfectly clear she thought Logan was the best candidate for me (as usual, not listening to a word I said) and had set about attempting to prove this by setting me up on another bad date.

All Chloe had done was proven that I could no longer trust her to help find me a decent date.

I'd barely put a step onto my landing when Logan's door flew open. Staring at him wide-eyed, I waited for him to say something. Instead he just glowered at me. *Still in a mood, I see.*

"All right, then," I said, and walked sedately over to my door. My heels made a helluva noise, echoing around the stairwell. It must have been what alerted Logan to my return.

"You're early," he grunted as I put my key in the lock.

"I am."

"Why?"

I nearly jumped out of my skin at the sound of his voice at my ear. I glanced over my shoulder, and sure enough he was almost pressed against my back. "Just because. *Dad.*" Angry, I pushed open my door and stepped in, hoping he would take the hint and piss off.

I was to be disappointed.

Logan caught the door and ushered me inside. "Did he do something to you?"

"Where is Maia?" I said, as he shut my door behind him.

"She's sleeping. I've locked her in."

"Oh good," I said, walking away from him. "If there's a fire, at least her chances of escape are narrower."

"She can unlock it from the inside," he said through gritted teeth as he followed me into my kitchen.

"Logan, I am not in the mood for whatever this is." I reached into my fridge for a bottle of wine.

The wine was promptly pulled out of my hands, and I grunted in annoyance as Logan set about opening the bottle and pouring me a glass. He slid the glass along the counter toward me with so much aggression I was lucky there was any wine left in it. "Speak," he demanded.

I grabbed the glass and moved away from him so I could take a somewhat calming sip.

"Grace," he warned.

My answer was a filthy look before I put the glass on the counter and started to unbutton my jacket. This was my house after all. I could make myself at home. "I don't know if you realize this, Logan," I snapped as I jerked open my buttons. "But I don't actually have to tell you anything about my life." I threw my coat at a stool that sat in the corner of the room and turned back for my glass.

The silence from Logan made me look at him.

His gaze was on my body, and I couldn't quite work out what the sudden darkness in his eyes meant.

"Logan?"

"Is that what you wore?" he choked out. "For him."

I glanced down at my dress. It symbolized all the hope I had been feeling about tonight and Colin, because it was the sexiest thing I had in my wardrobe, and I didn't wear it for just anyone. It was a black satin calf-length dress that fitted me like a second skin. It had thin straps and a sweetheart neckline that revealed more cleavage than any of my other dresses. I was wearing a sexy push-up bra that did wonderful things to my modest cleavage.

I'd pinned my hair up to show the dress off at its best.

Although it was far less revealing than the clothes I'd seen Logan's women wearing, I suddenly felt quite exposed with him looking at me like that.

I blushed and took a swig of wine.

"Was he worth it?" He gestured to my dress with a look of angry distaste in his eyes.

My own temper rose in answer. "There's nothing wrong with this dress."

"Well, he could be in no doubt what you were offering when you turned up in it. So what the hell happened? Or was it the true definition of a quickie?"

I sucked in my breath, hurt. "Get out of my kitchen."

He marched around the counter toward me. "Not before you tell me what that bastard did to you."

"It's none of your business. For the fifteen hundredth time."

"I beg to fucking differ." He stopped inches from me, towering over me, deliberately trying to intimidate me into answering.

I looked up at him, trying to shoot sparks at him with my eyes. "You're being ridiculous. I am not your sister!"

Logan jerked back as if I'd hit him, surprise rounding his eyes. After a minute he said hoarsely, "Believe me, I know you are not my sister."

What did that mean? I shivered under the heat of his regard and felt gooseflesh rise on the upper curves of my breasts. My nipples tightened against my bra. Trembling a little now, I skirted around him, putting some distance between us.

"I just want to know if he hurt you," Logan said, no longer sounding angry.

"No, he didn't." I finished off my wine and turned, but I braced myself against the wall, unable to hold myself up against the confusion I felt.

The tension in the room was unbelievably thick, and I was starting to wonder if the sexual part of it on my side wasn't just on my side. In fact, I was starting to wonder if the tension wasn't entirely made up of sexual frustration, period.

I looked up at Logan from under my lashes. He'd turned to face me, but every muscle in his body seemed to be stretched taut. "No, he didn't," I repeated quietly. "But he was only after one thing."

The muscle in his jaw ticked. "What did you do?"

"I told him I didn't do one-night stands because when I went to bed with a man I wanted him to do whatever he wanted to me, and for that I needed to know and trust him."

Logan's face went blank. "You said what?" he asked flatly.

"I was being funny." I shrugged, suddenly not feeling so funny anymore.

"Aye, well, I'd expect a phone call from him tomorrow. Saying shit like that to him, wearing that fucking dress . . ." He was angry again.

And like always, his anger ignited mine. "Why are you acting like a complete sod to me tonight?"

"Are you really that fucking clueless?" Logan shouted, wearing a look of disbelief.

"Apparently so!" I shouted back.

"Well, here's a damn hint!"

I barely had time to blink at his yell before his body was pressing mine hard into the wall. He captured my wrists in his hands and pinned them, holding me completely captive. Breathing heavy, his face but an inch from mine, he stared down into my eyes and said hoarsely, "Tell me to get out, Grace."

My skin was flushed. In fact, my whole body felt like flames were licking at every inch of it. I could feel my breasts swell up against the tight confines of my dress, and the tingling between my legs had increased to an insistent throb. I breathed Logan in, my breath hitching as I felt his erection. There was a pleasant flip in my lower belly, and I squeezed my legs tighter together at the rush of slickness between them.

"Grace." His head dipped toward mine. "Tell me to leave."

"No," I whispered back, relaxing into the wall, and he melted into me with a groan. "I want you to stay."

He looked into my eyes as if searching for the answer to something. "If I stay I'm going to fuck you."

I trembled in reaction to his bluntness and licked my lips before I moved my feet, widening my legs so he could fit just right between them. His eyes flared at the movement, and I reached up so our lips brushed as I whispered, "I'm counting on it."

CHAPTER 13

Logan MacLeod could kiss.

His lips were hot against my lips as his tongue slid against mine. Stubble from his beard scratched my skin as he deepened the kiss and ground his lower body against me. My nipples instantly hardened. I'd never been kissed like this before. With such voraciousness. Like he couldn't get enough of me.

I let out a little gasp of excitement as he released my lips to trail his down my throat, traveling lower to the rise of my breasts. He squeezed my wrists as I arched against his mouth. In answer he released his hold on my hands and pulled back to stare into my flushed face. My skin felt inflamed and much too tight.

My lower belly flipped at the hunger in his heated gaze.

I'd never felt so wanted in my life.

And to be wanted by him . . .

"Logan," I pleaded.

His eyes flared at my plea, and he slipped his fingers under the straps of my dress. With a deliberate slowness that had me panting, he lowered the straps of my dress, tugging on them until the front of it was bunched under my bra. He followed this by tugging my bra down to expose me. Cupping my breasts in his large hands, he stared into my eyes and gave me that sexy little smirk of his. His head descended, and I cried out as his mouth wrapped around my nipple. I reached for him, my arms curling around his neck, drawing him closer. I moaned, my head falling back against the kitchen wall as he licked and sucked and tormented before moving on to my other nipple. My senses were overwhelmed. His scent, his heat, his hardness, and strength. I was surrounded. I'd never felt this way before. Like I might burst out of my skin if he didn't come inside of me.

I writhed against him, and Logan groaned against my breast, the sound reverberating through me deliciously. In answer he pressed his body deeper into mine and lifted his head to kiss me again. This kiss was harder, wetter, much more out of control. I instantly wrapped myself around him, and my fingers curled in the hair at the back of his neck as I licked and sucked and flicked my tongue against his, our kiss so deep I wasn't aware of anything but him.

All I knew was that I wanted more and I wanted it now.

My hand slipped under his T-shirt, and I traced his hard stomach before sliding down inside his jeans.

He broke the kiss on a hiss, pressing into my hand as I tried to curl it around his erection against the constraining confinement of his jeans.

I pulled my hand out and began unzipping him. "I want you inside me," I whispered hurriedly. "I need you."

He gently brushed my hands away from his erection and slipped his own hand under my dress. As his fingertips trailed along my inner thigh, he asked against my mouth, "Are you ready for me, Grace?"

I nipped at his lower lip and sighed. "I'm so ready for you."

"Fuck," he groaned again, his fingers pushing under my knickers. "You are full of surprises."

"Huh-uh?" I said on a whimper as he slid two fingers inside of me.

I pushed onto them.

He pulled back to stare into my eyes as he fucked me with his fingers. "I never thought you'd light up for the likes of me."

I gasped, barely cognizant of what he was saying, as I clutched his arm, afraid he'd stop what he was doing to me.

"Jesus, you're killing me." His lips skimmed my jaw until his mouth stopped at my ear. "I'm going to fuck you until you see stars."

I came around his fingers, my cries of release swallowed in his kiss.

As I shuddered against him, I kissed him and sucked on his tongue. His answering growl spurred me on until it descended into the dirtiest kiss I'd ever experienced.

I felt his warm, rough hands on my outer thighs as they brushed my skin, pushing my dress up to my waist. Logan gripped the fabric of my knickers and tugged, and they slid down my legs. I kicked them away, not daring to break the kiss, and the sudden air between my legs increased the tingling need he was building in me again.

We both reached for his jeans, and we shoved them and his boxers down to his ankles, freeing him. Logan pulled back from the kiss, and I glanced down to check him out.

He was big.

Bigger than I'd had inside me before.

"Oh God," I breathed.

Logan's eyes darkened. "All for you, babe," he said as he gripped my legs, spread them, and thrust up into me.

"Logan!" I cried out in pleasured pain, his throbbing heat overwhelming me. All of my focus was on the sensation of his thickness inside me, and I struggled for breath as my body tried to adjust and relax. Logan held still against me, breathing heavily, as though he was attempting to gain a little control.

I didn't want control.

I wanted more. I pushed my hips against him and he eased me up against the wall so I could wrap my legs around him. It shifted him deeper inside me, and my fingers bit into his shoulders. "Logan!" I arched my head back, and Logan took it as an invitation.

His mouth tugged on my nipple, and my inner muscles clamped

around his cock and snapped whatever control he was holding on to. He pounded us into the wall, thrusting into me hard, gliding in and out of me with increasing frenzy.

He lifted his head, and our eyes met as he kept his promise to fuck me hard. As he watched me, his eyes blackened. "Grace." His voice was guttural. "I'm . . . close . . ." he panted.

At that I felt his thumb press down on my clit, and the combination of his cock inside of me and him rubbing my clit blew me apart. My release triggered his as my inner muscles rippled around his dick. Logan gritted his teeth, his eyes on me, his muscles strained, and he let out a deep belly grunt as his hips jerked against me in climax.

The world slowly came back to me as the euphoria of my orgasm faded. Suddenly I was painfully aware of Logan's chest rising against mine as we struggled to get our breaths back, of his heavy weight against me, of his lips touching my neck.

I breathed him in, afraid to let go.

When he pulled back from me, I could only stare into his eyes, hoping I would be able to read in them what he was thinking. But I couldn't. Instead I held perfectly still, wrapped around him, as he pressed the softest, sweetest kiss to my mouth. My lips tingled as he gently pulled out of me and lowered my legs to the floor.

"Are you on the pill?" he said softly.

I froze at the unexpected question.

And then it hit me.

I'd let him inside me without a condom.

How could I have been so stupid? "I'm on the pill," I whispered, because I was, but that wasn't the point!

Some of the tension he'd been carrying melted out of him as he bent down to pull on his underwear and jeans. I stared at him as he zipped himself back up and then took a step toward me.

What was he going to do next?

I had no idea what was going on here.

To my surprise he took hold of the hem of my dress and slowly lowered it back down into place. And then he grasped the straps of both my dress and bra and gently tugged the upper half of my clothing up until I was covered.

Legs trembling, I could only stand there in my state of shock as he trailed his fingertips across my cheek. "Did I hurt you?"

I shook my head.

In answer Logan took my hand in his and led me through the flat to the bathroom. "I'll let you get cleaned up and then we need to talk."

Locking myself in the bathroom, I did as he suggested, my skin burning as flashbacks from the sex hit me again and again. I leaned against the sink and stared into the mirror at my flushed cheeks, my too-bright eyes, and my hair, which was tumbling out of the grips that pinned it in place. What was going on with Logan? He was acting affectionately, but strangely for someone who had just had mind-blowing sex.

And he couldn't deny it was mind-blowing. I felt how hard he'd come. Just as hard as I had.

I flushed again.

What did "we need to talk" mean?

There was only one way to find out. Butterflies alive and well in my belly, I kicked off my shoes in the hallway and tried to walk calmly into the kitchen, where Logan was sitting on a stool at the counter.

I slid onto the stool next to him.

He turned his head to meet my gaze, and the look in his eyes told me everything I needed to know.

Everything I didn't want to know.

And the rejection, the pain, was awful.

It was this burning ache in my chest . . . quite unlike anything I'd ever felt before.

Logan lowered his gaze, appearing so solemn, that the ache intensified and began to crawl up my chest toward my throat until it felt like a hand choking me.

"This can't happen again, Grace," he said, confirming all that I'd seen in his eyes.

And I'd never felt loss like it. It was different from the pain of walking away from my family. I'd deliberately lost them.

I didn't want to lose Logan.

It hurt, and that hurt was only magnified by the loss of something else. Hope.

Before this I hadn't even realized that underneath my claims of logic and rationality I'd clung to the *fantasy* of Logan and me, but I had. That fantasy had sustained me in a way that I knew probably wasn't good for me in the long run, but it had made each day a little brighter and filled with anticipation.

I couldn't respond past the constriction in my throat.

"I have to focus on Maia. Every day I'm reminded that I've lost out on fifteen years of being her father, and I still haven't scraped the surface of the damage Maryanne did to her. I need to make up for it, Grace, and the only way I can do that is by giving her all of me right now. She deserves that. She deserves to be number one. I can't be in a relationship at the moment."

The sudden flashback of Logan moving inside of me no longer inflamed my skin. Instead I felt cold. I felt vulnerable.

Humiliated.

Stupid.

Oh, so bloody stupid.

Why did I give him that part of me when I knew all along what he wasn't saying, what he was hiding behind his excuse of Maia—he couldn't be in a relationship *with me.*

"Grace," he said when I didn't say anything, his beautiful eyes asking me to understand. "I should never have with you . . . I acted on impulse. I have to stop." He ran a hand over his head, clearly frustrated with himself. "I have to take control of my life. Be a fucking man. Look where impulse has gotten me. It put me in jail, for Christ's sake."

Anger opened up my throat and vocal cords. "Are you comparing having sex with me to what you did to get yourself imprisoned?"

"Of course not."

"Oh good," I said, as I slid off the stool away from him. "I might have taken exception to that."

"You're pissed." He sighed. "Shit, Grace, I never meant to—"

"Fuck me? Yeah, I got that memo." I was suddenly desperate for him to leave before I was humiliated further by crying in front of him. "You can go now, Logan."

He stood up, his features tightening. "Don't be like that. Please. You've been so good to Maia and me—you have to know that you are the last person I'd ever want to hurt. I'm a dick, okay." He held up his hands in surrender. "I shouldn't have done it. I care about you, and I'm attracted to you—of course I'm fucking attracted to you; look at you—but I had no intention of crossing that line with you and spoiling what the three of us have. You know how Maia has been acting when she gets even the sniff of a woman in my life. I can't do this. Please understand."

I narrowed my eyes, too hurt to hear his explanation of why not. All I really wanted to know was why. "Why did you, then?" I said, unable to hold that hurt inside. At least my anger seemed to be stemming the tears. "I was content in the knowledge that you didn't reciprocate my feelings for you, so why did you cross the line?"

Remorse blazed in his eyes. "I let jealousy get the better of me," he admitted hoarsely.

I gave a huff of disbelief. "So you're saying you got upset because another boy was playing with the toy you hadn't had a chance to play with yet?"

"Don't," he warned. "Don't make this worse. I had no idea how you felt about me."

"Oh please, Logan. That may have been true when we first met, but we have been past the antagonistic-neighbor routine for a while now."

The muscle in his jaw ticked. "I suspected you were attracted to me, but nothing deeper. I never imagined you could."

"Because that's me the shallow hookup girl. You know me better than that."

"Apparently, I don't," he snapped, eyes dark with anger. "But if you want me to take full responsibility for this, then I will. I've been an arsehole, I hurt you, and I hate that I've hurt you. I do. I am sorry," he ended on a whisper.

I shook my head and wrapped my arms around my waist, turning away because I could feel the tears start to come now. "I'm the idiot that forgot you like your quick fucks to come hassle free, with an ever quicker good-bye."

"Jesus—"

"Don't. Just go. There's no point to arguing. You were right before. I should have asked you to leave then. I'm asking you now."

After a moment I heard him walk toward the kitchen doorway.

I batted at my tears and turned around. "Logan."

He stopped, looking back at me almost hopefully.

"I don't want you back here," I said, squashing that hope. "Maia is always welcome and I will be civilized to you for her sake, but you and me . . . our friendship is officially over."

He tensed, an incredulous look in his eyes. "You're killing me here, babe."

Tears blurred my vision. "Please." I looked away, swiping at the drops as they fell down my cheeks.

"Okay," he said softly, and I heard him walk away.

At the sound of my flat door closing, I burst into tears, tightening my arms around myself as if it could somehow keep the pain from spilling out all over.

CHAPTER 14

There are moments in life that change us irreparably. Sometimes those moments are grand and dramatic, tragic or beautiful in their intensity. Sometimes those moments are quiet and small, like footsteps fading behind a closed door. The subtlety of those moments can sometimes camouflage their impact.

And sometimes the impact is felt profoundly, but the quietness of the moment is lost on everyone else around you, adding loneliness to the equation.

That's how I felt the next morning as I sat staring at my computer.

I'd fallen in love for the first time.

And he didn't love me back.

I no longer felt whole. I felt like I'd given a piece of myself away but there was no reciprocation to fill the emptiness it had left behind.

My family's lack of affection had been with me for so long that as I'd grown it had become a part of me. Every piece of me I'd tried to give to them had chipped away at me until I was this lonely teenager with a ten-mile-high wall of defenses and insecurities.

Aidan and Chloe had spent years helping me rebuild myself.

And I'd just handed a piece away without thought.

Was that really Logan's fault?

He had told me weeks ago that he didn't want to be in a relationship because he was concentrating on Maia. And look at how we were first introduced? His bed had seen more women in it than the bunks in a rock band's tour bus.

I feared I had acted selfishly with blinders on.

Before I could stew any longer in my misery, my phone rang. I wiped the tear tracks on my cheeks and picked up. "Hello," I said, grateful I sounded normal.

"Is this Grace Farquhar?" a woman asked. Her American accent was dented here and there with Scots.

"Speaking," I replied, hoping it wasn't one of those bloody call centers.

"Oh, hey, this is Joss Carmichael. Jo gave me your number."

Joss Carmichael? As in . . . "J. B. Carmichael?"

She gave a husky laugh. "Joss is fine. I was wondering if you're free to chat about possibly editing this manuscript I'm thinking of self-publishing."

Was she kidding? Her phone call could not have come at a better time. Distraction was exactly what I needed. "I can talk now if you like."

"Great. So I checked out your Web site, and your credentials and that all sound fantastic. Your rates are reasonable, you're well educated, and you have a solid clientele who have continued to come back to you. I even downloaded a couple of the books you've edited, and I'm really impressed."

I flushed with pleasure at the compliment. "Well, thank you."

"You are absolutely welcome. My only concern is that you've edited contemporary and historical romance but no other genre. This manuscript is for an adult dystopian paranormal romance. The first in a series. It's a little out there. A little dark and twisted. Like *moi*," she joked.

I chuckled. "That sounds great. I read all different genres and love dystopian and paranormal, so I understand the narrative and structure for those genres. But of course I understand if you'd prefer to work with an editor who has edited in the genre."

She was silent a moment. "That doesn't bother me. I'm happy to work with you on it, but . . . I need to know you're going to be brutally honest with me. I need an editor who isn't afraid to tell me how it is. You sound awfully *nice*, Grace."

"I'm not nice," I hurried to reassure her. "I mean, I'm nice, but I offer constructive criticism when needed. Believe me I've even had therapy to help me do it," I cracked, and then blanched, wondering why I said such a stupid, stupid thing!

Thankfully, Joss chuckled. "I hear you."

Thank God she had a sense of humor.

"Okay. Why don't we give this a shot, then?"

I grinned, feeling a little bit of light prick the darkness. "Really?"

"Really." I heard her smile in the word. "So . . . when can I send you this manuscript?"

"Oh, just let me check my calendar."

From there I booked Joss in. "I'll send you the invoice for half when I receive the manuscript and the other half you can pay when you're satisfied with the work I've done."

"Perfect. And listen, we should meet up for coffee soon. I've heard a lot of great things about you."

J. B. Carmichael wanted to meet up with me for coffee? "Uh . . . sure. That would be great."

"Fantastic. I'll call you."

I got off the phone and slumped back in my computer chair.

I got that call because of Logan.

With a sigh I got up and walked into my sitting room, where a pile of Maia's homework books sat on my coffee table, along with one of five fiction books she was juggling at the moment.

I had Maia in my life because of Logan.

". . . I hate that I've hurt you. I do. I am sorry."

The truth was I believed he was sorry.

I sighed and reached for my keys.

Logan MacLeod wasn't fully responsible for breaking my heart. I'd had a hand in it too.

It was strange being in Fire when it was empty. The low-lit club owned by Joss's husband had multiple levels, each decorated differently, and each one played a different genre of music. The main club floor was in the middle, where I knew Logan's office was. When I'd buzzed at the door, the janitor had let me in.

Logan was waiting for me at the edge of the dance floor. He looked surprised but pleased to see me. I glanced over at the janitor and the staff member who was wheeling drinks into the bar. Logan noted my look. "Let's go into my office."

I followed him off the dance floor, up a few steps, and along the back wall to where a door was barely visible from the dance floor. He led me inside. There was a huge desk with a computer on it. The desk was covered in papers. Behind the desk were rows of filing cabinets. It was pretty bland, and there were no windows.

Logan needed someone to decorate his office.

"Is everything okay?" he said, bringing me back into the reality of the situation.

I stopped mentally redecorating and took a deep breath, ignoring the raging butterflies in my belly. "I wanted to apologize for the way I reacted last night."

"Grace, you—"

"No, let me," I insisted. "You've been perfectly clear from the moment we met about who you are. And you were also extremely clear about the fact that Maia comes first. And so she should. I'm glad you're making her a priority. You're right—she deserves it. And I get it. I really do. I get it more than most that you feel guilty every day about missing out on being her dad all these years. I understand why you want to focus all your energy on her, and I'm ashamed by how selfish I was last night. We were both in that room, both making that choice. It's not all on you."

Relief made him sag against his desk. "Thank you. That means a lot."

I nodded.

"I still shouldn't have done what I did."

"As I said, we both made that mistake."

His eyes flashed like he was annoyed by my word choice, but he lowered his eyes to the floor, hiding the reaction.

Silence fell between us, awkward and heavy.

"I better go, then," I said, needing fresh air.

"Friends?" Logan said.

I nodded reluctantly and forced a grin. "Although you might not see as much of me for a while because I just took on a new client. Jocelyn Carmichael called me today. Looks like I'm going to be very busy."

"Congratulations, Grace. You deserve it."

"Thanks."

We looked at each other, not quite knowing how to do this. In the end I gave him a pathetic little wave and turned to leave. I was just pulling the door open when I felt his hand on my shoulder. I stopped and turned to him and was immediately pulled into his arms.

He held me tight, tucking my head against his chest, and I let a moment of weakness overtake me. I sank into his hug, breathing him in.

A lump of tears formed in my throat, and I abruptly slipped out of his embrace and hurried from the office without meeting his eyes.

I took the hot mug of tea from Aidan, feeling exhausted.

My hope was that I was all cried out.

After leaving Logan I'd immediately gone to Aidan, hoping he wasn't in training. I was in luck. He opened his door and I burst into tears.

Once I was inside he'd managed to get the story out of me through my sobbing. He was the first person to whom I admitted that I'd fallen in love with Logan MacLeod.

Now he sat down on the sofa next to me and gave me a reassuring smile. "It hurts now, Grace, but you'll get over it. I promise you that."

I gave him a doubtful look. "It doesn't feel that way now. How can you be so sure?"

He took a deep, shuddering breath, seeming almost nervous. "Because once, a long time ago, I was in love with you."

I almost spilled my cup of tea all over myself.

I stared at him in shock, probably doing a fair impression of a codfish.

"How?" I whispered, and then cleared my throat to be heard. "When? How? What?"

Aidan leaned over to pat my knee in comfort. "Years ago. All through university."

Pain rippled through me when I remembered the drunken night we'd slept together. We were in our third year at university. I'd just been dumped and Aidan had commiserated with me. We'd gotten smashed on cheap wine and ended up having sex. We'd decided to pretend the whole thing hadn't happened.

"Oh God," I breathed, just thinking about how he must have felt. Like I felt right now! "I didn't know," I begged him to believe me. "I didn't . . . I would never have had—I didn't mean to hurt you."

His answer was to haul me into his arms, cuddling me close. "Grace, I know that. I knew it then too. But it all worked out. I met Juno and my feelings for you changed. I love you, but I'm not *in* love with you anymore. And the point is . . . you'll meet someone, too, and you'll get over Logan."

I nodded, getting his point, but I was still reeling from his revelation. "Do Chloe and Juno know how you used to feel about me?"

"Yes."

Juno knew? I would never have guessed. She didn't treat me with jealousy or anger or any feeling that would be completely understandable. I huffed in disbelief. "Juno is a very special woman."

Aidan chuckled. "Don't I know it." He gave me a squeeze. "Someone will come along who loves you back, Grace, the way you love them, and it will change everything. You just have to be open to loving someone new."

I pulled back from him to stare up into his face. "How very wise you are, Dr. Aidan," I teased. "And thanks for dropping that bombshell on top of the destruction Logan caused."

He grinned. "I was trying to help, believe it or not."

I sighed and nodded, feeling a little kernel of something familiar start to bloom inside of me.

Hope.

"I know. And believe it or not, I think you helped." I slumped against the sofa and felt the ache still throbbing in my chest. "But if you don't mind, I'm not done with the whole broken-heart bit yet."

"Finally," I snapped as Chloe picked up her phone. "I have tried calling you all day."

"I know," Chloe huffed down the line. "Jeez. I was at work. Give me a moment, will you?"

"Aidan was in love with me and you didn't tell me."

There was silence.

"Chloe?"

"How did you find out?" she asked incredulously.

"He told me!" It took everything within me not to throw my phone at my kitchen wall. "Why didn't you?"

"Because he asked me not to."

"You should have told me."

"And what would the point have been in that? You didn't feel that way about him."

"No, I didn't, but . . . Chloe, I slept with him years ago."

"I know," she said softly. "I was there to pick up the pieces."

"Oh God." I sank onto a stool. "It's awful of me, but I wish he hadn't told me. I don't think my emotions can handle it today."

"Why did he tell you?"

I sighed, letting the ache fill me up as I started to blubber down the phone to her about Logan.

"Oh, sweetheart." Chloe sighed. "I'm so sorry. And as for Aidan, he was just trying to help. I mean, look at him. Seven years ago he was a mess over you, and now he's mad about Juno."

"True," I sniffled. "It does make me hopeful."

"I get exactly where he was coming from telling you. However, I'm going to come at it from a different point of view, so don't kill me."

"All right," I said in trepidation.

"Back then you had no clue Aidan was in love with you because your low self-esteem and insecurities make you absolutely oblivious when it comes to the opposite sex."

"Thank you for that dismal analysis."

"You're welcome. Anyhoo, what I'm saying is . . . if you didn't know how Aidan really felt about you, who is to say you know how *Logan* feels about you? You're clueless."

"What are you trying to say?"

"I'm saying I wouldn't give up all hope on Logan yet. A man doesn't have sex with you against a kitchen wall because you happen to be the nearest woman in the vicinity. Well . . . not a man who looks like him anyway."

"He has admitted to being attracted to me, but attraction and love are two very different things."

"You're right. But when they come together, they can be explosive . . . say . . . like hot, possessive sex against a kitchen wall."

I dropped my head, banging my forehead against my kitchen counter.

"What are you doing?"

"What are *you* doing?" I groaned. "Aidan was more help with his 'I used to be in love with you' story. I do not need hope where it pertains to Logan MacLeod."

"Ugh. Being in love makes you a grumpy cow."

I glowered even though she couldn't see me. "You owe me for keeping Aidan's feelings a secret. I'll let you know when I think of something for you to do to make it up to me, but right now I'm getting off the phone before I kill you."

"And how, might I ask, would you kill me down a phone line?"

"The power of wishful thinking." I hung up on her and threw my phone on my counter. "I need to get more pessimistic friends," I muttered.

The following Saturday evening I let Maia into my flat. She grinned at me and then turned to smile at her father, who was hovering in my front doorway rather awkwardly.

"Thanks again for doing this," he said, referring to the fact that Maia was staying with me for the night because he had to work at the club for some big deejay event.

"Of course."

We stared at each other—me trying to think of something to say next and him probably trying to think of a polite way to get out of having to say anything else.

"I hope you have a great event."

"Thanks. You too. I mean . . . do you have anything fun planned for tonight?"

"Oh, aye," Maia chimed in. "Grace is taking me to get a tattoo, and then we're going to get high and crash this party she's been talking about all week."

I threw her a look. "You're funny."

She wriggled her eyebrows at me. "I know."

Smothering my grin, I turned back to Logan, who was smirking at his daughter. "Just make sure you go to Cole for the tattoo."

Her eyes widened. "Are you serious? I can get a tattoo?"

He cocked his head, his eyes bright with affection. "Of course . . . when you're fifty and old enough to know better."

Maia scowled. "You have a tattoo."

We all looked at the sword on his arm, and Logan's face darkened. "You can blame Cole for that one too." He glanced up into my inquisitive face and gave me a sharp nod. "See you later." He looked past me to Maia. "Be good."

I shut the door on his retreating back and followed Maia into my sitting room.

"That was weird," she mumbled.

I guessed she was referring to Logan's comment about his tattoo. "Hmm."

"I mean, what's going on between you two? That was beyond awkward out there, and it hasn't escaped my notice that Dad and I don't have dinner here anymore."

Until this moment I had assumed we were getting away with it. Why I assumed that when Maia was intelligent and observant, I don't know. Call it wishful thinking.

"There's nothing going on." I walked into the kitchen, hoping that was the end of the matter.

Idiot.

"I don't believe you."

"That's your prerogative," I said as I picked up the bowls of snacks I'd set out. "Get some of these, please."

Maia followed me into the sitting room, where I was laying out snacks on the coffee table. Although we weren't getting tattoos and doing drugs tonight, we did have plans. Shannon had arranged a girls' night in and had invited Jo, Joss, and a few of their other friends to my place.

"Grace, just tell me one thing."

"Hmm?"

"Are you and Dad okay?"

I looked at her concerned face and paused for thought. I didn't want to lie to her. As a duo we were not okay. Technically, however, I was *going* to be okay and Logan *was* okay. "Yes."

Although she didn't look completely convinced, Maia let it go and helped me put more snacks out.

Half an hour later my doorbell rang, and I blinked as a stream of attractive women of different ages moved past me into the sitting room.

Shannon grinned at me as she stood among the crowd. "So you've met Jo." She gestured to Cole's sister, and we smiled at each other. "And the first person I'm going to introduce you to is Joss."

A woman around my height with long dark blond hair and tip-tilted eyes took a step forward from the group. She had an arresting, pretty face and a chest I was envious of. She also did not look thirty-five. I'd assumed someone had just done a really great job on her author picture, but nope, the mother of three was young and gorgeous in real life too. "It's nice to finally meet you, Grace," Joss said in her husky voice as she held out a hand to shake mine.

"Uh, you too." I shook her hand. "I told you I'm a big fan, right?"

"She has all your books," Maia piped in. "Maybe you could sign them."

"I can do that." Joss grinned wryly and stepped back.

"I love it." A leggy, curvy brunette grinned. Another American, by the sound of her accent. "You're such a rock star to book geeks." She flushed, her unusual eyes growing round as she stepped toward me. "I didn't mean to be insulting." She shook my hand enthusiastically. "I'm Olivia. You can call me Liv. Fellow book geek. I work at the University of Edinburgh Library."

I was momentarily hypnotized by her. On first glance her face seemed almost plain, but then she smiled and it transformed her. Plus, she had the most stunning hazel eyes. They were so light they were almost gold. That, combined with all her curves and the riot of dark hair tumbling around her shoulders, and *I* was beginning to feel plain. "It's lovely to meet you."

"I'm Ellie, Joss's sister-in-law." As I shook Ellie's hand I found myself looking up. She was just as tall as Jo, and just as pretty as the other women, but in a far more subtle, girl-next-door kind of way.

"And I'm Hannah, Ellie's sister." Despite the difference in eye color, I could see the similarities between them in their features. However, whereas Ellie could have been a fashion model with her tall, slender figure, Hannah was just slightly taller and had a lot more in the way of curves. She had the kind of figure women all over the world would die for.

"I've heard lots about you from Maia," I said. "It's lovely to meet you." I gestured to the snacks. "Please help yourself. Can I get anyone a drink?"

After taking their orders, I went to the kitchen, where Maia and Shannon helped me put together the drinks. We found the women seated in the living room, laughing over something.

"What's funny?" Shannon said as we settled in among them.

"I just got a text from Nate," Liv said. "My husband," she explained to me. "We left the men with the kids approximately half an hour ago and I'm already getting texts. It would seem that Belle and January are fighting over Sophia."

"Tell Nate to tell the girls that Sophia is not a doll," Hannah said.

"That's exactly what I'm texting to Nate. You'd think between him, Braden, Marco, Cole, and Cam, one of them would be able to deal with an argument between two girls."

Jo snorted. "Especially Nate."

Liv threw her a dirty look. "Not funny."

"What am I missing?" I said.

"Nate was a manwhore," Hannah supplied helpfully. "Before Liv, of course."

"I'd rather hope so," I said, making Joss snort.

"Should we be saying the word 'whore' in front of Maia?" Ellie asked, her brows puckered in concern.

"Well, you've done it twice now, so I reckon the question is redundant." Maia shrugged.

Shannon grinned at us all. "Did I mention I love my niece?"

We laughed, and I felt something warm bubble up inside me as I saw Maia's eyes brighten. This was the person she was always meant to be. Being with Logan was changing her, giving her confidence to be herself.

Which was proving to be a smart-arse, sarcastic, hilarious, sweet kid who had a habit of making everyone around her fall in love with her.

I watched as Maia settled in with us, not caring she was a fifteen-year-old among women whose ages ranged from twenty-six to thirty-six. She was comfortable and happy listening to the ladies joke about their jobs and their husbands and kids, and I understood why. These women were more than friends. They were all a family. And their warmth drew people like Maia and me in. We were helpless before it. The very definition of a moth to the flame.

We'd gotten onto the subject of movies when Jo said, "I don't think I've been to the movies in about two years. That's ridiculous."

"That is," Liv agreed. "Nate and I have a date night every two weeks, and we go see a movie once a month. We just went to see that new one with that hot real-life ex-marine. Bad movie but yum to the male eye candy. Nate had to wipe the drool off my chin."

Joss wrinkled her nose. "Oh, I rarely get to see movies like that. Braden refuses to watch movies where the men think they're prettier than the women."

"No. Braden doesn't watch those movies with you because he takes possessiveness to a whole other level," Ellie teased.

Joss rolled her eyes. "Look, if your brother is happy pretending that I find no man but him attractive, we're going to leave him to his denial. Although the truth is, no one does it for me like Braden does it for me." She raised a finger and pointed at us. "That does not leave this room. I like to keep him on his toes. Ego in check."

"Like they don't find other women attractive," Hannah huffed. "I swear I've heard Marco growl—yes, growl—under his breath if I so much as share a smile with a good-looking guy, and yet I'm supposed to believe he watches reruns of *Dark Angel* for the plot? I don't think so."

"Hey, *Dark Angel* is one of the most underappreciated TV series of all time," Liv argued.

"For a reason," Hannah argued back.

"They're all the same," Jo interjected. "Cam has this new colleague. I happened to mention he was good-looking, and he suddenly felt the need to"—she glanced at Maia and then back at us, giving us a knowing look—"*prove* himself."

"You mean have sex," Maia said.

Jo curled her lip. "Well, there's no getting anything past you, is there?"

"Believe me, I've seen and heard a lot worse."

The humor in the air dissipated, and an awkward silence fell over us all. Maia's cheeks were reddening, and I was just about to open my mouth to change the subject for her when Jo beat me to it. "Actually, I mentioned this guy was good-looking because I was thinking of you, Grace. You're single, right? He's single too. I was just saying to Cam how it might be fun to set you up on a date. I've never played matchmaker before."

"Ooh." Ellie nodded, eyes glittering. "Do it. And then you can update us on every date. It'll be fun."

"Have you forgotten what it's like to date?" Joss said wryly. "And you want her to share that excruciating time with all of us?"

Ellie made a face at her. "It was just a thought. And anyway . . . you've only ever dated one man."

"And he was enough, believe me." Joss turned to me. "You can tell Jo to stick the cute single guy up her ass. I'll back you up."

"That didn't sound right at all." Liv was choking on laughter.

"Get your mind out of the gutter." Shannon gestured with a nod of her head to Maia. "Impressionable minds are present."

But Maia wasn't paying much attention. Instead she was staring stonily into her empty glass for some reason.

I frowned, wondering what had been said to upset her.

"Uh, thanks for the thought, Jo, but I've been on six incredibly bad dates in the past few months, and I'm feeling a little gun-shy. Maybe some other time."

"Aka never." Hannah grinned. "Poor Jo. That career in matchmaking didn't last long."

"You're all shits," Jo said in response to their teasing, but her voice was filled with laughter. "Now, where is the loo, Grace?"

I showed her the way and then wandered into the kitchen to get more drinks. I wasn't in there but two seconds before Shannon sauntered in. She sidled over to me and smiled. "They're great, aren't they?"

I nodded, understanding she was talking about the women. "They're wonderful. They love one another a lot, don't they?"

"Fiercely," Shannon agreed. "You know, I thought finding Cole made me the luckiest woman alive until I met his extended family and realized it was more than that. He's a freaking miracle. They all are." She glanced out the door. "They're how family should be. They're a tribe."

I thought of Logan and how in all of our conversations he hadn't discussed his parents or his other sister much. I already knew they hadn't supported Shannon when she needed them, so I guessed their family wasn't a close one. "You and Logan are close. But just with each other?"

Shannon looked back at me. "My parents and my sister, Amanda, are kind of selfish. Logan was the favorite, and he hated the way I was treated differently. He tried to make up for it as we grew up. He's always been there for me. When he found out how they'd treated me while he was in prison he wasn't happy, but he wanted us all to be a family. I've been trying . . . So has he . . . But then they reacted the way they did to Maia, and he's had enough."

I frowned, feeling my heart rate pick up. "How did they react?"

"Logan didn't tell you he told them about Maia a few days ago?" Shannon seemed surprised.

I shook my head.

"He wanted to wait until she was settled. He's been putting off my parents for weeks." She sneered. "Now they've done what they always do and are acting like judgmental shits because Logan has disappointed them."

I felt anger start to burn in my blood. "Does Maia know?"

Shannon shook her head. "No, and as far as Logan's concerned, she doesn't have to know. She hasn't asked about them in a while. Hopefully, she still won't, and that will give him time to cool his own anger. He wants to explain it in the least hurtful way possible. She needs to know that it's not about her. Our parents are just like this."

I looked down at the counter and saw my fingertips were digging into the wood. I felt awful that Logan had had to deal with that and I hadn't been there to help him. "I should have known," I muttered.

"Hard to do when you're avoiding him."

Glancing up sharply at her, Shannon stared back at me with a knowing look in her eye.

"Logan told me what happened between you."

I raised an eyebrow in surprise. "He did?"

"Not in detail, of course, because"—she shuddered—"he's my brother. But he told me. Mostly because I wouldn't let up until he did. He's been acting like a grumpy bastard with everyone but Maia this last wee while. I finally badgered him until he told me what was up. Turns out it's you." She grinned. "Like I didn't already know it had to do with you."

"What do you mean?" I said warily.

Shannon leaned in to me, expression guileless. "Before you . . . Logan didn't smile a lot or laugh in that big hearty way he used to laugh." Her eyes were bright with tears now. "Prison changed my brother, Grace. You should have known him before it. He was . . . He was this big lovable joker, everyone's friend. Everyone wanted to be his friend. He just had this . . . this *light* around him, you know?" She dashed at her tears with the backs of her fingers. "He's not like that anymore. He doesn't trust easily. His smiles don't come easily. His laughter definitely doesn't . . . or it didn't . . . or it doesn't . . ." She shook her head as if in confusion. "He started to smile and joke around more when you and Maia came into his life." Shannon placed her hand on mine and squeezed it. "He hasn't smiled much lately."

I couldn't breathe at what she was suggesting. I didn't want her to think something that wasn't true. "Shannon—"

"I really like you, Grace. And I very much like the idea of you and my brother together. Just so you know." Her hand tightened on me. "Please be patient with him. He's been through a lot."

I felt for her. I really did. And that's why I had to disabuse her of these notions before she got her hopes up regarding Logan and me. "Shannon, I'm not Logan's type."

"I don't believe that." She shook her head stubbornly.

"He's also focusing on Maia right now."

"I think he's hiding behind that."

Dear God, she was beyond stubborn. She was a mule. "Logan and I . . . We won't work. We're too different. Honestly, I think right now we're better off staying away from each other."

A noise drew my attention to the doorway, and I saw a flash of a body and dark hair before it disappeared. I frowned.

Maia?

"Do you think she overheard?" Shannon said, sounding concerned.

"Dammit." I heaved a sigh. "I better talk to her so she knows it isn't about her."

As I shut the door on the last of my new friends, I leaned against it and wondered how best to approach Maia. After she'd overheard what I'd said about my friendship with Logan she'd been quiet and mostly unresponsive. The girls knew something was up, and not too long after made their excuses to leave.

Bracing myself, I went to find Maia.

She was in the guest bedroom, apparently having decided to abandon me and the mess in my sitting room. "There you are," I said, leaning against the doorway.

She was sitting on the bed with a book in her lap.

"Maia, we need to talk about what you overheard."

"About the fact that you hate Dad?" she snapped.

I felt a sharp pang in my chest just at the thought of anyone ever thinking I hated Logan. "I do not hate your father."

"Then what's going on?"

"It's complicated, Maia. And it's between your father and me. We've decided to spend some time apart, but that doesn't mean my friendship with you has to change. You understand that, right? I'm not going anywhere."

Although she looked no less upset, Maia gave me a reluctant nod.

I would have slumped with relief against the doorframe if I'd thought for one second that was the end of it. And I knew when she stiffly told me she'd like to read her book that she wasn't quite finished being pissed off at me.

I left her to it, hoping her bad mood with me wouldn't last too long.

CHAPTER 15

"Get back here!"

My head jerked up from my laptop and I stared at my sitting room wall. Logan was shouting. Loudly enough for me to hear every word.

I'd just put my feet into my slippers and had grabbed a cardigan, intent on investigating, when my front door slammed open and shut. Feet stomped down my hallway and came to a stop before me.

"Maia, what on earth . . . ?" I stared, aghast at the sight of her tear-stained face.

"I'm staying here. I *hate* him!"

I sucked in my breath. "Don't ever say th—"

I was cut off abruptly by the sound of my door slamming open and shut. Again.

Logan's stomping feet were louder. Maia scurried farther into the sitting room at the sound of his arrival. He came into the room, eyes dark with anger. "Don't you dare walk out of the house like that, and definitely don't ever bring Grace into this."

"Logan . . ." I was shocked by his attitude. "What the hell happened?"

"Maia was caught with a boy in an empty media room at school." His whole body bristled with tension.

My eyes bugged out as I turned to Maia. "Please tell me there's been a misunderstanding."

"We were only kissing," Maia said belligerently as she swiped at her tears.

"The headmaster said it was a little more than kissing!"

"Logan, perhaps you—"

"It's none of your business!" Maia yelled at him. "Stop pretending to care!"

"Maia!" I shouted.

She flinched, her eyes round with shock at my outburst.

I'd never used that tone with her before. But she'd never stepped over the line before. "Do not ever disrespect your father again by saying such nonsense. Apologize."

The look she gave me was strangely assessing. She sniffled and said, "Are you saying you're on his side?"

"Maia, fooling around with some boy in a classroom at school is wrong, and you know it. You're a smart girl. Why on earth would you act like this? Is there something more going on here?" I took a step toward her.

She shrugged, looking unsure of herself now. "Layla dared me to do it."

I glanced over at Logan, and I knew exactly what he was thinking before he said it. My expression told him I agreed with him. "Maybe we should curb how much time you spend with Layla."

"Dad," Maia whined, looking startled by his suggestion.

"Ah, so I'm 'Dad' again. Ten minutes ago I was to 'stop acting like your father since I'd been absent for most of your life.'"

Although he didn't show it, I knew how much her words must have hurt him and I couldn't cover the disappointment on my face as I turned to her.

She winced and lowered her gaze. "I didn't mean it." She looked up at Logan, eyes pleading. "I'm sorry. It was just . . . It's embarrassing! Why did the head teacher have to tell *you*? But I'm sorry, okay? I didn't mean it."

Maia suddenly looked terrified, as if frightened Logan would turn away from her.

Instead his features softened. "Come here."

Slowly she made her feet take her to him, and as soon as she was within reaching distance, Logan pulled her into his arms and kissed her forehead.

Maia relaxed into him and hugged him back.

As touched as I was by his understanding, I wasn't distracted from the main issue at hand. "We need to talk about who this boy is and how you are never, ever going to do this again."

Pulling away slightly from Logan, Maia blushed. "Do we have to?"

I looked at Logan. "How would you feel if Maia and I discussed this alone?"

He actually looked relieved. "Fair enough . . . but"—he tugged gently on her arm, drawing her attention back to him—"whatever the discussion may involve, the outcome will be this: You won't do this again, or, when the time comes that you're old enough to date, I will scare the absolute shit out of every boy that even so much as smiles at you. Understood?"

Maia stared wide-eyed at him and nodded quickly.

"Good." He nodded, satisfied, and then walked out, leaving me to it.

"I won't do it again," she said hurriedly. "Promise."

"You have to understand that when you act like that with boys—"

"Grace, not to be a bitch or anything, but I know, all right? I've seen a girl a year younger than me having sex with an older guy in my stairwell back in Glasgow. And I've seen other stuff too. And the guys don't respect the girls. I know all that. It was just a dare. And no matter what the headmaster said . . . it was just kissing. I'm not . . ." She blushed. "I'm not ready for anything else."

Relief made me sag against my sofa. "You have no idea how happy I am that you said that."

She chewed on her lip a moment and then said, "How old were you when you lost your virginity?"

"I still have it," I lied. "And if you're sensible, you'll hold on to yours for a long, long time."

Maia rolled her eyes. "Aye, and Santa is real."

"He is. So is the Easter Bunny. And babies are dropped off at the doors of mums and daddies everywhere by giant storks. Now nod like you believe me."

She giggled and nodded.

"And my work here is done."

"I can't believe you thought these would help make me feel better." I raised the DVDs at Chloe as she sauntered back into my sitting room with two glasses of wine.

"What?" She frowned at my tone. "You've been moping around with a broken heart for quite long enough. I thought these would help you get over it."

"I've had a broken heart for approximately two weeks, but thank you for your patience." I dumped the DVDs on the coffee table. "How are *The Notebook*, *Sleepless in Seattle*, and *Love and Other Drugs* supposed to help me? They're all about two people falling in love. With each other. La-di-da. I hate them already."

"They're supposed to act as a reminder of hope." She smirked at my grimace. "These films aren't just about two people falling in love. They're about two people who fall in love but there are all these obstacles in their way and it's a struggle . . . but in the end they do end up together."

I took a massive gulp of my wine. "I really wish you'd give up on the idea of me and Logan, Chloe."

"Nope."

"I'd really consider it, if I were you."

"Why?"

"Because I'm going to kill you if you don't."

"Pfft." She waved my threat off. "You don't scare me, Grace. I could snap you like a twig."

I stared at her in indignation. "I'd like to see you try."

"Move the coffee table and I will."

"Fair enough." I got up off the chair and the doorbell rang. I narrowed my eyes on her. "You were just saved by the bell."

"I'm shaking in my boots."

I threw her a grin before hurrying out of the room to answer my door. To my surprise I found Logan outside.

"Have you seen Maia?" he said without preamble.

Taking in the frantic expression on his face, I felt my heart rate start to pick up speed. "No. I thought she was going to Layla's after school today? Have you called her?"

He shook his head. "She's not picking up."

"Well, let me try." I turned on my heel and heard him follow behind me into the sitting room.

"Chloe, this is Logan. Logan, this is Chloe." I introduced them quickly before rifling through my bag for my phone.

"Is everything all right?" Chloe said.

"Hopefully." I rang Maia's number and waited. It went straight to voice mail. I looked over at Logan, who deflated at my expression. "Do you have Layla's parents' number?"

He shook his head. "I didn't think to do that. Fuck." He ran a hand through his hair, and I could see the panic in him mounting.

"Chloe"—I turned to my friend, who was watching Logan with a mixture of concern and curiosity—"open up your Facebook."

"Why?"

"Because you have Maia on your Facebook. Maybe she posted something."

"Well, if she's up to no good, do you really think she would be that stupid?" she said as she looked through her bag for her phone.

"Yes. Even intelligent teenagers can be idiots sometimes."

Chloe nodded and started flicking through her phone as Logan and I looked on impatiently. Her eyes grew round as she read something and then she gave us an "uh-oh" look.

"What?" Logan said gruffly.

"They're trying to get into some club in Tollcross."

"It's Thursday," I said dumbly, disbelieving that Maia would act this irresponsibly.

"It's student night," Logan said. "How the fuck does she think she's going to get into a nightclub? I'm going to kill her." He started toward the door.

"I'm coming with you!" I turned back to Chloe as I grabbed my keys. "I'm sorry. We need to cut this short."

My very understanding friend quickly gathered her things, and I said good-bye to her outside my building and left to catch up with Logan. I found him marching past the university toward the Meadows. "Logan . . ." I tried to match stride with him.

"Why is she acting like this?" He glared at me. "She's not like this in the house. We're great. We don't argue. We're fine. But then she's out of the house and she's kissing boys in media rooms and trying to get into nightclubs, not picking up her phone, making me worry. I got another phone call from school," he told me. "Yesterday. She missed two morning classes."

Dread moved through me. "Clearly this is deliberate. It's not like her. She enjoys school. And she's happy with you, Logan. I know she is."

"Then why?"

I shrugged. "Maybe it's about her mother . . . or . . . We don't know everything she's been through. We don't know what's she dealing with. Perhaps she should see a school counselor."

"I don't want to force her to do something she doesn't want to do. Well . . . except drag her out of this bloody nightclub."

"Maybe we can try to be calm when we find her?" I suggested gently.

"Calm? Grace, it's nine o'clock on a Thursday night. I've been trying to call her for the last two hours and was just seconds from calling the police when I knocked on your door."

"When was she supposed to be home?"

"She said she was having dinner at Layla's so she'd be home around seven thirty."

"It took you more than an hour to come to me?"

Logan glanced at me. "Things have been strained between us. I didn't want to bother you."

"It's Maia. You're never bothering me when it comes to Maia."

"Right." The word was laced heavily in sarcasm.

We fell into an awkward silence, compounded only by the silence of the almost-empty park around us.

"Are you okay?" he said, no longer sarcastic but concerned. "Maia mentioned she was going to Layla's instead of yours after school because you had a doctor's appointment."

I blanched. "Oh . . . yes. I'm fine."

"That was the least-fine-sounding fine ever. What's going on?"

"Nothing."

"Grace—"

"Logan—"

"I will keep asking until we find Maia, and after I've dealt with her, I'll make you talk," he warned, sounding completely serious.

I looked up into his eyes and saw the steely determination in them. *Oh shit.*

"Fine . . . It wasn't a doctor's appointment. I had an appointment this afternoon at the health clinic."

"For?" He sounded impatient now.

"A sexual health check." I stared ahead, not wanting to see his reaction.

After a moment's silence he said, "Because we had sex without protection?"

I heard something in his voice I had never heard before. Something a lot like hurt. I couldn't help but look at him, and I found him staring at me in angry incredulity. "Logan, you've slept with a lot of women."

"I use protection."

"You didn't with me."

"Only you though!" He clenched his hands into fists at his sides and picked up speed.

I hurried to stay with him, my heart beating frantically. "I don't know what to say. I didn't intend to hurt your feelings."

"Hurt my feelings?" he sneered. "You didn't hurt my feelings, Grace. But at least I know exactly what you think of me."

"I don't think badly of you. I just think you've slept with a lot of women and I was being safe. You can't blame me for that!"

He stopped suddenly, and I stumbled to a halt to face him. His breathing had increased exponentially. "You must think I'm an irresponsible fuckup. Do you honestly believe I don't get health checked? Of course I fucking do. I had a health check six weeks ago. I'm clean. I would have told you otherwise."

"You were with the American after that," I said, my voice quiet with pain at the idea of him being with her. "Only days before me."

Logan caught the pain because his features instantly softened, remorse lighting his eyes. "Grace . . ." He raised a hand as if to reach for me, but I turned away and started walking toward Tollcross.

"Let's just forget it, all right? We have Maia to worry about."

We didn't speak the rest of the way to the club, the tension mounting between us.

When we turned down the wide alley where the entrance to the club was, we took in the line of young people outside, searching for Maia.

"There," I huffed out in relief, hurrying along the line to where she was standing close to the front. My eyes almost bugged out of my head as she turned to smile at Layla and I saw what she was wearing.

She did not own that dress.

It was short, it was tight, and it was no, no, no, NO!

"What the hell are you wearing?" Logan snapped, shooting past me. Obviously, he agreed with my assessment of the dress.

Maia's cheeks flushed at the sight of us, but she didn't look nearly as guilty as she should.

Logan wrapped his hand around her arm and tugged her out of line. She came willingly enough but whined, "Dad, you're embarrassing me."

This stopped him, and he turned back around to glower at the girls who had been standing with Maia. One was a tall, very pretty brunette; the other a small, curvy, cute brunette. I presumed these were the infamous Layla and Leigh. "You two, come here!" Logan pointed his finger at them and then at the ground by his feet.

The tall brunette, whom I knew was Layla from Maia's description, sauntered toward us with Leigh trailing at her back. She was wearing a dress similar to Maia's, so I could guess from whom Maia had borrowed the dress. "My, is this your dad?" She grinned, raking her gaze over Logan in what was a clearly inappropriate and lascivious way.

Logan's face darkened, his anger heightening.

I sought to intervene. "Layla, Leigh . . . Let's get you home."

Layla cut me a dirty look. "Are you Grace?"

"I am. And I take it that it was your idea to bring Maia to a club?"

She shrugged. "So what if it was?" She stared at Logan again. "It was worth it to see him."

"Stop it," I said quietly, my voice filled with derision. It made her blush in a way no yelling or snapping would do. "You are fifteen years old, not thirty. You're being irresponsible and ridiculous."

"Grace." Maia sounded mortified, but I couldn't care less. I did not like Layla's influence on her.

"I'm not sure you're a good influence on Maia."

"You're not her mum," Layla huffed. "You're just a nosy, skinny English bitch."

"That's it." Logan stalked past us, and we watched as he spoke to the doorman at the club. The doorman nodded, and Logan pulled out his phone. He returned to us a few seconds later. "There is a cab on the way for you two," Logan said to Layla and Leigh. "And that huge bloke behind me is going to make sure it takes you home. You"—he pointed at Layla, and she blanched at the anger in his eyes—"stay away from my daughter from now on."

He walked around me and grabbed Maia's arm. "We're going home."

"Dad—"

"Don't push me, Maia."

Thankfully, she didn't.

Logan was seething as he marched her home through the Meadows, and I hurried to keep up. "Is this the person you want to be?" he suddenly asked her, his voice filled with disbelief. "Irresponsible? Childish? Immature? How could you do this tonight, Maia? I've been worried sick."

"I knew you wouldn't let me go if I asked," she said quietly.

"You're damn right. You're fifteen. That club is for eighteen and overs. Not to mention it's a bloody dive."

"I just wanted to spend time with my friends."

"Oh, and some friends they are." He snorted in disgust. "Did you hear how she spoke to Grace? After everything Grace has done for us, you're okay with one of your friends speaking to her like that? Disrespecting her?"

Maia pulled her arm out of his hand, her face suddenly red with her anger. "And what does Grace care? She's not our friend anymore!"

I felt like I'd been punched in the gut. "What the heck does that mean?"

Eyes bright with tears, she stopped, and we halted. "I just want things to go back to how they were. When it was the three of us."

Logan looked dumbfounded. "Is that why you've been acting like this?"

She shrugged. "It's the only way to get you two to spend time in the same room together. Before . . . well, it was like we were a family."

"I don't understand." Logan scratched his beard, appearing confused. "Are you and I not a family?"

Maia's lips trembled, and I could tell she was very close to crying. "Aye, of course."

"Good." Logan started walking again. "As head of this family, I'm grounding you for two weeks."

"But, Dad . . ." Maia hurried to catch up with him.

"No 'But, Dad' anything. You ever pull anything like this again and it will be a whole month."

I followed slowly after them, listening to Maia try to talk Logan into lessening her sentence. My heart was beating fast again as I started to put the pieces of the puzzle together. Logan had missed it, but I hadn't.

Maia wasn't pissed off that Logan flirted with other women because she wanted all of his attention. I thought of her annoyance when I announced I was going out on a date. Of how upset she got when she overheard me talking to Shannon in the kitchen about Logan.

Maia MacLeod didn't like Logan flirting with other women because she'd already chosen the woman she wanted in his life.

Me.

Maia was playing matchmaker.

Bloody hell.

CHAPTER 16

The day after Maia's irresponsible venture to the nightclub—which I now realized was a deliberate act to get Logan and me in the same place because she wanted us to be a couple, and I still didn't know how to talk to Logan about it—I was in my sitting room with my laptop doing one last read-through of a manuscript before I returned it to the author. In a moment of procrastination I flicked to my home page and a news article jumped out at me.

DANIELLE BENTLEY'S CANCER FIGHT?

My heart leapt into my throat as I clicked on the headline.

There was a picture of Gabriel and Danielle Bentley up in the corner of the article. They were both dressed in evening clothes, suggesting they'd been at some well-to-do event. Gabriel, as always, wore a solemn expression on his handsome, rugged face. There was more gray in the hair combed precisely back from his temple than I remembered and a few more lines at the corners of his eyes and around his mouth. As always, he was dressed immaculately in a tailored tux from some expensive designer.

All the old feelings of neglect, rejection, and anger flooded me as I stared at the picture of my mother and father. And just as suddenly as I was hit with the overwhelming crush of them, I was hit with the massive feeling of failure.

I'd truly thought they didn't have that power over me anymore. Or at least not so much.

But there they were on my screen, and I felt like the little girl they'd abandoned all over again.

My eyes scanned the tabloid article.

Inside sources have revealed that the wife of world-renowned London-based media tycoon and business entrepreneur Gabriel Bentley has been diagnosed with breast cancer. A spokesperson for the family has neither confirmed nor denied the rumor.

I knew what that meant. It meant my mother was sick and she didn't want anyone to know she was infallible.

The same inside sources also revealed that estranged daughter, Gracelyn Bentley, has still not returned to the homestead to be by her mother's side. Rumors surrounding Gracelyn Bentley's split from the family have circulated for years, but as yet the truth behind her departure remains within the family fold.

In a state of shock I somehow got myself to the bathroom. I felt the bile rise up in my throat and flipped the lid on the toilet seat. I coughed it up, but no vomit followed it despite the roiling in my stomach.

A cold sweat broke out over my skin, and I flopped back against the bathroom wall, pulling my knees up to my chin. I couldn't stop trembling.

I wished I could stop trembling.

Stop trembling!

My mother had cancer. Possibly dying?

And now the press were finally interested to know where the Bentleys' only daughter, Gracelyn Bentley, had disappeared to. I knew there had been rumors at first—family staff who couldn't keep their mouths shut, most likely—but after a while the press weren't really that interested. There were children of British rock stars up to far more scandalous and nefarious things, whereas Gracelyn Bentley was the quiet, studious girl with doe eyes who didn't do anything of significance to capture their attention.

That's how Gracelyn had been described once in the press.

But I wasn't Gracelyn Bentley anymore. I'd legally changed my name to Grace Farquhar. Though I imagined if the press were really interested, it would be easy enough to find me.

I shivered at the thought.

They wouldn't find the girl with the doe eyes anymore.

I'd worked hard to become my own person and not a shadow of the girl lost in the manipulations, cruelty, and neglect of her family.

If the press went searching for Gracelyn . . . they went searching for a ghost.

Or was she?

I squeezed my eyes shut and tears leaked out under the light pressure. Just like that the sob rose up from deep in my gut and I couldn't control it. I couldn't stop it.

My mother most probably had cancer and my father hadn't reached out to tell me. And he knew where I was; he knew my surname. Farquhar after my grandmother on my father's side. She'd died when I was eight, but some of my happiest childhood memories were when I was with her. She represented real family to me. She represented everything I wanted and hoped to someday have for myself.

My mother had cancer and I couldn't go to her because they hadn't asked me to.

They didn't want me to.

And the horrible, awful truth was . . . I didn't know if *I* wanted to go to her.

All the ugly things she'd ever said came flooding over me . . .

"That's right. Keep eating that piece of cake if you want to get fatter than you already are."

"An A in history? And why would I care if you're able to memorize facts about a bunch of people that are dead?"

"Don't tell me you lost your virginity. He must have been desperate."

"If you don't stop telling tales about Sebastian, I will send you to boarding school. As if any of his friends are hard up enough they'd need to force themselves on you."

And the last, the most horrifically cliché . . .

"I was doing you a favor, Gracelyn. You reached too high. You can't seriously believe that you can have what I can have. You need to lower your expectations."

Swiping the tears from my eyes, I slowly got up from the bathroom floor. I couldn't let them do this to me all over again. Reaching for my phone, I started to dial Aidan's number and stopped.

He wasn't the one I wanted to pour my heart out to.

His arms weren't the ones I wanted wrapped around me.

And for that I started to cry again, because the one person I wanted was only a few feet away . . . and I couldn't go to him.

Looking around at a bunch of people I didn't know, I wondered if I'd made the right choice coming to this party at the Carmichaels'. Joss had invited me when we'd had our girls' night in, and at the time I thought it would be rather exciting to attend. The party was for Ellie's stepdad, Clark Nichols, celebrating his sixty-fifth birthday. I had discovered that although Braden wasn't related to Ellie's mother, Elodie, and Elodie's husband, Clark, the two were as close to parents for him as any could be, and thus the reason he was hosting the event.

Somehow I'd managed to put myself together for the party at the Carmichaels' huge, stylish town house on Dublin Street after the news I'd been dealt that afternoon, and the truth was so far the party had been a distraction. But now that I'd been introduced to all the people Joss loved, the news kept creeping into my head like a curtain blowing in the wind and allowing bright light to peek into the room every now and then when all I needed was the dark.

I'd been introduced to Elodie and Clark, a lovely, warm older couple whose teasing, bickering banter made me laugh. I'd also met their son and

Hannah's younger brother, Declan, and his shy wife, Penny. Moreover, I'd been overwhelmed by my introduction to the husbands of my new friends. The only one not present was Cole, because he had the flu, and he and Shannon were staying at home. Cam, whom I'd already met and blushed over, was there with Jo. It was from there that things got . . . well, yes, *overwhelming*. I met Liv's husband, Nate.

I really hoped my face wasn't on fire when I met him.

Like Cam, he was almost forty and didn't look it. Unlike Cam, with his rough-around-the-edges attractiveness, Nate was pure Hollywood gorgeous with his thick dark hair, smoldering dark eyes, and sexy dimples.

Then there was Marco, Hannah's husband. Tall didn't cover it. Muscular didn't quite cover it. Strikingly handsome didn't cover it. I knew from Hannah that Marco was half Italian American, half African American, and all I could say was that the results struck me dumb with reticence as I shook his hand.

The only husband I wasn't quite so shy with was Ellie's husband, Adam. He was the kind of man who grew more good-looking as you talked to him because he oozed a warm charisma that was incredibly appealing. He put me at ease immediately.

Until I met his best friend—my landlord, Logan's boss, and Joss's husband.

Braden Carmichael.

"I've heard lots of good things about you, Grace," Braden said as I shook his hand. He stared down at me with just the slightest kick of a smile on his lips, and as I stared up into his pale blue eyes I shivered. Braden was in his early forties and he wore it well. I'd always found it annoying that so many men grew better-looking with age, and I had a feeling Mr. Carmichael was one of them. His dark hair was peppered with gray that only made him look distinguished. Unlike Nate, Braden didn't have perfect features, and yet somehow what he did have made for an extremely compelling face.

More than that, there was an aura around him—confidence, power, and a sheer force of will that poured out of him. Of all the gorgeous men I'd been introduced to that evening, in my opinion, Joss's husband was the most appealing.

He was also one of the most intimidating men I'd ever met, and I lived next door to Logan MacLeod. I was glad Logan wasn't at the party because he was with Maia. I didn't think the room could take having him and Braden in one place together.

No wonder they were friends. They shared a likeness that became more apparent as Joss and Braden talked with me.

"I heard Maia's doing well and that you're a big part of her transition," Braden said as Joss tucked herself into his side. He wrapped his arm around her automatically, as if she naturally fit there.

"Logan's made Maia's transition smooth. I'm just . . ." I shrugged. "There for her."

"She's being modest," Joss said. "Anytime I've hung out with Maia and Shannon, all Maia talks about is you and Logan." Something glittered in her eyes, something like amusement, and I wondered for a moment if she'd picked up on Maia's desire to see me and Logan as a couple.

"Well, all I know is that it is a special kind of person to take a kid under their wing that isn't theirs." His gaze drifted across the room, and I glanced over to see whom he was staring at.

Elodie.

Joss lifted Braden's hand to press a light kiss on his knuckles. He looked down at her and pulled her tighter to his side before focusing those pale eyes on me again. "Logan is a good friend. Maia was a massive shock for him and I'm grateful for what you've done for them. If you ever need anything, Grace, you let me know."

I felt like I'd just been officially welcomed into their fold by the Godfather. I blushed and mumbled my thanks.

"I know what you could do." A face appeared beside me, and I slanted a look to the side to see Ellie had come up behind me and popped her head into the conversation.

I grinned at the mischievous look in her pale blue eyes. Huh. She and Braden had the exact same eyes.

"And what's that?" Braden's face had softened with affection as he waited for his sister's answer.

Ellie slid her arm along my shoulders. "Did you know that this beautiful lady is single?"

Joss snorted at the mortified look on my face.

"Point being, Ellie, other than to embarrass Grace?" Braden said dryly.

"James Llewellyn-Jones," Ellie whispered.

Braden frowned. "My lawyer?"

She nodded. "He's gorgeous, he's successful, he's single, and he's here. Perhaps an introduction would be in order."

My heart started to beat hard with embarrassment. "Oh no, really, you don't have to do that."

Joss was scowling at Ellie now. "Really. You *don't*," she said pointedly, widening her eyes at Ellie, as if trying to send her a message. I just didn't know what that message was. Apparently, neither did Ellie, who appeared adorably confused by Joss's eye gesturing.

"What's going on over here?" Jo sidled up to us, grinning.

"I thought Braden could introduce Grace to James. The lawyer." Ellie grinned back.

Jo immediately glowered. "Or *not*," she said pointedly.

"What the hell am I missing?" Braden asked them.

"Nothing," Joss assured him. "Your sister just has *stupid* ideas."

"We knew that when she decided to marry Adam," he said.

"I heard that." Adam stepped up to the group. "And my rebuttal is your wife is the one with stupid ideas. She allowed you to breed. *Three* times."

"Hey, our kids have got more of me in them, so there's no worries on that account," Joss said.

"Bull. Beth, yes, Luke, no. That kid is Braden's spit and we all know it. The world is fucking doomed. You better keep your eye on wee Ellie," Adam said with a teasing gravity.

"Oh, don't worry. I'm grooming her to be just like me." Ellie smiled at her husband.

Braden looked at Adam. "You're right. The world is doomed."

For whatever her reasons, Joss slipped me out of Ellie's matchmaking clutches and guided me across the room in the opposite direction of James Llewellyn-Jones to refill my champagne.

Twenty minutes passed during which I was introduced to a bunch of people whose names I would never remember since my memory bank had been filled up on the names of the Carmichael & Co. Clan that evening. Ellie didn't badger me about the lawyer she wanted me to meet, so I assumed she'd been talked down by either Jo or Joss, who both seemed strangely opinionated on the matter.

It was just a coincidence then that when I reached for the last vol-au-vent someone else did too.

"Oh, I'm sorry," a masculine voice said, and I followed the hand that had been reaching for my pastry up to a pair of lovely gray eyes. They belonged to a good-looking man around my age. "I insist you have it," he said, giving me a teasing smile.

I really wanted that vol-au-vent. "Then I insist I do too."

He laughed, watching me as I took the snack and started to nibble at it.

"I'm James." He continued to smile at me.

I swallowed the tasty little morsel, blinking rapidly. "Not Llewellyn-Jones?"

He raised an eyebrow. "I'm famous?"

I smiled weakly, searching the room for Ellie, who had obviously put him up to this. I found her, but instead of looking gleeful to see James talking to me, she looked stricken. She shot a look across the room at Jo, who was shaking her head in annoyance at her.

What the hell was going on with that lot?

"Is something the matter?" James said, looking over his shoulder to follow my gaze.

"No, not at all. Braden mentioned your name earlier. That's how I knew who you were."

"Saying only good things, I hope?"

I felt uncomfortable, awkward for some reason, like the two of us were under a magnifying glass. I did my best to hide the feeling. "Well, there was some mention of tax evasion and terrorism, but other than that . . ."

He grinned. "And can I ask what your name is?"

"Oh, it's Grace." I held out my hand. "It's nice to meet you."

His hand had just slid into mine when I felt this peculiar prickling sensation on the nape of my neck. Some instinct made me glance over my shoulder.

Logan stood in the doorway of the room, his eyes boring into me.

For a moment I was breathless as our gazes held across the room.

And then, just like that, he gave me that annoying chin nod of his before looking away. I followed him with my eyes as he strode across the room toward Braden. A number of other women followed him with their eyes as well. He cut quite the figure in his suit trousers and black shirt. He'd left the shirt open at the neck, and the sleeves were rolled up, displaying his tattoo.

"Do you know Logan?" James said, drawing my attention back to him.

I thought I did.

"Not very well." I reached for my glass of champagne, suddenly not so very distracted from my worries.

"So what do you do, Grace?"

I let myself be carried away by the conversation, hoping that it would take me somewhere else for a while, but unfortunately it was too late. My chest ached so badly because I couldn't manage to steer my thoughts away from either my mother, father, Sebastian, or Logan. The pain was only compounded when Logan came into my line of sight beyond James, and I saw him flirting with a pretty blond woman whose name I couldn't remember.

I lowered my gaze, pretending to laugh at what the lawyer was saying. I didn't know what he was saying. I could barely remember what he'd just said. There was a whooshing sound in my ears, and I felt like I was observing myself in this conversation from a distance.

I don't know how I managed to last as long as I did, but suddenly the room was too warm, too loud, too everything. "I'm sorry," I interrupted James. "Could you excuse me for just a minute? Sorry." I spun around and walked away, moving through the crowd in the main living area of the town house. The hallway was packed with people, too, but when I glanced upstairs, all was silent and dark.

I knew it was a little intrusive, but I needed some peace and quiet for a moment, and Joss had relayed to me that her children were with Jo and Cam's and Nate and Liv's, being looked after by Olivia's father, Mick, and his wife, Dee. They'd been cracking jokes about the two of them being brave to take on six kids for the evening.

While no one was paying attention, I went upstairs onto the first floor. Light from the moon pouring in through the large window on the front of the house illuminated my way, and I hurried into the first room I came to.

I left the door open a crack, allowing a little light into the room, and shapes leapt out at me in the darkness.

It was the nursery for Joss and Braden's youngest, Ellie. She was only one year old. I walked quietly over to her crib and saw the night-light on the dresser beside it. When I switched it on, pale blue stars began dancing around the walls of the room as the night-light spun slowly around. Noting the large comfy-looking chair in the corner by the window, I zeroed in on it and sat down to catch my breath.

I stared at the stars circling the room so far above my reach and suddenly felt a bit like a cat trying to catch a beam of light in its paw. Why did I keep doing this? I wondered. Why did I keep letting my parents do this to me? Hurt me like this.

A creak on the floorboard made my breath catch. The door opened slowly, and a tall figure slipped inside. A star of light caught his face, and I tensed.

"Grace?" Logan stepped inside, shutting the door behind him. "Are you okay?"

"I'm fine," I whispered.

He walked toward me, and my muscles grew more strained at his nearness. "You're not fine. I was watching you downstairs. Something has happened." He stopped a few feet from me, and I stared up at him.

"It doesn't matter."

"Of course it bloody matters," he snapped, and took another step toward me. "Tell me what's going on."

"Where's Maia?" I said instead.

"With Shannon and Cole. Stop changing the subject."

"My name isn't Grace Farquhar," I blurted out.

In the dim glow of light I saw his eyes narrow. "What the fuck?"

"I mean it is Grace, but it didn't used to be. I used to go by Gracelyn Bentley. Only Aidan, Chloe, and Juno know that. Now you."

"Grace," he whispered, concern deep in his voice. "I don't understand."

"Have you heard of Gabriel Bentley?"

"The guy with the media empire?"

"Yes." I don't know why I was telling him. Perhaps I was a glutton for punishment—confiding in a man, seeking affection from him, when I knew there was no hope of its real return. "He's my father, Logan."

"Jesus," he said hoarsely, and took another step toward me. "What . . . ?"

"He was always busy, always working, never had time for me, only for Sebastian, whom he was grooming to take his place in the business. He was a little old-fashioned that way. I gather he never thought I'd be of much use in business because he never bothered with me." I gave a huff of bitter laughter. "I wish my mother had been the same, but unfortunately her neglect came with a constant stream of criticism. I wasn't a size zero. I wasn't pretty enough, sexy enough, witty enough, fashionable enough. I was boring. I was pathetic. I should never have been born." My breath caught, remembering the day she'd said that to me. "I was never good enough, Logan. And I wish it didn't still bloody well . . . hurt." My voice cracked on the last word as tears spilled down my cheeks.

Suddenly Logan had lowered to his haunches in front of me, one hand on my knee, the other cupping my face as he stared at me with growing concern.

I shook my head, unable to stop the flow of tears or the feeling of being transported back to how I'd felt at twenty-one years old, when my whole world seemed to collapse around me. "I'm sorry." I sobbed. "I just . . . I'm sorry."

He pulled me toward him, and I buried my head in the crook of his neck, the pain that had been pressing on my chest pouring out of me as I cried. Logan's hand tightened on my nape.

"You're scaring me, babe," he said hoarsely. "Tell me what's going on. Please. Let me fix it."

I shook my head and eased away from him, but he refused to let me go. "You can't help."

"Try me." He cupped my face in both hands now, and his thumbs swiped gently at my wet cheeks.

Just like that I got lost in his eyes. "My parents were in the newspaper today. There hasn't been a press release from them yet, but inside sources are saying that my mother has breast cancer. She's fighting breast cancer."

"Shit." Logan eyes filled with sympathy. "They didn't tell you."

"They didn't tell me," I confirmed. "Clearly they don't want me there. But do you want to know the truth?"

He nodded solemnly.

"I don't even know if I want to be there for her. She made me feel worthless my whole life. Between my father's indifference and her cruelty, I was a bit of a mess as a teenager. When I got to university Aidan suggested I talk to someone . . . a therapist. So I did. And it really helped. It really did. So I thought when I went home I'd be able to cope better. But I made the mistake of taking my boyfriend home with me after I graduated. We'd met in my last year at school. I'd thought myself very much in love with him." I remembered it. The utter soul-destroying pain of it. "I was supposed to be out meeting up with an old school friend. He stayed behind at the house. But my friend canceled, so I came home early . . ."

"Oh fuck," Logan whispered, and I heard the empathy, the pain he felt for me.

"It's such a cliché." I swiped at my tears, throwing him a bitter smile. "The mother sleeping with her daughter's boyfriend. She told me afterward that she did me a favor. That he would never have stuck with me in the long run because I wasn't good enough. She was saving me the heartbreak of getting in too deep with him. I was so enraged I told my father."

Logan tensed.

"Yes. Vengeful little me. I wanted to ruin her. I wanted to take everything from her. But my dad didn't care." I shook my head, more tears welling up. "They'd been having affairs for years. Sebastian was the one who told me. He spilled that as he acerbically told me to get my head out of my arse and in the real world. I was too soft, he said. I needed to grow up and grow a pair.

"I hated them. All of them. I hated the way they made me feel, and I hated that I wanted to hurt them for hurting me. I didn't want to become like them."

"So you left?" Logan said.

I nodded. "Left it all behind. Them, the money, and my name. I came back to Edinburgh and moved in with Aidan and a few other friends. I thought my family didn't have the power to hurt me anymore. Turns out they do." I gave a huff of incredulous laughter. "How wrong is it that I'm not sure I want to go to my possibly dying mother, but I want her to want me to?"

"It's not wrong." Logan pulled me close again. "It's not wrong at all."

I wrapped my arms around his shoulders and held on for dear life as the old wounds were ripped open, bleeding more tears. "Why don't they love me?" I whispered into his neck.

I felt Logan's chest shudder against mine as his arms tightened around me. He gently tugged on my hair, pulling me back to look at me, and my heart stuttered at the sheen of emotion in his eyes. I found my tears slowing to halt at the blazing mix of anger, tenderness, and helplessness I saw in his gaze.

The whole world just disappeared.

Logan's gaze dropped to my mouth and gently, slowly, he tugged my head to his and pressed his lips to mine. The kiss started soft, quiet, as though meant to comfort and soothe, but I was desperate to feel anything but the pain, and so I deepened the kiss, pushing for more.

Just like that we caught fire.

Our tongues stroked, our grips on each other grew desperate, bruising, and I was ready to tackle him to the floor.

And then my mother's words penetrated.

Logan's rejection after we had sex followed quickly on its heels.

Remembering it, I found myself hating him a little. I pulled out of his hold, abruptly standing up. He had to drop to a knee to stop himself from landing on his arse.

Staring down into his questioning eyes, I realized I didn't hate him. I hated myself for allowing his sympathy to turn into more than he'd meant it to. "I never asked for that kind of pity."

"Grace, it wasn't pity. It was just a—"

"Mistake," I finished for him. "You're right. This was all a mistake." I'd let another person into my heart and he couldn't love me. He cared. I knew he cared. But it wasn't love. It wasn't what I needed.

My lip started to tremble, but I refused to give in to more tears. "Will you call me a cab?"

"I'll take you home."

I cut him a look that made the muscles in his jaw clench. "I don't want to be around you right now."

He reached for me, and I flinched back. Logan lowered his hand to his side in defeat. "I don't want to leave you like this."

"I'll be fine. If you call me a cab."

I stayed upstairs while he did as I asked. He returned a few minutes later to tell me one was on its way and was close by. "Will you tell Joss I'm just not feeling well?"

He nodded, watching me carefully.

I hurried down the stairs, letting my hair fall forward, hiding my face from the guests in the hallway. I moved past them without looking at them and darted outside. Logan was right behind me.

"You shouldn't be alone, Grace," he said as I strode down onto the pavement to wait for the cab I could see approaching up the hill.

I glanced over my shoulder at Logan, who looked surprisingly lost. "I'm not. I'm going to Aidan."

His face darkened at my announcement. "Aidan?"

I didn't answer. Instead the cab pulled over and I practically threw myself in it. "Raeburn Place," I said quickly, thankful when the car pulled away from the curb.

The cab passed Logan as he stood on the pavement, his eyes filled with frustration and worry as they locked with mine. He mouthed my name.

I looked away and sank back against the seat.

"You all right?" the driver asked.

I realized I must look a fright with my tearstained cheeks and red eyes. I closed said eyes and said, "I will be."

And despite what an utterly heartbreaking, shitty day it had been, in a weird, twisted way, the reminder of Logan's rejection had put steel back in my spine. I had to remember that I didn't need Logan. I'd been perfectly fine without him before he came into my life.

I didn't need my family. I'd gotten on better without them these last few years.

I just had to keep reminding myself of that.

I opened my eyes, thinking of the three people who always helped with the reminder.

A feeling of calm started to settle over me as the cab carried me toward Aidan and Juno. Slipping my hand into my purse, I pulled out my phone and rang Chloe.

"What's up, chick?" she said chirpily.

"Can you meet me at Aidan's?"

She was silent a moment. "What's going on? You sound like you've been crying."

"Just meet me there?"

"Why? What's going on?"

I pressed my forehead against the cool glass of the back passenger window, watching the city pass me by. "I just really need you right now. I need my family, yeah."

"I'll be there in ten."

CHAPTER 17

The only way I could avoid Logan completely was by camping out at Chloe's flat. I'd dart home to get showered and changed when I knew he was working and then I'd go back to Chloe's.

There were five missed calls on my phone from him, including a voice-mail message I couldn't bring myself to listen to.

When Maia called, I picked up. I fed her some rubbish about Chloe having had an argument with Ed and I was keeping her company for a little bit, and I felt awful for lying. I think Maia knew. I tried to make up for my absence by chatting on the phone with her for ages, listening to her as she spun plans for her summer holidays, which were fast approaching.

I honestly thought that I was going to get away with my lie.

Poor naive me.

"So you and Dad had a fight, didn't you?" Maia said abruptly upon the third night of my stay at Chloe's.

I already felt guilty enough lying to her the first time. "It's not just about that."

"What did he do? I bet he didn't mean it."

"Maia, it's not just about Logan and the differences we're having at the moment. I'm just . . . I'm going through some stuff and . . . well . . .

Chloe is to me what Logan is to you. I like being around her when I feel like this."

"And that Aidan guy?" she said with so much suspicion I laughed.

"Yes, but that Aidan guy is just a friend. One of my best friends. He's engaged, you know."

"Hmm. So you say."

I laughed again. "I promise."

There was a moment of silence, and I realized it was due to Maia plucking up the courage to say, "Don't you like Dad?"

Too much.

"It's not that simple. Maia, I love you, but I can't talk to you about this stuff. It's between me and your dad."

She was quiet again.

I bit my lip, worried I'd hurt her. "Maia, please under—"

"You love me?"

My heart squeezed at the whispered question. "Of course I do. It's kind of hard not to. It's really rather annoying how adorably lovable you are."

She snorted, and the silence fell again. And then . . . "I love you, too, Grace."

I smiled and then immediately felt like a coward and a bit of a shit for hiding out from Logan and thus avoiding Maia. "You know what? I'll be home tomorrow. You should come over for dinner."

"Just me though, right?" she said dryly.

Remembering those first few weeks when Logan and Maia had spent all their free time in my kitchen, I felt a wince of regret. "That would be best."

We talked a little more about other things, mostly about how Layla wasn't talking to Maia because Maia called her a gossip and how now poor Leigh was stuck in the middle. As I listened to her blather on, I once again assumed I'd escaped any more Logan conversations.

But the last thing Maia promised before she hung up was, "I'm going to make you like him again."

. . .

I was walking up the stairwell the next afternoon, having just dropped off Mr. Jenner's shopping for him, when Logan suddenly appeared, hurrying down the stairs toward me. He halted when he saw me, his expression blank.

And then he gave me an abrupt nod and started to move quickly past me. I turned, frowning. Although I'd known things would be uneasy between us, the reality of it was quite different. I didn't like it. "Are you all right?" I called after him.

He stopped again and looked back at me. "I got a call from the school. Maia is in trouble."

Worry whooshed through me, making me momentarily forget the awkwardness of being in Logan's company. "What do you mean?" I started down the stairs after him.

"Are you coming?" He raised his eyebrows in surprise.

"It's Maia."

He nodded, and I hurried out of the building after him. As we walked, he talked. "The history teacher has been accused of having an affair with a married colleague. The rumors are all over the school, and they think Maia started them."

Anger and disbelief coursed through me. "Oh, I think we both know who started them." Logan met my gaze, and we stated in unison, "Layla."

The rest of the walk to the school was completely silent and incredibly tense. I knew Logan was furious that anyone would attempt to pin a "crime" on Maia when she wasn't the one responsible, and I was trying to work out how I could contain his anger so he didn't inadvertently get himself and Maia in more trouble.

When we got to the school, the headmaster, a Mr. Bruce, almost didn't let me in his office because I wasn't family, but Logan did that deadpan-staring thing that intimidated a person into doing almost anything he wanted them to do. We strode inside Mr. Bruce's office only to discover Maia sitting, pale and anxious. Beside her was a petulant Layla, and standing across from them was a redhead in her late thirties and a guy around my age. Our eyes caught and met for a moment, his expression turning from brooding to arrested as his gaze washed over me.

"Layla's parents can't get out of work," Mr. Bruce said as he followed us in and shut the door. He marched around to his desk and sat down, gesturing to us to take the other empty seats in the room. "So we shall commence. Mr. Tatum, Mrs. Rogers, this is Mr. MacLeod, Maia's father and his erm . . . friend Miss Farquhar. I've asked you here because there is a vicious rumor circulating the school community that Mr. Tatum and Mrs. Rogers have been involved in an extramarital affair on school grounds. We all know the rumor to be a repugnant lie started by an irresponsible student. Layla has named Maia as the culprit, and as you can guess, Maia has labeled Layla the culprit. In order to satisfy some very uneasy parents, I need the student responsible to issue an apology. They will also receive a suspension. If I don't get to the truth today, I will suspend both Layla and Maia. Am I clear?"

I glanced at Maia, who was staring at her feet, looking like she wanted the ground to open up and swallow her. Layla was staring at her cuticles as though bored out of her mind.

Shifting my attention, I looked over at the two teachers in question. On closer inspection Mrs. Rogers was attractive, and Mr. Tatum definitely was. It was clear to me why shallow little Layla had chosen these two as her victims. My gaze met Mr. Tatum's again, and I found myself directing my words to him. "I'm a good friend of the family and I know Maia well. In fact, only a few weeks ago, while she was having dinner with me, she mentioned Layla had imagined there was something going on between yourself and Mrs. Rogers. Concerned, I asked if it were true and Maia said of course not, that Layla was just bored and inventing drama. I asked Maia not to repeat the rumor, and she promised that she would not. I believed her and I still do."

Mr. Tatum nodded gravely at me. "I'm inclined to believe her too." He looked at Mr. Bruce. "Layla has demonstrated inappropriate behavior around me and has been warned. I noted it and made sure management was aware of it."

"Maia's behavior of late hasn't been great though," Mrs. Rogers added.

"It's been getting better again," Mr. Tatum disagreed. "And I've noticed friction between the girls in my class."

"You've got it in for me, Mr. Tatum." Layla narrowed her eyes on him.

"Quiet," Mr. Bruce said sternly. "Layla, were you the one who started the rumor? If you admit it, I'll cut the length of your suspension."

"Layla, please," Maia suddenly said. "Tell the truth."

Layla rolled her eyes. "You're such a boring bitch lately."

"Don't speak to her like that," Logan interjected, and Layla flinched at the warning in his voice. He held her gaze, his expression fierce, and it seemed someone was able to pierce that indolent arrogance of hers. She blushed and bit her lip, looking down at her feet just as Maia had done a moment ago.

"Layla?" Mr. Bruce said.

She refused to speak.

He gave a weary sigh. "Then I have no recourse but to punish both girls."

I clamped a hand down on Logan's arm, anticipating his reaction. Putting pressure on his arm, I forced him to be quiet without saying a word. "Perhaps we can work something else out that's a little more fair."

"Fair?" Mrs. Rogers snapped. "I had to explain this nonsense to my husband."

"I know Maia wasn't involved," I told her. "So if she's to be punished, I want to make sure it's not a suspension that blackens her school record."

"What are you suggesting?" Mr. Tatum said, seeming willing to hear me out.

"It's the end of school. Isn't there an event that they could volunteer to work on?"

There was silence as they mulled it over. Mr. Tatum looked at the headmaster. "There is the end-of-term service . . . but I have something else in mind."

"Oh?" Mrs. Rogers wore an annoyed expression, as though pissed off he was contemplating my idea.

"Next semester I'll be hosting the fund-raiser for Armistice Day in November. It's always a stressful event for me on top of my work . . . so why don't I just leave it to these two ladies to organize it for me?"

"But—"

Mr. Tatum held up a hand to cut off Rogers's coming complaint. "If they screw it up, the suspension still stands."

I looked over at Maia and Layla. "How does that sound?"

Maia nodded glumly.

Layla glowered at me. "How do you think it sounds?"

"Attitude," Mr. Bruce warned. "If Mrs. Rogers agrees, then this will be your punishment."

We all looked at the teacher in question. She glared back at us but eventually nodded.

Logan shook the headmaster's hand and then the teachers', thanking them. Maia sidled up to me and clasped my hand. "Always saving the day," she whispered to me.

I squeezed her hand. "I'd do anything for you."

She smiled cheekily and then looked pointedly at her dad. "Anything?"

I groaned. "*Almost* anything."

We were heading out of the office when Logan caught up with us, Mr. Tatum at his side. The teacher immediately held out a hand to me. "It was nice to meet you."

Our eyes met and held again, and I felt a little zing of attraction. "You too. Thank you for being so fair."

"I don't believe Maia had anything to do with it."

"Nice, Mr. T.," Layla snapped at him as she strode past us, eating up the ground with her long legs.

"I guess we're not friends anymore!" Maia called after her sarcastically.

Logan put his hand on her shoulder and squeezed. "She was never a very good one anyway, Maia."

"Um . . . do you have a minute to talk privately?" Mr. Tatum suddenly asked me.

I could feel Logan's and Maia's eyes burning into mine. "Uh . . . Yeah, sure." I looked back at them. Maia was glowering. Logan's expression was carefully blank. "I'll catch up with you."

Logan had to budge Maia to get her to move, and as soon as they were out of earshot, I turned to Mr. Tatum, curiosity written all over my face.

He grinned, a boyishly charming smile that I had to admit I liked a lot. He didn't look a thing like Logan, and I decided I also liked that fact. "Maia's a good kid. I get the impression she's been through quite a bit. She talks about you and her dad a lot."

I smiled softly. "She's a very special person."

He nodded. "She thinks the same of you. That's why I know your name is Grace and you are a freelance book editor."

I laughed. "What else has she been telling you?"

"Apparently you make good homemade pizza."

"I do," I agreed with mock arrogance.

He chuckled. "She said nothing of your modesty, however." He cleared his throat. "Look, I hope you don't think this is forward, but I've written an historical fiction novel that I'd like to send out on query to a few publishers, and I was wondering if I could hire you to edit it before I do."

Surprise moved through me at the request. I honestly hadn't known why he'd asked me to stay back with him, but for some reason that had been the last thing on my mind. "Oh . . . um . . . I have a pretty tight schedule at the moment, but why don't you give me your e-mail address and I can send you some recommendations for other editors?"

He looked disappointed but nodded. "Sure. I understand. Thank you. I'll give you my number instead."

I rummaged through my purse for my phone. "Okay. And thank you again for helping me out back there, Mr. Tatum."

"It's Patrick," he corrected with a soft smile that definitely verged on flirtatious. He rattled off his number to me once I had my phone in hand. "Call me so your number will come up on my phone and I'll know who you are."

I did as he said.

"You do know that was just a cheap ploy to get your number, right?" He grinned mischievously at me.

My lips parted. "What? Even the 'I've written a book part'?"

"No. That part was true. But if I can't get to know you while you edit my book, I'd really like to get to know you over a coffee or something." His smile widened at my surprised expression. "Think about it. Please." Patrick glanced at his watch and sighed. "I'm taking detention today, so I need to go." He started walking backward, smiling at me the whole time in a way that left no doubt that he was flirting. After the last few days, it was a very nice feeling to be found attractive. "I'll await your call, Grace."

I waved my phone at him and spun around, grinning from cheek to cheek as I strode down the hallway.

It was funny how that giddy feeling completely evaporated as soon as I caught up with Logan and Maia on the Meadows. There was an awkward silence upon my approach, and I knew Maia was desperate to ask me what her history teacher wanted with me.

"Why weren't you at work?" I said to Logan, diverting the conversation immediately.

"I'm working tonight."

"Do you want Maia to come to me?"

"Nope."

"Who is looking after her, then?"

"I don't need looking after," Maia huffed.

"Shannon," Logan said.

"How is Shannon?"

"Fine."

I shivered at the chill Logan was giving off. I felt like we were meeting all over again. However, his monosyllabic, gruff way with me was even more unpleasant this time around.

I thought of Patrick, who actually seemed attracted to me. Maybe Aidan was right after all. Maybe there really was hope.

Upon our return to Nightingale Way, Maia followed me into my flat and Logan disappeared into his own.

"What did Mr. Tatum want?" Maia said immediately.

I wrinkled my nose at her. "You really are getting very nosy."

"Well?"

"Maia."

"Dad's upset."

I huffed. "Not about that, I assure you."

"You know, for a smart lady, you can be pretty dumb."

I narrowed my eyes on her. "Watch it."

It was her turn to wrinkle her nose. "You can't date my history teacher, Grace."

"If you must know, Mr. Tatum asked me for a favor." I slumped down onto my armchair and stared up at her as she glared down at me in irritation. I tried to keep my tone gentle. "But if Mr. Tatum was to ask me on a date, or if anyone was for that matter, it will be up to me whether or not I decide to say yes. Maia, I'm not stupid. I know you're hankering after something to happen between your dad and me, but it's not going to happen. I'm sorry."

Tears sprang into her eyes, making me feel guilty as hell.

"Maia." I stood up, but she'd already spun on her heel and dashed out of my flat.

I heard the slam of Logan's front door and slumped back in my chair, wishing my life weren't so freaking complicated and that I didn't care so damn much about one fifteen-year-old girl and her annoying father.

CHAPTER 18

I t would suffice to say that I could not get to sleep that night. I tossed and turned for hours, until eventually I gave in and got up to do some work.

At around four in the morning I was in my sitting room stretched out on the couch with my laptop, working on Joss's manuscript. I was having the best time with it. The lady knew how to bloody well write a good book. This was when my job was amazingly fun, because I got to read a great book and then advise on little things that I thought might help make it greater.

I was lost in Joss's compelling heroine and whether a scene she'd written that let the reader dive a little deeper into the heroine's psyche should perhaps be brought forward in the plot so the reader could connect with her a little faster, when—

BANG! BANG! BANG!

I jolted up on the couch, my laptop almost sliding off of my lap at the sound of a fist banging on my front door. Wary, I got up, placing my computer aside, and hurried down the hallway on tiptoe. I peeked out of the peephole, and my heart leapt into my throat.

I unlocked the door, yanking it open to reveal Maia standing there in her pajamas with hair disheveled and face pale. "What's going on? Are you all right?"

She shook her head. "Dad's having a nightmare."

Worry instantly moved through me. "A nightmare?"

Maia nodded. "He's thrashing around and all sweaty I'm really worried."

"Okay. One second." Pulse racing, I rushed back into the flat, grabbed my keys and slippers, and hurried out to Maia. Following her into Logan's, I whispered, "Does this happen a lot?"

Her wide eyes met mine. "Not at first, but the last few weeks he's had a few. I'm frightened to wake him because I saw this movie once where this guy had nightmares all the time and he could be, like, violent in his sleep. But I can't leave him like that. It's really bad tonight. It's been going on for ages."

"Right." My gaze was automatically drawn down the hallway to where his room was. "Go back to bed, sweetheart. I'll make sure he's all right."

Maia sagged with relief and exhaustion. After giving me a grateful hug, she returned to her room.

Filled with trepidation, I started down the hall to Logan's room, and sure enough I heard a noise like a pained grunt. Moving faster now, I pushed inside his domain, my eyes taking in the shadow of furniture in the dim light. Logan was curled up in the tangle of his blankets as if he were contained in a small space and not a huge bed. Everything about his body language suggested he was trying to protect himself, and the vulnerability of it caused a painful streak to radiate across my chest.

He jerked suddenly, his face tightening in sleep, and he gave another pained grunt. I switched on his bedside lamp, and the light exposed the sweat glistening on his face and the dampness of his T-shirt.

I felt anxious about waking him, unsure how he would react, but I couldn't bear to watch him in pain like this. "Logan," I said, resting a hand on his shoulder. "Logan." I shook him.

He flinched but didn't wake up.

I bent closer, my lips at his ear. "Logan, you're having a nightmare, sweetheart. Wake up." I shook him harder and jumped back as his whole body jerked.

Violet eyes blinked up at me in confusion and shock.

Logan's chest heaved with exertion.

"You were having a nightmare," I told him softly.

"Jesus," he whispered, running a hand over his damp short hair. Then something changed in his expression. "Maia?"

"She's fine," I assured him. "She was worried, so she came to get me."

"Fuck." Logan huffed and sagged against his pillow, his fingers curling into his hair. "Fuck."

"I'll go get you some water."

When I returned to his room, he'd propped himself up against his headboard and taken off his sweat-soaked T-shirt. He looked exhausted, and that was almost enough to distract me from his well-defined abs.

"Thanks," he said, taking the water I handed to him.

There was a small part of me that wanted to embrace our awkwardness of late and just be done with him. Walk out and not look back. However, there was a much larger part of me that was worried sick about him.

That part won.

"Scoot over," I said.

Our eyes met and I held my breath, and despite everything, I hoped he didn't reject my offer of friendship.

He didn't.

Once he'd moved over a bit, I propped myself up against the headboard and stretched my legs out on the bed beside him. "How long have you been having nightmares?"

There was silence from my left, and I was about to press him when he finally replied, "Since I got out."

I ached for him. "Logan," I whispered, turning my head to look at him.

Our eyes met again, and I hurt for him even more at the sight of his stubborn expression. "I'm fine, Grace."

"You're not fine."

"Look, they come and go. I hadn't had one in a while, but lately . . ."

"What are they about?"

He gave me a wry smile that didn't reach his eyes. "Prison, of course."

"Specifically?" I insisted.

"I don't want to talk about it."

"I'm not leaving until you do."

Logan sighed heavily. "Why are you even here?"

I glowered at him. "Because despite everything, I do care about you. I don't like the idea of you having nightmares, and talking about them might help make them go away."

His face softened. "I appreciate that, babe, but I don't think this can be as easily solved as all that."

"At least try."

"I'm in a tiny dark room," he said abruptly. "There's absolutely no space for me to stretch out. I'm curled up in it just to fit. Yet somehow, magically," he said with dry disgust, "there's room for feet to kick at me, knives to stab at me . . . faces to . . ." His eyes lowered, the muscle in his jaw clenching.

"Faces, Logan?" I pushed.

When he looked up at me, his eyes were blazing with turmoil. "I let shit happen in there that I shouldn't have, Grace."

Hearing so much pain in his voice was unbearable for me. I reached for his hand and threaded my fingers through his. His grip tightened around it. "There's something in particular," I deduced softly. "Something haunting you."

He scowled at the wall.

After what seemed like forever, he finally began to speak. "There was a kid. Nineteen. Stupid, cocky little kid. But he wasn't a bad kid. I know bad. It seeps out of them. You feel it in the air around them, something heavy and dark that creeps over you and makes you shudder like someone is walking over your grave.

"Not this kid. It was all bravado. Got himself thrown inside for being

200 · SAMANTHA YOUNG

an accomplice in an armed robbery. He used to swagger around, trying to convince everyone this was where he belonged, but he was scared and you could fucking smell it on him. Like blood in shark-infested waters."

I felt a little sick just imagining where this was going. "What was his name?"

"Danny," he said, his voice hoarse. "Danny Little. Tried to get every fucker in the place to call him the wee man. I tried to tell him he was pushing too hard, pissing the guys off . . ."

"Was he your friend?"

Logan frowned. "I think *I* was *his*. He told me everything about himself. About his mum and his wee sister. How he was just trying to take care of them, make life better for them since their old man had passed away. A fucking cliché of tragedy, this kid.

"Just a kid, Grace. I should have protected him."

The agony in his voice brought tears to my eyes. "Logan . . ." It almost sounded like a plea.

He turned to me, guilt written all over him. "I knew they were circling. I didn't do enough. They got to him . . . kept threatening to rape him. I told him it was just a bullying tactic, but they tormented him with the threat until they attacked him. They didn't rape him, but they promised him that they would next time. I just told him to keep strong, that they were bluffing, toying with him. I wasn't . . . I didn't do enough."

I felt sick. My hand tightened in his in reaction.

"He killed himself a few days later. Stole a shank from someone. Slit his wrists at night in his cell."

"I'm so sorry," I whispered around the lump in my throat.

"I could have done something." His hand was holding mine so tight now it was almost painful. "I . . ."

"You are not to blame for what happened to him."

"Those words mean nothing to his family. If it were your son . . . those words would mean nothing to you."

I couldn't say anything because as much as I didn't believe he was to blame, I knew he was also right. "You take too much upon yourself." I brushed my thumb over the back of his hand in comfort. "All you see is the bad when there is so much good."

He turned his head to stare at me, his eyes on mine before moving across my face, caressing my mouth and traveling back up to my eyes again. There was such tenderness in his expression it made me a little breathless. "Sometimes it's hard to believe you're real."

Suddenly feeling like we were venturing into dangerous territory, I loosened my grip on his hand and pulled away a little.

Tightness appeared around his eyes at my withdrawal. "I'm a selfish bastard."

I shook my head.

"I'm a selfish bastard," he insisted gruffly. "I want to bury myself inside you, and I'm not sure I can keep holding myself back from doing it."

My breath caught at his confession, and I couldn't ignore the burst of aroused tingles between my legs. But I could run from them. I sat up, prepared to do just that. "I told you I don't do casual sex."

He sat up, too, now. "Grace, there is nothing fucking casual about how I feel about you."

Suddenly all my sympathy was crushed beneath my anger. "You have a funny way of showing it."

"It didn't seem fair."

"What?" I asked, completely confused.

His brows dipped together in consternation. "I got out of prison and I had these great people willing to help me. And if that wasn't enough, I got Maia. My kid could have been anyone, Grace . . . But it wasn't anyone. It was Maia. Funny, smart, sweet, beautiful. My kid. A kid with so much will and determination she adjusted to life with me in weeks. There is so much to be proud of there."

"And you think you don't deserve her?"

"I know I don't. But I could handle it because there was one thing I couldn't have and it made me feel like there was a balance."

My heart rate increased. "What are you talking about?"

"You."

I felt the world tilt around me. I wasn't sure I'd heard right. "Me?"

"The day you told me and Shannon that you didn't care about my time in prison. You didn't judge me for it." He stared at me soulfully. "I wanted you then. But you didn't look at me the way a woman wants a man. I'm pretty sure all you felt toward me was annoyance. And that worked for me because I didn't deserve someone like you. Later, when I started to realize you were as attracted to me as I was to you, I buried it. And after we had sex, it wasn't just about Maia. If I got to have you and have Maia . . . It was too much—much more than I deserved."

"I was a form of self-flagellation." I looked away. "You hurt me to hurt yourself. Is that what you're saying?"

"It sounds fucked-up when you say it."

"That's because it is fucked-up." I swung my legs off the bed and stared hard at the wall. "You should see someone, Logan. Talk to them."

"You mean a therapist?" He sounded incredulous.

"Yes. I used to see one. It helped."

"I'm not the talking-it-out kind of guy."

"You're talking to me." I glanced over my shoulder at him.

He gave me a sad smile. "Because you're Grace. You're the only one I talk to like this."

Tears pricked my eyes and I looked away.

The bed shifted, and I felt the heat of him at my back. I shivered at the feel of his breath on my neck as he brushed my hair out of the way with one hand and wrapped his other arm around my waist, bringing me back against his chest. "I don't want to fight this anymore. I'm so fucking tired of fighting." He pressed a kiss to my neck, and I squeezed my eyes shut. He might have been tired of fighting, but I wasn't.

He'd hurt me so badly.

Just like my family.

Until now I didn't even realize how bloody angry I was with him.

"I'll talk to Maia," he said softly in my ear. "I can make this work and still focus on her."

"Maia wants us to be together," I told him flatly. "She's been trying to push us together from the start."

Logan tensed. "You're joking?"

"Nope. I guessed as much after the night we dragged her home from the club. She's admitted it to me."

He pressed his forehead against my shoulder. "Are you telling me all the huffy shit she pulled wasn't about other women—it was about the fact that the other women weren't you?" I could hear the rumble of amusement in his voice, and I willed my body to stop reacting to it.

"Yes."

He chuckled and pulled me against him, his fingers slipping under the hem of my T-shirt. "My girl has got good taste."

I jerked out of his arms, pushing myself off the bed. I turned to stare down at him incredulously. "Do you think that's it? All you have to do is say you want me and I'll come running?"

Logan frowned. "That's not . . . I'm just trying to be honest."

"You rejected me, Logan," I whispered, feeling the pain of it all over again. "When I was at my most vulnerable. I know right now you're feeling a shitload of guilt over things that you couldn't control, and I'm sorry for that because I don't believe that you deserve to feel guilt over that. But this"—I gestured between us—"it's not happening. You humiliated me."

He pushed the duvet away to get out of the bed, and I backed up as he came toward me. I slammed up against the wall as he pressed his hands to either side of my head, caging me in. His chest moved up and down with his rapid breaths. "I never meant to hurt you, babe," he promised, his voice deep with sincerity. "I thought I was protecting you."

"From what?"

"From ending up with someone like me."

I shook my head, looking away so I didn't have to see all the self-recrimination and pain in his eyes. It always called to me. It always begged me to soothe him, and I wasn't sure I could fight the need to do it.

"Do you know how fucking beautiful you are?" he whispered, pressing his cheek against mine, his stubble prickling my skin in a way that sent delicious shivers rippling through me. "And I don't just mean this." He slid a hand up my waist, his thumb brushing the underside of my breast. My nipples tightened, my body betraying me. He pulled back and tipped my chin, forcing me to meet his gaze. I sucked in my breath at the need in his eyes. "You are the kindest, funniest, most compassionate woman I have ever known. The fact that you're gorgeous and the classiest fucking woman I've ever met just makes it harder not to want you. And I want you, Grace. Never doubt that I have wanted you since the moment you snapped at me about that thong." He came closer, his lips almost touching mine. "And I've needed you since the moment you took my hand at Maryanne's."

"Logan . . ." I shook my head. "I can't. I can't . . . I . . . I don't trust you anymore. Not with me."

He squeezed his eyes closed, pain tightening his face. "Don't say that."

I almost whimpered at the hurt plea. "I can't help it."

When he opened his eyes, I saw the panic in his eyes melt suddenly, only to have determination take its place. "I'm going to make this right."

"Logan, please . . . Let's just forget it."

We stared into each other's eyes, the air between us thick with emotion and arousal. His hand slid down my waist and his grip hardened. He brushed his lips over mine, causing my mouth to tingle. Finally he responded with one word that sent shivers cascading down my spine.

"Never."

CHAPTER 19

There was no mistaking the determination in Logan's eyes when I shot one last glance over my shoulder before fleeing inside my flat. I'd hurried out of his flat only to find he'd followed me. He stood in his doorway, saying nothing because his eyes said everything.

Logan MacLeod wanted me.

Logan MacLeod was determined to have me.

I'd slammed my door shut behind me with the hope of slamming that look behind me as well. But I couldn't shake his expression from my mind. There was a part of me that was thrilled. It would be foolish to deny that I wasn't. I was only human, and the man I'd previously fallen in love with had told me he'd wanted me all along. There was a triumph in that. However, the triumph was overwhelmed by my fear.

There had been many times in the past when I'd been ready to give up on my hellish family, but then my father, Mr. Neglectful, would suddenly show an interest in me, manipulate me, and I was right back in their fold again. Sometimes I worried that the only reason I'd stayed away from them for so long was because my father had given up on me as much as I'd given up on him and them.

I didn't want this situation with Logan to be another example of my weakness. The man had hurt me more than I thought it was possible to be hurt. Just because he suddenly showed interest in me didn't mean I should run right back into his arms. As much as he claimed to want me now, I had to wonder if I was just a balm for his own fear. I had been there to help him through a tough time in his life. I feared he was confusing gratitude for something more, and that when he finally realized I really wasn't his type after all, my heart would be crushed into dust.

But was that my insecurities talking? Perhaps Logan really did have genuine feelings for me.

The fact of the matter was that I couldn't really know for certain.

"Ask the history teacher out," Aidan had suggested upon my relating the new development in the Logan and Grace Saga.

"Are you nuts? Say yes! Let that gorgeous man throw you on his bed and have his wicked way with you a million times over." Chloe had fervently fought in Logan's corner when I told her.

"Do what makes you happy," Juno had said sweetly but ever so unhelpfully.

Since my friends' conflicting advice did nothing to help me, I sought to avoid the matter altogether by joining Shannon, Jo, and Joss for coffee the next afternoon. Shannon turned up covered in paint splatter. She was an art student at Edinburgh College of Art. It was Jo's day off from working with her uncle Mick in his painting and decorating company, and Joss, as a full-time author, had the flexibility to use her time however she pleased. Elodie was babysitting little Ellie for her.

I met them at Black Medicine, this cool coffee shop in Old Town, and as soon as I saw their concerned faces I wished that I could back up and leave the coffeehouse. It was apparent immediately that they would be no help in my attempt to ignore the Logan situation.

"We just wanted to check in with you," Shannon said as I took my seat with them. "Joss said you rushed out of her party without saying good-bye, and Logan looked upset. And, of course, he called me." Her look was pointed.

Taking in their expressions, I just knew it.

Logan had enlisted them.

The bugger.

"Oh dear God." I let my head fall back as if in supplication to an unmerciful deity. "Why me?"

Joss snorted. "Yeah, doesn't it suck when gorgeous, funny, loyal Scotsmen fall in love with us?"

I shot her an evil look. "Your sarcasm is unwanted at the moment."

She grinned. "Maybe I wasn't being sarcastic. There was a time when I wished Braden would back off."

Jo shot her a look. "But like Grace, you were in denial. Secretly you wanted him. Obviously." She pointed to Joss's wedding rings.

My next glower was directed at Jo. "I'm not in denial. I'm perfectly aware of my feelings for Logan because said feelings were crushed under his big stomping feet not too long ago. Perhaps I just don't want to repeat the experience."

Shannon placed a hand on my arm. "Grace, I know my brother. He doesn't make the same mistake twice. He wouldn't hurt you again."

I stared pleadingly at her. "I just wanted a coffee."

"Well, you're getting a coffee with a side of lecture," Joss said.

"You are very lucky I have a fear of confrontation and alienating people I care about."

Joss considered this and then cocked her head at Jo. "That sounded vaguely confrontational to me—don't you think?"

Jo nodded solemnly. "There was definite aggression in her eyes."

"According to Logan, you have no problem confronting him." Shannon smirked.

I closed my eyes at their teasing. "There's no place like home."

"I think that incantation requires ruby slippers," Joss said.

I snapped my eyes open. "I shouldn't make friends with smart women. They're obnoxious."

"That was definitely confrontational," Jo informed Joss.

I immediately got up out of my seat. "If I'm going to sit through an hour of this, I'll need that bloody coffee."

By the time I got home my head was ringing with their voices.

"Logan is loyal to a fault. He'll always have your back."

"Braden trusts Logan. That says a lot about him; I promise."

"I've never seen Logan so happy as he has been with you. When you're fighting I know because he's a broody, snappy bastard. You affect his mood."

"Oh, that's when you know a man is in love with you."

"Give him a chance. Just one more chance."

"Maia adores you. Doesn't that count for something too?"

"Just think about it, Grace. Really think about it."

When I'd gotten up to leave, Joss had taken one look at my deer-in-the-headlights expression and announced ruefully, "I told you we should have gone subtle. She looks like she's about to upchuck."

"Ellie said this would work." Shannon had stared at me nervously.

"And we listened to Ellie, why?" Jo had said, sharing a similar expression.

"Because she's the best at this cheesy-love stuff," Joss had replied. "But I'm thinking reverse psychology would have worked better in this case."

"Okay." I'd sighed, grabbing my purse. "I am not an experiment in matchmaking. I appreciate the thought and genuine concern behind whatever the hell this was, but my head hurts and I feel a little sick, so I'm going home."

They had offered me worried, apologetic good-byes, and I'd hurried out of there.

But the damage was done.

They had filled my head with descriptions of Logan's best qualities, reminding me of all the reasons I had fallen in love with him in the first place. As much as I had grown to care about these women, right then I was irritated with them for making my life just that little bit harder.

I hated to admit it, but when Maia turned up at my door that evening, a part of me wanted her to go away. That part of me was the part that was secretly wondering if she had also been enlisted by Logan to break down my defenses.

I stared warily at her.

"Um . . . can I come in?"

I stepped aside slowly. "You *may*," I corrected her automatically.

Maia grinned at me and strode inside the flat. I followed behind her, my whole body tense with anticipation.

Spinning around to face me, Maia wrinkled her nose. "I'm bored. School is finishing, I have no homework, and Dad is working overtime. Entertain me, Grace." She pouted comically.

My whole body deflated with relief. Maia was just being Maia. I was never so thankful. "What would you have me do?" I grinned.

She blew air out between her lips and looked around the room thoughtfully. Her eyes stopped on my DVD collection and her face lit up. "Let's go the cinema."

I considered my workload and then I considered how difficult it was for me to work at the moment because I kept thinking about the man next door. I could do with the distraction. "Okay. Do you have something in mind?"

"There's that new action flick with Nick McGuire."

Nick McGuire was the new action hero of the moment in Hollywood and very, very pretty. I knew exactly why Maia wanted to go see the film, and it had nothing to do with well-sequenced car chases. I rolled my eyes. "Fine."

We decided to walk into Morningside, where there was this wonderful art deco theater we both loved. You could either buy a ticket for an ordinary individual cinema seat, or you could purchase an armchair or sofa. We bought tickets for a leather sofa to share and headed inside.

"I need the loo," Maia announced as I took my seat on the small sofa. "I'll be right back."

"Get some popcorn on your way back." I handed her some money, and she nodded before disappearing out of the theater.

The trailers were finishing up and Maia still hadn't returned. Sometimes the lines for refreshments could be terribly long, but she had been gone for quite some time and I was getting worried.

I'd just bent down to get my phone out of my bag when the leather of the sofa creaked and the whole thing depressed with someone's weight.

Much more weight than the weight carried by a slender fifteen-year-old girl.

I sat up, and the light from the cinema screen lit up Logan's face. His body pressed against mine on the small sofa.

My heart started to pound. "What are you doing here?" I whispered frantically.

His eyes smiled. "Maia decided against the movie."

I was going to kill her. "That little traitor."

Logan shrugged his shoulder against mine. His heat was soaking into me along with his delicious cologne. "She's on my side in this, Grace."

I glowered at him. "Apparently everyone is."

There was a glint of remorse in his eyes. "I'm sorry about the girls today. They are, too. It was overkill."

"And this with Maia? What do you call this?"

"Necessary." The deep, determined rumble of that one word made me shiver. He really needed to stop creating that kind of reaction in me.

I cursed my body. "You're not playing fair."

He gave me a slow, seductive smile. "No. I'm definitely not."

Someone behind us shushed us, and I turned to look at the screen.

The film had started and I hadn't even been aware of it. That was pretty much how the next ninety minutes went.

If anyone asked me about the film, I'd have no clue what to tell them because, other than a make-out scene, I paid little attention to anything but the man beside me.

The force of the attraction between us was never so evident as it was in that dark theater. I had to give Logan his due. He didn't try to seduce me with touch. He let his presence do all the work. My senses were on high alert beside him. My body reacted to the heat of his and my skin felt on fire from the beginning of the movie until the end. His knee pressed against mine out of sheer lack of space, and my whole being was focused on that point of contact. The pressure of the touch expanded, crawling up my leg until it almost felt like his fingers were trailing over my skin. During quiet scenes in the movie, I could hear the soft inhale and exhale of his breath beside me. Sometimes his cologne would linger into my space and activate memories of the night we had passionate sex against my kitchen wall.

That was the worst.

Because I remembered feeling him inside me.

I squeezed my legs together, trying to deny the rush of arousal, but I couldn't.

It only increased when Nick McGuire started making out with his beautiful sidekick and heroine. The film wasn't R-rated, so it cut to another scene, but clothes did come off and we got to watch a gorgeous couple in nice underwear glide against each other before it did.

I saw Logan's hand curl into a fist on his knee, and I had a suspicion I knew what was going through his mind. Was he willing himself not to touch me?

I couldn't breathe.

When the film finished I shot up out of my seat and brushed past people, muttering apologies as I tripped over the belongings they had scattered on the floor at the foot of their seats.

Once outside the theater I gulped in the fresh, cool air of the summer night and turned to stare at Logan as he joined me. I didn't know what to say.

"Let me walk you home."

Since we were both going that way, it seemed childish and petty to deny him.

For a while we walked in silence, the tension crackling between us.

"You could have left," Logan suddenly said.

He was right. At any time I could have stood up and walked out of that theater. "Apparently, I'm a masochist."

He grunted at that. "I'm quite sure that was an insult."

"Logan . . ." I sighed wearily. "Let's not talk."

"I'd prefer not to. Right now I'd prefer to be kissing that fucking sweet mouth of yours."

I flushed and stared at him, wide-eyed. "You can't speak to me like that." I glanced around, making sure there were no bystanders to his flirtation.

"Babe."

"Don't 'babe' me. In fact, quit with the 'babe' thing completely."

"Fine. I'll quit with it if you can tell me you didn't feel that inside the theater. Tell me while I was getting hard just sitting next to you, breathing you in, that you weren't thinking about what it's like to have me inside of you. Tell me you weren't thinking about me fucking you. Because I couldn't stop thinking about it. I want to fuck you and then I want to make love to you . . ." He drew closer to me as I kept walking, trying to walk away from the words that were making my heart rate speed out of control. "And I want to repeat it over and over for the rest of our lives."

My breath stuttered, but I kept walking.

Until suddenly I wasn't.

I blinked at the abrupt movement as I was jerked sideways down the alley between two boutiques. Logan loomed over me, pressing me against the cold, shaded brick wall. "Tell me."

My lips parted to deny him, but I couldn't.

He kissed me, crushing my mouth beneath his in an angry, desperate kiss that curled my toes in my shoes. I hated that the scratch of the bristle of his short beard sent goose bumps of arousal up all over my body. I hated that my breasts swelled with need, pushing up into his chest, pleading despite everything for his touch. I hated that my skin flushed and I tingled between my thighs.

I hated that I kissed him back just as desperately.

At the press of his erection against my stomach and the simultaneous brush of his thumb against the side of my breast, the jolt of lust that moved through me had the effect of reminding me of where I was and whom I was doing this with.

I gave Logan a gentle shove, and he immediately let me go.

His chest heaved as he stared down at me, more than a glimmer of triumph in his eyes.

I huffed and pushed past him, darting back out onto the safety of the street.

He caught up with me, and I felt his question without him having to voice it.

"So there's attraction between us," I said quietly, feeling vulnerable and, for some strange reason, lonely. "It doesn't mean a thing."

"Oh, it means something," he disagreed, and I could hear that damned determination in his voice, along with not a small hint of cockiness. "You told me yourself, babe. You don't light up for just anyone . . . and you become a blaze whenever I put my hands on you."

"I really don't like you right now."

Logan grinned. "That's okay. As long as you love me, nothing else matters."

"You are so arrogant," I huffed. "Have you always been this arrogant?"

"Don't confuse arrogance with confidence."

I made a face and stomped ahead, grumbling under my breath at the way his long legs easily caught up with me.

I didn't shake him the whole way back to our building, and as I put my key in the lock of my flat, he pressed his chest into my back, his lips whispering across my ear. "I'm looking forward to repeating the best sex I've ever had."

My breath caught at his confession, my body screaming to give in to him. Instead I turned the key and shoved inside my flat, slamming the door behind me so I didn't have to look him in the eye and show him how much I still wanted him.

CHAPTER 20

"**Y**ou really should think about giving me a key."

I stared balefully at Maia as she stood on my doorstep the next morning. "I don't give keys to traitors."

She grinned sheepishly. "Can you blame me for helping a guy out?"

"Yes. Yes, I can."

Rolling her eyes at me, Maia disregarded my glare and swept past me into my flat. "Do you have any cereal? Dad and I have run out."

"I'm making scrambled eggs if you want some," I grumbled, shutting the door and following in her wake.

She glanced up from the now-open fridge door as I wandered into the kitchen. "Did you say something about eggs?"

"I'm making them. Do you want any?"

"See, you can't stay mad at me for long."

"Oh, I'm still mad—just not mad enough to see you go without breakfast."

"Then that's not really that mad." She shuffled up onto one of my kitchen stools. "You look kind of tired."

I looked a fright. I'd barely gotten any sleep. Again! I'd managed to fall asleep at around five o'clock in the morning out of sheer exhaustion, and then Maia had banged on my door four hours later. "It's Saturday. Shouldn't you be sleeping in, like every other teenager in the country?"

She bit her lip, the cockiness she was picking up from dear old Dad suddenly disappearing. "I couldn't sleep. I was worried about you."

I immediately stopped pretending to be annoyed at her. "Maia, you don't need to worry about me, sweetheart. I can take care of myself."

"But can you?"

I slid onto the stool beside her. "What does that mean?"

As she stared at me with those violet eyes of hers, I realized that they were so similar to her father's and yet so different. There was a tinge of darkness in her eyes, but they hadn't yet grown the hardness that Logan's had. It was a hardness that melted whenever someone made him laugh, and I shook off the disturbing realization that although his laughter was rare, it was less so with me.

Maia sighed wearily, the gesture so much older than her years. "I know you care about Dad. I just don't know why you're making this so hard for him."

"There are things you don't know, Maia." I didn't want to tell her that Logan had hurt me. I didn't want her to ever think badly of him.

"I'm not stupid. I know he's not perfect," she insisted. "If he hurt your feelings, then I know he's sorry."

"Maia, please . . ." I buried my head in my hands, suddenly feeling the urge to cry. "I can't talk about this with you."

There was silence, and for an awful moment I feared I'd hurt her feelings.

"Grace . . ."

At the tightness in her voice, I lifted my head to look at her. The tinge of darkness in her eyes had spread until there was a whole lot of black in among the violet. An unwelcome shiver rippled over me in reaction.

"Do you remember when I first got here and you asked me what I'd been through?"

Mostly Logan and I got Maia the same way every day—funny, sarcastic, and warm. But there were days when she'd brood alone in her room or cry for no good reason at all. I chalked it up to being a teenager and the drastic change of direction her life had taken. I chalked it up to the fact that her mother had abandoned her.

I'd been waiting for Maia to open up about it.

Now I wasn't so sure I could handle the truth.

"I know you're worried about what happened to me when I lived with my mum."

I nodded again, a choking sensation developing in my throat.

Maia stared me straight in the eyes, her own glistening. "It wasn't good, Grace. But it wasn't as bad as you think. Mostly she just wasn't there for me. For ages it didn't matter because she was my mum, and when you're wee, you love your mum no matter what."

I nodded, remembering that unconditional love I felt for my mother when I was a child. Day by day as the years passed my mother had chipped away at that love until I was only clinging to the idea of it.

"She would lock me in my room for hours when she had a guy over." Maia's haunted eyes made me reach for her hand and hold on tight. "I'd have to sit in there listening to them having sex, and then he'd leave and Maryanne would get high or drunk and forget about me. I'd need the toilet or I was hungry and I'd bang on my door, but she was out of it and I'd be stuck in there." Tears slipped down her cheeks, and my own eyes stung in answer to them. "Afterward I wouldn't talk to her because I was hurt, and she'd feel really bad and she'd take me out for lunch and buy me something. She'd sit with me the whole day making me laugh, and I'd start loving her all over again." Maia brushed impatiently at her tears. "But she'd just repeat it."

"Oh, Maia." I squeezed her hand, not knowing what to say because I knew there were no words to soothe this kind of wound.

"She messed around with these really dodgy guys, Grace. They treated her badly. They spoke to her like she was nothing, and sometimes they hit her. For years she protected me from that. That's why she'd lock me in my room, so they either didn't know about me or they couldn't get to me. But I heard it all. Heard her crying out in pain sometimes . . ." She grew silent in reflection.

I stared at her, willing the rising anger inside of me down.

I wanted to punish her mother for doing this to her.

I closed my eyes, more tears falling as I realized Maia would carry this pain for the rest of her life.

She would always, always feel like an unloved, abandoned child whenever she thought of her mother.

"Grace." Maia's grip on my hand tightened, and I opened my eyes. More tears sprang to her eyes when she saw how upset I was, and this little sob burst out between her lips. "Grace."

In answer I got up and pulled her off the stool and into my arms, and I held her while she cried, her tears soaking my bathrobe.

Eventually she pulled away from me and wiped at her cheeks. She looked at the floor, her dark eyelashes glistening. Heaving a shaky sigh, she shook her head. "I didn't tell you to upset you. I was trying to tell you why you should be with Dad."

I touched her chin, gently lifting it so I could see her eyes. "Tell me."

The sudden determination in her gaze reminded me so much of Logan. "I didn't just decide to leave Maryanne. She stopped protecting me. She stopped pretending to love me. That guy . . . the junkie that was in the flat with her."

Fear knotted my stomach. "Yes?"

"That's her boyfriend Dom. He's been her boyfriend for a while now. He . . . He tried to touch me when Maryanne was out of it."

I jerked away, my rage hot in my blood, my skin, my nerves—

"He didn't," Maia hurried to assure me. "I didn't let him. But Maryanne didn't believe me when I told her. That was it for me. I was done pretending that we loved each other. I was done pretending I didn't hate her for what she was doing. I was done pretending I wasn't ashamed of her." Her eyes blazed with her anger and guilt.

We were mirror images.

Still learning to deal with the tangle of emotions and damage created by our parents.

I knew then I would die before this girl ever thought I didn't love her.

"When Maryanne mentioned Logan was my dad, I took the newspaper article. I kept it. The day after she slapped me for telling her Dom tried to touch me, I started looking for Dad. I got on the computer at school and Googled him. There was an article about him and the nightclub. I went there and told some janitor guy I was a family member and someone had passed away and I needed to find Dad. He gave me Dad's address."

I raised an eyebrow at that information. "Did you tell your dad?"

She smirked. "Yeah. I mean, he's glad I found him, but the guy shouldn't be randomly handing his address out. Dad had words with him."

"I imagine he did."

"I didn't know what to expect with Dad. I just hoped it would be better than what I had with my mum. I was scared there, Grace. I was really scared."

"I know," I whispered, hating that she'd gone through that.

"I'm not anymore." She stepped toward me, light suddenly melting away the dark in her eyes. "Dad makes me feel safe. I feel like we've been with each other since the beginning, and I never thought that would happen. It's like a miracle." She gave an embarrassed laugh. "It's sounds really cheesy."

I shook my head. "No, it doesn't."

"You're a huge part of that. You've given me a home too."

I started to cry again.

Big giant watering pot.

"And yeah, I want you and Dad to be together because I want us to be a family. I've never had that. But I really just want you to be happy too. I've seen what's out there, and Dad is one of the good ones and he really cares about you. I don't understand why you won't give him a chance."

I stared at her, feeling her hope pressing heavily upon me. "I would do anything for you, Maia MacLeod, but I can't do that. If things work out between your dad and me, it would have to be because I trusted him. It would fall apart if I did this because on paper it makes sense for us all."

She gave me this smile, this small smile that made me pause. "Grace, how can you learn to trust Dad if you won't give him the chance to win that trust?"

And just like that, with that one sentence, I felt a strange mix of defeat and relief.

Maia packed a small bag that afternoon and Shannon came to collect her. It was embarrassing that they were both in on my decision, and as much as I tried to convince Maia that there was no need for her to give Logan and me privacy because nothing was going to happen, she wouldn't listen. And neither would a very giddy Shannon.

Thus I was left to pace the sitting room in Logan's flat while I waited for him to return from work. The nervous butterflies in my stomach would not stop flapping their wings at one another, and more than a few times I changed direction toward the exit, ready to give up before even trying.

As I paced the room, I took it in and how different it was since the first time I walked in there. There had been unpacked boxes lying around and not a stick of furniture except for the L-shaped leather sofa. And, of course, the television was mounted on the wall opposite it.

Now he'd added the armchair Maia had gushed about to the room. It was this huge black velvet snug chair with a matching footstool. Both Maia and I could fit on it at the same time. Along with the television on the wall there was a silver-framed mirror above the sofa that I'd picked out when helping Logan with Maia's room. On the wall by the door were photographs that Maia had put up. There were two of Logan and Shannon when they were younger, a photo of Shannon with Cole, a selfie of Logan and Maia that Maia had taken on her phone, and another photograph that caused the ache in my chest to throb.

It was a photograph of me with Logan and Maia at the dinner with Jo, Cam, Shannon, and Cole. Shannon had told the three of us to scoot together and she'd taken the photo on her phone.

Now it was hanging up on Logan's wall.

I knew it was Maia's doing, but still . . .

In addition to the photograph, luxurious curtains framing the window gave the room more warmth. They were cream trimmed in navy, and I'd bought matching scatter cushions for the sofa to tie it together. A coffee table sat in the middle of the room, a rug underneath it.

Altogether it was a very different room.

It was a room in a home.

And he'd done it for Maia.

Like always, the thought made me melt more than just a little.

The front door opened and slammed mid-melting.

I tensed.

"Maia?" Logan's deep voice boomed through the flat without him having to even raise it. "You fancy Chinese tonight?"

His footsteps padded toward the sitting room. "Maia?"

He appeared in the doorway and drew to a stop at the sight of me.

I shrugged, giving him a nervous smile and feeling very close to passing out. "She's staying at Shannon's."

Logan raised an inquiring eyebrow as he took a step into the room. "For any reason?"

"To give us some privacy so we can talk."

The corners of his mouth turned up just a fraction. "Is my night looking up, Grace?"

I rolled my eyes at the wicked rumble in his words. "Not in that way. I said *talk*, Logan."

He gestured to the armchair as he sat down on the sofa. "Then let's talk."

222 · SAMANTHA YOUNG

"You're sure you're not too tired from work?" I said, hoping to stall.

Logan knew exactly what I was up to and he shook his head, mirth in his expression. "I'm perfectly *energized*."

I narrowed my eyes at the innuendo. "I'm so glad I'm getting to see this side of you."

"Oh, you haven't seen anything yet, babe."

"You're filthy."

He leaned forward, practically stripping me naked with his gaze. "You haven't seen anything yet, babe," he repeated slowly.

I shivered and squeezed my legs together. "Can we be serious?"

"I am being serious."

"Logan."

"Grace."

I huffed and stood up. "I'm trying to tell you something here."

"Then tell me."

Crossing my arms over my chest, I glowered down at him. "Now I'm not so sure."

He stared up at me, all flirtation and teasing out of his expression now. "Tell me."

I sucked in a huge breath and shakily released it. Locking eyes with him, I hoped I could say what I had to say without any misunderstanding between us. "I talked to Maia today."

"Is she okay?"

I smiled at his immediate concern. "She's fine. She's very persuasive."

Hope brightened his eyes. "Do I need to increase her allowance?"

I laughed lightly and looked at my feet. "Maybe."

"Grace?"

When I looked into his face again, I shivered at the utter longing I found there. I knew if I wasn't careful I could find that kind of attention addictive. "I still don't trust you completely."

He nodded carefully, tentatively, as though he didn't want to scare me away.

"But Maia pointed out I'd never learn to trust you fully if I don't give you a chance to earn it."

"That is one smart kid."

I smiled. "Yeah. She is. And I don't want her to get hurt in this, so I need you to really think about this, Logan. Put aside the fact that I happened to be the person who was here for you when this huge change happened in your life, and put aside my closeness with Maia. I need you to really think about me, just me, and if I'm really the woman that you want." I felt naked saying those words, so naked and vulnerable. "Will you do that?"

"I haven't confused the situation," he said. "Why would you think that I had?"

"Look at me." I huffed in frustration. "I was there, Logan. I saw all the women who came and went from your flat. They were my opposite in every way."

He shot to his feet, and I stumbled back at the sudden movement. "Aye, do you know why? I didn't want serious, Grace, so I slept with women I knew I couldn't see myself getting serious with. I didn't want the complication." He took a step toward me, and I forced myself to remain still. "You want the truth? There have been a few women over the last eighteen months who I sparked with . . . that spark of potential. I walked away. I didn't take their number and I certainly didn't sleep with them. Because I didn't want serious. I didn't want reality. I just wanted oblivion."

Seeing the pain in his eyes made me move toward him. "Logan . . ."

"But you"—he shook his head—"I can't walk away from you even if I wanted to. And I don't want to. You are reality and sweet oblivion wrapped up in one annoyingly argumentative, always-bloody-right, classy, gorgeous-as-fuck package."

I held my breath at his beautiful words.

"Does that answer your question, your doubts?"

I nodded slowly.

"So are we doing this?" He started to prowl toward me.

I panicked a little and backed up. "I'm going to try, but we're taking it slow and we need to—ahh!" I cried out as I suddenly found myself hefted up over Logan's shoulder. "What are you doing?" I yelled at his back as my hair swung against his delicious bottom.

"That was reality. It's time for oblivion, babe."

"No sex! We have to talk!"

He stroked his hand over my bottom. "I want inside you."

Suddenly I found myself falling through air. I landed with a soft *thump* on Logan's mattress and stared up at him in a panting, disheveled, and very aroused state.

"And you want me inside you." He unbuckled his belt slowly, the blaze in his eyes turning me into a hot, flustered puddle on his bed.

"You are so very cocky," I whispered.

"Take your top off," he demanded, *cockily*.

I crossed my arms over my chest and glared up at him. "No."

He grinned. "Take your top off, babe."

"I don't take orders."

"In bed you will."

My eyes widened, my heart thumping hard in my chest. "Are you into that kind of thing? Whips and dominance kind of thing?"

"Whips? No. Tying you to a bed and knowing you trust me enough to be tied up while I do whatever I want to your body? Yes. Canes? No. Spanking you? Yes. St. Andrew's crosses? No, a little too dramatic for my taste. Playing out sexual fantasies? Yes. Fucking you in every sexual position known to man, yes, yes, and yes."

I gaped up at him. "You may want to ease me into this very sexual frankness you have going on. I'm not used to it."

"You like it, or you would have walked out of my flat ages ago." He unbuttoned his shirt and threw it aside, revealing his sculpted chest and strong arms. "Now take off your top before I rip it off."

I didn't even dare to question that his threat was real. Logan Mac-Leod was Mr. Alpha in the bedroom, apparently. Although I'd enjoyed a good alpha in the fantasy of romantic books, I'd always thought I'd hate it in real life. But I was finding there was a balance. Logan wasn't nearly so alpha outside his bedroom, but inside . . . Turned out that an alpha in the bedroom wasn't nearly so scary as I'd thought. In fact, I found it really rather hot.

I grabbed the hem of my sweater and pulled it up over my head, throwing it behind me as I lay back down on the bed. In answer, Logan put his knees on the bed at either side of my hips, straddling me so he could skim his hands up my waist to cup my breasts over my bra.

I arched my back, pushing them into his hands. Logan kissed me, deep and hard, as he deftly unclipped my bra at the back. My hands traced every inch of his chest while we kissed, reluctantly letting go when he gently pushed me back on the bed and slipped my bra straps down my arms. His gaze drifted from my face to my naked breasts and the heat in them made my breasts swell, my nipples tightening. I wasn't big chested like the women who had come before me, but under his heated gaze I no longer felt insecure about it.

I could see it written all over his face: Logan liked me just the way I was.

I felt that flutter in my lower belly and knew that if he slipped his hand between my legs he'd find me wet and ready for him.

He touched me, cupping my breasts again, squeezing them gently, thumbs rubbing over my nipples as he deliberately stirred my arousal instead of shaking it. He was intent on teasing me and I was intent on letting him. His breathing grew heavier and I could feel the hard press of him through his jeans. Amusement sparkled within me as I realized he might break before me.

Logan saw the look and his gaze darkened with tenderness and determination. I sighed at the gentle brush of his lips against first my right breast and then my left. He tormented me with whispered touches, trying to force me to beg, but despite my nails digging harder into the muscle in his shoulders, I held strong until my whimpers of need broke his will. He finally closed his mouth around my nipple, flicking his tongue over it, before sucking hard.

A larger ripple moved through my belly, and I cried out softly, throwing my head back against the bed.

Logan lavished attention on both nipples until they were swollen, until I was desperate for him. I cried out now, begging him, and he pulled back, easing off the bed to stand over me like some pagan sex god. The dark hunger in his eyes was my undoing.

"Are you wet for me yet?"

My lips parted at the shockingly stripped sexual question, and I felt my cheeks flush.

Logan's eyes narrowed. "Tell me you're wet for me, Grace."

The demand only made me more so. "I'm wet for you," I whispered.

The muscle in his jaw clenched with determination as Logan leaned over to unzip my trousers. He hooked his fingers into the waistband of them and my underwear and he tugged. I lifted my lower body, and he removed them with quick ease. Once he'd divested me of them, gently caressing my calves and outer thighs, he lowered my legs and opened them as he glided his hands up my inner thighs. He put a knee to the bed and moved up my body so he could slip two thick fingers slowly inside my channel. My knees fell open and I gasped at the sensation. He pulled them almost all the way out, and I tilted my hips to meet them as he slid them back into me.

"Logan," I groaned, undulating against his touch. "Oh God, I need you."

His fingers disappeared, and I snapped my eyes open to watch him. He got off the bed, his jaw taut with dwindling control, and pulled a condom out of his jeans pocket before removing them and his boxers. I watched, every inch of me on fire, my inner thighs trembling, my breathing harried, as he rolled the condom up his huge straining cock.

My legs fell open automatically as Logan lowered himself over my body, nudging against my center as his hard torso brushed against my breasts. He kissed me gently, trailing his fingertips up my outer thigh in a way that caused me more shivers and hot impatience.

My hips jerked at the touch of his thumb on my clit, and he growled possessively from the back of his throat. And then he was kissing me, a series of wet and drugging kisses as he played with my clit. I touched him, too, caressing his shoulders, his back, his abs, strumming at his nipples in a way that made him shudder and press harder on my clit.

When he slipped two fingers inside me again, I broke the kiss, moaning as my back arched into his caress.

"You are so fucking sexy." He peppered kisses along my jaw as he thrust his fingers in and out. "The things I'm going to do to you, babe. I'm going to make you mine, every single piece of you." Our eyes locked, his filled with sexual promise. "No holds barred, Grace. Not with me. I'm going to fuck you like there's no tomorrow, and you're going to let me."

My belly squeezed and my inner muscles clamped around his fingers. Logan's eyes darkened and he pressed them deeper inside me. His voice lowered and he leaned down to brush his mouth softly over mine. "But right now I'm going to make love to you."

Tears sprang to my eyes at the vow in his voice. A vow for so much more than great sex. I wrapped my arms around his back, sliding my hands over his smooth, hot skin. "Come inside me, Logan." I whispered the invitation, and there was so much more in it that I meant to give. Logan heard it, and triumph gleamed in his eyes.

His fingers slipped out of me, and his hands circled my wrists. He raised my arms above my head and tightened his hold on me. Looking deeply into my eyes, he moved. I felt him hot and hard against my center, and then suddenly there was pressure as he pushed inside, eased by my slickness. He surged deep in me, his hands moving up from my wrists so his fingers could tangle through mine. Like this, he held me as he gently rocked inside me, taunting me toward climax and then yanking me back.

"Faster," I pleaded.

A smile tugged at Logan's lips. "We're making love, Grace."

"We can make love"—I panted—"a little faster."

I raised my hips to punctuate my point, and Logan slammed back into me. I cried out at the deliciously growing pressure building inside of me. His teeth gritted, his muscles straining as his thrusts came harder, but he maintained an excruciatingly slow pace. He let go of my wrists to cup my arse, tilting me higher so he could slide in deeper. My hands gripped tight to his hips in response.

Our eyes stayed connected the whole time, the power of the intimacy between us overwhelming in its intensity.

The feeling inside me was building upward in a spiral, coiling tighter and tighter until my whole body tensed over a cliff edge. His fingers dug into my arse, his hips jerking harder and faster against mine as we neared what we were desperately reaching for.

One more push. "Logan," I pleaded.

Another.

"Ohhh—" The tension inside of me exploded, an orgasm unlike any I'd ever had before flowing through me.

My lower body shuddered against Logan's, and I watched as he stiffened, his neck arched, his teeth gritted, and his eyes flared with fierce pleasure as his own climax moved through him. He jerked against me, his hold on me almost painful as he came.

Logan's chest heaved as he tried to catch his breath. Those extraordinary eyes of his washing over my face as I lay there, my muscles warm and languid from the most amazing orgasm of my life.

"Trust me yet?" he said between pants.

I smiled at his sneakiness. "Don't ask me serious questions when I'm on a post-orgasm high, Logan MacLeod."

He grinned and settled over me, cupping my face with his hands. His lips brushed over mine softly, my mouth tingling at the gentle touch. "How many orgasms do you think it will take to get you to trust me?"

I giggled. "Hmm . . . I don't know if orgasms are the way to go regarding trust. Addiction . . . yes."

"Addiction?" He raised an eyebrow, looking far too pleased with himself. "First addiction, then trust?"

I opened my mouth to argue the complete lack of sense in that and then I frowned. "Why am I arguing about this?" I threw my arms out wide and let my legs fall farther open. "Ply me with orgasms if you think it will do the trick."

His whole body shook against mine with his laughter.

CHAPTER 21

Two orgasms later I lay on Logan's sofa, freshly showered (the location of the last orgasm) and eating the Chinese food he'd ordered.

He was sprawled out on the other end of the sofa, our legs tangling in the middle.

Logan was looking more than a little satisfied, I thought rather smugly, as he ate a huge mouthful of fried rice.

"Food good?" I said, a teasing smile on my lips.

Amusement sparked in his gaze. "Someone worked me hard. I'm starving."

"I don't recall being the demanding one."

He raised an eyebrow. " 'Faster, Logan, faster.' "

I blushed and kicked at him, causing him to laugh, unrepentant.

"You're a swine." I huffed, my cheeks still on fire.

"I'm not complaining, babe," he said, still chuckling.

I eyed him, unable to deny the warmth spreading across my chest. I'd never seen him like this, so relaxed and content. *Is it me?* I really wanted to believe I had the power to affect his moods as much as he did mine.

His smile disappeared. "What are you thinking about so hard?"

I covered my real thoughts with a lie. "How I gave in way too easily."

Laughter danced in his gaze again. "It was pretty fast. Your heart really wasn't in the fight."

I rolled my eyes. "You know I avoid drama, and battling you was just drama I couldn't be bothered with. It was easier to give in and try it out than it was to fight you off."

"You make me sound so appealing."

It was my turn to grin. "You're all right."

"Just all right?" He lowered his plate to give me the full blast of his sensual focus. "Do I have to remind you already about the three orgasms?"

"You're counting my orgasms? Really, Logan." I snorted.

"Pretend all you want. We both know I blew your fucking mind."

I giggled. "You have quite the ego, sweetheart. It wouldn't be good for me to stroke it too often."

He flicked me a wary look. "I hope we're just talking about my ego and not other parts of me."

I frowned, teasing him. "I didn't know there were any other parts worth stroking."

"One huge fucking part that was inside you not too long ago."

He made my cheeks flare hot again, but I was getting used to his frankness. "Oh, that part," I murmured, my voice a little husky with the memory. "Hmm, I do rather enjoying stroking that part."

Logan's eyes warmed with delight at my flirting, and I couldn't stem my own pleased smile.

Oh, this was not good—that overwhelming feeling of contentment I felt whenever I made him happy.

I felt a momentary stir of panic.

As if he sensed it, Logan wrapped a hand around my ankle and squeezed. "This is going to be great, Grace. It's going to be better than great."

I nodded slowly, letting his touch soothe the tension that had crept so quickly over me.

232 · SAMANTHA YOUNG

We were silent a moment as his thumb brushed over my skin. When he finally felt like I'd come back from my fear, he let go to continue eating.

"So Maia is at Shannon's?" he said.

I thought about the two little matchmakers. "Yes. You did a wonderful job inviting all the women in your life to play matchmaker."

He grunted. "Believe me, it didn't take much. Apparently, they've had their eye on you for me since Shannon told them that was what *she* wanted." He cut me a dry look.

I laughed. "I bet it just sticks in your craw that you're giving her exactly what she wants."

Logan shook his head. "Honestly, not really. I couldn't be happier that Shannon likes you so much. She's my only real family now. I want you two to get on well."

At the mention of his family, I felt a burn in my blood. "Your parents still haven't come around to the idea of Maia?"

"It's worse than that." His eyes flew over to the wall with the photographs on them. "My parents take their good old time coming around about things. It took them ages to come around to the fact that Shannon wasn't making a mistake by getting engaged to Cole. It took them ages to come around to even forgiving her for my prison time when it wasn't even her damn fault. And it has taken them all this time to come around to the fact that it isn't my fault or Maia's that she wasn't a part of my life until now." Anger tightened his expression. "They want to meet her."

"What do you want?"

"I want to tell them to fuck off." His plate clattered onto the coffee table, appetite clearly destroyed by the topic. "They've never been the best parents, and they've pissed me off a million times with their treatment of Shannon . . . and they've done it again. To my kid. A kid who has been through a fucking war . . . a kid whose feelings you can't play with because her feelings have already been crushed to hell by her own mother. They knew this. I told them this and still they held out on her as grandparents. Now because they're ready they think they can just waltz into her life?"

I sat up, putting my own plate down so I could scoot closer to him. I rested my hand on his thigh, drawing his gaze. Our eyes locked, and like always, my whole body zinged pleasantly in reaction to our connection. "I understand you're pissed off at them, and honestly, I am too. I don't want them in Maia's life. But that's not my decision, and it may be yours . . . However, you have a very smart girl on your hands, and she's already lost out on so much. Perhaps you should give her the choice. Be honest with her about them, about their attitude and about the possibility that they could hurt her . . . and then let her decide for herself."

He stared at me a moment before leaning in to brush his mouth over mine. My lips tingled as they parted under the sweet kiss. When he pulled back, he cupped my face and brushed his thumb against my lower lip. "I can't imagine my life without you in it."

My breathing stuttered at the confession, and I felt that happiness swamp me again.

Just as quickly the panic set in.

Logan was filling my head and my heart and my body with him.

What happened if he walked away again?

Suddenly I was jerked toward him, my hands fluttering against his chest to catch myself. I stared, wide-eyed, into his face, which was now but inches from mine. "I'm not going anywhere," he promised, his voice gruff. "I'm going to do whatever it takes to make you trust me so I never have to see that fear in your eyes ever again."

I closed my eyes at his sweet promise and leaned my forehead against his jaw. "I'll try too. It's just going to take time."

"I've got all the time in the world, Grace. All the time in the world for you."

The sun felt wonderful on my skin. The waves were crashing to shore. I had no worries, no responsibilities, just never-ending white sands.

Life was perfectly, gloriously cliché in its utter heavenliness.

"*Grace.*"

I squeezed my eyes shut tighter against the sound of the masculine voice in my ear.

"*Grace.*" *The voice became more insistent.* "*Grace, wake up.*"

Suddenly my sun lounger was flipped on its side and I awoke with a jolt. Breathing hard, I blinked against the darkness of my bedroom, and as my eyes adjusted to the light, my heart only started to hammer harder against my chest. Logan was sitting on my bed.

"What?" I whispered in worry, leaning over to switch my bedside light on. Logan was sitting on my bed wearing nothing but a pair of faded old jeans. I forced my gaze to his face. "What's wrong? Has something happened?"

His violet eyes were hot on me, his silent presence potent.

My breath caught.

My lower stomach clenched against the burst of tingles between my legs.

"Logan?"

He placed a hand slowly on either side of my hips and leaned forward until his face was so close to mine our lips were almost touching. A fierce hunger flashed across his face, and I gasped, feeling arousal shoot through my body.

He wanted me.

Suddenly he grasped me by the nape of the neck and hauled me against him. His mouth captured mine. I instantly melted into him and wrapped my arms around him, my fingers pressing into the muscle beneath his hot skin.

His kiss was hard, demanding, almost punishing, and I reveled in it. Logan groaned, the reverberations causing my nipples to tighten in reaction, and I shuddered. My reaction ignited something inside of him, and he shoved me roughly onto my back before hauling the covers off me. I stared up at him in aroused astonishment as he tugged on my pajama shorts. He slid them deftly down my legs along with my underwear and then he was braced over me, nudging my thighs apart as he stared down into my eyes. Logan's hands encircled my wrists and he pinned my

arms above my head as he pressed his jeans-covered erection between my legs.
"Grace," he whispered hoarsely, the word filled with need.

"Logan," I pleaded.

His right hand left my wrist to draw down his zipper. He shoved his jeans
low enough to release his erection and then returned his hand to my wrist to pin me
to the bed.

Suddenly I wasn't underneath him. I was across the room, watching him
glide his body into a woman. Was it me? Was I having an out-of-body experience?

The headboard rattled against the wall as Logan fucked me toward climax.

"Logan, oh God!" a woman I recognized cried out, and I tensed.

It wasn't me he was with.

I felt sick. Terrified.

No!

"No!" I cried out, my head jerking up from my pillow.

My eyes adjusted to the dark.

It was a nightmare.

Just a nightmare.

"Grace." The mattress shifted beneath me, and light suddenly poured
into the room. A second later Logan was braced over me, his concerned
gaze on my face.

I immediately burst into tears.

"Jesus," he muttered as he pulled me up into a sitting position so he
could wrap his arms around me. "What's this?" he asked, tucking my
head under his chin.

I shook my head, trying to control the tears. I didn't want to tell him.
The whole nightmare screamed of my insecurities, and I still wasn't sure
enough of our relationship to know that it wouldn't send him running for
the door.

"Hey," he said, his voice low and soothing but also firm. "I talked to
you about my nightmare. I trusted you. Trust me, Grace. Please. I can't

stand to see you cry." His arms tightened around me, and he whispered hoarsely, "I don't want to lose you."

I turned my face from where it was pressed against his chest so I could speak. "It will freak you out."

"You didn't run from me, and what I had to say wasn't easy."

When he put it like that, there was actually really no comparison between what bothered us in our dreams. Mine was a distasteful, hurtful family drama. His had been death and guilt.

I suddenly felt very small and foolish. "Now you're really going to think I'm an idiot."

"Just tell me."

I sucked in a huge breath, my stomach fluttering with butterflies. "I had this dream about you before anything happened between us. Before we were even friends."

"Okay."

My cheeks flushed. "It was a sex dream."

"Really?" He sounded extremely pleased with himself.

"If you must know, it disturbed the hell out of me at the time." I sniffed haughtily.

He grunted. "I'm sure it did. I'm surprised you could look me in the eye afterward."

"It wasn't easy."

I felt him shake with laughter. "Okay . . . so tonight's dream?"

I tensed again, and he felt it, his arms tightening around me. "It was the same dream to begin with . . . but just as you're about to . . ."

"About to?"

"Come inside me," I muttered, still not quite sexually forthright enough to say the words without a little bit of modest embarrassment. "Suddenly I was across the room, watching on. I thought at first I was having some sort of out-of-body experience, but then the woman cried out and . . . I saw who it was."

Logan was tense now. "Who was it?"

I shook my head, feeling sick all over again with the memory. "My mother."

"Jesus Christ," Logan bit out immediately.

I pulled away from him so I could look him in the eyes. "I know you wouldn't betray me like that. That's not why I'm crying."

He cupped my face in his hands, his eyes dark with worry. "Why *are* you crying?"

"Because I finally feel like there is a chance I could be really happy . . . and I thought I had let go of them long ago, but these past few months . . ." The tears spilled down my cheeks. "She has cancer, Logan. She hasn't asked for me. My father hasn't. And it was his pattern, you know . . . Whenever she hurt me, I'd do something rebellious. I'd decide I was dropping out of high school and he'd suddenly fly home from a business trip to tell me how proud he'd be if I graduated top of the class. And it worked. He manipulated me. Made me believe that he actually cared. And then she'd hurt me again and I decided I wasn't going to a top university. Community college would do me. Dad would come home, give me presents, sweet-talk me, and suddenly I was going to Oxford. Then she hurt me again and I changed my mind and accepted University of Edinburgh. Dad didn't mind too much since it was still a good school, but he came back to try to change my mind.

"When she slept with my boyfriend, Dad tried to manipulate me then too. But I was too hurt and disgusted by them this time. It didn't work. I left. And he gave up." I stared up at Logan, pleading with him. "How could he do that? He just gave up. He never came for me. He has never sought me out. And now my mother has cancer and they just . . . they don't want me there."

"Do you want to be there?"

"I want them to want me to be there," I admitted, ashamed they still had that hold over me. "I thought I was over it, Logan. I'm so mad at them and mad at myself. I'm not a child anymore. I shouldn't feel like this."

"It doesn't matter what age you are. Parents have more power over us than anyone." He drew me closer. "They don't deserve you, Grace." He pressed a soft, comforting kiss to my lips. "Perhaps you should talk to someone again?"

I stared up at this beautiful, caring man and gave him a small, watery smile. "I'm talking to you." I mirrored his words to me from not that long ago.

"And you always can." The words were heavy and deep with promise.

CHAPTER 22

Six pairs of pretty eyes stared at me, together conveying a mixture of curiosity, teasing, delight, and expectation. Chloe, Shannon, Joss, Jo, Hannah, Ellie, and Olivia sat in a semicircle in my sitting room.

It was two days after my decision to give Logan a chance, and I'd called them all for a reason. Probably not the reason they were hoping for.

I wasn't much of a gossip.

"Thank you all for coming, guys. I've asked you here—"

"To thank us for pushing you to give in to Logan? You're welcome." Shannon grinned.

I smiled serenely. "Oh, no. You're here despite that."

Joss snorted. "Gotcha."

"This is actually about Maia's sixteenth birthday. Logan feels it would be better if I organize it—"

"And of course you said yes because you *looovve* him," Chloe interrupted.

The girls tittered at her immaturity.

I rolled my eyes. "Anyway, I was wondering if you ladies would like to help me organize a sweet sixteen birthday party."

"Of course!" Shannon nodded enthusiastically, and the other girls smiled and added their own agreements.

"Okay, so I think we're all on board with helping you organize the best sweet sixteen any girl has ever had, but first please give us some details about you and Logan," Olivia said.

Shannon made a face. "Not too much detail. He's still my brother, and I can guess what put that look of pleased satisfaction on his face. I don't need the details."

Looking around at their inquiring faces, I gave a long-suffering sigh. "Fine. I have agreed to give a relationship with Logan a chance so he can earn back my trust. It's been two days so far, and we're still working on it."

"And the sex?" Chloe persisted. "Is it as good as the first time? He looks like he would make it good every time."

Shannon made a gagging noise.

"He's not good at it." I shook my head, watching their faces fall. "He's fantastic at it, and that's all you need to know on the matter."

"Frankly, that was too much for some of us," Shannon muttered.

Chloe raised an eyebrow, apparently unimpressed. "And not enough for others."

"Best you've ever had, huh?" Joss said, a knowing, almost sympathetic glint in her eye. "You're so fucked."

"Literally," Ellie agreed.

The girls laughed while I tried to quell the rising panic inside of me.

"Let's change the subject before I have to tell my brother we're the reason Grace is backing out of a relationship with him." Shannon pushed my cup of tea closer to me. "Take a calming sip, and let's get on with planning Maia a birthday party."

I did as Shannon suggested and focused. "It's the summer holidays now and I don't know who Maia's real friends are after the whole drama she had with the history teacher, so it will be difficult to invite school friends to the party. Honestly, though, I was thinking Maia might be happier this year with just a family affair. I know sixteen is a big birthday, but it has been a difficult year and I think low-key would work best."

"Agreed," Shannon said. "When it's her eighteenth, she can invite whoever she wants."

"Exactly." I flipped open the notebook in front of me. "So, if you're all up for it, I thought Maia would like it if you all were there with your kids. She's never had a big family party before, and I think she'd love it."

"We're definitely up for that," Jo said, her eyes bright with kindness. "We'll be there."

"Hyper kids and all," Olivia added.

Hannah grunted. "Just remember you asked for it."

"You know Braden would probably let us host it on the bottom level of Fire," Ellie said.

"Or there's D'Alessandro's," Hannah offered. "It's Marco's uncle's restaurant. He'd give us the back room for a private function and he'd even cater it."

"Yeah?" I said, pleased. "Maia loves the food there. That would be perfect."

"I'll get Marco to call him tonight. When is it?"

I gave her the date, two weeks from now. "What about decorations? Maia's not a girlie girl, but I would like to make an effort."

"Metallics," Joss suggested. "As a non–girlie girl myself, you can't go wrong with silvers and golds and bronzes for decoration."

"Okay." I nodded, scribbling that down.

"But make sure it's sweet sixteenth stuff," Shannon said.

"Right. What about music?"

"Deejay?" Olivia suggested.

I mused over it. "Do you think we could get him to play alternative rock?"

"Forget a deejay." Chloe waved the idea off. "We'll get an iDock and some speakers and plug an iPhone with all her favorite stuff on it into it."

That was the music sorted, then.

"Is that it, then?" I stared at the list I'd made.

"Ooh, why don't we put up a projector screen?" Ellie said. "Right across the back wall. At first we can just use it for slides of photos of Maia with us. We'll take sneaky shots over the next few weeks when we're with her, and then afterward we can stick on a film for the kids. We could rent a really big one for the back wall. Make a statement."

We all liked that, so I wrote down "Rent projector."

As we sat talking and throwing out more ideas, laughing and getting sidetracked, I relaxed completely as I realized these women were genuinely invested in making sure Maia had the best birthday ever.

We were in the middle of discussing whether it would be too much to hire some kind of entertainment act when Logan came striding into my sitting room.

"Hello, ladies," he said, and brushed his hand over Shannon's shoulder as he passed her.

"Where's Maia?" I said. He was supposed to be with her, distracting her.

Logan leaned down and kissed me softly on the lips before settling on the arm of my chair. "I dropped her off at the tattoo parlor. Apparently, Cole said she could spend the day learning about the world of tattoo artistry."

"Oh, yeah. I forgot about that," Shannon said.

I wrinkled my nose. "Should she be spending the day in a tattoo studio?"

"Why not?" Hannah shrugged. "They're only smoking crack and tattooing babies."

I made a face. "I see sarcasm runs in this family."

Shannon chuckled. "She'll be fine, Grace. She's with Cole. There's no one more responsible. I promise."

Logan rubbed my shoulder. "You think I would have left her there otherwise?"

"No, of course not," I assured him. "I'm just a little frazzled. There's a lot going on."

"How are the plans coming along?"

I dove into explaining what we'd come up with so far.

His eyes brightened as the girls jumped in with all their ideas.

"Sounds perfect," he said once we'd finished. He peered down at the note-book and the guest list I'd written out. He frowned. "Be sure to add my mum, dad, and Amanda."

"What?" Shannon snapped immediately.

Logan shot her a warning look. "I'm not happy about it either, but Maia wants to meet them and they want to meet her."

"Oh, *now* they want to meet her. So! It's not up to them."

"No. It's up to Maia. I gave her the choice."

"And whose bright idea was that?"

I winced. "Uh . . . well . . . that would be mine."

Shannon sighed heavily. "Grace, I know you mean well, but you don't understand what our parents are like."

"I can guess. And I'm worried about Maia meeting them, too, but she is old enough to make this decision herself."

"I explained it to her," Logan said. "I told her exactly what they're like so she knows what's she getting into. She still wants to meet them, and we're going to let her."

His sister shook her head and lowered her gaze. "It's a mistake."

An awkward, tension-filled silence enveloped the entire room, and the girls looked at one another, wondering what to do. Jo watched Shannon in concern and reached for her hand and squeezed it. "I think we're done here for today. Come on, Shannon. We'll go look for Maia's birthday presents."

Shannon nodded and started to get up.

The others did, too, the mood completely ruined.

I glanced up at Logan, who was watching his sister. Feeling my gaze, he looked down at me. "I'll be right back," he muttered.

Logan led his sister and the others out of the room, each of them throwing me smiles and waves. I waited anxiously for Logan to return, worried about Shannon and worried about Maia meeting his parents. His sister's negative reaction was just too strong to not warrant concern.

A few minutes passed and I decided to clear up the cups of tea and biscuit plates while I waited. I was in the kitchen, organizing cups into the dishwasher and china ones into the sink to hand wash them, when I heard his footsteps.

At the press of his body against my back, I melted into him.

Logan wrapped his arms around me and rested his chin on my shoulder. "Is she okay?"

"She will be." He turned his head and pressed a kiss to my neck. "We'll talk about it later." His lips moved up to my ear. "Right now we're going to forget everything else but each other."

My skin flushed at the recognizable rumble in his voice. "Now?"

"Now." His hands coasted down to my hips, and he deliberately ground his erection against my backside. "We've had to be quiet the last few times with Maia in the flat. Now we're all alone . . . and I want you to be very, very loud."

"Loud?" I breathed.

"Loud." His hand slipped down and he tugged on the hem of my summer dress. "I like this. Ease of access."

I giggled, the sound cut off when his hand slipped under my dress and into my underwear. I gasped as he brushed his fingers over me before moving them down and then sliding two of them inside of me. He played me like that until I was panting and whispering his name.

"I want you louder than that," he said, his own breathing coming fast with his increasing arousal.

He removed his fingers and then curled them around the fabric of my underwear and pulled them down. They fell to the floor, and I stepped out of them. "My room?" I said.

"Here. Add to the memories." His words, the heat of him at my back, the sound of the zipper on his jeans sliding down, sent a bolt of pure lust through me, and my fingers curled into the kitchen counter in front of me with anticipation.

"Spread your legs, babe."

My gosh.

I whimpered and did as he demanded.

He put his hands on my outer thighs and skimmed his fingertips upward, over my skin, eliciting goose bumps and delicious shivers all over me. He caressed my hips before turning his attention to my bum. His touch was delicate as he smoothed his hands over my cheeks. "I love this arse."

I jerked in shock at the gentle touch where I'd never been touched before.

Logan pressed a kiss to my jaw. "One day," he said, his voice dark with promise.

The thought filled me with equal parts trepidation and excitement.

He felt the shudder of thrill that went through me at the thought and he groaned. I felt the heat of his hard cock brushing across my arse, teasing me, tormenting me, as his hands slid out from under my dress to pluck at the buttons down my chest. His fingers were fumbling as his arousal grew.

"Logan," I begged, as cool air drifted over my chest.

His hands slid under my bra, his fingers and thumbs pinching my nipples. I cried out at the sharp streak of lust that spiked toward my center.

"Please." I wanted him inside me. I wished he'd stop teasing. "I need you."

The words were Logan's undoing. He slammed inside of me, and I keened at the deep invasion, my back bowing with the overwhelming sensation of being filled to full. He slid out a couple of inches and thrust back inside, and I found myself gripping tighter to the counter to steady myself against the force. The kitchen filled with the sound of our heavy breathing, our groans and grunts, the wet slap of flesh as he fucked me, but it wasn't enough for him. His fingers dug into my hips as he pounded into me from behind, groaning as I pushed back into him in perfect, but rough, rhythm. My panting got louder as he continued to knead my breasts and pinch my nipples.

"Louder, Grace," he grunted, reminding me I could be.

I let all the "Oh Gods" and whimpers and cries that I'd been holding in out as he played my body toward climax.

"Logan!" I screamed, an orgasm to beat all others exploding through me, my inner muscles squeezing and pulsing around his cock as he continued to ride me to his own climax.

He came with a deep groan, his mouth on my shoulder, his hands gripping my hips even tighter to his as he rocked up into me, shuddering as he came.

My limbs were no longer working. The only thing holding me up was the kitchen counter and the man inside of me.

"Loud enough for you?" I panted, feeling completely spent.

I felt his grin against my skin, and then he touched my chin, turning my head so I could meet his gaze over my shoulder. There was a ferocious hunger there I knew all too well. "Not nearly. And we've got all afternoon to blow the roof off this place."

I shivered at the thought. "You're insatiable."

He nodded and pressed his nose against mine. "I can't get enough of you."

"You're blaming me," I teased. "You're just randy."

Logan's body shook with amusement, the movement causing lovely sensations of friction inside of me. "I wasn't like this until you."

I snorted. "I don't believe that."

His expression grew serious. "Believe it."

An excited shiver rippled over me. I was stunned that I made him feel that way. Not knowing how to react, I turned my head to avoid his gaze. His hands now rested on the counter in front of me, barricading me against him and it. My eyes traveled over them and caught on the tattoo on his right forearm. I circled my fingertips over it. "You never said what it means."

He rested his chin on my shoulder. "Cole gave me it. I asked him for a tattoo and he asked me to trust him enough to choose one for me." He sighed heavily. "It's the Celtic symbol for justice."

A smile pulled at my lips. "He believes you did the right thing by Shannon."

"He would." Logan huffed. "Of course he would."

"He wants you to be at peace with it." I kissed my fingertips and pressed them to the tattoo. "I knew I liked him."

"I was pissed at him when he did it."

"And now?"

"I'm trying to make it fit me."

I turned my head slightly to lock gazes with him. "You don't need to try. It already fits."

His reply was the sweetest kiss anyone had ever given me.

CHAPTER 23

"So I've joined the summer program at the library and the summer program at Meadowbank Swim Center," Maia announced.

It was the day after planning Maia's sweet sixteenth with the girls and things felt like they were moving very fast. I felt like I was trying to swim out of this crashing, joyous wave, while Logan and Maia were content to keep me there . . . seeing as they were the wave. Apparently, after all my protestations, there would be no taking things slowly for my sake or Maia's. Maia didn't want to go slowly, and Logan certainly didn't.

Already the pair of them were in my kitchen eating the pasta I'd put in front of them. It was as if we'd traveled back in time to a few weeks ago, only now, every time I looked over at Logan, he stared back at me with undisguised heat in his eyes.

I swear I'd blushed more around that man in the last seventy-two hours than I had in the many combined embarrassing moments of my childhood.

"Swimming?" Logan said.

Maia nodded. "I used to like swimming when I was wee, and I need some kind of exercise."

"Good idea, then."

"And the library?" I said, smiling.

She grinned at me. "They have a great YA program." She shrugged, seeming a little shy. "I thought I might meet some friends there. You know . . . better ones."

"Best news I've heard all day," Logan said

Maia looked down at her plate, a small smile of pleasure on her lips. It appeared she'd caught my disease—a state of overwhelming happiness whenever Logan MacLeod was pleased with us. She shrugged. "I thought it would keep me busy this summer."

"Speaking of busy, Joss has sent me another manuscript. I just sent her the last one back." I shook my head, still spinning in amazement at her. "How does that woman write so fast when she has three small children?"

Logan smiled over at me. "Don't start the hero-worshiping just yet. I've been over there when she's writing and it's all Braden. He gives her a few hours a day, finds some way to distract the kids."

I sighed at the thought of Braden Carmichael. "I've never seen a man so in love."

Logan cleared his throat, and I looked over at him. He glowered at me. "No need to be hero-worshiping him either."

I struggled to contain my laughter, my fight only made worse when I looked over at Maia and found her grinning mischievously at her dad. "I can see why Grace likes him, Dad. I mean, he's a wee bit old and all that, but the man has presence."

I snorted, losing my struggle. "A wee bit old and all that. Maia, the man is only in his forties."

"That's old to me."

"Oh, how you will change your tune when you're my age and approaching your forties."

"You're only twenty-eight, Grace."

"A few weeks ago you said that was old."

"It is. But there are levels of old. I'm pretty sure Dad wouldn't want you if you were Braden's age."

"Wrong," Logan said, scooping up some pasta. "I'd want her any way I could get her." He said it with such casualness before popping food into his mouth.

There was nothing casual about the words, however, or the intent behind them. I stared at him, my lips parted in surprise as I struggled to draw breath in quite so easily as before.

Sensing my gaze, Logan looked over at me and then at Maia. "What?"

Maia pressed her lips together at his obliviousness to the significance of what he'd said. She cocked her head and gave him a condescending smile. "You're adorable, Dad."

I burst out laughing.

Logan stared at his daughter and me in puzzlement. "What just happened?"

"You know what just happened?" Maia sat back on her stool to look from me to him. "This." She shook her head in amazement, a gesture that conveyed maturity beyond her years.

"What's this?" I said.

She shrugged and started to eat again. "I'm just happy."

Something like panic clutched my chest.

Logan stared at Maia, arrested. Slowly his gaze drifted over to me, and I saw gratitude, thankfulness, and something much more alarming in his eyes. Determination.

His determination met the worry in mine and battled with it.

But I'd been worrying my whole life, and now I had something so important to worry about not even Logan's strength and persistence could defeat it.

I worried for Maia.

I worried that somehow Logan and I would mess this up and Maia would get her heart broken all over again.

· · ·

People walked past us in a massive blur, laughing, talking, bumping into us every now and then. Princes Street was always busy, and on a warm summer day like today, it was even more so as residents and tourists and visitors shopped. Afterward they wandered down into the gardens to sit and soak up the sun, or hide in the shade of the towering Edinburgh Castle.

I felt comfortable on the streets of Edinburgh. Unlike London, Edinburgh fit me like the perfect pair of shoes. I felt all at once anonymous and well-known to the city. No one looked my way because I fit the streets like I'd been born to them.

As I walked down Princes Street with my hand clasped tightly in Logan's, I lacked my usual comfort, my usual perfect fit.

Logan wasn't anonymous. Logan was Logan. He demanded you notice him, even if it wasn't deliberate on his part. And so walking down the street, claimed by this man as his, I was aware of the looks he drew, mostly from young women, and sometimes their eyes would glance from him to me and I had to wonder if that was a question in their eyes.

Why was *he* with *her*?

"So we're going into Topshop why?" Logan said as we neared the fashion retailer on the corner of Princes Street.

"Because I still need to buy Maia a birthday present."

He squeezed my hand. "I told you the laptop could be from the two of us."

"And I said, 'Let me give you money, then,' and you told me to bugger off."

Logan grunted. "For good reason."

I stopped him and turned to face him. "The laptop is a wonderful gift, and it should just be from you. I am going to buy her a bunch of non–girlie girl stuff, and you're going to suffer through it since you insisted on spending the day with me."

With my hand still in his, Logan put his, and thus mine, behind my back and jerked me against him. He drew me into that sexy low-lidded gaze of his. "With the arrangements for the party, Maia being on school holidays, you working a million manuscripts at a time, and me working, I've barely had a chance to get you to myself. I'm grabbing time with you while I can get it. Even if it does involve shopping."

"You have seen me," I argued quietly and pointedly, my cheeks heating at the reminder of how many times he'd "seen" me in a week. "It must be a record or something."

His lips twitched with amusement. "As fantastic as that is, babe, sometimes I want to spend time with you when we're not having sex."

"What a revelation," I teased.

He gave me a deadpan look before leading me into the store. "Shop."

I snorted at his demand but started looking around. Seeing the mounting boredom on Logan's face, I moved a little faster and picked up some cute sarcastic slogan T-shirts I thought Maia would approve of, a pair of skinny jeans, some fashion jewelry, and a purse.

"You're spoiling her," Logan murmured as he stood at the checkout with me.

"She deserves a little spoiling. And look who's talking, Mr. Laptop."

Without warning, he kissed me. And not just a brush of lips against lips. It was a full-on, tongue-in-my-mouth, luscious, wet kiss.

"What was that for?" I whispered, perfectly aware of the burning stares from the retail assistant and other patrons.

Logan didn't answer, but the expression on his face . . . the look in his eyes . . . the emotion they conveyed were so overwhelming I had to look away.

I wanted to believe so much in that look on his face, and yet I was still terrified too.

The girl ringing up my presents for Maia stared at me with open envy. I squirmed at her assessing stare and looked down at my purse.

There it was again.

Why was *he* with *her*?

My mood plummeted, the high of buying Maia gifts slowly flowing out of me as we wandered back down Princes Street.

"Let's grab something to eat," Logan said, and I nodded absentmindedly. "What do you fancy?"

"Anything."

He led us uphill off Princes Street and hailed a cab. As soon as we got inside it, he gave the guy our home address. I stared at him in question.

Logan shrugged. "Maybe if I get you home you'll relax. You've been tense the whole time we've been out."

My lips parted in surprise at his observation. I didn't realize he was that perceptive. "I'm fine," I lied.

His expression darkened. "Don't lie to me."

"It's nothing," I assured him. "It's silly. My own insecurities. I'm working on it, but I can't work on it if you take us home."

"Tell me what's going on in that head of yours."

I glanced over at the cabdriver, but he didn't appear to paying much attention to us. "It's silly."

"You said that already."

Heeding the warning in his impatient tone, I blurted out, "I feel like people are staring at us and wondering why the hell you're with me."

Logan stared at me in shock. "Fuck," he bit out, the muscle in his jaw twitching. "Your mother really did a number on you, didn't she?"

I flinched at the reminder. "I said I'm working on it."

"I've changed my mind, mate," Logan suddenly said loudly to the driver. "The Caffeine Drip."

"I love that place," I murmured.

"I know." He took my hand in his, his grip tight, possessive. "And when we go in there, I want you to think of one thing." He bent his head, his lips inches from mine. "When I walk anywhere with your hand in mine, I'm proud as fuck that a woman like you is with me."

I felt the sting of tears in my eyes and nose. "I kind of like you, Logan MacLeod."

His grin was wicked and slow. "You kind of *more* than like me, Miss Grace Farquhar."

I *tutt*ed. "You really are far too cocky for your own good."

His breath whispered hot across my ear. "You kind of more than like my cock . . . iness."

I blushed and swatted him away, but he only pulled me closer into his chest so I could feel his laughter against me.

CHAPTER 24

"I t looks busy, guys," Maia said as we approached D'Alessandro's a week later.

"It's a Saturday, but we'll be fine. I booked the table a few weeks ago," I lied, as Logan and I lured her into the restaurant under the pretense that we were having a quiet birthday dinner together.

Logan pulled open the door. "Ladies first."

Maia stepped into the restaurant wearing one of the slogan T-shirts I'd bought her and the skinny jeans. I'd managed to talk her into wearing some jewelry and a pair of heeled boots to dress it up a little, and I'd insisted on putting waves in her hair. She looked so pretty. And so not aware of what lay before her!

I felt like a big kid, giddy for her reaction.

"Ah, Logan, Grace." Marco's uncle Gio greeted us from behind the host's desk, having apparently been waiting for us himself.

A few days ago I'd met with Gio and his wife, Gabby, to give them the decorations and work out logistics for Maia's party. They'd very kindly rented out the back room of the restaurant to us at a crazily discounted price.

"And this must be Maia?" He held out his hand.

Maia shook it, seeming bemused by the attention of the owner of D'Alessandro's.

"Come, come. I'll show you to your table." His eyes twinkled with mischief.

We followed him through the front room and down a narrow hall that immediately opened up into a large room.

"Surprise!"

Maia jolted to a halt at the cries of our new friends and her new family. All of the girls were there with their partners and kids, as promised, and Ellie's mum and dad were there, too, along with Jo's boss and Olivia's dad, Mick, and his wife, Dee.

The children were jumping up and down with excitement as Maia stared around the room in shock.

Streamers hung from the ceiling and every nook and cranny. A massive silver banner printed with HAPPY SWEET SIXTEEN, MAIA was draped along the back wall. Tables were set up around one half of the room, a large buffet of food on one of them, a stack of presents on another. As discussed, we had a projector on the wall adjacent to the banner wall, and at that moment pictures of Maia with all of us were flicking on a slide show. We had a couple of Pixar movies to put on it later to occupy the younger children. Chairs and beanbags were placed in front of it for the kids.

"Oh my God," Maia whispered.

Logan put his arm around her and pulled her in to his side. "Happy birthday, sweetheart."

She looked up at him in teary-eyed awe. "Dad . . ."

He kissed her forehead. "Grace and the girls put this together for you."

"But it was your dad's idea," I added.

"I don't know what to say."

Before we could reply, an older couple stepped out from the group, followed by a woman who didn't look that much older than me. She had dark hair and pretty features that reminded me of Shannon.

I knew immediately who they were.

"Maia." Logan put his hand on her back and led her forward. "This is my mum and dad and my other sister, Amanda."

Not wanting to intrude, I skirted around them and strode into the room with Gio at my side, trying, unsuccessfully, not to worry about Maia. "The place looks great," I said. "Thank you again."

"No need. We're happy to host it. Marco's told us all about Maia and Logan. He's doing a good job in a tough situation." I watched Gio walk over to Marco and Hannah, wondering if Logan realized how much people admired and respected him.

Before I could muse too long over the question, Shannon came forward to hug me.

When she pulled back, her brow was wrinkled with worry. "The place looks great."

"She said with a frown," I teased.

She nodded her chin in the direction behind me. "They've barely said two words to me and Cole."

"Why? I thought you had worked out your issues."

Shannon sighed. "A few months ago I asked Logan to walk me down the aisle. Logan asked me to discuss it with Dad first, and of course Mum and Dad fell out with me. And then the whole Maia situation blew up."

I hissed, "It is kind of a kick in the teeth asking your brother to walk you down the aisle."

She blanched. "I know that. Don't think I didn't stew over it. But I want my life with Cole to be honest and real, and having my dad walk me down the aisle when he's never really believed in my relationship with Cole, and he's definitely never really believed in me, seemed hypocritical. It didn't feel right."

"So you asked Logan," I said. "Well, I think that was brave."

"Thanks, Grace." She smiled sadly. "Some people at school think I'm a shit when I tell them."

"They don't know what you went through and how your parents weren't there for you when you needed them the most. They can't judge. No one can. It's a difficult situation you're in, and ultimately you have to make the decision that sits right with you."

She nodded, expression grave as she looked past my shoulder again. "I don't want them to hurt her. They have this wonderful way of acting like good parents only to disappear as soon as you disappoint them even slightly."

Cole drew up behind her, wrapping his arms around her waist and drawing her back against him. She was so short next to him, he looked like a warrior come to protect her. "You okay, shortcake?"

She nodded and clutched his hand. "I'm just doing my usual freak-out." Her eyes widened slightly. "They're coming over here."

"Should we abandon Grace to them or hang tough?" Cole whispered dramatically.

He succeeded in making her giggle. "I couldn't live with myself if I abandoned Grace to them."

"And Grace would never talk to you ever again," I muttered under my breath, all my muscles stiffening as I watched Logan and Maia approach with the rest of the MacLeods in tow.

Thankfully, Maia was smiling, and her grandparents seemed genuinely happy to be with her.

Logan got to us first. He made a point of kissing Shannon's cheek and nodding at Cole before sliding his arm across my shoulders and drawing me into him.

I studied Maia on closer inspection, and although she didn't look upset, she did look slightly overwhelmed. I put my hand out to her subtly, and she immediately grabbed it and burrowed into my side. Logan's parents and sister watched this interaction with interest and something that seemed a lot like suspicion. I braced myself.

"This is my girlfriend, Grace," Logan said.

Very quickly I schooled my features.

It was a surprise to hear myself called that. Yet . . . I found it was a good surprise. I liked the sound of it. This last week Logan had worked very hard to exorcise my demons and insecurities.

I doubted there was a woman alive who felt more wanted than I did right then.

"It's nice to meet you." I held my hand out to his mum first, a petite woman with red hair and violet eyes. She was young-looking and still very pretty, and could probably pass for Shannon's sister. Logan's other sister, Amanda, had inherited her dark hair and eyes from her father, although his hair was peppered with gray.

He shook my hand after Logan's mum did. "And what do you do, Grace?" he asked immediately, the question containing more than a hint of interrogation.

Logan tensed against me.

"Grace is a freelance book editor," Maia piped up. "She's really good at her job. She has bestselling authors as clients."

I smiled down at her gratefully. "You make me sound cooler than I am."

She shot me a look of mock horror. "Are you suggesting books aren't cool?"

"Ooh, you walked into that one," Cole teased behind me.

I shot him a look over my shoulder, and he grinned unrepentantly. "Thank you, Mr. Walker, for the narration."

"You're very welcome."

"So how long have you been dating?" Amanda stepped forward. Unlike with her father, there seemed to be just curiosity in the question.

"A while," Logan replied vaguely. "And before you ask, it is serious. But this party is not. Question time is over. The birthday girl has guests to greet." Logan led us toward the rest of the tribe, diplomatically making his point. His parents and sister had been invited, they were welcome to get to know Maia, but other than that they had no rights to know any-thing else about our lives. Not yet.

"You're kind of wonderful," I whispered in his ear.

"Just realizing that now?"

I pushed at him playfully, and he laughed, hugging me closer. We watched on in delight as Maia was engulfed by the Carmichaels, Walkers, MacCabes, Sawyers, and so forth. The kids clambered for her attention while she received hugs and kisses from the adults.

"You're going to crush her," a tall girl with curly blond hair and blue tip-tilted eyes said, hovering over Maia protectively. Eleven-year-old Beth Carmichael had inherited her father's height, her mother's hair and eye shape, and her dad's pale blue eye color. She was an extremely pretty child, even if she did wear this constant expression of weary disdain that was hilarious on a little girl.

Maia had met Beth when she babysat for Joss and Braden a few weeks ago. According to Maia, the eldest Carmichael child had adopted her as one of her own.

"Okay, we're done." Beth fluttered her hands at everyone. "Let her breathe, but most importantly, let her open her presents." She grinned and stepped back, nodding her head encouragingly at Maia.

I snorted.

Maia smirked. "I think you need to sort out to your priorities, Beth. Breathing always comes before presents."

We tittered while Beth made a face. "Uh . . . only just. Presents are, like, the most important part of a birthday."

Joss, who was holding her baby daughter, Ellie, in her arms, shot her husband a look. "What are you teaching our children?"

"Nu-uh!" Their eight-year-old son, Luke, crossed his arms over his chest and shook his head stubbornly at his sister. "The best part is the food!"

"What are *you* teaching our children?" Braden countered.

Logan pressed his forehead to the top of mine and chuckled.

"Can we just do something?" Maia said. "So . . . you know . . . everyone will stop staring at me."

"Why?" Beth seemed genuinely bemused by this. "You're the birthday girl. You should get all of the attention. It's the third-best part, after the food."

"You're not my child," Joss joked.

Beth put her hands on her hips. "You can't run from it, Mother."

Everyone laughed, Braden's laughter the loudest.

Joss grinned and wrinkled her nose at her daughter. Beth stuck out her tongue and grinned back. "You can't either," Joss reminded her.

"I'm younger. I probably could."

"You run, baby. I'll run after you." She winked at her, and Beth smiled before turning her attention back to the still-overwhelmed Maia. I felt happy for Joss and Beth but envious of their teasing. I couldn't imagine what it would have been like to have grown up in a home where my mother not only loved me, but treated me like a friend.

"Presents," Maia suddenly announced, seemingly having caught the persistence in Beth's gaze.

"Yay!" Beth clapped and ran for the table with the presents. "Open mine first! Please, please, please!"

Braden caught Logan's eye across the room. "She loves buying people presents."

"You better hide your credit cards," Logan warned.

"I sleep with them on me."

"And with one eye open," Joss cracked before following everyone over to the presents.

"Hey, we didn't miss anything, did we?"

I spun around out of Logan's grasp, delight washing through me as Aidan, Juno, and Chloe strode across the room, carrying birthday presents in their hands. "Guys, you made it."

Aidan engulfed me in a tight hug. "Long time, no see." He pulled back, his gaze questioning. "Are we okay?"

262 · SAMANTHA YOUNG

"Of course." I shoved him gently. "Don't be an idiot. I've just been busy."

His gaze moved over my shoulder. "So I see."

Juno butted in. "Give me a hug."

I was just pulling back from hugging Chloe when Logan appeared at my side. Chloe being Chloe, she hugged him whether he wanted to be hugged or not.

After shaking hands with Juno, he offered his hand to Aidan, and as they greeted each other, they eyed each other with masculine wariness.

I was really glad I hadn't told Logan that Aidan used to be in love with me.

"So," Aidan began, and I immediately tensed at the mischievous glint in his eyes, "she chose you over the history teacher after all."

Logan glanced over at me. "I didn't know the history teacher was an option."

"He wasn't," I said quickly, and then glowered in warning at Aidan.

He just smirked until Juno hit him on the arm.

"A word, Grace."

"A word, Aidan."

Logan and I spoke in unison.

"Just . . . give me a minute to talk to Aidan," I said.

Without waiting for a response, I grabbed Aidan by his T-shirt and hauled him out of the room into the hallway. Well, not exactly *hauled*. You didn't and couldn't haul Aidan anywhere. "What are you doing?" I hissed.

"Nothing." He shrugged. "I'm just not convinced about this guy. I want him to know that you have options."

"I don't have options," I whisper shouted. "The history teacher is not an option."

"That's not what you said a few weeks ago."

"A few weeks ago I was hurt. Logan is trying to make up for that. People deserve second chances, Aidan."

He nodded, concern for me swimming in his eyes. "They do. But, Grace, you have a habit of giving people fifty chances."

"Look, I know you mean well, but this . . . Logan isn't like my mum and dad and Sebastian. He won't hurt me intentionally."

"He could still hurt you, intentionally or not."

"Yes, but so could anyone," I said, suddenly making the realization myself. "The history teacher could have if I'd given him chance. Even you could have, Aidan."

He frowned. "He's not like your usual blokes."

I laughed. "No, he's not. And I never felt about them the way I feel about him."

Slowly Aidan's shoulders relaxed and his eyes warmed. "So what you're saying to me is 'keep your big nose out of it.'"

"Never. You're my family, Aidan. If you didn't care, I'd hate it. But Logan and I need to work all this out for ourselves without you pushing his buttons."

"Gotcha."

We wandered back into the room only for Logan to grab my hand and lead me over to the table where Maia was opening her presents. "When she's done, we talk."

"Logan, it was nothing," I tried to explain, but he was already focused on Maia and ignoring me for the moment.

I let her delight distract me as she opened present after present. She received books, gift vouchers, makeup, DVDs, chocolate, and other gifts galore. The tribe spoiled her rotten.

"Dad, did you see?" Maia ran up to him after thanking everyone. She'd left her presents in the care of Beth, who had organized her brother to clean up the wrapping paper while she tidied the gifts into a neat pile.

"I did." He smiled down at her, his eyes crinkling at the corners attractively. "Having fun so far?"

Eyes wide, she stared around at the room. "I've never had this many presents before, let alone a party." She turned to me, eyes bright with excitement. "I got eighty pounds in gift vouchers for the bookshop."

"Nice," I said. "We'll go tomorrow if you want."

She nodded, looking dazed.

"You all right, sweetheart?" Logan said.

"I just don't know what to do next."

"I've got something." He disappeared behind the table and brought up his present.

I grinned as Maia opened her mouth in surprise. "Another one?"

"From me." He gestured her over. "Open it."

"There's another present!" Beth yelled at everyone, drawing attention back to the table.

"Horsey!" Belle, Jo and Cam's daughter, cried out excitedly, running for the table.

Beth eyed the rectangular-shaped parcel and then Belle, this time dubiously. She shot a look at Jo, as if to say, *What are you teaching your child?*

I had to wipe the tears from my eyes, I was laughing so hard.

Jo narrowed her eyes on Beth. "She's just going through a horse phase." She turned back to look at Joss and mouthed, *Smart-arse.*

Joss just grinned.

"What is it?" Maia said, and I turned back to her. I wanted to see her expression when she opened it.

"Open it and find out."

Carefully, Maia tore open the paper and turned the box around so she could read the front. Her jaw literally dropped at the sight of the laptop.

"Happy birthday, sweetheart," Logan said softly.

She immediately burst into tears.

His eyes flew to me.

Good tears. Good tears, I mouthed, waving my hands at him frantically.

He rounded the table at my direction and pulled her into his arms.

"I think it's cake time," Elodie announced, her years of experience as a mother shining through as she deftly drew attention away from Maia while she composed herself. "Let's go, kids. Let's get the cake for Maia." They followed her, chattering at her the whole time, and I marveled at the way she could take in everything and have multiple conversations at once.

I stepped forward toward Maia and Logan, and I was only about a foot away when Logan reached out an arm and jerked me into the huddle. They both wrapped an arm around me and I held on tight to them.

"You're going to make me cry now," I whispered over the lump of emotion gathering in my throat.

"Good. That will make me feel like less of an idiot." Maia sniffled.

Logan and I pulled back, and I cupped her tear-streaked face. "You are not an idiot. You're a sweetheart."

She wiped her face and gazed up at her dad as if he were a hero come to life. "Thanks for the laptop, Dad."

Wetness shimmered in his eyes, and he could only nod.

My fingers curled into his T-shirt, and I fought hard not to cry at the sight of his emotion.

"Maia, why don't you go show Beth the laptop," I suggested softly, realizing Logan needed a minute.

Maia seemed to realize that, too, and did as I asked.

In turn I took Logan's hand, led him out of the room and into Gio's office. "Are you okay?"

In answer he pulled me into his arms and just held on tight.

We stood there for a while not saying a word.

"You're mine," he suddenly whispered.

I stilled. "What?"

Logan drew back just far enough so he could cup my face in his hands. "Did you consider going out with Maia's history teacher?"

Surprised by the sudden turn in conversation, I shook my head. "Aidan is just being an arse."

"Did you?"

"Logan—"

"You're mine," he said, his words fierce. "I'm yours. I'll never let anything or anyone come between that."

I shivered at the sweet possessiveness in the words and clung to him tighter. "I don't want anyone else but you."

He closed his eyes as if in relief and leaned his forehead against mine.

The silence wrapped around us, this time only emphasizing our closeness, our connection, and the wordless promises we made to each other.

CHAPTER 25

It was one of those perfect mornings. Not too hot, but the sunlight was pouring in through the window. Earlier I'd woken up in my boyfriend's bed after a night of sweet lovemaking. We'd had breakfast with Maia and then she'd gone off to the YA summer program at the library and Logan had left for work.

I'd returned to my flat, where I was working on Joss's new manuscript and eating leftover croissants from yesterday's trip to my favorite bakery. For the first time ever, I was able to throw off my inner angst over . . . well . . . everything . . . and I was just enjoying my work and life.

I should have known it would all go to hell.

The knock at the door was the signal of the start of it.

The man standing on my doorstep was the "hell" part.

"Father," I said softly, shocked by the surrealism of him standing on my small but clean landing.

Gabriel Bentley stood there in a crisp white—most probably designer—shirt, lightweight leather jacket, and dark trousers. He was shiny and clean from the top of his perfectly combed hair to the gleaming black Italian loafers on his feet.

But the shiny and clean were only skin-deep

My fingers curled around my doorframe. "What do you want?"

"May I come in?" he said, pushing his way past me.

I felt the panic rise up from my chest, a choking sensation wrapping around my throat as I closed the door and followed him inside my flat.

I found him in my sitting room, looking around, taking it all in.

"What do you want?"

He gave me this weary sigh in response to my snappish tone. "Your mother is sick. She has breast cancer."

Hearing him say the words out loud suddenly made it so real. "I know," I said. "I saw an article in the news."

My father jerked his head back as if I'd slapped him. "And it never occurred to you to come see her?"

I fought off a wave of guilt. "Last time I spoke to her she told me she never wanted to see me again."

"To be fair, you did tattle on her to me about her lover," he chastised.

Dumbfounded, I shook my head. "One—he was not her lover. He was my boyfriend. Two—do you not hear yourself? I will never understand your mutual lack of respect for each other and your marriage."

"On the contrary, I have a healthy respect for your mother." Looking saddened, he sat down on the arm of my sofa. "I just wished you'd inherited her realism. You get hurt so easily, Gracelyn. It's hard to watch."

"My name is just Grace," I reminded him coldly.

He nodded. "Grace."

"Why are you here?"

The sadness melted just enough for that steely determination of his to shine through. "I'm here to convince you to come home. The media have shown some interest in the fact that you're not home, standing vigil at your mother's bedside."

I sneered. "Of course. It's all about appearances with you."

He had the audacity to look hurt. "I am the head of a media company. Image is everything. But I do need you for more than that. She's sick, and I don't know what to do."

Try as I might, I couldn't ignore the niggle of sympathy I felt or the ever-increasing guilt. "Is she dying?"

"She's fighting it. But it's a difficult battle. Sebastian has stepped up to take a more hands-on role in the company so I can concentrate on getting your mother the best treatment possible."

I crossed the room, my legs shaking too much to stand any longer. Once I was seated across from him, I somehow found the courage to ask the question I wasn't sure I wanted the answer to. "Has she asked for me?"

I received only silence as my father looked at the floor.

"That would be a 'no,' then." I closed my eyes, fighting the pain of her rejection. Like always.

"*I* am asking you." He stared me straight in the eye and gave me that coaxing smile he'd always given me when he was intent on getting me to do whatever he wanted. "I have missed you."

I eyed him suspiciously. "I never would have known that what with all the e-mails, calls, and cards you sent over the last seven years."

He frowned, seeming perturbed by my stubbornness. "The lack of communication goes both ways."

"No, it doesn't. I was betrayed by my mother, and you and Sebastian brushed it off like I was a child who needed to grow up and understand the ways of the world—as though betrayal is just a part of life. Well, it's not. I know that now. I have people who care about me, and they would never betray me like she did. Like you all did."

My father cocked his head to the side in thought. "Are you talking about this man, this neighbor of yours? Logan MacLeod. The ex-convict and his long-lost child."

I sat back, the panic rising within me again. "You've been looking into me?"

"Of course I have. You're my daughter. I didn't let you go off into the world entirely by yourself. You needed space from this family and I've given it to you, but I've also been watching over you. I know all about you. I know about the rugby player, Aidan Ramage, and his fiancée, Juno. Canadian, yes? And, of course, your best friend from college, Chloe. I know you all go to Skye every year for a weekend in the summer and Paris for a weekend in the winter. I know you, *Grace*."

"That doesn't mean you know me."

It didn't.

But I was also completely thrown off-balance by the news that he had always been looking out for me. Looking out for me or into me—the result was the same. My father hadn't completely abandoned me.

I didn't know how to feel about that.

"I know you well enough to know you've been taken in by an ex-con." He stood up, towering over me, no longer the weary father but the intimidating businessman. "I know you enough to know betrayal is something you cannot stand for. You've abandoned your family over it. And now you're opposed to returning to us because of this Logan and his daughter. I think it's important, then, that you know he's manipulating you. He's not what you think he is."

"Enough!" I jumped to my feet, my anger boiling in my blood.

My father flinched back, shocked that I would use that tone with him.

Shocked, because he was wrong.

He did not know me.

I wasn't afraid anymore that speaking out would turn him away from me. "You don't know the first thing about Logan."

"Oh. Do you?" He stepped toward me, his cheeks reddening with his rising temper. "Why don't you ask him about the American blonde he's sleeping with? Ask him why she was at his club during the day while he was working there. *Twice. This week.*"

It was like a punch to the gut. It actually winded me.

How did my father know about the American? He could only know if what he was saying was true.

But surely there was an explanation . . .

"Get out," I gasped, slumping down onto my sofa, curling into myself for protection.

"All right." His voice was soft with sympathy now, real or faked. "But once you see reason, you can find me at the Balmoral Hotel. I'm staying there until you agree to come home with me."

It was an understatement to say my father had sucked all of the happiness out of my flat when he'd left. It was like my family had radar or something!

"Oh, look, Grace is truly happy. Let's go shit all over it!"

I barely moved from my sofa for the rest of the day as I went over and over everything my father had said. The confusion, the guilt, the sadness . . . it was all so much.

I needed to talk to Logan.

That afternoon, around dinnertime, he and Maia walked into my flat together. I knew Maia had been going to a friend's house after the YA program and that Logan had agreed to pick her up after his work. That meant I'd been stewing, and knowing that I'd have to stew for hours, until this moment.

As soon as they walked into the living room, I looked at Maia. "Could you give me and your dad a few minutes alone, sweetheart?"

Maia took in my expression, concern in her eyes. But she nodded. "I'll go next door."

"Grace, what's wrong?" Logan asked as Maia left the room.

When I heard the door shut, I stood up. "My father was here today."

"What?" Logan marched across the room and took me by the arms. "Are you okay?"

"No. He wants me to come home. To be with my mother. She really is sick."

"Breast cancer?"

"Yes."

"Fuck." Logan's grip on me tightened, and he tugged me closer. "You told him no. He's off his fucking head if he thinks you're going home with him."

I blanched and pulled out of his hold. "He did his usual. He tried to manipulate me." I glanced over my shoulder at Logan, whose own concern seemed to have quadrupled since I pulled away from him. "He said you saw the American. Sharon, was it? He said she visited the club twice this week. During the day. How did he even know about her?"

Now it was Logan's turn to blanch.

My stomach fluttered unpleasantly. "Did she visit you?"

"It's not what you think. I saw her once this week. If she visited before, I wouldn't know about it. I didn't tell you because I didn't want you to get upset over nothing. She was there to see if I wanted to rekindle things one last time before she left the country. I told her about you and she left. End of story."

My heart was pounding at the thought of that woman being anywhere near him. For Christ's sake, I could still hear her screaming his name from his bedroom next door. I gritted my teeth against the memory. "If it was nothing, you should have told me."

"And upset you over nothing? You're starting to trust me. I didn't want to fuck it up."

"Clue in, Logan. It's better to hear that shit from you than someone else. Least of all my goddamn father!"

"This is what he wants!" Logan yelled back, gesturing between us. "To fuck us up so he can sweep in and manipulate you into going home with him!"

"Yes, it is," I said, lowering my voice. I sagged against the back of the sofa and stared up at him balefully from beneath my lashes. "Don't keep something like that from me again."

"I won't. I promise." He rounded the sofa and put his hands on my hips, drawing me against him. "Tell your dad to go home, Grace, before he causes any more trouble."

The slamming of my heart became a sledgehammer pounding. "I'm not sure I can."

"What?" He stared down into my eyes, his filled with incredulity.

"Logan, you know I've been carrying this guilt, this weight, over my mum's cancer. The fact that I feel like this means something. I need to work it out, and if that means talking to my dad again, then so be it."

"You know what the guilt means, Grace? It means you're not a soul-less bitch like the woman who gave birth to you. It's as simple as that. Don't let him draw you back into that world."

"I'm trying not to. I feel panicked just at the thought of it," I confessed. "But, Logan, what kind of person does it make me if I don't go to my possibly dying mother's side?"

"What are you worried about? What the world thinks of you? What we think of you? Or what you think of you? Because at the end of the day, babe, the only opinions that matter are your own and those of the people you care about."

There was a huge part of me that knew Logan was right and another huge part of me that hyperventilated at the mere thought of letting the Bentleys back into my life. Yet there was also this small voice inside of me that kept telling me Logan was biased. He couldn't give me advice because he had a stake in the outcome.

Although I knew Aidan did too, I called him that night as Logan and Maia sat in my sitting room watching a movie after dinner. I closed myself in my bedroom with the phone and dialed my oldest friend's number because he had been there with me through the trauma of my mother's betrayal and my family's apathy toward me.

He also had a far less hotheaded reaction to drama than Logan.

"Oh shit," Aidan said once I'd finished telling him about my father's visit.

"So what do I do?"

"I can't tell you what to do."

I stared at my phone in horror for a second and then put it back to my ear. "The whole point is for you to tell me what to do!" I hissed.

"No, it's not. I can't make this decision for you. No one can. It has to feel right for you. All I can tell you is that not one of us will judge you for whatever choice you make. Just do what you have to do."

We talked for a little longer before I finally hung up, feeling no more and no less confused than I had when I'd called him. I was just getting up off my bed when the bedroom door opened and Logan stepped in.

"You okay?" he said, wary.

I nodded. "I was just talking to Aidan. Asking for his advice."

Apparently it was the wrong thing to say. Logan's expression darkened. "So you take his advice but not mine?"

"It's not like that."

"Oh? I'm to feel all right about you running to dear old Aidan whenever you have a problem? Is this something I should prepare myself for in the future?"

I gaped at him. "Logan, where is this coming from? You know Aidan is one of my closest friends."

"Yeah, and while you're pushing me away, you're running to him."

"I'm not pushing you away." I jumped off the bed and hurried over to him, only just realizing how much the news of my father's arrival had shaken him. "Logan, I went to Aidan because he can be rational about this. He can step outside of our friendship and give me advice without being biased."

"He can do that because he's not fucking fighting for you." He dragged a hand over his face, looking suddenly exhausted. "That's all I feel like I'm ever doing . . . fucking fighting for you."

Tears stung my eyes at the sight of the hurt in his. "I'm only thinking this over. And you know going back to London would only be for a bit. It wouldn't be the end of us."

"No. It means the end of everything you've built since escaping their manipulative, sick, bloody world. They are toxic. They will hurt you again, Grace, and there will be nothing I can do to stop it. I can't let that happen. I can't let you do this."

I grabbed his hand, hoping the gesture would soften what I was about to say. "Whatever I decide, it's up to me, not you."

He ripped his hand from mine. "See, that's the difference between you and me. I thought that since I love you, when shit like this comes up, we discuss it . . . because it affects us both."

Surprise, amazement, joy, panic, euphoria, fear, excitement, trepidation . . . It all flooded through me at the sound of those three words falling from his beautiful mouth.

In fact, I felt so much I couldn't find the strength to reply.

And he was waiting for a reply.

And not just any reply.

"Nice, Grace," he bit out, and disappeared before I could get my mouth to work.

CHAPTER 26

I love you.

I love you.

I. Love. You.

What was so difficult about those words? Nothing! I'd said them to people before!

Somehow, however, they'd grown to fifty times their normal size when Logan said them. They were so big there was no way around them, and I couldn't see anything for the hulking shadow of each damn letter.

I was frightened to say them back to him.

That night I lay in my bed, and each time I tried to force my body up and out so I could go to him next door and just blurt out the words, I was stopped by that fear.

Yet, as the next day wore on with no sign of him or Maia, the words percolated, and common sense started to punch the crap out of my fear. By the time I returned with some shopping for Mr. Jenner, I was determined to turn back out of the apartment building and find Logan.

He said those momentously large words to me first.

He made himself vulnerable to me.

He took that step without having to be asked.

And surely he was just as scared of being rejected? Of putting it out there and it all going wrong?

If Logan could be brave, then I could be brave.

Because of course I loved him.

I felt like I'd loved him forever.

I had just dumped my own food shopping in the kitchen and was hurrying back out of the flat when I heard, "Grace!"

Running up the stairs toward me, Maia was frantic, her eyes alert with panic. I hurried to her just as she reached the landing. "What's wrong?"

"It's Dad," she huffed, out of breath. "Shannon just called me. She's been trying to call you. Her ex is back. The one who beat her. Dad's gone AWOL."

And just like that, nothing else mattered, *nothing* but finding Logan. I rummaged in my bag for my phone, which I'd stupidly switched to silent. Sure enough, I had a dozen missed calls from Shannon. I flicked through the numbers and hit Logan's. "Come on, come on," I muttered as it rang. My hopes fell as it went to voice mail. "No," I hissed, and hung up. I rang Shannon back.

"Oh, thank God, Grace. Have you seen Logan?" she said without preamble, panic clear in her voice.

"We're just checking the flat." I nodded to Maia to do so, and she immediately set about unlocking Logan's flat.

I followed her inside as she called out to him. "Shannon, what's going on exactly?"

"My ex," she said softly, a tremble in her voice. "Ollie. He contacted me. He's out of prison and he's in Edinburgh. He wants to meet me."

"Are you bloody well kidding me?" I snapped, outraged.

"No Dad." Maia shook her head, coming down the hall toward me.

"He's not there," Shannon said, obviously having heard.

"Have you checked the club?"

"That's where I was. God, Grace, I would never have told him, but he was there. I didn't have a class today and sometimes I take lunch to Logan when I don't. The school admin office had a letter for me, and I opened it up in Logan's office. It was from Ollie. When Logan saw my reaction, he snatched the letter off me before I could stop him. And then he just left and he won't answer his phone. Oh fuck, Grace, what if he does something? I can't let this happen to him again." She started to cry, and there was a loud rustling sound. "Grace?" I heard Cole say. "Look, I want to murder this guy for contacting her more than anyone, but he's not worth it. Do you have any clue where Logan is?"

I tried to breathe over my mounting fear. "There would be nowhere specific, but he knows people, Cole. He could be trying to track down Ollie. Our best bet is to try to do the same and get there first."

"It could be too late. He's been missing for a few hours."

"Oh, Jesus, don't say that . . . this . . . How is Shannon? Is she going to be okay?"

"She's not afraid of that piece of shit anymore. She's just afraid for Logan. I don't know . . ."

His words faded for me at the sound of the front door opening, and both Maia and I spun around, relief pouring over us at the sight of a haggard Logan stepping inside the flat.

"Cole, he's here." I cut off whatever he had been saying. "Logan's home."

"Thank fuck. Is he okay? Did he do anything?"

"Dad!" Maia hurried past me and threw herself at him.

Logan immediately wrapped his arms around her, squeezing his eyes shut. I saw the strain on his face, but also the love. And I knew. "No, Cole. He didn't do anything." *He wouldn't jeopardize his life with Maia.*

"Good. I'm coming over and I'm bringing Shannon. We need to talk."

I agreed and hung up.

For a moment I could do nothing but stare at father and daughter, the sudden relief from such fear causing the adrenaline levels in my body to just drop. I felt exhausted.

By everything.

Maia eventually pulled back from Logan and he cupped her face, swiping her tears away. "I'm okay," he promised her. "We're okay."

"Shannon thought you'd gone after that bloke."

His jaw clenched and he shook his head.

He hadn't gone after him, but he was fighting the urge.

"Maia," I said, "I'm going to take your dad next door for just a minute or two. Is that okay?"

She frowned, clearly not too happy with me hijacking him and leaving her out of the loop, but she nodded.

"Grace." Logan held up a hand, his expression horribly blank. "Not now."

Although I was hurt, I glowered through it. "Yes, right now."

His answer was to brush by me, not even looking at me. He strode down the hall into his bedroom and closed the door behind him.

Tears welled up in my eyes as I stared at the closed door.

I knew what he was doing.

Shutting me out because he thought I'd shut him out.

"Grace?" Maia touched my hand, staring up at me with sympathy and concern.

So what did I do?

Did I avoid confronting him? Take my hurt and let it fester just as he did his?

He was in that room, probably stewing over every moment he'd spent in prison because of that bastard who had attacked Shannon.

And that was bigger than my hurt feelings.

I grasped Maia's hand as I dug my keys out of my bag. I handed them to her. "Go next door, sweetheart."

She gave me a watery, relieved smile before leaving the flat.

I in turn threw my shoulders back, preparing myself for battle as I marched down the hallway and pushed open his door.

He looked up from his perch on the bed. He was sitting on the edge of it, elbows on his knees, hands clasped tightly together. His eyes flashed at my intrusion. "Go home, Grace."

"No." I slammed the door shut behind me and crossed my arms over my chest. "I've never been afraid of you, Logan MacLeod, and I'm not starting now. I'm not leaving you."

"Is that it?" he sneered. "I'm only interesting when I'm playing the wounded ex-con? First it was Maia; now it's Shannon's fucker of an ex coming back. And here you are all concerned again."

I winced at his cutting tone. "I'm going to let that slide since you're having a particularly bad day."

"Kind of you."

"Logan, don't. I've spent all night and all day berating myself for just standing there like an idiot when you told me you loved me. I was just coming to see you when Maia came rushing up the stairs in a panic over this news of Ollie."

He shook his head and looked at the floor. "Don't. I don't want to hear it."

Anger spilled into my blood, momentarily eclipsing my sympathy and concern. "Don't you dare," I said, voice soft, but my tone drew his head up. "Don't you play the rejected hero because I failed to say the words you bloody well know I already feel. You've known I've been in love with you since my reaction to you walking away after you screwed me against my kitchen wall!" My chest heaved as I tried to draw breath.

Logan lost the blank look in his eyes. "Are you ever going to let me live that down?"

"I have!" I yelled, because yelling felt better than crying. "My point is that I have let it go because I love you!" I sagged with relief at saying the words. "As much as it scares the absolute shit out me, I love you more than I have ever loved anyone. I didn't shut you out, Logan. I was just taking a moment. But this." I gestured to him, feeling the sudden wetness on my cheeks. "This is shutting me out, and I'm scared shitless all over again."

"Because you think I'm going to go off half-cocked and finish what I started with Ollie?" His eyes blazed with fury and confliction.

"No." I shook my head. "You love Maia way too much to endanger your relationship with her. You would never damage that."

His shoulders dropped and he stared at me wide-eyed. He looked so much like a little boy lost that my tears spilled faster for him. "You believe that?" he said hoarsely.

"I know it."

Suddenly he was across the room and I was in his arms and he was kissing me hard, desperately. He pulled back, holding my head in his hands as he stared into my eyes with the fierceness that I loved. "I love you so much," he said, voice gruff. "Don't ever leave me, Grace. Don't ever leave me."

My lips trembled as I shook my head at the idea. "I won't," I cried softly. "I love you. You're my family. I won't leave," I promised, and I knew then I never would. "I don't want to be anywhere but here with you."

He wrapped his arms around me tight, and I buried my head against his chest, soaking him in. "I nearly lost it," he confessed. "I was in an already shitty mood because of our fight, and then seeing that letter . . . The audacity of that fucker to contact her . . . I had to walk around, had to walk it off and remind myself of everything I had to lose. He took so much from her, Grace, and he took two years from me and more. He doesn't deserve to be walking free around the streets of Edinburgh."

"I know," I said, my fingers curling tighter into his T-shirt. "But he can't do anything anymore. You have a life now. You have a daughter who adores you and a girlfriend who would do anything for you both." His arms tightened at that. "And Shannon." I laughed softly. "Oh my gosh, your sister is happier than most people ever dream of being. She has school and she has you and she has Cole. Ollie can't take any of that away."

"You're right." He gently moved me back so he could stare into my eyes. "I just wish the mere mention of him didn't fuck with my head."

I touched his cheek, brushing my thumb over the bristle of his short beard. "I'm discovering that these things are ingrained so deep in us that there's a possibility they won't ever really go away." I gave him a sad smile and I knew he knew I wasn't just talking about his demons. "I thought they would, but it seems it's going to be a constant battle. Some days, some years even, will be better than others. But I'm here for you and you're here for me, and that's all we can ask for."

His fingers curled into my waist, his grip almost bruising. "Does that mean you're not going back to London?"

"No, I'm not. But"—I heaved a sigh—"I still need to talk to my father."

Although Logan didn't look too happy about that announcement, he said, "Just be careful."

"Always."

He kissed me softly, a kiss that was just growing in hunger when the doorbell rang seconds before we heard it open.

"Logan!" we heard Shannon yell.

We pulled back from the kiss. "Tonight," he promised.

Anticipation zinged through me. "Can I be loud?"

His eyes flared with heat. "When Maia goes to sleep I'll come over."

"Logan!" Shannon sounded more frantic.

"We better get out there."

Shannon and Cole were in the sitting room, and Cole gave us a knowing look when we appeared. I rolled my eyes at him and he grinned. His fiancée, on the other hand, flew at her brother, much like Maia had done earlier.

Logan hugged Shannon tight, whispering soothing words to her. She pulled back, swiping at her tears. "You had me so worried." She punched him on the chest and walked back to Cole, burrowing into his side.

"I just had to walk it off," Logan told her. "Sorry for worrying you."

"Okay, I'm just jumping right into this," Cole said. "This guy wants to meet with Shannon to apologize—that's what his letter said. Well, we're going to let him."

"Are you out of your bloody mind!" I beat Logan to the punch.

Everyone stared at me in shock.

"Well?" I huffed, crossing my arms over my chest.

Cole raised an eyebrow at Logan. "So much for the quiet type."

Logan smirked, a wicked glint in his eyes. "Oh, she knows when to yell at the appropriate times."

Cole snorted while Shannon gagged.

"Can we get back to the matter at hand?" I said, gesturing to Cole. "You can't seriously think it's a good idea to put Shannon in that position."

"I can speak for myself," Shannon said, not unkindly. "Look, I don't want to meet with him. I don't want his apology. I'm not looking for closure from him. At. All. That's his crap and he's not forcing it on me. But Cole doesn't think ignoring him will work."

"Agreed," Logan grunted.

Cole held up his hands as if assuring me. "We just *pretend* that Shannon's meeting him. We'll make it somewhere public but open. I'm thinking the Meadows. And instead of Shannon he gets me, Braden, Cam, Nate, and Adam."

"What about me?" Logan's jaw clenched.

"No." Shannon shook her head. "The guys are only going to warn him off. There will be no violence . . . just a warning. Logan, he took two years of your life. You have no way of knowing how you will react to that."

"I'm going," he said. "I want to face that fucker, and I want him to know I'm still here. I won't do anything but—"

"You don't know that," Shannon argued.

"See that," he snapped, pointing to the laptop on his coffee table. "That belongs to my daughter, my daughter who is right now next door waiting on me, just like she's been waiting on me her whole life. And this." He grabbed my hand and held it against his chest. "I've been waiting on *this* my whole life. I am not going to jeopardize either of those relationships for that sniveling little fucker. But I am going to look him in the eye and he is going to know that he didn't beat me."

Shannon's lips trembled, but there was a light in her eyes, a light that I saw more and more in Logan's lately. She nodded and then covered her mouth to try to stifle a sob.

"Shannon?" Logan stepped forward, looking confused.

"You're okay," she sobbed out. "You're okay."

And that's when I saw realization dawn on Logan's face, and before Cole could get to her, her brother pulled her into his arms and held her while she cried.

I stared at Cole, somewhat confused. In answer he walked toward me and put a hand on my shoulder, gently guiding me out of the room and out of the flat.

"What's going on?" I said once we were on the landing.

Cole's eyes were bright with emotion as he stared down at me. "You have no idea," he said hoarsely, "how much guilt my girl is carrying over what happened to Logan. As much as he's told her over and over again that it wasn't her fault, she couldn't let it go." He smiled at me—his love and his relief for her in his eyes. "I think this means she's letting it go."

The door opened and Maia stepped out of my flat. "Is everything all right? I heard yelling earlier."

"That was Grace." Cole shoved me playfully. "Can't shut this one up."

I grimaced at him. "You're funny."

"I am delightful," he responded, and then grinned at Maia, who blushed. That only made Cole grin harder.

I shoved him for teasing her. "Grow up."

"Never." He shook his head and stared at Logan's flat door again. "How long should we give them?"

"Give who? What's going on?" Maia said.

"Shannon and Logan," I replied, heading toward my door. "Let's go in and have a cup of tea." I glanced back once last time at next door, feeling the beginnings of something I hadn't felt in a long time. Contentment. There was still a ways to go to getting there, but it didn't seem so far out of reach anymore. I smiled as I stepped inside. "They'll come get us when they're ready."

CHAPTER 27

I timed my confrontation with my father perfectly.

By that I mean I did it at the same time as the guys were going to confront Shannon's ex. I couldn't bear the idea of pacing back and forth in my flat, waiting for Logan to return and tell me everything was going to be all right, so I decided I'd distract myself with the emotional nuclear weapon that was my father.

Maia, who now knew about my father's visit and Logan and the guys' decision to meet with Ollie, assured me she'd be fine keeping Shannon company. It might have seemed like bad parenting to let her in the loop, but she was bright; she knew these upsetting things were happening, and it was just making her feel worse not knowing the details.

This was Maia.

As much as I hated the reasons why, she was mature enough to handle it. And honestly, she was a wonderful solace to Shannon.

I left Maia with her aunt at her flat and then I jumped in a cab.

The driver dropped me off outside the Balmoral Hotel. The huge building loomed over me, intimidating me, taunting me.

I had the concierge ring up to his room, and they sent a hotel staff member to take me to his suite. Of course it was the best suite in the hotel: the Royal Suite.

I was led inside the foyer of the suite and left there.

"Hello?" I called out.

"Oh, you're here. Come in."

I followed his voice into a large sitting room. The Balmoral Hotel was a period property with the massively high ceilings and grand architecture of the Victorian era. The focal point of the room was a beautiful fireplace that Gabriel had crackling despite the warmth of the summer air outside.

I had been hot with nerves before. Now I was practically melting.

"Sit." He gestured to the armchair across from him. It was a nineteenth-century reproduction Louis XV chair, and I was almost afraid to sit on it. As per usual, nothing but the very best for Gabriel Bentley.

Once I was seated, he smiled. I could see immediately that he thought he'd won. "May I offer you a drink?"

"No, thank you," I sucked in a huge breath and exhaled slowly. "I'm here to tell you to go back to London. Without me."

His smile immediately died, his brown eyes darkening to black. "You can't be serious."

"I'm very serious."

"Your mother has cancer, for Christ's sake!"

I winced at the reminder. "Yes. But I had to ask myself what was harder to live with—the guilt that I'd feel not going to see her, or the venom that would reenter my life by allowing her back into it. By allowing you all back into it."

He scoffed. "Such drama."

"No, Gabriel," I said, my use of his name cementing my coming point. He flinched. "You are not my family anymore. You stopped being my family a long time ago . . . if you ever really were."

"Forgiveness is divine," he reminded me.

"Yes, it is." I stood up, letting all the anger and hurt and rejection flow out of me, and for the first time it was directed at one of the people who deserved it. "And what am I to forgive? Your complete and utter neglect? How you were never there so you never saw how she treated me?

Her constant criticism and insults? How she tore me apart from the moment I could walk? I'm to forgive this. But not for you. I will forgive it all for me. For my sake."

"Your mother was trying to prepare you for our world. She's a realist!"

"She's a bitter, cruel, conniving bitch!" I yelled back. "Cancer doesn't erase that, Gabriel. Sickness doesn't automatically erase people's sins. My mother is not a realist. She's a woman who woke up to realize her husband didn't love her like she loved him and so she learned to play the game and play it well instead of running as far and as fast as she could from you. Because she's mercenary and the money will always be more important than her happiness. And if she couldn't be truly happy, by God, I wasn't going to be either. I took the brunt of her bitterness. You unloved her, so she unloved me!" I pounded my fist against my chest as he stared up at me in horror. "I took your insults, your slaps, your betrayals! All of it meant for you!"

"Gracelyn . . ." he whispered.

"Grace." I sucked in my tears and straightened my shoulders. "And I'm done wondering what I could have done to make her love me. It isn't my fault she's not capable of it. I know that now." I nodded, knowing it but not quite feeling it. I could only hope that one day the words would sink into my bones. "I won't let her hurt me again. Or her twisted little shit of a son who thought it was all right to set his mates on me because he thought rape was so damn funny."

Gabriel stood up slowly, eyes narrowed. "What are you saying?"

"I'm saying your precious little boy liked to let his drunken friends into my room when I was teenager. Luckily for me, I got away before anything truly horrific could happen."

"No." He shook his head. "Sebastian wouldn't . . ."

"Sebastian is a male version of your wife. Believe me, he did. He learned from Danielle how to treat me, and she only encouraged him."

He gazed at me, disbelieving. "You are saying all this happened under my roof without my knowledge?"

I sneered. "Don't pretend to care now. It's too bloody late."

"I don't know what you want from me." He shrugged. "I thought I'd given you everything. Now I just don't know what you want from me."

Like always, he would play the sad martyr . . . another weapon of manipulation.

But it wouldn't work. Not this time.

"I want you to go home to London."

He stared at me as if he didn't recognize me.

Good.

I didn't want to be the person he knew before.

"You would really ignore this? Ignore your mother's cancer?"

"I'm not ignoring it. I'm sad for anyone who has to fight that battle, but with her the sadness is begrudgingly given." I strode toward the door and stopped to look back at him "I'll tell you what, Gabriel. If Danielle asks for me, I'll come to see her. But just to visit. Not to stay, not to care for her . . because we both know with utter certainty that she would not reciprocate the kindness. This is good-bye, Mr. Bentley."

He looked away, the muscle twitching in his jaw, as realization poured over him that he wasn't going to win this one. There would be no reuniting of this family so he could wave to his public and his shareholders and tell them all was right in his world, and if all was right in his world, then all was right in his business.

"She won't ask for me," I said. "And I thank God she won't. Her presence in my life is a snake bite. I'm still not done sucking the venom out of me from last time. Another bite might prove fatal."

And with that sad summation of my relationship with the woman who had once been my mother, I walked out of the hotel room, feeling heavy of heart but knowing I'd done the only thing I could live with.

CHAPTER 28

I'd love to say I went back to Shannon's flat and kept my cool and was strong, filled with British stiff-upper-lipness.

The truth is, emotional flood that I was, I burst into tears as soon as Shannon opened the door, and spent the next ten minutes alternating between hugs from her and from Maia.

Finally I calmed down enough to tell them everything I'd said, and when I was done they both stared at me in awe.

"One day, when I'm older and I can hack it, I hope I'm brave enough to confront my mum like you did your dad," Maia said.

Well, that just made me cry again.

"Oh dear," Shannon said upon the return of the human watering pot in her sitting room. "I think I'd better make some tea."

Once she'd left the room, I wiped at my tears and tried to focus. "Any word yet from Logan?"

Maia shook her head. "Nope. I have to admit, I'm starting to get worried."

The butterflies that had become my constant companion these last forty-eight hours suddenly grew fiercer.

We sat in silence for a minute or so until I said, "They should be back by now."

"I know," Shannon agreed, coming back into the room with a cup of tea for us all. I took the warm cup gratefully. "I've texted Cole, but I haven't heard anything back. We've all been worried about Logan's reaction, but you guys do know that Cole is a trained martial artist, right?"

My eyes bugged out of my head. "No. No one did impart that pivotal information. You don't think he would . . . ?"

Shannon shrugged. "He promised me he wouldn't. But Cole has protective instincts a hundred miles long. He knows everything that Ollie did to me." She ran a hand through her hair, a ringlet springing back defiantly from the tug of the action. "I should never have agreed to this."

The door opened at that exact moment, and Shannon sprang to her feet as Logan and Cole strode into the room. There was a heavy, dangerous air around them.

"What happened?" Maia said, getting to her feet as I did.

"He got the message," Logan said, features tight with grim fury. "Without violence. Although I had to hold this one back the whole time." He jerked his thumb over his shoulder at Cole.

Cole looked ready to explode.

Shannon took a tentative step toward him, whispering his name.

Logan looked at Maia and then at me. "Let's leave these two alone."

I gathered my things as Maia hugged a very distracted Shannon good-bye. I touched her shoulder as I passed her and grabbed Logan's hand.

There was no point saying anything to Cole. His eyes were locked on Shannon, and I had a feeling I knew how he was going to expend all that unused energy inside of him.

I blushed at the thought and held tighter to Logan.

"Are you okay?" I said as soon as we were out of the flat.

"Aye," he assured me. "I'll tell you everything when we get home. Are you okay?"

"She was brilliant," Maia threw over her shoulder as she led us out the building. "But I'll let her tell you how it went."

"Maia was there?" He frowned at me.

"No," she said, "but I wish I had been."

Since no one felt like cooking that night, we grabbed some fish and chips while we were out and took them back to Logan's. We snuggled up in his sitting room, eating, while he related what happened.

His eyes glinted with triumph. "You should have seen his face when he saw these six blokes walking toward him. And then he saw me. By then it was too late. We were right in his face."

"Were there other people in the park watching?" Maia said, her eyes bright with excitement at the thought of the drama.

Logan nodded. "Aye, we definitely had an audience."

"The six of you are quite a sight," I muttered, my lips twitching with amusement at the thought.

He chewed on a chip and then swallowed. "The first thing Ollie said was, 'Where's Shannon?' Cole just lunged for him. Luckily, I'm fast. But I had to keep ahold of him the whole time."

"So what else did he say?"

"Ollie basically said that he wanted to apologize for what he'd done. That he was a different person."

"What did you say?"

"I said Shannon didn't want his apology. She had moved on, had a life, a family, and a fiancé. Cole may have thrown a few expletives at him at that point. And then I told Ollie that Shannon never wanted to see him again and that if he tried to contact her we'd call the police." He smirked. "And then Braden stepped forward and told him Shannon had a family here now and that family would protect her. He said it was best Ollie returned to Glasgow."

"Is that it?" Maia grimaced, clearly disappointed there had been no fists involved.

Logan grinned at her. "It wasn't what he said, Maia. It was how he said it."

I shared a knowing smile with him. "These people are good people."

He winked at me, obviously in agreement.

"Well, as long as this guy pisses off and leaves Aunt Shannon alone, I guess that's all that matters." Maia shrugged, shoving a piece of fish in her mouth.

"Don't use the word 'piss.'" I shook my head at her.

"Bugger off?" she suggested, her mouth full.

I wrinkled my nose. "Chew before you talk."

She swallowed and bugged her eyes out at Logan. "She's bossy tonight."

I shrugged. "It's been that kind of day."

"You still haven't told me what happened with your dad."

"Later," I said, with more than that promise in my eyes.

Understanding, his own gaze grew heated. He looked away before Maia caught on. "Movie?" he asked her.

"Sure." Maia put her plate on the coffee table and wandered over to the cabinet with the DVDs. "I guess this is as good a time as any to tell you I've got a date next Saturday."

Logan choked on a chip.

"A boy from the swim program?" Logan stood in my bedroom doorway with his arms crossed over his chest. "And I've just to say yes?"

I sat on the edge of the bed wearing a sexy blue silk nighty, and that was the first thing he said to me upon his arrival. I had to stop myself from laughing.

"Well?" he said.

"She's sixteen, Logan. She said that he's also sixteen. It doesn't sound like the end of the world. He could be nineteen and riding a motorcycle."

"I have to meet him."

"That's your prerogative. But you will not scare him away."

He glowered at me. "I thought that was part of my job."

I chuckled. "A gentle warning perhaps—not a full-blown threat."

He seemed to consider this, and then he sighed. "You're sure she's not too young?"

"She behaves older than most girls her age, and far more responsibly."

"Maybe you should have the sex talk with her just in case. You know, scare her off."

I stood up, smoothing out the short nightdress. "If anyone should be getting the sex talk, it's you." I gestured to my attire. "This should be getting a different reaction than it's getting. I've checked . . ." I glanced over my shoulder at my bum and deliberately plucked at the material covering it. "And it seems to accentuate all the right places, so I don't think I'm doing anything wrong. That would be y—" I looked up again only to discover he'd silently crossed the room until he was inches from me.

His heated gaze made me shiver.

"Does that mean you like it?"

His answer was to drag the nighty up over my head and throw it on my chair. Once I was naked, he lifted me up into his arms and threw me none-too-gently on the bed. I watched, my excitement mounting as he stripped out of his clothes in lightning-fast time.

Suddenly he was braced over me, kissing me like there was no tomorrow. I gripped Logan's waist as the kiss grew hungrier. I could feel the hard, insistent press of his erection against my belly. He groaned, his lips drifting from my mouth, across my chin, down my jaw. He kissed his way down my body, his mouth hot, desperate, and I held on, caressing his muscled back, sliding my hands up toward his shoulder blades as he moved downward.

When that hot mouth of his closed around my left nipple, my hips slammed against him in reaction. "Oh God." My thighs gripped him as I urged him closer, my back arching for more as he first licked me and then sucked hard.

I felt a wet rush between my legs. "Logan."

He groaned again and continued to suck and tease and torment me, until I felt the coil of tension tighten in my lower belly.

"Logan —" I was breathing hard now, clutching his head in my hands as he circled his tongue around my areola. "More."

Suddenly he was moving, sliding down my body, his hands cupping and shaping my breasts as he descended, his lips trailing wet kisses down my stomach. I shivered at the touch of his tongue across my skin and relaxed in anticipation of his destination, my legs falling open.

He kissed me, flicking his tongue lightly, deliberately missing my clit, teasing me. And then I felt his fingers slide inside me, and I whimpered with need. Logan looked up at me, his eyes hot with his own desire. His fingers slipped out of me and then back in. My hips pushed against them, trying to catch his rhythm.

I bit my lip as my orgasm built.

"Let it out, Grace. I want to hear you."

He slipped his fingers out of me, but before I could mourn the loss, he parted my labia and circled my clit, teasing it, pressing it . . . and then he sucked it.

I let it out for him, crying his name loudly in my pleasure as he continued to lick me. "Logan!" I panted, feeling my orgasm near the edge, "Oh God, yes. Yes. Yes!" I burst apart, crying out his name as my eyes fluttered shut. The orgasm rolled through me in waves, and I pulsed and pulsed against his mouth until finally I was satiated.

I felt him move up my body, and when I eventually pried my eyes open he had his hands braced on either side of my head again, his lower body pressed to mine. His expression was dark with promise and lust . . . and something much, much deeper. "My God, I love you," he said, the words so thick with emotion they were barely audible.

I forced energy into my arm and lifted my hand to brush his cheek. "I love you just as much."

He shook his head. "Not possible, babe."

I smiled. "Is it a competition?"

"Fact." He nudged his hard-on between my legs, and I shivered in reaction. "No man alive loves a woman as much as I love you. I never thought I would feel this way about anyone. I didn't think it existed. Not for me."

"You're going to make me cry, and I need to stop crying," I whispered. "I love you just as much. Never forget it."

He nodded, leaning down to brush his mouth over mine. "Do you trust me?"

"Yes," I said immediately. "Completely."

"Still on the pill?" He nibbled on my lower lip before looking into my eyes in question.

Confused, I nodded.

"And you trust me?"

"I already said yes."

In answer he kissed me deeper, wetter than before, and as I sank into the beauty of it, he pushed inside of me.

He gasped against my mouth at the feel of being inside of me sans protection. His eyes darkened as he pressed deeper, and my muscles squeezed around him. He eased almost all the way out of me, and then slid back in, his thrusts gentle and slow.

The friction started within me again.

We locked gazes as he moved inside of me, and I was overwhelmed by the connection between us, by the love. It spurred my arousal on like nothing else could, and before I knew it I was coming again.

Logan kept pumping into me, chasing his own climax, the tension straining his muscles as he fought to hold it off as long as possible. When he pressed a thumb to my clit, I realized why.

He wanted me to come again.

In the privacy of my bedroom, Logan MacLeod whispered all the dirty things he was going to do to me in explicit deal. Just as he demanded I come once more, my inner muscles tightened around his cock and his lips parted, his hips stilled, and with a deep groan that sent satisfaction rumbling through me, he shuddered as we reached climax together.

CHAPTER 29

Eight months later

The sound of banging slowly seeped into my ears, jerking me out of my warm, wonderful sleep. I kept my eyes shut, refusing to be completely pulled out of it.

"Dad! Grace!"

The heavy arm around my waist shifted, and a groan rumbled right near my ear.

"Dad!"

"Maia?" Logan said sleepily into my ear, sounding confused.

"Door," I mumbled.

"Wake up! It's the wedding today!" She ended that on a giggle.

"Fuck." The arm started to disappear from my waist, and I fumbled to catch it.

I pulled his body back in to mine, my back against his front. "No."

I heard his throaty chuckle. "Babe, we need to get up."

"Wake up!"

"We're up, Maia," Logan called back.

"I've got coffee for you. Are you decent?"

He leaned down to brush my hair from my face and whisper in my ear, "Are we decent?"

"I am. You're definitely not," I mumbled, still refusing to open my eyes.

"In ten seconds I'm coming in!"

"Damn." I opened my eyes, squinting against the light. "I feel like I've had three hours of sleep."

"That's because you have."

I turned and sat up, watching as Logan got out of bed and quickly shimmied into a pair of jeans. He threw a T-shirt at me.

Oh, yeah, I was naked.

I started to pull it on when I noticed his tie still wrapped around my wrist. "Shit." I tugged at it frantically, not wanting Maia to see it.

Logan laughed and sat back on the bed, pushing my hands away. "Give us just a few more seconds, Maia," he called out to her.

"Ugh," she said. "That told me more than I needed to know."

"Get it off," I whispered, as he struggled to untie the knot.

He was shaking with laughter. "Where's the other one?"

I lifted my wrist and frowned. "You must have taken it off." I glanced warily at the bedroom door. "I thought Maia was staying with Shannon last night?" Just the thought of her hearing what we got up to in this bedroom made me blush in mortification from head to toe. A few months ago I'd given up my flat to move into Logan's, and we'd been very creative about sex ever since, finding time to have amazing, very loud sex whenever Maia wasn't home. The times she was home were the times Logan loved to watch me bite my lip to keep the cries of pleasure inside.

"She was," he assured me as he untied the tie.

As soon as he did that, I whipped on the T-shirt.

"I'm coming in before the coffee gets cold."

"Come in," Logan said once I was covered and the tie was hidden.

Maia pushed open the door and stepped in carrying two mugs of coffee. My lips parted at the sight of her. She was already dressed in her bridesmaid outfit.

"You look beautiful," I said.

She grinned, handing me my coffee. "Now, don't go getting all watery on me, Grace."

"She's right." Her dad leaned up to press a kiss to her cheek as he took his coffee. "You look gorgeous, sweetheart."

She blushed and smoothed her now-free hands down the pale pink dress. It was so subtle a pink it was almost oyster. It had little cap sleeves, a sweetheart neckline, and a slight swing in the skirt. The skirt hit her knees, so you could see the beautiful oyster-pink platform peep toes she was wearing. Her hair had been styled into this elaborate updo with coils and curls pinned in place with little pearls and diamantés.

"You look so grown-up."

Maia smiled shyly at me. "Do you think Charlie will like it?"

Her father growled at the mention of the boy who had been seeing Maia for eight months now. I didn't know what he was so concerned about. Charlie was the opposite of a bad boy if ever I had met one.

"I'm sure he will. What are you doing here? Clearly you've been at Shannon's." I gestured to her.

"Aye, the hairstylist and makeup artist did my hair and makeup first, so I thought I'd grab a cab and come back home to make sure you two were up. Thankfully I did, or you'd still be sleeping."

"On that note, I'm going to take a shower." Logan dumped his now-empty coffee mug on the bedside table and hurried out of the room.

"Is he nervous about walking Shannon down the aisle?" Maia said after he'd gone.

"Nope. He's honored."

I watched Logan walk his sister down the aisle a few hours later, my chest bursting with pride. I still thought it was incredibly brave of her to choose him over her father, and I was pleased to see that despite the upset it caused, her parents were still in attendance. Apparently, their father had come around, and understood why it meant so much to Shannon for Logan to be the one to give her away.

They'd also been there for Maia so far.

Not surprisingly, Maia, knowing what they were capable of, kept her defenses higher around them, having been taught too young what it was like to have someone care for you one moment and stop caring the next.

But the MacLeods were trying.

Shannon had only a flower girl, a bridesmaid, and a matron of honor. She had Maia as bridesmaid, Cole's niece, Belle, as flower girl, and her friend Rae was matron of honor. I'd met her only once before. Rae worked with Cole at the tattoo studio, and she herself was a tattooed biker-looking chick who somehow made her dress look biker punk.

It might have been the motorcycle boots Shannon had allowed her to wear.

Both Shannon and Cole had written their own vows, so I had mascara blobs around my eyes by the time they were finished. I was glad to see I wasn't the only one affected, however, as I could see Ellie, Jo, and Hannah dabbing away at their eyes. Only Olivia and Joss were dry-eyed, but their beaming smiles lit up the whole church.

I'd never known people like them, I thought as I stared around the room at the women and men and children who had invited Shannon and Logan into their lives and just as easily took in Maia and me.

"Need a hanky there?" Aidan whispered in my ear beside me.

Juno, who sat by his side, jabbed her elbow into his stomach to quiet him.

Chloe, who sat on my other side, handed me a tissue.

I rolled my eyes at their gentle teasing, but I was glad they were here with me.

All of my family in one room together.

"Okay, let's ditch this place and get out of here," Shannon announced upon rushing over to us, dragging Cole with her.

The reception hall was huge because they had a lot of guests, but those of us who were family and close friends had pushed two tables together and were sitting around them, talking and drinking, relaxed now that the ceremony and dinner was over.

We stared up at Shannon, amused.

Her dress—a white, figure-hugging, calf-length forties-style number—was still pristine. As were the five-inch Kurt Geiger bridal shoes she was wearing. However, her cheeks were flushed, and her hair was falling loose of the clips the hairstylist had used.

She looked overwhelmed.

"I mean it." She nodded. "We need to get out of here. My cheeks hurt, my feet hurt, and I'm fed up talking to people I hardly ever talk to instead of the people I want to talk to." She gestured to us.

"I tried to tell her this is what it would be like," Cole said as he wrapped his arms around her waist and drew her back against him.

"Let's just go to the Walk or something." She referred to a pub that I knew Cole favored on Leith Walk.

"Nope." He kissed her cheek apologetically. "We're stuck here."

"That doesn't mean you have to traipse around after everyone else," I said, pushing an empty chair toward her. "Sit down with us. If anyone wants to talk to you, they can come to you."

Her eyes brightened at that, and she immediately whipped off her shoes and padded over to me barefoot. Logan pushed a chair toward Cole, and he gave up and decided to join us too. "What the hell," he muttered. "It's our wedding."

"We should have done that at our wedding," Joss said to Braden.

Her husband held Baby Ellie in his arms, swaying her gently as she took everything in. Shannon and Cole had deliberately held the wedding and wedding supper early so the kids could all enjoy it. "Probably," he said. "But I quite enjoyed how tortured you were by it all."

"You're such a romantic," she said dryly.

He winked at her and she rolled her eyes.

"Everyone should do what we did," Hannah said. "Marco and I invited just you lot, and it was perfect."

"Oh no. I like the whole big wedding thing," Ellie disagreed. "I love weddings."

"We know," Joss, Jo, Liv, and Hannah said in unison.

Ellie glared at them, and Adam put his arm around her, pulling her in to his side. "Ignore them, sweetheart."

"You love that I love weddings—don't you?" she said to him, wide-eyed, still somehow managing to pull off this adorable thing even though she was in her late thirties.

"Absolutely," her husband managed to say with a straight face.

Braden ruined it by grunting loudly in disbelief.

"Well, Grace and I will probably just make it a small do," Logan announced, causing the whole two tables to quiet.

I stiffened and felt Chloe's hand grip my knee in reaction to the announcement.

Maia gasped. "Are you getting married?"

"At some point," Logan said, looking confused by everyone's sudden alertness.

"But have you proposed?" Shannon leaned across the table, eyes bright with excitement.

"At some point I will." He stared across the table at me, apparently looking for help.

I could only stare back in shock.

He had not mentioned marriage to me.

"Why does Grace look like she's just hearing this for the first time?" Olivia asked, amusement in her expression.

"Because she is," Chloe answered beside me. She would know, because she'd be the first person to hear about it.

"Och, Logan," Jo snapped at him. "You can't go announcing these things without talking to the bride-to-be first."

"Bad form, mate." Nate shook his head.

"Well . . ." Logan looked at them all and then at me before coming to the realization that he'd gone about it all wrong. "Fuck."

"Logan MacLeod, there are children present." Elodie harrumphed.

"Apologies," he said, almost sheepishly.

I laughed at the fact that no one else, absolutely no one else on the planet could intimidate Logan, but Elodie Nichols could make him feel like an errant schoolboy.

Our eyes met as he turned toward my laughter. His eyes asked me if we were okay. I smiled. "You just better make sure it's one hell of a proposal."

Everyone snorted and chuckled as Logan's gaze, his promise to do just that, seared from his eyes into my very soul.

"Way to hijack my wedding, folks," Shannon teased.

It snapped Logan and me out of our moment, and I put an arm around her, hugging her in apology. She waved me off, laughing, apparently too excited at the prospect of us becoming sisters to care.

As conversation moved on to other things, Maia rushed around the table to me, bending down to look me in the face. For a moment we just gazed at each other, and I felt everything she was feeling without her having to say anything. I reached up to touch her cheek, and her eyes brightened with tears.

Just like that my eyes filled up too.

Because we suddenly knew.

She and I . . . we had Logan and we had each other.

And that meant we were finally going to be okay.

I glanced over at Logan to find him watching us intently, like he knew what had passed between us. His eyes darkened with deep-felt emotion. His lips parted and he mouthed, *I love you.*

And as I mouthed them back, in that moment—in that moment I would never forget—I felt the rare sweetness of absolute rightness . . . of absolute contentment.

Of absolute family.

EPILOGUE

Four days later in Italy

Shannon

"It was good of Joss and Braden to give us the villa again," Cole said as we floated in the pool together. Spring in Lake Como was genuinely a mild affair, a bit like an early British summer, but today was an unusually hot day for the season and we were taking full advantage of it.

I bobbed gently against him, my legs wrapped tight around his hips, my arms around his neck. "I'm so glad we came back here." It had seemed like the perfect choice for our honeymoon.

Cole's hands kneaded my bottom, his low-lidded gaze making me tingle. "Me too. I have particularly good memories of this pool."

I laughed. "It's broad daylight. I only let that happen last time because it was dark."

"Does that mean you'll let me take advantage of you in the pool tonight, then?"

"Oh, you'll have to get me drunk first. I mean, look at you," I teased, smoothing my hands over his strong biceps. "Blech."

He shook with laughter. "I know it'll be a hardship for you, short-cake, but do it for me."

"Oh, all right, then." I laughed as he peppered my face with kisses and pretended to grope me.

"You're wearing too many clothes," he huffed.

"I'm wearing a bikini."

"Yes. Too many clothes."

Giggling, I held on tighter to him, urging my body closer to his as the water tried to gently separate us. "I think we should come back here for every big anniversary."

He slid his arms around my back, drawing me up against his chest so our lips were just an inch from one another. I stared into his beautiful green eyes, and like always, I felt contented with the soul-deep knowledge that I'd found my best friend and my family in this man.

"I think that's a great idea," he said softly, brushing his mouth over mine. "And when we have kids and they're older, we should bring them here too."

"How many do you want?"

He shrugged. "It doesn't matter to me. I'll be happy if we have one or five, boys or girls . . . As long as they have a piece of me and a piece of you in them, that's all that matters."

"Do you have to be so perfect, Cole Walker?"

"It's all part of my charm, Mrs. Cole Walker."

I flushed, my body tingling with arousal as it did every time he called me Mrs. Cole Walker. I didn't know why it was such a turn-on and a trigger, but it was, and I seriously regretted confiding it to him. I glowered at him. "You said you wouldn't." I squirmed as he cupped my ass, deliberately pressing me against him.

He grinned devilishly. "You are so fucking adorable."

I closed my eyes and shut out what he was doing to my body. There was no way we were having sex in broad daylight in a pool! "I want three kids!" I practically shouted to distract us both.

Just as I'd expected, Cole stopped teasing my body and stilled. "Three?"

"Mmm-hmm." I popped open my eyes to stare into his in earnest. "Boys or girls . . . I don't mind. Although I would like one boy with green eyes and strawberry blond hair."

His smile was slow and boyishly pleased. "Yeah? And when are we starting on making that happen, then?"

"Another few years?" I said. "I still want you all to myself for a while."

"Another few years," he murmured, staring at me with all the love and tenderness in the world. "We're going to have really cute kids."

I nodded, hugging him tight. "And smart."

"And kind."

"And talented."

"We really love ourselves, don't we?" he cracked.

I shook my head and stared into his eyes. *No, I just really love you.*

As if he read my thought, Cole closed the distance between us and kissed me so deep and so hard, I reconsidered the whole sex-in-broad-daylight thing.

Meanwhile, back in Edinburgh

Hannah

I couldn't remember the last time I'd come around to my parents' house and it wasn't chaotic. Mum and Dad had to like it that way because it was constant. I knew Mum well enough to know if it was bugging her, she'd tell us all to shove off.

"Dad, can I go upstairs and play the computer with Will?" Dylan said quietly, staring up at his father imploringly as we stood in the hall-way of my parents' house.

We'd only stepped foot in the door and already my nephew Will was attempting to drag my stepson up the stairs.

Marco stared down at Dylan, as did our son Jarrod, who was reaching out his short little arm for his brother with no hope of obtaining his goal. Dylan helped him out by reaching back and clasping his hand. "Only for a while," Marco said. "Your grandma Elodie has made lunch, and you're going to sit with the family and eat it."

"That goes for you too." Adam, my brother-in-law, stepped out into the hall from the sitting room.

His son, Will, who was only a few years younger than Dylan, grinned back at him. "Okay." He shrugged. It was becoming more apparent as the years went on that he'd inherited his easygoing nature from my sister.

Dylan nodded too and then followed Will upstairs.

"I thought I heard voices." Mum appeared beside Adam with five-year-old Braden in her arms.

I strode over to kiss her cheek and then steal Bray from her. "And how is this wee man?" I asked him.

"Fine," he said, chewing on a now soggy brioche roll my mum had probably given him. "Hungry."

Jarrod made this cute little grunting sound as he tried to push away from his dad to get to Bray. When it didn't work, he immediately burst into loud tears. For whatever reason, my son had decided he liked Bray the most out of all of his cousins. Unfortunately, Bray was too concerned with five-year-old boy things to care much for the attentions of a two-year-old.

"Oh dear." Mum smiled. "Let's put Jarrod in the playpen in the sitting room."

"Where's Will?" Bray asked.

"Upstairs."

"Down, Granny," he said.

Mum let him down, and he hurried upstairs as fast as his wee legs could take him.

"Hannah, sweetheart," Dad said, getting up from his chair to hug and kiss me. "How are you?"

"Good, Dad. Stressed with school. Nothing new." I smiled.

"Teaching." He grunted as he took Jarrod into his arms. My dad would know all about the ups and downs of teaching. He taught at university level. "Marco." He nodded congenially at my husband and then looked around us, frowning. "Where's Dylan and Sophia?"

"Dylan is upstairs with Will, and Sophia . . ." I glanced over my shoulder as Ellie walked into the room carrying my daughter in her arms. "Ran straight toward the kitchen."

Sophia adored her aunt Ellie and apparently had some kind of psychic radar for finding her.

Ellie came over to kiss me on the cheek, and Sophia buried her head against her aunt's chest, clearly stating, "I am refusing to budge." My eyes laughed into Ellie's. "How are you?"

"Good." She smiled. "We booked our family holiday this morning."

"Ooh, where are you off to?"

"Disney World," Adam answered, coming up behind his wife. He looked pained just at the thought of it. "Florida."

Ellie was grinning from ear to ear. "It's going to be fantastic."

"Fantastic," Adam murmured, making a horrified face behind her back.

Marco coughed, trying to cover a laugh, but he was fooling no one. Ellie shot him a sideways glance. "Is my husband making faces behind my back?"

Marco straightened his face. "Absolutely not."

"I don't believe you." She looked over her shoulder at Adam. "You are going to enjoy the magical kingdom, Adam Sutherland, end of story."

He stared at her and then turned to us. "The kids will love it—that's what matters. Even though I think Bray is still too young for it."

"Then we'll go again when he's older." Ellie shrugged.

Adam paled. "I need a drink."

"I'll get you one," Mum offered. "Alcohol, right?"

"I really love you, Elodie," he said.

She laughed. "I'll go get you a lager. Clark?"

"Yes, thanks, sweetheart."

"I'm just going to the loo," I said, brushing a hand over Sophia's hair as I passed her and Ellie.

I'd just finished up in the upstairs toilet and had opened the door to come out when I was blocked by Marco. He gently put a hand to my stomach and pushed me back inside, closing the door behind him and locking us in together.

"What is it?" I stared up at him in surprise.

In answer, he slid his hands across my stomach and down onto my hips, gripping them so he could tug me in to him. My own hands smoothed over his chest as I stared up into his beautiful eyes.

"Baby, what is it?" I repeated, growing more concerned by the anxious look in his eyes.

"You're not upset?" he said.

"About what?"

"About all the talk about Disney World?"

Realization suddenly hit me. I shook my head emphatically. "No. I'm not."

Although we both had full-time jobs, as a young couple living in a four-bedroom house in central Edinburgh, it wasn't financially easy. Of course we'd had a better start than most because my pseudo big brother Braden had gotten together with Ellie and they'd bought me a gorgeous flat in New Town. I'd sold the flat to put down a hefty deposit on our four-bedroom house, but we still had a sizable mortgage to pay as well as three kids to clothe and feed.

Expensive holidays to Disney World weren't exactly in the cards for us right now.

"We'll pick up a bargain and take the kids to Spain or something," I reminded him. "And even if we can't do that, we'll just take them on day trips around the country."

Marco nodded but still didn't look entirely convinced. "I don't want you and the kids to miss out on anything."

"Miss out on what?" I pressed deeper into him. "A beautiful house, a husband who loves me, a father who adores them. What exactly are we missing out on?"

"You're sure?" he said, his voice gruff now.

I slid my hands up around his neck and pulled his mouth down to mine. I teased my lips over his, brushing my top lip over his bottom, my bottom over his top.

He groaned, his grip on my hips turning almost bruising, and I felt his immediate reaction to me digging into my stomach.

My skin flushed hot and I kissed him, loving how I could turn him on so easily.

The kiss turned wet, deep, hard, hands sliding and touching and pulling to get closer.

The sound of my mother calling up to the boys that lunch was ready broke through our haze and we reluctantly parted. My breasts heaved in Marco's hands, and he kneaded them one last time before sliding his hands to a safer position on my waist.

"I guess that means you're sure." His voice rumbled with amusement.

I grinned up at him. "Baby, every day with you is a vacation."

His eyes warmed, filling with tenderness.

"Where are Hannah and Marco?" I heard my mum say loudly.

"Dunno," Will answered cheerily.

My eyes widened. "I'll slip out first and let you . . ." I gestured to his hard-on.

He closed his eyes. "My fault for choosing a hot wife."

I chuckled and slipped past him as he moved his back from the door. "I'll tell them you'll be down in a minute." I opened the door and looked back at him. "Uncle Gio. Naked."

Marco cursed and threw a hand cloth at me, and I laughed, fleeing the bathroom and slamming the door shut behind me. "I bet it works!" I yelled through the door, and laughed all the way downstairs.

Upon my arrival into the dining room, Dylan patted the seat next to him. "Hannah."

As always, my chest burst with feeling as I walked over to join my stepson. Dylan adored his dad, and of course he loved his mum to bits, but I was pleased to have earned his love over the last few years and the coveted position of being the person he most wanted to sit beside at mealtimes. Just as I was about to sit down, Sophia decided she'd missed me in the last ten minutes and refused to sit anywhere but on my lap. It was clear she hadn't realized that at four years old she was now much bigger than she was at two. But I didn't mind. Mum had already warned me there would come a time when Sophia wouldn't want to be seen with me, let alone sit on my lap, so I was determined to soak up her attention as much as possible.

The skin on my neck prickled and I knew my husband had entered the room. I looked over as he walked in with Adam, Adam holding Bray's hand while Marco carried Jarrod.

Marco took his seat beside me, shooting me a look that promised retribution later for our moment upstairs. Jarrod immediately reached for a lock of Sophia's hair, and she turned and tickled his neck in response, eliciting a giggle from him.

"Everyone ready to eat?" Mum asked the table, and as I glanced around at my family, I felt strangely emotional. I looked back at Marco, who seemed to sense it and was watching me carefully.

Like he always did. My feelings were a number-one priority to him, and he never let me forget it.

I thought of what he'd asked me upstairs.

"I am so sure," I whispered, and my husband reached out his free hand to squeeze my knee under the table.

Olivia

It was too quiet. Much, much too quiet in the house.

I was snuggled up on a huge armchair in the snug sitting room (the smaller of our two sitting rooms), where I was reading a book by an author Grace worked with. I got to a steamy part that made me flush and looked over at my gorgeous husband, who was lying on the couch reading a graphic novel (because he'd never stopped being a big kid).

My intention was to jump him when the thought occurred to me that either one of our girls might come running in and interrupt us. That's when I realized the house was much, much too quiet.

"Where are the girls?" I said to Nate.

He turned his head on the fat cushion he was resting against and peered at me over the glasses he now had to wear. He hated them. I thought they made him look adorable. Which was exactly why he hated them. "I thought they were in the living room watching a film."

"And that usually comes with singing or dancing or squealing of some sort." I got up off of the chair, leaving my book in my place. "I'll be back in a sec."

"Baby, can you get me a coffee while you're up?"

"Your lack of concern is wonderful." I rolled my eyes at him and disappeared out of the room.

What I found in the living room made me draw to a stop with a small gasp.

Playing on the large television screen Nate had mounted on our wall above the fireplace was our wedding DVD.

Lily and January sat on the couch, quiet as mice as they watched their mom and dad dance at their reception.

I stared at the image, too, at the way that Nate held me close and gazed into my eyes like no one else was in the room with us.

Clearly the girls were mesmerized by this, watching it as if they were watching a Disney Princess movie.

I felt heat at my back seconds before arms slid around my waist and drew me back against a hard chest. I relaxed against Nate, covering his arms with my own. He nuzzled my neck and whispered in my ear, "Good movie choice."

I grinned. "I haven't watched it in ages," I whispered back.

Lily turned, having heard us. She wore a look of apology. "Oh. We just found it."

January glanced over her shoulder at us. "Mummy, your dress is so pretty."

"Do you still have it?" Lily asked, eyes bright just at the thought of getting to wear it.

"I do. I'll show it to you, but you have to be really careful with it, okay?"

They nodded solemnly, my two little angels.

"Daddy, you're wearing a kilt there!" Lily giggled.

"I am wearing a kilt," he acknowledged as he shuffled me forward as if I were his puppet, making the girls giggle harder.

"Did you like wearing a kilt?"

He squeezed me harder. "I don't know. Did I like wearing a kilt?"

I shook my head. "You complained about it the whole day."

Lily paused the DVD and turned around on the couch to face us. Like always, January did what her big sister did. "Would you rather wear a kilt or a nappy?" She grinned like she'd thought of the funniest thing ever.

I shook with laughter, wondering if Nate regretted introducing our "would you rather" conversations to our children.

"Hmm." He actually pretended to ponder it. "I think I'd rather wear a kilt."

"Why?"

316 · SAMANTHA YOUNG

"Because it's warmer and less humiliating."

Lily giggled again, but Jan wrinkled her nose. "What does humil—humanaiting mean?"

"Humiliating," Lily corrected her. "It means embarrassing."

My smart, smart little cookie.

"Oh." Jan laughed, the dimples she'd inherited from her father flashing. "Yeah, a nappy would make you look silly, Daddy."

"I don't know."

I glanced over my shoulder to look at him. "A nappy, really?"

He grinned, his own dimples flashing. "I could pull off a nappy."

"Honey, I love you, and I think you are very handsome, but not even you could pull off a man nappy."

He snorted. "Maybe you're right."

"Mum, would you rather be married to Daddy or the man from the washing-up liquid commercial?" Lily grinned mischievously.

I bugged my eyes out at her as my kid gave me away.

Nate gently eased me around to face him. "What's this?" he teased.

I shrugged sheepishly. "He's very good-looking."

"So?" He raised an eyebrow. "Me or this washing-up guy?"

Now it was my turn to pretend to muse over it. "The washing-up guy does do the dishes."

"We have a dishwasher."

"He cleans kitchen countertops too."

"Hey, we had a deal. I give you two cute kids, you clean the kitchen."

"That's a pretty good deal, Mum." Lily smiled.

I made a face at Nate, who couldn't contain his laughter. "She's got you there."

"She's not got me there. *I* did the hard work to produce these two angels. That doesn't make sense at all. If anyone should be cleaning countertops, it's you."

"Mum, would you rather—"

"No, my turn." I bent down as far as I could with Nate's arms wrapped around me and brushed my nose over Lily's and then Jan's. They both giggled and waved me away. "Would you rather live in the sewers with enchanted animals and pretty elves and mystical sewer cities, or in a beautiful, peaceful forest with a bunch of pretty princesses and charming princes?"

Our girls looked at each other for a second as they contemplated it and then turned in unison and said, "Sewers!"

"Good answer." I nodded in approval.

"That was a tough one." Nate was pensive. "I was really having a hard time coming up with an answer to that one." He put a hand to his heart in a dramatic fashion. "Live in the dirty sewers with a bunch of lovable weirdos or traverse a beautiful forest with a gorgeous princess. It's tough. Really tough."

"Daddy!" The girls laughed at his joking, their giggles coming harder.

"You're lucky you're adorable in those glasses." I pressed into him, laughing when his eyes narrowed at the word "adorable." "Or I might just take offense to the whole gorgeous princess thing."

"I wouldn't," he whispered. "She was dull as dishwater and kept falling asleep."

"*Sleeping Beauty*!" Jan shouted, having overhead. "Can we watch *Sleeping Beauty*?"

"Yeah!" Lily shouted, dashing across the room to our DVD cabinet.

Nate looked from them to me and snorted. "Our wedding DVD has been bumped for *Sleeping Beauty*."

I pulled him away from the girls, snuggling into him once I had him at the doorway. When I was sure the girls couldn't hear, I whispered, "Perhaps there is something to the whole *Sleeping Beauty* thing."

His hands flexed on my hips, his gaze turning low-lidded and hot. "What did you have in mind?"

"I'm thinking sexual fantasy. Tonight." I brushed my lips over his. "Your choice? Do I play a damsel-in-distress fairy-tale style, or do we go with something a little more sci-fi?" I grinned suggestively.

"Never change," he whispered hoarsely. "You are absolutely fucking perfect the way you are."

"What are you talking about?" Lily called over to us nosily.

"Your dad is just remembering why he married me," I called back, and he grinned, those irresistible dimples flashing again, like they were wont to do at least thirty times a day.

Johanna

"Belle loves it here." I snuggled into Cam's side as the breeze from the water sent goose bumps up all over me. "I should have put on a jacket."

In response, Cam opened his and burrowed me into him, closing the jacket over me as far as it would go. "We should make an effort to come here more often."

I nodded, watching Belle play on the beach with our friends, Lyn and Peetie's daughter, Sara. Lyn and Cam's mum, Helena, pretended to chase them, and their giggles floated up into the air to join the caws of the seagulls above our heads.

I always loved Cam's hometown of Longniddry. I loved the nearby beach we were on, and I loved that my kid loved her grandparents so much. I loved that she was having the kind of life I'd always dreamed of having as a child.

"Cole and Shannon will be enjoying the sun," Cam said, a smile in his voice.

Belle shrieked as she spun out of Helena's reach only to go running straight into her Grandpa Anderson. He laughed and swooped her up into the air, and she giggled and cried out as he spun her around before releasing her to the sand again. Sara demanded the same treatment, and Peetie obliged as Lyn and the grandparents looked on. I followed Belle with my eyes as she ran on ahead a little.

As I gazed at her, she morphed into a little boy with strawberry blond hair, looking at the water in awe. It was a memory of the day I'd jumped on a bus with him and taken him to Balloch so he could see the loch for the first time. He'd been six; I was only fourteen.

"I still can't believe my wee brother is married."

"He's twenty-seven, Jo," Cam reminded me gently.

"He'll always be wee to me," I whispered, feeling a little emotional. "You'll get it with Belle. She'll always be six years old to you."

"Baby, are you all right?" He ducked his head to look at my face.

"It's silly." I shook my head, blinking back tears. "I just feel like . . . ever since I got everything I ever wanted, time has just sped up. Belle will be in high school before we know it. I love being a mum. I love us as parents. I don't want that to stop."

"It will never stop, Jo."

"I know, but look at Cole. It doesn't stop, but they don't need you the same way after a while."

Cam was silent a moment, I think surprised by my sadness.

But like always, he had the ability to surprise me too. "Do you . . . ? Do you want another baby?"

I tensed against him, afraid to look him in the eye and give myself away. "You're forty this year, Cam."

"And you're only coming on thirty-five. There's still time . . . if that's what you want?"

Hope began to bubble up within me as I turned to look at him. For months this had been pressing on me, but Cameron had never given any hint that he wanted to have another kid. It would be more financial stress. It would mean maybe having to look for another place to live. But I *really* wanted another baby. I wanted Belle to be a big sister like I had been, and to have her little brother or sister look up to her the way that Cole had looked up to me.

"Would you *want* another baby?"

Cam searched my eyes, a small smile starting to play on his lips.

"Yeah, I'd want another baby. I just didn't think it was something you wanted. You usually tell me when you want something, Jo." He was grinning now as he saw the excitement enter my eyes.

"I really want another child," I whispered. "I really do."

He nodded slowly. "Then we'll start trying."

"Just like that? No discussion?"

"It won't be easy." He stared off down the beach. The others had gotten farther ahead of us, and Belle and Sara were skipping down the beach hand in hand now. "But it's worth it."

I wrapped my arms around his neck, holding on tight. "I love you."

"I love you too."

I kissed him, a long, slow, sweet kiss filled with every ounce of love and gratitude I had within me that after all these years Cameron MacCabe still had the ability to make me the happiest woman on the planet. Tears trembled on my eyelashes, and when he broke the kiss they splashed onto my cheeks.

Cam swiped at them with his thumb. "Happy tears?"

"Very."

He grinned and hugged me tighter. "This will be fun."

"Adding another kid to the tribe?" I sniffled, chuckling.

"I meant the constant sex . . . but yeah, that too."

My laughter rang out down the beach as he tugged my hand and led me toward our family. At the sound of my laugher, Belle, blond hair flying wildly around her smiling face, immediately dashed back up the beach toward us.

Ellie

Leaning silently against the doorway of my mum's kitchen, I studied Adam's back as he stood alone at the sink washing the cups and mugs that couldn't go in the dishwasher.

For not the first time I thanked God I married a man who didn't mind kitchen duty.

"I can feel you there, you know," he said quietly, the words tinged with amusement.

I smiled and stepped into the room. "Hannah and Marco are leaving in a bit."

"We should probably head home too. I think Jarrod has worn out Bray."

Slipping up behind him, I slid my arms around him, crossing them over his chest as I leaned my cheek against his shoulder. "I was thinking . . ."

"Hmm, that's never a good thing."

"I'm serious."

Adam snorted. "So am I."

I rolled my eyes even though he couldn't see me do it. "You'll like this line of thought. I promise."

In answer he stopped drying a mug and turned so I had to rearrange my arms around his shoulders as he drew me chest against chest to him. I stared into his dark eyes, seeing a glimmer of discontentment in them. I'd seen that look a few times now over the past few weeks, and it was starting to make me anxious. It was only after we'd booked the kids' holiday to Disney World that I began to suspect what was wrong.

"I've been neglecting you," I whispered, brushing his hair from his face.

There were a few wrinkles around his eyes that didn't used to be there, but they only made him look rugged and interesting. Bloody men. Why was it so many of them got better-looking with age while we women had to work our arses off to stay looking young?

"Ellie?"

I shook my head, focusing. "I've been working on my paper, and I've been spending all my free time with the kids, and you've been busy. You and I haven't had any 'us time.'"

He nodded, something like relief entering his expression, and I was suffused with guilt.

322 · SAMANTHA YOUNG

"You thought I hadn't noticed?" I said.

"Like you said, we've been busy." He shrugged.

"Adam, I've noticed we haven't been on a date in months. I've noticed we haven't had time for more than a quickie in months." I pressed into him. "You have to tell me when you're unhappy."

"Els." He wrapped his arms even tighter around me. "I'm not unhappy. I've just missed you. I never wanted to be like my parents and ignore my kids, but I also would like some time with my wife every now and then."

"Me too." I smiled slowly. "That's why I asked Mum and Clark to take the kids tonight. We'll pop home and get them some overnight stuff, bring it back here, and then you and I can do whatever the hell we want."

Adam raised his eyebrows. "Are you kidding? Because if you're kidding, it's really cruel."

I giggled. "I'm not kidding. Just you and me, sweetheart."

He kissed me, a soft kiss that promised more, and then he pulled back to whisper against my mouth, "We'll drop off the kids' stuff and then we're going home so I can fuck you as hard as I want and you can come as loudly as you want."

A streak of arousal shot straight between my legs, and I nodded, speechless.

His eyes heated. "Let's go now."

I grinned and nodded. "I have another present for you."

"Please say see-through lingerie."

Laughing, I shook my head. "Better."

He looked doubtful that there was anything better than see-through lingerie.

"We'll do Disney World with the boys in the summer and have a ball with them." Because as much as he teased about the predicted chaos of the upcoming holiday, he loved hanging out with his boys. His real issue had been that he never got to see *me . . . alone*. "And afterward, you and I are going to Joss and Braden's villa at Lake Como for four nights. They said we could have it, and Mum and Clark are happy to look after the boys."

Adam stared at me a moment as if in disbelief. When he realized I was serious, he kissed me again, harder this time. We broke the kiss to gasp for breath, and he said, voice hoarse, "I fucking love you."

"Kind of hard to hate me, sweetie," I teased.

"You're not joking," he grunted, backing me up toward the door. "Home, kids' stuff, back here, home, screwing like teenagers. Now."

Well, he didn't need to tell me twice.

Joss

"Mum, are you writing?"

My fingers stilled on the keys of my laptop at the sound of my eldest's voice behind me. "Is this the room in which I write?" I said without turning around.

"You didn't look like you were writing."

I turned in my chair to find Beth hovering in the now-open doorway of my office. "Did the closed door and the sound of keys tapping not give it away?"

My eleven-year-old grimaced in a way that was so like me. "Dad's with Ellie, Luke is playing a video game, and I'm bored."

"I thought you were reading."

"I was, but my book is boring. Plus . . . it is a Saturday, you know." She put her hands on her hips and glared at me.

I felt that glare hit me in the chest and a little ache spread out from it. I tried my best to balance my writing and my life with my kids and with Braden, but clearly sometimes I got it wrong. "Go and get Luke ready and I will go get your dad. We'll go out for lunch and to see a movie. Sound good?"

"I really shouldn't have to drop these hints about how to be a parent,

Mum." She raised her eyebrow at me in this seriously schoolmarmish way. I honestly didn't know where she picked up this crap.

I raised my eyebrow right back at her. "Okay, smart-ass. Message received."

She grinned triumphantly and dashed off to get her brother.

I chuckled as I saved my document and shut down my computer. My kid was getting too smart for her own good. It was difficult to rein in the smart-assness, however, when she had a mother like me and a father like Braden.

Finding said father in the sitting room, I stopped in the doorway to stare at him for a moment. Braden's long and still deliciously well-kept body was sprawled over our couch. Our baby girl, Ellie, was sprawled across Braden's chest. They were both sleeping.

I pulled my phone out of my pocket and started taking pictures.

"What are you doing?" Braden mumbled sleepily.

I looked up from my phone to see him rubbing his eyes with one hand and stroking Ellie's back with the other.

"Putting a photo of you and Ellie sleeping on Instagram. My readers will love it."

Looking more awake now, he frowned. "What?"

"Didn't you know, babe? You're their favorite book boyfriend come to life."

"You've been sharing photos of me with your readers?" he grumbled sleepily.

"I had to get some use out of you. You've increased my social media followers. Oh look. Twenty likes already." I grinned over the top of my phone at him, and his eyes narrowed.

"You owe me for that."

My body warmed just at the thought. "What did you have in mind?"

He smiled, slow, wicked, and sweet. "I'll think of something."

"Will I like it?"

"Are you flirting with me while our child is sleeping in the room?"

I strode over to them. "She can't hear me," I whispered, bending down to my haunches to stroke her soft hair. "She's out."

"I thought you were writing."

I turned my attention from Ellie to Braden, falling like always into his pale blue gaze. "Beth misses me. Although she didn't put it quite like that."

"She wouldn't." He smiled affectionately. "She's too much like her mum to admit outright when she's missing someone. Always has to wrap up the feeling in sarcasm."

I chuckled. "It makes life entertaining for you."

"I wouldn't want it any other way, babe."

Leaning over, I pressed my lips to his, intending it to be a soft kiss, but like always, it turned deeper.

"Yuck!" Beth's voice broke us apart. "It's bad enough doing that in front of me, but in front of Ellie?"

At her loud entrance, Ellie stirred on Braden's chest and began to whimper at being awoken.

"Beth, your sister was sleeping," I admonished.

She immediately looked guilty and crept on her tiptoes into the room as if her now-silent entrance would undo waking up her sister. Coming right up to my side, she knelt down and put her hand on Ellie's back. "It's okay, baby girl," she said softly. "We're going to go out. You want to go out?"

Ellie reached sleepily for her sister, and Beth took her into her arms with ease and stood up. "I'll go get her changed."

I tugged on the hem of Beth's skirt. "Thank you, baby."

Once they were gone, Braden sat up, running his hands through his mussed hair. "We're going out?"

I nodded and sat down on his lap, mussing his hair even more with my hands. "Beth was bored."

He frowned as he wrapped his arm around my waist. "I could have taken the kids out, left you here to write."

"No." I kissed him again. "Beth was making a point. I need to spend more time with you and the kids. I *want* to spend more time with you."

"And tonight with me?" He brushed his mouth teasingly over mine.

"Every night with you," I whispered back, and he kissed me harder.

"Yuck!"

We broke apart this time to find Luke standing in the doorway with his arms crossed over his chest.

"Problem?" I arched my eyebrow at my eight-year-old.

"Yeah." He said it like it should be obvious. "You're not supposed to do that in front of your kids. That's what Beth says. She says it's, like, a rule."

Braden chuckled. "Son, the only ones making rules in this house are Mum and Dad. Got that?"

He nodded obediently but still looked consternated. "Perhaps it should be a rule?"

I bit back laughter at the hope in the question.

"Believe me, bud," Braden said, squeezing my hip for emphasis. "That's the one thing that's least likely to become a rule in this house."

"But there's a chance?"

I turned my face to Braden's neck to hide my grin from Luke.

"No. There is zero chance."

"When I turn eighteen, will I be able to make rules?"

Sensing where this was going, Braden chuckled. "Son, when you're eighteen, a no-kissing-girls rule will be the last thing you want to put in place."

"Maybe. But a no-kissing-Mum rule will definitely be put in place." He disappeared from the doorway and we heard him yell for his sister, probably going in search of her to complain about us.

"They're ganging up on us," I murmured ominously, staring after our son.

"Oh, they can try." Braden turned my face so he could kiss me again. When he pulled back, he grinned. "But they won't succeed."

I grinned at the humor in his eyes, the humor I shared, the connection *we* shared that got us through absolutely anything, and I knew always would. "We've got this."

"We've got this," Braden agreed, and then he kissed me once more as Luke walked back into the room, and our laughter bubbled against each other's lips at the sound of our son's outrage.

Grace

"You have to be nicer to Charlie," I whispered in Logan's ear as we walked hand in hand into the rugby stadium.

Maia walked ahead of us, clasping tightly to Charlie's hand as Chloe and Ed chatted to them about something.

Logan grunted. "I was nice."

"You barely said two words to him during the taxi ride here."

"What do you want me to say to him?" He frowned. "The only things I can think to say to him involve threats."

"He was a perfect gentleman with her at the wedding the other day. He's always a perfect gentleman."

As if he knew we were talking about him, Charlie threw us a look over his shoulder and blanched. Tall and lanky, he was cute in a very boyish kind of way. He was smart, funny, and stylish. He was wearing a pair of thick-framed black glasses that really suited his angular face, and he was dressed in a white shirt, a black waistcoat, and black tapered suit trousers with a chain dangling from one side of his waistband to the other.

"You could ask him about his band. Maia said the boys booked a gig."

"A band." Logan shook his head. "He went from Mr. Good Guy to Guy in a Band."

"I thought you'd be over this by now."

"I'm not over it because the longer they're together and the more she falls for the little bugger, the more chance he has of violating my baby girl."

I squeezed his hand. "You have to let her grow up and trust her to act responsibly."

His face snapped toward me. "What do you know? Has it happened already?"

"Oh dear God, fatherhood has made you crazy." I sighed. "Let's just talk about something else."

"Like what?"

"I don't know . . . maybe—"

"Hurry up, slow coaches!" Chloe yelled back at us, grinning.

I rolled my eyes at her, but Logan and I picked up speed and followed them down the stands. Juno waited in first-row seating for us.

"Hey, you." I hugged her close. "How are you?"

"Fine." She grinned at us. "Excited for the game."

"Who are you supporting, Grace?" Ed teased me.

It was a Scotland versus England game.

I made a face. "Funny."

"No, seriously?"

"I'm supporting Aidan," I huffed, and sat down with Juno on one side and Logan on the other. "Aka Scotland."

"Just checking."

"Chloe, please punch your husband for me."

"Ow!"

I looked down the chairs to her and grinned. "Thank you."

She winked at me and ignored Ed's grumbling.

"So is Aidan ready?" Logan said to Juno.

"As he'll ever be."

"The place is packed," Charlie noted from beside Maia. Maia was seated next to her dad, placing Charlie on her other side. Smart girl.

"It is that," Logan said, surprising me even more when he asked, "You a big rugby fan, Charlie?"

Charlie and Maia looked just as stunned as I felt. Charlie collected himself. "Not really, sir."

"Me neither. But it's different when you have someone to support."

"Oh, definitely," he hurried to agree. "Aidan's a cool guy."

Logan stared at him. "*I'm* a cool guy, Charlie."

Maia's boyfriend swallowed hard. "Of course, sir."

I groaned. "You almost had it. Then you ruined it."

Logan grinned unrepentantly.

"Did anyone bring any food?" Chloe yelled.

"Nope."

"Drink?"

"Nope."

Chloe threw us a disgusted look. "You did well, guys."

"Go and get us our usual drinks," Juno called down the row to her. "We've still got time."

My friend pulled out her purse.

Logan nudged me with his shoulder. "Want anything to drink?"

I bit my lip and stared up at him. "Maybe just water."

"You don't want a beer or wine?"

I shook my head.

Juno scowled. "We always get a beer to salute Aidan as he comes out."

"I know. I just don't feel like having one today."

She grunted. "What? Are you pregnant?"

I blushed so hard my face felt like it was on fire.

"Oh my God, you're pregnant!"

"WHAT?" Maia yelled.

Logan was silent as he stared at me in shock.

"What? What did I miss?" I heard Chloe ask.

"Grace is pregnant!" Maia cried out, and she at least sounded happy.

"Logan?" I reached for his hand. "Are you okay?"

"You're pregnant?" he said, his voice low. "Pregnant, pregnant?"

I giggled inappropriately. "Is there any other kind of pregnant?"

"There's a pregnant pause," Juno supplied helpfully.

"Are you a little bit pregnant or pregnant, pregnant?" Logan said, absolutely ignoring everyone but me.

"A whole lot pregnant."

I jumped in surprise as he lunged at me, hauling me off my seat as he stood up. My feet left the ground and I clung to him as he held me tight, his face buried in my neck.

Eventually he lowered me to the ground and pulled back to cup my face in his hands.

"I take it you're happy, then?" I smiled, tears shining in my eyes.

"Understatement, babe," he whispered.

"I want a hug!" Maia pushed up against us, wrapping her arms around us both in the tight confines of the row.

I laughed as Logan slid an arm around us both and grinned like a little boy.

"Uh, move over, people!" Chloe huffed, ducking under his arm to get to me. "Let the best friend through."

"This really has nothing to do with you, Chloe," Logan teased her as she snuggled into me.

"Oh boy." She shook her head at him as if she felt sorry for him. "You really need to learn faster than you're learning. The best friend . . . that would be *moi*"—she gestured to herself—"is always included in everything that is not the actual sex."

"And that's the moment ruined for me." Maia wrinkled her nose.

Logan snorted. "I think it's just ruined, period."

Chloe stuck her nose up in the air. "I'm not listening to your negativity. I'm going to go and get water for my beautiful and glowing best friend. I thought there was something different about you tonight."

I nodded. "Uh-huh. Sure you did."

She pushed back out of the circle and grabbed for Ed, dragging him out of the row and back up the stairs in search of drinks.

After hugging Juno and Charlie, I sat back down on my seat, this time with Logan's arm around my shoulders.

We were silent as we all took in the significance of the news and of the moment.

And then Logan said, "Best rugby game ever."

"Nothing can ruin this moment," Maia added.

"Not even England beating Scotland?" Juno teased.

"Not even Charlie," Logan said pointedly.

"Aw, thank you, sir," Charlie said, sounding genuinely pleased.

At that I burst out laughing, falling into belly-aching giggles, and the sound was so infectious I took Logan, Maia, Charlie, and Juno with me.

ACKNOWLEDGMENTS

Writing the conclusion to this series has been nothing short of insanely emotional. These characters have become like family and saying good-bye to the series has given me both joy and sadness. The *On Dublin Street* series has been a journey, and I've been very lucky to share that journey with some wonderful people.

A massive thank-you to my fabulous agent, Lauren Abramo. You believed in it from the start and have worked incredibly hard for it and for me, as well as encouraged, supported, and driven me from day one. Thank you for all that you do. I can't wait for what's over that horizon!

To my editor, Kerry Donovan: I remember the day I got your e-mail about *On Dublin Street*. You made a dream come true. Thank you for loving these characters as much as I do, and for making each book better than I ever thought they could be. It is a complete and utter pleasure to work with you.

A huge thank-you to Erin Galloway and the entire team at New American Library for all your hard work on the series. You are all rock stars.

Moreover thank you to Anna Boatman at Piatkus for really believing in the series and in me. It means a lot to me. And thank you to Clara Diaz and the team at Piatkus for working so hard to get the books into the readers' hands.

These last few years writing the series have been a roller coaster of a ride, and along the way, I've gained new friends, readers, and bloggers. Thank you to those readers and bloggers, to Club 39, to Samantha Young

(Official), and to everyone who has ever sent me a tweet, an e-mail, or a social media message letting me know how much you've enjoyed the series. I cherish every single one.

And finally I must thank my friends and family, who remind me what is important in life. Every one of you has impacted this series in some way. Your humor, your heart, your struggles, your compassion, and your strength have touched me and in turn touched the pages I write upon.

Don't miss the exciting
stand-alone contemporary romance
from bestselling author Samantha Young!

HERO

Available now from Piatkus.

Read on for a special preview.

E than led me into Caine's office the next afternoon and I was surprised to find Caine not behind his desk but standing in front of the floor-to-ceiling windows staring out over High Street and Atlantic Avenue to the harbor beyond.

With his back to me, I stole that moment to fully appreciate Caine Carraway without him knowing it. So yeah, I couldn't see his face, which was the best part, but with him standing with his hands in his trouser pockets, legs braced, shoulders relaxed, the view was delicious enough for me. His height, those broad shoulders, and let's not forget that ass.

That was a mighty fine ass.

When the seconds ticked by without a response from him, I began to feel like a high school nerd waiting for the captain of the football team to pay attention to her.

I didn't like that nearly as much as the view of his ass.

"You rang?"

Caine turned his head slightly in profile. "I did."

"And I assume there was a reason?"

He faced me and I felt that flush of attraction as his eyes swept over me. "You would assume right." He sighed and strolled over to his desk, his gaze raking over me speculatively as he did so. "Do you own a suit, heels?" His scrutiny moved to my face. "Makeup?"

I looked down at my clothes. I was wearing jeans and a sweater, and no, I wasn't wearing makeup. I had good skin. I'd inherited my olive skin from my mother, and despite those darn freckles sprinkled across the crest of my nose, it was blemish free. I rarely wore foundation or blush, and because my eyes were so light and my lashes so dark, I only wore mascara when dressing up for an occasion.

I knew I wasn't glamorous, but I looked like my mom—I had her apple cheekbones, blue-green eyes, and dark hair—and my mom had been very pretty. No one had ever looked me over and considered my lack of makeup with disdain before.

I frowned. "Weird question."

Caine relaxed against his desk in much the same pose as he had used the last time he pinched his lips at me in his office. And he *was* pinching his lips and inspecting me. I felt like I was being judged and found wanting, which was insulting normally but somehow even worse coming from a guy who looked as put together as he did.

Sexy jackass.

"I couldn't change Benito's mind," Caine informed me. "That little bastard can hold a grudge."

If I weren't so deflated by his news I would have laughed. "Bu—"

"So I thought about it," he said, cutting me off, "and you can try working for me. You'll need to invest in some appropriate clothing, however."

Um . . . what? Did he just . . . ? "I'm sorry. What?"

"Benito informed me that it kills him but he just can't take you back after your behavior with a client lost him such big accounts. You're the biggest disappointment of his thirties and before you went insane you were the best PA he ever had. The disappointment of your behavior on-set, and I quote, Broke. His. Heart."

"Oh yeah, he sounds devastated."

"Despite his flair for the melodramatic, it seems he has high standards and he has led me to believe that before you acted like an insane person you were intelligent, efficient, and hardworking."

"Insane person?" That word had been used as an adjective to describe me twice now.

He ignored me. "I need a PA. Ethan is a temp and my previous PA has decided not to return from maternity leave. I have a job opening and I'm offering it to you."

Dumbfounded.

There was no other word for how I was feeling.

How could this man go from never wanting to see me again to offering me a job that meant I was going to be in his face? *A lot*.

"But . . . I thought you didn't want me around."

Caine narrowed his eyes. "I need a PA who will fulfill all my wishes and demands immediately. That's not easy to find—most people have social lives. You, however, are desperate, and the way I see it, you owe me."

I sobered at his reminder of the past. "So what . . . you get to act out some kind of vengeance by working me into an early grave?"

"Something like that." He smirked. "It'll be a comfortable grave, though." He told me the salary and I almost passed out.

My mouth parted on a gasp. "For a PA job? Are you serious?"

I'd get to keep my apartment. I'd get to keep my car. Screw that . . . I'd be able to save enough money to afford a deposit on my apartment.

Caine's eyes glittered triumphantly at my obvious excitement. "As I said, it comes with a price." His grin was wicked and I suddenly felt a little breathless. "I'm a hard man to please. And I'm also a very busy man. You'll do what I want when I want and I won't always be nice about it. In fact, considering what your surname is, you can pretty much guarantee I won't be nice about it."

My heart thumped at the warning. "So you're saying you plan to make my life miserable?"

"If you equate hard work with misery." He considered me as I considered him, and that damnable little smirk quirked his beautiful mouth again. "So . . . just how desperate are you?"

I stared at him, this man who held up an armored shield so high in the hopes that nothing would penetrate it. But call it intuition or call it wishful thinking, I believed I could see past that shield of his—like I could feel the emotion he fought so hard to hide. And that emotion was anger. He was angry with me, whether because of my father or my sudden intrusion into his life, and this job . . . this job was his way of taking back control, of making me pay for throwing him off balance. If I took it I had no doubt he was going to do his best to test my patience to the limit. I was a pretty patient person normally. No way I could have worked with someone like Benito and not have been. But I didn't feel like myself around Caine.

Not at all.

I was defensive and scared and vulnerable.

It would be a huge risk putting myself in his control.

However, I knew it was a risk I would take. And not just because he was offering me more money than I would ever make anywhere else, nor because this job would look great on my résumé. I would take this risk because I wanted him to see I wasn't anything like my dad. I wanted Caine to see that if anything, I was like *him*.

I jutted my chin out defiantly. "I worked for Benito for six years. You don't scare me." *You terrify me.*

Caine slipped on that intimidatingly blank mask of his and pushed up off his desk. I held my breath, my skin prickling as he prowled across the room. I had to tilt my head back to meet his gaze as he came to a stop inches before me.

He smelled really, really good.

"We'll see," he murmured.

I felt that murmur between my legs.

Oh boy.

I stuck out my hand. "I accept the job."

Caine's eyes dropped to my hand. I tried not to tremble as I waited for him to decide whether or not he wanted to touch me. Swallowing my misery at his reluctance, I kept my gaze unwavering.

Finally he reached out and slid his large hand into mine.

The friction of the rougher skin of his palm against the soft skin of mine sent sparks shooting up my arm, and arousal tightened my muscles, including those in my fingers.

Surprise flared in both of our eyes.

Quite abruptly, Caine ripped his hand from mine and turned his back on me. "You start Monday," he said, his words curt as he made his way to his desk. "At six thirty. Ethan will give you the particulars of my morning schedule."

Still shaken from the sizzle that had just passed between us, I said hoarsely, "Six thirty?"

Caine glanced over his shoulder at me as he shuffled some papers on his desk. "Is that a problem?"

"It's early."

"It is." His tone brooked no denial.

Six thirty it was, then. "I'll be here."

"And dress appropriately." I bristled but nodded at the command. "And do something with your hair."

I frowned and touched a strand of it. "What do you mean?" I wore my hair long with a slight wave in it. There was nothing wrong with my hair.

Annoyed, Caine turned to face me. "This isn't a nightclub. I expect your hair and clothes to be stylish but conservative. Image is important, and from now on you represent this company. Slovenly hair and clothes do not reflect the company image."

Stylish but conservative? Slovenly hair and clothes?

I contemplated him and how pompous he could be. *You have quite the stick up your ass, don't you?*

He glowered as if he'd read my mind. "Tomorrow you'll receive employment contracts. Once you sign those I'm your boss." When I didn't

342 · *Excerpt from* HERO

answer he said, "That means you act the way I want you to act. That means you shelve the attitude and the twenty questions."

"Should I shelve those next to 'personality'?"

Caine did not look amused. In fact, the look in his eyes bordered on predatory. "That would be wise."

I gulped, suddenly wondering why I'd thought it was smart to poke the tiger. "Noted." Already I could tell this arrangement between us was not going to be easy, but I just had to remember my endgame here. "I guess I'll see you Monday, Caine."

He lowered himself into his seat without looking up at me. "Ethan will provide you with all the information you need before you leave."

"Great."

"Oh, and, Alexa?"

I froze but my pulse sped up. He'd never said my name before.

It sounded nice on his lips. Very, very nice.

"Yeah?" I whispered.

"From now on you will refer to me as Mr. Carraway and only Mr. Carraway."

Ouch. Talk about putting me in my place. "Of course." I took another step toward the door.

"And one other thing." This time I halted at his dark, dangerous tone. "You never mention your father or my mother, ever again."

My heart practically clenched at the pain I heard in his voice.

With a careful nod, I slipped out of his office, and despite the way he threw me off balance, I was more determined than ever that this was the right decision. Somehow this was where I was meant to be.

Don't miss the other passionate and
heart-breaking New Adult titles
from Piatkus!

Turn the page for more . . .

piatkus

COME TO ME SOFTLY

A.L. Jackson

A second chance at life . . .

A second chance at love . . .

Jared Holt never thought he deserved either – until he found both
in the arms of Aly Moore. Aly has loved Jared for as long as she
can remember, and she's more than ready for the future they're
making together. But Jared can't help remembering his own family.
And he'll never forgive himself for what happened to them.
How can he allow himself the very happiness he once destroyed?

To live a life worthy of Aly, Jared knows he has to stop running and
finally put his past to rest. But when he decides to face his demons
head-on, he encounters more than he bargained for: a dangerous mix of
jealousy, lies and dishonest intentions. When those intentions threaten
Aly, Jared loses all control, giving in to the rage that earned him his
bad-boy reputation years before. And he'll fight to protect her no
matter what it costs . . . even if he destroys himself in the process.

HARDER

Robin York

Caroline still dreams about West. His warm skin, his taut muscles, his hand sliding down her stomach. Then she wakes up and she's back to reality: West is gone. Before he left, he broke her heart.

Then, out of the blue, West calls in crisis. A tragedy has hit his family – a family that's already a fractured mess, Caroline knows what she has to do. Without discussion, without stopping to think, she's on a plane, flying to his side to support him in any way he needs.

Though they are together once more, things are totally different. West looks edgy, angry at the world. Caroline doesn't fit in. She should be back in Iowa, finalizing her civil suit against the ex-boyfriend who posted their explicit pictures on a revenge porn website. But here she is. Deeply into West, wrapped up in him, in love with him. Still.

They fought the odds once. Losing each other was hard.
But finding their way back to each other couldn't be harder.